Friend & Foe

Friend & Foe

A Hew Cullan Mystery

~

Shirley McKay

Polygon

This edition published in Great Britain in 2015 by
Polygon, an imprint of Birlinn Ltd
West Newington House
10 Newington Road
Edinburgh
EH9 1QS

www.polygonbooks.co.uk

9 8 7 6 5 4 3 2 1

ISBN: 978 1 84697 322 2

British Library Cataloguing-in-Publication Data
A catalogue record for this book is available on request from the British Library

Typeset by IDSUK (DataConnection) Ltd
Printed and bound by Clays Ltd, St Ives plc

For all those 'little, nameless, unremembered, acts of kindness'

To my friend John Beaton
and in memory of Jane

Prefatory Note

Friend & Foe follows on from the third book in the series, *Time & Tide*, where Hew was sent to Ghent by the coroner, Andrew Wood, to find out the source of a Flemish windmill washed up in a shipwreck in St Andrews bay. Hew returns to his position at the college of St Salvator as lecturer in law, a post with no real purpose that brings little satisfaction. Working for Wood when the will takes him, Hew has remained his own man, while the coroner's motives are not always clear. King James VI meanwhile has lost his grip on both his court and kingdom, following the Ruthven raid of 1582.

St Andrews Castle Ground Floor c1583

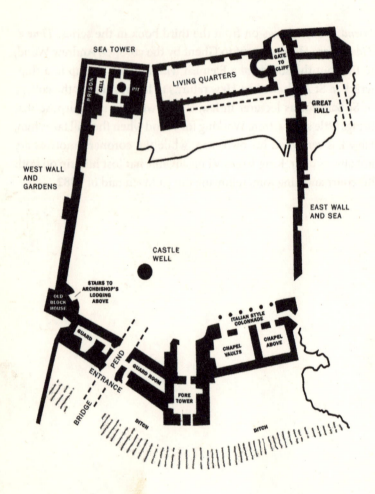

SEA TOWER

PRISON CELL

PIT

LIVING QUARTERS

SEA GATE TO CLIFF

GREAT HALL

WEST WALL AND GARDENS

EAST WALL AND SEA

CASTLE WELL

STAIRS TO ARCHBISHOP'S LODGING ABOVE

OLD BLOCK HOUSE

GUARD

PEND

GUARD ROOM

ENTRANCE

BRIDGE

DITCH

FORE TOWER

ITALIAN STYLE COLONNADE

CHAPEL VAULTS

CHAPEL ABOVE

DITCH

St Andrews Town Plan c1583

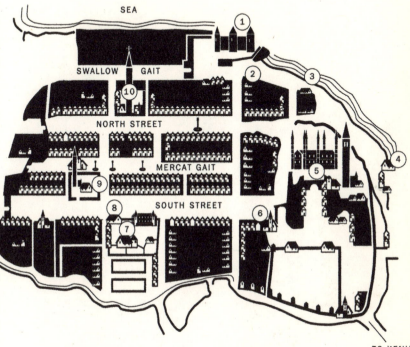

SEA

SWALLOW GAIT

NORTH STREET

MERCAT GAIT

SOUTH STREET

TO KENLY
GREEN

1. Castle

2. House of Giles and Meg

3. Kirk Heugh

4. Harbour

5. Cathedral and priory

6. College of St Leonard

7. College of St Mary

8. House of Andrew Melville

9. Kirk of Holy Trinity

10. College of St Salvator

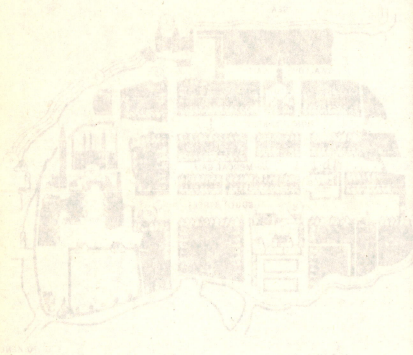

Chapter 1

A Merry Month

Quhair thou was wont full merilye in May
To walk and tak the dew

Henryson, *The Testament of Cresseid*

St Andrews, Scotland
May 1st, 1583

To those who watched, the house appeared asleep. But though the doctor and his wife had long since gone to bed, both were wide awake. Giles Locke lay still and thoughtful, muffled in his quilt. He heard Meg's footsteps cross the floor, through curtains she had closed on him against the cold night air, and felt his wife's departure with a sense of dread. The doctor sighed and shifted, finding out the place that held the scent and shape of her, willing her return. Matthew Locke slept on, his soft lips pale and puckered, plump and moist with milk. Meg blew out the candle flame, and let the darkness close.

In a loft upstairs, the doctor's servant Paul closed up his folding bed and dressed in bilious green. He listened to his mistress moving through the house, coming to the kitchen, past the sleepy maid. Canny Bett slept upon a sheepskin bolstering the hearth, wrapped up in a blanket blackened by its coals. Canny's limbs were slack, her mouth half-open still, a quarrel in full flight when sleep had over-taken her, her red cheeks pinched and scorched. She had left an egg to roast in the embers of the fire. Canny did not stir as Meg explored the shelves, collecting things to fill a basket, small glass bottles, cloths and cups.

The house looked out upon the castle on the cliff. In daylight, it looked out upon the grey washed sky, on cliff tops bright with thistle heads and clumps of summer moss and white-flecked seabirds circling, on mellow stone and high arched windows, glancing on the street. The ringing out of hammermen, the hoarse cries of the fisherwives, the grumbling of the baxters and the brewers with their loads, forged a solid thoroughfare between the house and cliff, the castle falling back to bask upon its rock. At night, the forecourt stilled. The castle overlooked, its black hulk rising blankly from the darkened precipice, seabirds curling mute, invisible in crevices. Pinpoint pricks of firelight moved across its walls.

On the corner by the Swallow Port, a yellow lantern burned. Meg ducked beneath its light to turn into the Fisher Gait, and hurried out of sight. There were lanterns, too, outside the cookshops and the taverns on the far side of the Mercat Gait, and in the wynds and closes leading to the South Street, across the southern boundaries of the town. Here the yellow smoke gave way to natural light, the watered-grey, soft glancing of a quarter moon. Meg continued landward, keeping to the narrow path towards her brother's house. From time to time, she strayed closer to the shore, or through a copse of trees, conscious of a shadow at her back. She came into a barley field, and shook the drops of water from the morning rose, wiping with a cloth each sharp green stalk and leaf, milking the wet linen out into a cup. When the cup was full, Meg passed the water through a funnel drop by drop into a coloured glass – amber for barley, olive for the rose – sealing it with parchment and a plug of wax. She let a drop of barley water settle on her tongue, knowing she was watched. She had felt it at the sea-port to the harbour, and on the landward path that led out to the barley field. The gulls had woken up, and swept towards them, shrieking, through the pink-shot clouds. Meg took pity on the watcher: 'You may go now, Paul.'

2

'On my life, I cannot,' answered Paul. Paul had spent the last hour hiding in a sheep trough, the evidence of which was plain upon his hat. He gave up all pretence of coming there by chance, to shake the matter off. 'Doctor Locke insists on it. And he will have my carcass cut up on a slab, he will carve my corpse up as one of his experiments, if I neglect his charge.'

'He will do no such thing. And when were you inclined to do as you were told?' Meg brushed aside this argument, as Paul brushed down his hat.

The servant stood his ground. 'Twould ding his heart to shards, if harm should come to you.'

'What kind of harm,' protested Meg, 'can come to me, upon my brother's land? Where I have lived and wandered, since I was a child?'

'I ken that, mistress, yet he fears—'

They both knew what the doctor feared. Paul bit back the words. 'He telt me to lie low.'

Meg accepted with a sigh, 'Aye, and so you did. No matter, you shall stay, and help collect the dew. For that may serve you better than to lour among the sheep. Then, when we are done, you shall take some to your lass.'

'I have no lass,' he lied.

Together, they filled bottles, kneeling in the grass, until the sun broke tentatively through the clearing sky. The light brought lads and lasses laughing through the trees. Children gathered blossoms, trailing chains of buttercups and armfuls of white flowers. A girl ran through the barley field with petals in her hair, followed by a young man fumbling with his breeks. Paul's gaze fixed on the couple longer than was decent, and the lass stood still to flounce at him, poking out her tongue. The young man snatched his quarry from behind. He pulled her out of sight, into a clump of trees.

'There are violets in the wood. She will like those too,' Meg broke upon Paul's thoughts.

He spluttered, 'As I swear to you—'

'For certain, you must not,' said Meg. 'There can be no shame in it, that you should have a lass. Or is there some impediment, prohibiting the match?'

His mistress was a soothsayer, who saw into the heart of things. Paul had no idea how she could read his mind. He blurted out, 'It is the widow Bannerman, an honest, proper wife. But I must prove my worth to her, and she is brave and delicate, and till I am assured of her, I would not have my love laid bare for a' the gaping world. I cannot, for the life of me, think how you came to ken of it.'

'It was not hard to guess. You have trimmed your beard, and cut and combed your hair. And you are wearing your best clothes, my brother's gooseturd riding coat, and Kendal breeks and hat. And here we are in May, the merry lovers' month.'

Paul turned a livid purple, clashing with the green. 'Master Hew was good enough to give me his old coat. But do you think the colour is too keen? I must be bold, yet circumspect, if I would prove my worth to her. In truth, the case is intricate.'

Meg suppressed her smile at the language he had borrowed, like his bright green coat, from her brother Hew. 'True love often is. But I know Jonet Bannerman, and she will like you better, in your own, true, proper self. And if you wish to please her, take to her this water from the morning rose.' She offered up the dew, in a phial of coloured glass.

The morning light, it seemed, had worked to calm Paul's fears. He accepted eagerly. 'This water shall speak worlds to her. I thank you, with my heart. You will not tell the doctor, though?'

'Will not tell him what?' Meg teased. 'That I caught you spying? That you left my side? That you go a-Maying? That you have a lass?'

'All of those,' admitted Paul. 'Especially that one last.'

'I will not say a word.'

Meg's smiles gave way to thoughtfulness. She watched Paul set off down the track, the bottle of elixir warming in his hand. Daylight burned the vapour from the early dew. The lusty lads and lasses went about their day, the children brought their blossom homewards from the fields. The world became quite still. Meg took off her shoes. She felt the blades of barley sharp against her feet, and found her cheeks were wet, despite the morning sun.

From the fore tower of the castle on the rock, the sergeant of the garrison looked out. He saw the bridge across the fosse, the stables and the cookshop, and the house of Doctor Locke, its chimney wisping smoke into the white-veined sky. He saw the woman turn the corner from the Fisher Gait, a basket on her arm. Tam Fairlie left his post, running down the stair to rap at Patrick's door. Patrick lay unbuttoned in a borrowed archer's coat, on the great bed of estate. His face looked sickly still, and in the morning light a little wan and flushed, pink-white, blotched and mottled like a bulbous flower. He perspired a little, though the air was cool.

The chamber had been dressed in shades of blue and green. That was Patrick's doing: 'For what would you have else, the colour of a cardinal?' and for his present purposes, the colours seemed to suit. The curtains round the bed were of a thick dark damask, green leaves stitched in silk. In places, they had faded to a dirty olive-grey.

'Olives,' Patrick said. 'Ewe's milk cheese and figs. *Ficus* is the fig. And *fica* is the common Latin for a woman's orifice.'

It pleased him to refer such matters to the Latin tongue, as though the lick of scholarship brought polish to the sin. To Tam's mind, Patrick talked too much.

'What you, as a soldier, like to call her scabbart. Her scabbart is so called, because she is the sheath, where I put my sword, and not because of scabs. She *may* be scabbed, of course.'

'Olives and suchlike are your steward's job,' said Tam.

'He asks too many questions, and he tells too many lies.' Patrick closed his eyes and sank back on the bed.

He did not look like a man with the mettle for the task, however bold he boasted of it, dressing up bare appetites in rags of foreign words.

5

'Succats, and sweet almond cakes, and flagons of red wine,' he added to the list.

The sergeant sighed. 'Aye, I will see to it.' Though Tam had never tasted olives, and had rarely eaten figs, he knew how to procure them with a minimum of questions – answered with his fists. 'And make a bonny brothel of the brave bed of estate,' he muttered to himself.

His master rallied, 'Say you? What was that?'

'She is here, my lord, waiting at the gate.'

'She has come too late. I have not the strength for her.' Patrick slumped again.

Tam Fairlie was accustomed to his moods. 'As you will, then,' he shrugged, 'I can send her away.'

'Ah, no, not at all.' Patrick shook his head, and sat up in the bed, smoothing out his coat. 'For we must take our remedy, though it may be bitter to us. I shall go up to the chapel now, while you prepare the chamber. After she has left me, I shall want my bath.'

Tam grunted, 'Aye, my Lord.'

In his latter months of sickness, Patrick had begun to bathe, a witless, witches' remedy, that he could not effect without calling on the garrison. Six strong men it took to carry in the vat, and fill it up with water, scalded on hot coals, and six men more to empty it, and lug it down again, while Patrick shifted, slippery, huddled in his closet. The closet had a stench and savour that the high draught of the chimney piece did little to disperse. It was like looking into a man's heart, and Tam felt sickened there, not by the dark stench of the close stool but the dark-filled rancour that was Patrick's soul.

'Pray dress the walls with carpets, and the bed with flowers,' Patrick rumbled on.

'The bairn has brought the May.' Tam cursed the words, and God, who had not stopped his tongue, as soon as he had spoken them. The bairn brought in the flowers and sunlight, and the song of birds. If Patrick did not see it, then the man was blind; and Patrick

6

was not blind, he saw the bairn too plainly, and what she meant to Tam. The mention of the child made Patrick stir and frown, like a sleeping leopard, startled from his dreams. 'Ah, yes, your little lass. The chamberlain has telt me that she is a thief.'

'Then he is a liar.' Tam made his protest brief and loud, to drown his beating heart.

Patrick said, 'Perhaps.' Like the leopard in the sun, he opened up an eye, lazily considering. 'But be that as it may, he caught her at the sugarloaf.'

Tam faced him, stiff and proud. 'She is six years old.'

'So I said to him.' Patrick lacked the will to follow to the pounce. 'And yet it is a fault in her,' he scratched his back and yawned, 'that ye must amend. I hear her, sometimes, at her play. And sometimes I am set to think, the castle is no place to keep so small a bairn.'

Tam was in a black mood then, before he reached the gate. The sentinel was Harry Petrie; Tam had seen to that. He did not trust the Richan boy, his long ungainly limbs and pale insipid looks, the queer way that he spoke to them: 'He's gaan to blaw agin the nicht,' when he meant the wind. What sort of fool said that? 'John Richan is a pestilence,' Tam had telt to Patrick. Patrick had smiled that smile of his, cunning like a cat. 'Ye maunna damn the man, Tam, for his Orkney speak. His father is an officer, in service to the earl.'

Patrick in the chapel, fallen to his knees, whispering his prayers up through the coloured glass ... Patrick's gross allegiances were troublesome to Tam. He sailed his skift through narrow waters, closely to the wind. Robert, earl of Orkney was uncle to the king, and no one could be certain where his leanings leant, to king or to conspirators, the English or the French. They kent he was a bastard though, and that in every sense. Patrick made the earl his ally at the parliament. He had in mind a marriage for his middle daughter with the bastard's son.

'Besides,' Patrick said, 'the boy is an expert at shooting the bow.'

'What use were his arrows in a blockhouse built for guns?'

'If we had powder, Tam, if we had shot. But powder and shot are for kings. And pistoletts are pepper pots that scatter far and wide. You cannot hope to best a perfect archer's eye. The arrow at his heart strikes deadly, straight and pure. I will stand you one sound bowman for all your fleet of guns,' said Patrick, who kenned no more of battle plats than Tam did Latin prayers. 'He may be of use to us.'

So that was how it was.

Tam had trained the boy. He trained him up, by night and by day, for endless drills and exercises woke him from his sleep, until his green limbs bent and buckled at his bow, his sapling arm hung slack. And what use was an archer then, that could not lift his bow? No use at all, the sap.

At sunrise, Tam had sent John Richan out to see the surgeon. 'Show him your sore shoulder, son.'

The boy had answered warily. 'Ye telt me to keep watch.'

'And now I tell ye, go.'

The Richan boy had glanced the question back at Harry Petrie, and Harry Petrie nodded at him, whittling with his knife. Harry was a man that kent when he should speak, and when to turn his head away, and when to haud his tongue, that no amount of buffeting could teach the Richan boy. Harry was a proper man, a soldier born and bred.

Now Harry stood there talking to the porter at the gate, smiling at the lass, who made her way unsteadily across the wooden bridge. For form's sake, Tam called out, 'Ho, there, stranger! Stand!'

The silly wench blinked back at him. 'But surely you maun know me, Tam? I came as I was asked.'

'Oh aye, I ken you now. It is the physick wife, that brings his lordship's remedy,' Tam informed the world. The porter gave a nod, and let the woman pass. Tam took her arm and hissed, 'What mean you, wench, by coming late? We looked for you at dawn.'

The woman shook him off. 'I went to gather dew. And I will not have you call me, as I were some whore, that walks about at night.' She answered him, with spirit. 'Will Patrick take his physick now, or no?'

She looked, in light of day, a decent sort of wife. She came from a good family, she had told Tam once; scholars, men of learning, who had taught her secrets they had found in books. Though he had not believed her, he approved her plan. She was a subtle lass. 'What medicines have ye brought?'

'A pill to purge his stomach. Water for his eyes.'

Though Patrick's eyes were sharp enough, none sharper bar his tongue.

Tam had kept her talking as they passed the guardhouse, partly to distract her, partly for appearances, to satisfy the crowd. The castle's inner courtyard was a town within a town, and at this time of morning filling up with traffic, soldiers cleaning weapons in the sunlight on the green, stable boys and scudlars gathered round the well. Tam Fairlie scowled and snarled. 'Are none of ye at work today, that you must chat and clatter, littering the square? Here comes the physick wife.'

The woman clutched his sleeve. 'Tam, I am afeart.'

'What are ye afeart of, lass?'

'For that he is sick. I cannot make him well.'

'A lass like you? For sure you can!' He brought her to the place that Patrick had prepared for her, the cold north-western tower that looked out to the sea.

She whimpered, shrinking back. 'You never said in there. I will not wait in there. You cannot make me, Tam.'

She was, after all, a silly witless wench, and Tam could well have shown to her the error of her words. Instead, he murmured soft to her, and coaxed her like a bairn. 'See, lass, tis a play, a wee bit dressing game.' He opened up the door so she could see inside. A fine fair shift and cloak lay folded on a ledge, together with a girdle and a coronet of flowers.

'Put on the dress, and Patrick will come for you. You are his queen of the May.'

Tam whistled as he put the final touches to his lordship's room. He had brought a banquet, balanced on a tray, of sweetmeats, wine and fruits. He bent the boughs of hawthorn that the bairn had fetched and bound them to the bedposts, making up a bower. He lit candles in the passage next to Patrick's closet, where his lordship wrote his letters, did his easement, took his bath, and knelt on winter nights to say his blackest prayers. A thick curtain on the south side closed it from the draughts. Behind this, came a scuffling sound, which Tam put down to rats. At once, he drew his sword and pulled the curtain back.

'Mercy, but a poor blind clerk, helpless and unarmed!' A timid voice cried out. A figure flew up flapping, from the stool of ease, floundering and fummilling, falling on its knees. 'Murder! Mercy! Oh, my life!'

Tam put up his sword. 'Master Ninian Scrymgeour,' he acknowledged pleasantly. Patrick's privy secretary, stripped of breeks and spectacles, grovelled on the floor. 'Here ye are, a-scummering,' Tam said with a smile.

Scrymgeour squinted, whimpering, 'Mercy, who is there?'

'It is I, Tam Fairlie, Sergeant of the guard.' Tam found the missing spectacles, and gave them to the clerk. The clerk received them gratefully. With one damp hand he felt for them, and clasped them to his nose, and with the other pulled and pummelled at his clothes. 'Dear me, I thought . . . I thought . . . I thought to fetch a letter, that my lord has had me write for him, to take it to the town.' He gestured to the ink and papers on a little desk.

'And thought to use his close stool?' Tam supposed.

'I have not been well,' Scrymgeour said, defensively. The closet bore this out. 'And you yourself are here because . . .?'

'To mak the place secure for him. The physick wife is coming to advise his regimen. His lordship has instructed that they manna be disturbed.'

'Quite so, quite so. I see ... I go ... I am ...' The small clerk turned bright pink, and clutched a sheaf of papers tightly to his chest. He asked no further questions in his haste to leave, but scuttled past the banquet and the flower-decked bed. Indeed, his sight was limited, a pitiful impediment, to plague a privy clerk. He saw the world but dimly, through thick slabs of glass.

'Have you done your office, now?' Tam pursued him playfully.

'Ah, yes, aye, indeed.'

'Then go about your business, sir. And take the scummer pan.'

Chapter 2

The Physick Wife

The physick wife stood naked in a pleasing coolness, shown to none but God. She felt that God approved of her, stripped and cleansed of sinfulness, His shrewd eye winking kindly on her bare white breasts. The cell had a monastic feel, with solid, whitewashed walls and one long shelf of stone. A man had made his bed on it, for you could see the hollow worn smooth by his head. There was a hole above it where they passed his food, like a little tunnel to the other side. Standing at the window she could see the sea, the blank face of the cliff, leading to the jetty, blackened by the tide. A seagull perched to keek at her, parked up on the sill cut deep into the rock. She darted at it, laughing, 'Aye, then, keek your fill!' The bird took fright and flew from her, leaving her bereft. Supposing God abandoned her? She said a prayer, in case. The words became a song, that echoed through the tower, and were soothing in the stillness, like a kind of spell.

It was too cold to stand still for long, whatever God might think. The sea tower facing northwards seldom felt the sun. The woman bundled up her clothes and put them in her basket, taking up the costume laid out on the shelf. The first thing was a shift of fine white linen lawn, with little whitework flowers. A dark green band of velvet clinched it at the waist, and shaped the full white softness of her breasts and hips. The best part was the long green cloak, which swept down to the ground, and she felt warm and safer gathered in its folds.

She had unpinned her hair, taking off her cap and shaking loose the curls, just as Patrick liked it, but she would not wear the crown. The tight-lipped buds and blossoms brought the stench of death, carrion scent of darkness, dank and sweet decay. No one but a witch brought hawthorn in a house. The very sight and stink of it might make a person sick. She thrust it in the channel where the thick walls met, hidden out of sight, and settled on the ledge, hugging close her secret through the thin white shift.

It was Tam she thought of when she closed her eyes. Tam Fairlie smelled of leather, sweet earth, sweat and smoke. Tam was Patrick's man. He had found her at the market, where she sold her flowers. Nettles, garlic, violets, sweet herbs, who will buy? And she had not supposed that he would stop to look at her, but she had caught his eye. 'What is it that you want, sir?'

'What have you to sell?'

Her basket wares were roots and posies, seaweeds, flowers and ferns. But for those that wanted, she had other charms. She learnt them long ago, when she was a lass. She had suffered as a bairn from a fearful kind of palsy; they had sent her for a cure to a man called William Simpson. William was a cousin, on her mother's side. Some said he was carried off by gipsies as a bairn, some that he had gone to sea, and trained to be a doctor in the foreign schools, some that he had learnt his magic from the faerie queen. However he had learned them, he taught his charms to her. The first time it had happened, he had given her a potion, sending her to sleep. After it wore off, she found herself full stiff and raw, and sorely black and bruised. There were blood spots too.

'The guid neighbours took you,' William had explained, 'off to elfin-land. If ye stayed too long there, you wad go to Hell. I risked my life for you, to take you back again.' He had added, oddly, 'Dinna tell your dad.'

The next time William came to her, he took her hard and cold. But while he had his way with her, and she closed her eyes, she could see quite plainly there the elfin folk and court; the faerie queen had shown her terrors and delights.

In all the years she had been coming to the town, the physick wife had met with many sorts of men, but none of them had proved so hard to please as Patrick was, so fond of make-believe. He had something in him that reminded her of William. It made her sore afraid, for how the play might end.

She had not sat for long before the key was turned, and Patrick came to find her. He was wearing yellow hose, with a feather in his cap and a Kendal archer's coat, a longbow in his hand and a quiver at his belt, too heavy and too broad for him, so that he buckled slightly underneath the weight. His limbs were weak and withered while his belly hung distended, like a sack upon a stalk. She should not have giggled, but she could not help herself. She disguised it, quickly, with a little gasp. 'Are you come to save me, sir?'

He took her hand in his. 'I am Robin Hood.'

He teased her with the arrow shaft. The flint began to burrow, deep inside her dress. The physick wife shrank back.

'I liked the other play,' she protested, weakly. 'When you dressed up as the bishop and you blessed me, on my knees.' They had gone up to the chapel. He had worn his bishop's cloak, and he had knelt behind her, on the quiet stone. And since he was God's servant, it could not be wrong. There were three sorts of bishop, he had told her once; one that was a lord, and one that served a lord, and one that served the Lord. Which of them was he? He had laughed at that. He was laughing at her now.

'Did I say something daft?'

Patrick shook his head. 'I liked that play too. But this is a May game. A Robin Hood play.'

They were lying on the bed in the bishop's private chamber, and around them lay the remnants of their May Day feast. The walls were hung with tapestries, blue and green and grey, and she could not dismiss the thought that somehow they were peeking at her, through the flowers and leaves. 'Tam Fairlie keeps the watch,' Patrick reassured her. She closed her eyes, and thought of Tam, standing watchful, somewhere near. She thought she would not mind it if he took her for himself.

14

She felt sleepy now, gorged on Patrick's wine, the jewel bright cups of claret he had made her drink. She had not wanted to. The wine was on a flowery carpet, like a faerie feast. There were sweet-meats too, quince and honeyed figs. It did no good to Patrick to consume such richness; she had tried to tell him: 'You must take your physick for to make you well.'

Patrick had refused. 'I have drank your physick, both the foul and fair. It does me no good. I am dying, no doubt.'

'Do not say that.' She did not know a cure. Sometimes, he made water, and it came out black. She told him, 'That's a good sign, the badness pissing out.' But she shuddered at the thought of that black polluting her.

He fed her fruits and jellies, teasing on her tongue. She was empty, always, hungry for a herring or a bit of bread. She wished she had them now. She did not eat or drink enough. 'You are skin and bone.' His words made her afraid. For both things could be broken, could they not?

'There is food enough here to last for a year,' she tried to distract him. 'Here in the castle, I mean.'

If the town was like a world, then the castle was a town, and Patrick's bed of state was like a private stronghold high up in its walls. To climb it there were steps, yet Patrick struggled still to mount it, as he struggled to mount her. He caught her at the waist and held her close and hard, that she could feel his hot breath on her neck, his wheezing dry and labouring. He was laughing at her. 'We would not last long.'

She did not see why not. The castle had a well, in the centre of the yard, though Patrick would not drink the ale brewed from the water there; he drank from vaulted cellars that were stocked with wine, and when the stocks ran dry, more were brought in boats.

'The walls are not so strong as you suppose. And many times afore they have been built and blasted, and they will not stand a siege.' The worst threat, Patrick told her, was the sea. And how could that be? A narrow metal ladder ran down from the cliff top, sheer onto the rocks and the jetty down below. From there they brought provisions when the gates were closed. And no man could have scaled it with a blade between his teeth, before his hopes and bones were driven down and dashed; the coast was closely watched.

Patrick shook his head. The constant, slow artillery of water, he explained, the patient revolution of the waves, would wear the walls away. What was sand but stone? What was man but dust?

'Not in a year, Patrick,' she protested stubbornly. 'The walls will not be worn out in a year.'

'Aye, mebbe not.' He had closed his eyes. 'Long before that, I shall be dead.'

Long ago, he said, archbishops lived like kings, and they had many palaces, and kept many whores. They drank their wine from cups of gold. A cardinal was murdered here, taken at his prayers. And those who drew him out had all met dreadful deaths. One falling from his horse; the horse had kicked his face, and shat into his mouth, as it bubbled, bright with blood. 'That was God's revenge on him.'

She sensed that he was sporting with her. 'The cardinal was bad, though, was he not?' Patrick merely smiled at that, showing yellow teeth.

The bed was decked with hawthorn flowers. 'I dinna like the May,' the physick wife complained. 'It smells like rotting flesh.'

Patrick snatched a clutch of petals from the bough and crushed them in his fingertips, breathing in the scent. 'It smells,' he concluded, 'like a woman's placket.'

He meant a women's sex; her placket was her apron, a pocket in her dress. She wriggled from his grasp. 'You will not hurt me, Patrick?'

'Why would I do that?' He took out another arrow from the quiver at his side, and began to stroke her with the feathered end. 'You are my quiver-case.'

'I am all a-quiver,' she replied, obligingly. 'Will you close the drapes?'

The curtains round about were heavy, thick and worn. They did not look as though they had been often drawn. She imagined they

16

were laced with moths, creased into the faded cloth, feasting on the flowers.

'What is the matter? Are you cold?'

Tam would stand outside the door, a little upwind of her cry, frowning as the sun rose higher, polishing his sword. Perhaps it was Tam Fairlie's bairn, the feylike, faerie child, whose eyes she felt still at her back. The child had brought the May, a harbinger of death. She swallowed thickly, fearful. Surely, it was God, who looked down on her nakedness, saw her bared and brazen, brought to Patrick's bed.

'Patrick—'

'No more words.'

Once Patrick was asleep, the woman crept out from the sheets. She folded up the white lawn shift and left it by his side. Her clothes were in the basket – kirtle, cap and shoes. She sought, but could not find, the partner to her sock, a sky-blue scrap of silk. Patrick frowned on nether hose. He liked to nuzzle bold and bare her warm soft placket through her skirts, to find her muff and burrow there. The sock was not in her basket, nor beneath the bed; she dared not lift the quilt. The drowsy dullness of the wine was turning to a throb. Her foot would rub and blister on the long walk home. She felt a wave of sickness as she met the sunshine, dizzily descending, feeling for the steps.

Tam Fairlie stood on guard at the entrance to the stair. He would take her to the gate, and set her on the bridge. By the time she turned the corner, he would already have forgotten her.

'Patrick is asleep. I left his medicines at his side. He did not want to take them,' she confided.

Tam Fairlie did not care. He had taken out a purse and was counting out the coins. 'I know where I can find you, if he asks for you again.'

'I dinna ken . . .' The physick wife whimpered.

He glanced at her then. 'Why is that?'

''Tis that . . . he hurts me sometimes. And I do not like it. I think he does not mean to, that he is not well.'

She knew it was not Tam who had listened at the lock. She saw how he considered her, neither cruel nor kind. 'How am I to cure him, Tam?'

'How should I know? Use your charms.' He brought out an extra shilling. 'Or, if you will not, I can find some other lass.'

'I did not say that.' She took the money quickly, hid it in her basket. It was business, after all. 'I have lost a sock.'

Tam had turned his back.

'A short footsock of sky-blue silk. Mebbe I dropped it back there in the tower?' She knew that she had not. 'Or mebbe in the square.'

Tam went on ignoring her.

'Perhaps it has been picked up by your little lass.'

This produced an answer, for he turned on her and scowled. Dismayed, she trailed off lamely. 'I should like to have it, if she has.' They had come down to the gate, where the sentinels kept watch. She felt hot and shamed, discarded like a cloth. She clutched the sergeant's sleeve. 'That man is staring, Tam.'

'Is that so?' Tam took off a glove, and struck the soldier full force in the face, with his open hand. The young man staggered back. Within a moment, he stood full upright again, staring straight ahead. He made no start or cry, nor raised his fingers up to touch the place, already turning purple on his cheek. The woman felt a thrill, a sudden flush of pride, that she had the power to work the sergeant's fist. Tam Fairlie pushed his red face close into the boy's. The soldier did not flinch.

'What was it you were thinking, son? Thinking you could go with her?'

'I wasnae thinking that.'

'What is your name, again, son?'

'John Richan, sir.'

The sport was cheap enough, yet it did not grow stale. 'Reekie, is it?' Tam inquired.

'Richan, sir. Fae Orkney.'

'Oh aye, I forgot that. Mind me, what it means?'

The soldier answered, 'It means bruck.'

'An' wit wad that mean now, in a proper tongue?'

'Bruck is a word that means . . . trash.'

'Do you mean shite, son?'

The soldier shook his head.

'Trash? Then it reeks, does it no? Trash reeks? In guid plain Scots, ye are a piece of shite.'

Harry Petrie, hearing this, had come out from the guardroom on the western side; there were chambers built on both sides of the gate, and Harry kept the left one, closest to the bridge. He stood quiet, watching, resting on his sword, while the sergeant poked. 'How is your sore arm?'

John Richan dropped his gaze. 'The surgeon couldna help it, sir. He couldna find a lesion on the place where it was hurt.'

'Imagine that! All cured!' The sergeant marvelled cheerfully, and clapped him on the back. 'Awa ye go and practise then. Shoot arrows at the butts.'

'*Aw, sarge.*' Harry Petrie murmured, quiet, at Tam's back. For only Harry Petrie ever spoke up for the Richan boy, and dared, or cared enough, to come to his defence. Tam Fairlie let it pass. He jabbed the Richan boy, hard in his sore shoulder. 'See you gang an' practise, son. Else you will spend your rest hours sleeping in the pit.'

He let his quarry drop, and winked across at Harry. 'Show this guidwife out, and send her safely home.'

The physick wife was pleased. For it was fit and proper she should have a convoy, and a bonny one, at that. She let the soldier take her arm and help her cross the bridge, careful at the middle, where the planks were loose, and she almost slipped. He saw her safe, and smiled at her. 'What is it that they call you, then?'

The physick wifie preened. 'Alison. It's Alison.'

'Now that's a bonny name.'

19

Chapter 3

First Light

Four miles south at Kenly Green the servants brought the May to cheer Hew Cullan's house. The lass threw back the shutters to admit the sun, stippling grey stone windowsills in pink and yellow stripes. She set her master's breakfast table out in the great hall: manchet bread and butter, coddled eggs and milk. A little pot of primroses to welcome in the spring fetched warmth and freshness to the dark green cloth. The tower house wanted light. It had seen more cheer when Matthew was alive, though he had lived secluded with his daughter Meg, while Hew was off in France. Meg had made its beating heart, had kept the cold months warm with cinnamon and gingiber, and cooled the summer haze with lavender and rose. Once Meg had left to marry, and the old man died, the heartbeat had been stilled. Meg had not returned there since her bairn was born. The kitchen shelves were crammed with jars from her distillery, the gardens overblown; the apple racks were filled, the sweet plums spiced and bottled, left to gather dust.

A wife was wanted, plainly, to restore the place to life. Now that Hew was master, living at the tower, he barely made a home of it, extending to the house the same reserved politeness he had shown its servants, speaking to his tenants there as if they were his guests. For all that, he turned out to be a canny host, for he did not neglect the business of the land. He made the luckless miller's son a present of a pig, that left the miller's widow squealing in dismay, and the miller's children squealing in delight. When winter came in hard, he saw that no one starved.

The house was quiet now, for strangers seldom called, and those who did were *unco*, sinister or serious. Once, it was the crownar came, the sheriff Andrew Wood, crafty as the rabbit they had served up in a pie. The crownar had a look about him shook you to the bones, and left behind a taste so sour that you would not be hurrying to ask him back for more. The shakebuckler he brought wi' him was left to stand on watch, and ne'er a scrap nor drop of drink allowed to pass his lips, that made a body thankful not to work for *him*. After, Hew had gone abroad, through far-flung fields and foreign wars, to a town called Ghent. He fetched hame wi' a soldier laddie – Robert Lachlan was his name – bonny, braw and bold and full of brag and crack, that livened up the place. The lassies sulked for weeks when Robert Lachlan left.

Only one such came by now, and that was Master James, the nephew of the grand reformer at the Haly Trinity, who breathed his gloom and hell smoke thick upon the town. Hew asked him here for Nicholas, he said, '*to cheer him up.*' The three men talked for hours on things they read in books, though precious little comfort to be found in them. So she had telt the cook; the cook had said, more exercised and expert in such things, that yon was brought to Nicholas to mak him ripe for death, and doubtless, he prepared for it, for he was frail enough. Three husbands she had buried, so she ought to ken. Nicholas Colp was Hew's old friend, librarian and secretar. He laboured under strain of a sair afflicting sickness, though ye couldna fault him for it; he did not complain. He rarely came below, but lived up in the library, wrapped up in his paper mantle, wanner than a ghost. He was dying, then. Even Doctor Locke, who never spoke a straight word where a wrangled one would do, had telt them plain and simply, '*It will not be long.*'

'He is waiting, you see,' the cook prophesied gloomily. 'Once Nicholas lies cold, the maister will away. He will not bide here, at the house.' And Master Hew grew so remote, so quiet and subdued, there was a steady rumour he was turning to the kirk. His father, had he kent of it, would start up from his sepulture, for that was not the purpose he intended for his son; his father was no founder or supporter of reform. Yet when they dared to ask him for a feast at Yule, with carol songs and dances set to fiddles in the barn, Hew readily agreed to it, and answered with a smile, and that would set the Melvilles spinning in their turn. Hew kept his counsel close. He had sent them down a hogshead, but he had not come himself.

The serving lass returned with collops of cold beef, to find the hall abandoned and the table bare. Her master had gone up to breakfast in the library, dropping crumbs and smearing butter over his best books. *Kittill as a bairn*, the weary lassie sighed. However long she schooled him, he would never learn.

'The world is light and lunatic.' Hew broke the loaf in two, and gave one half to Nicholas, who was perched upon a high stool at his writing desk, adding annotations to the margin of his page. Nicholas was making a vernacular translation of George Buchanan's dialogue on the law of kingship, *De Iure Regnis apud Scotos Dialogus*, at his friend's request. Hew had sought to occupy him through those dark wracked hours from which he found no rest; he had no personal interest in the finished text, which he could read as easily and well in the original. And though Buchanan's warnings were offensive to the king, who had never taken kindly to the censure of his tutor, it could scarcely matter here. If Giles Locke's last predictions were correct – and it was rare enough for the doctor to commit himself – Nicholas would not live out the year. By giving him a purpose, Hew hoped to prove Giles wrong.

'Hmm? How so?' Nicholas was used to such incursions. He fished out a crumb of bread, which had fallen in his ink pot, with the blunt end of his pen and a mild air of reproof.

'All of them, a-Maying,' grumbled Hew. 'Frivolous and furious with love. The lasses, up at dawn, and out into the fields, have come home giddy-headed, and with muddy feet. I ask them to fetch butter, and they bring me buttercups, or whatever they may cry

22

them, those curdle-coloured flowers. Even James Melville – our ain honest James – is marrying today, and his uncle has resolved to treat us to a homily, upon the marriage state, as soon as they are come home from the grand Assembly. The world whirls mad with love, and skips a frantic jig, and none but you and I stay scathless and untuned to it.'

The laughter in his tone drowned out a darker note, for Hew had been reflective and withdrawn these last five months. He had taken up a room in St Salvator's College, where he now spent half the week, an arrangement to which he had once been bitterly opposed. He gave lectures on the law, spoke the Latin grace, and took supper on a Thursday of mutton, sops and prunes, with the phlegmatic mathematician Bartie Groat.

In his spare hours, he resorted to St Mary's on the South Street, where he had embarked upon a course of ancient languages – Sanskrit, Chaldee, Hebrew, Greek – under the instruction of James and Andrew Melville, from which he brought home copious reams of script for Nicholas to copy out, in a careful hand. And therein, he told Nicholas, of these contorted languages, were mysteries enough to last him for the while.

Nicholas was not deceived. He had known the world for long enough and suffered too acutely there to fail to know a man who had a troubled conscience, or to suppose that with such work Hew's spirit might be quelled. He sensed that Hew had lost both head and heart, and sent his quiet sympathies, to one who like himself loved recklessly and hopelessly and who, through no grave fault, found blood upon his hands.

Hew wiped butter from his knife, and tucked it in his belt. 'Now, I must be gone. Today there is a contest at the butts, in honour of the May, between our college archers and the students from St Leonard's. I am called to judge.'

'You might look in on Meg's physick garden as you make your way,' Nicholas suggested.

'Aye, and why is that?'

'No reason, but for solace of an early summer's day, to see the sweet herbs flower.'

Hew sensed a deeper purpose lay behind the words. But Nicholas had closed his eyes, and he would not be drawn. Since he had seen his friend fall headlong into danger there, he no longer shared the substance of his dreams.

'Go, you will be late. Your archers will be waiting for you. I am done with kings,' he referred to the Buchanan, 'and by your leave and grace, I intend to rest a while, before I turn to tyranny. You will find me wrestling with it, when you next return.'

'As I hope.' Hew hesitated, 'You will still be here?'

'Where else would I be?'

There were two paths from the walkway built around the house; one passing by the stable block up to the beaten track, the other to the gardens, through a walk of trees. To the west of Kenly Water both paths crossed and merged, and followed by the burn in its steady slow meanderings, until it reached the dam. On a morning such as this, when the haar had lifted and the rose began to bloom, it was no hardship, Hew decided, to take the garden path. He wandered through the boughs of yew and holly trees, the rowan and the ash, watching over all with ancient powers restorative, their histories extended long into the past. From the orchards on the south side came the hum of bees, sipping at the cups of the cherry and the plum, and the scent of apple blossom, faintly on the breeze. Beyond the kitchen gardens, with salad greens and roots, and rows of beans and cabbages, strawberries and leeks, the physick garden slept in the shelter of high walls, the cool house and distillery, where Meg had made her remedies from summer herbs and flowers. Hew opened up the doorway through the garden wall, and found his sister, barefoot, in a bed of leaves.

She looked as she had looked when he returned from France, expecting a bit lass, to find a grave grown woman, wild and dark and strange. Hew stopped short and shy of her, a shadow forged of mist

24

and sunlight, dancing in the grass. Only when she spoke to him did she seem flesh and blood.

'Hew. What brings you here?' The question he should put to her.

'Nicholas,' he said. 'I know not how, he knew that you would come today. He must have second sight.'

Meg took his answer seriously. 'He has. For he knows me better, than I know myself. I had not meant to come.' Already, she was pulling on her shoes, twisting up her hair to tuck into her cap. Hew felt he had disturbed her, stolen something from her, in her natural state.

'He sees beyond this world, since he is balanced in his frailty so close to the brink of it.'

This simple explanation made no sense to Hew. Nicholas had premonitions, which his friend dismissed as bodily afflictions crept upon the mind, to mortify the spirit, as they bound the flesh. Nor would he allow that Nicholas was close enough to parting from this life, when he himself was not prepared or willing yet to part with him. But Nicholas possessed a subtle power of sympathy, an imaginative force, which allowed him to transcend and see into the heart of things. It was Nicholas who gave instruction how Meg's garden should be kept, to give a perfect harmony of wildness and intent. Nicholas had kept the garden, as he knew Meg wanted it; his heart had felt the moment when she would return to it. As Nicholas grew more detached, more distant from the physical, the more he came to know, and understand the world.

Meg said, 'I have come too far and I have stayed too long.'

'Have you come alone?'

The question was a delicate one, and Hew pursued it cautiously. Meg suffered from the falling sickness. It was unthinkable that Giles would let her out alone, to tramp through morning dew, at dawn, to catch her death, and equally unthinkable that he would hold her back.

'Giles sent Paul,' confided Meg. 'We parted at the barley field, once the sun was up. I came out for the morning dew, and felt my heart was grening then to come back to the garden here, and see how it was kept.'

'Nicholas has kept it for you. Has he kept it well?' Her brother smiled at her.

'He has kept it perfectly. There is a careful order to it, patiently disposed and gentle in its touch, that nature does not feel the hand by which she has been led, and is content to settle under its restraint. But at this time of year, there is so much to be done. The broom buds to be bottled, waters to be stilled; seeds and winter plantings brought out from their glass, all this month and next to gather in the herbs. It is too much for Nicholas.'

'Then you must come and see to it.'

'I cannot bring my child with me,' Meg said, with a sigh, 'nor leave him long behind.'

'For certain, he must come,' pressed Hew. 'Wherefore should he not?'

'The road is rough and steep for him. It is too far to come. Besides which, things are different now. There is no turning back.'

Meg seemed so pale and sad, her brother was perplexed. 'How does the child?' he asked.

To his relief she broke into a smile, warming her wan face.

'Matthew is quite perfect. We have loosed his swaddling, for the summer months. His sapling limbs spin furiously, wild as any plant. He is the bright flower of my heart, and the very apple of his father's eye. By now, he will be breakfasting. He will have an egg. He will wriggle in a napkin, on his father's lap, striving with a small fat fist to snatch at Giles' spectacles, while his father reads to him, in Latin and in Greek, and fails to notice milk sops in his hair and beard, and Canny Bett looks in on them, to tut and roll her eyes. He will not want his Minnie for a while.'

Hew laughed at this. 'Does Giles truly read to him in Latin and in Greek?'

'In equal measure, both, to see to which he is more naturally inclined. I sometimes think he looks upon us both as an experiment. Is it so wrong to feel . . .'

'Wrong to feel what?'

'It is no matter,' Meg retracted. 'I have been confined and wintered far too long. I had forgotten quite how much I miss the garden here. Now the hours move on, and I must go back.'

'I will take you,' promised Hew. He let discretion veil her tears, and went back to the house, to see about a horse.

To Meg, Hew lent a fine red roan, while he rode on Dun Scottis, who had spent the morning slumbering in peace, and showed no sign of waking to the summer day. At best, the horse was sluggish, and at worst, recalcitrant.

'I don't know why you suffer him,' said Meg.

'Because he is a friend. And he wants the exercise, whatever he may think.'

'He is a thankless friend.'

'The most persistent kind.'

They rode on at a gentle pace, where the track was broad enough to travel side by side, coming past the corn mill, decked with summer flowers. The children were at play, tying ribbons to a pole.

'I never saw so many people celebrate the May, since I was a bairn. Perhaps it is the sun,' Hew smiled. The morning mists had broken on a cloudless summer's day.

His sister shook her head. 'It is not the sunshine, but the absence of the Melvilles, at the Kirk Assembly, lifts a heavy cloud. Their sermons are a shackle that have kept us all subdued.'

Hew protested, 'Ah, but that is harsh! For they are good men, Meg, and ardent in reform, Andrew, in particular, the scourge of all hypocrisy, of which you should approve. He brings fame and honour to the university, and a sense of order to the town.'

'He is the scourge of all,' corrected Meg. 'I have heard him preaching in the kirk of Holy Trinity, and nothing you can say of him will make me doubt him less. His language is vindictive, wrackful, and intemperate. I cannot help my feelings, Hew. I wish you were not friends with them. It makes you sad and serious.'

'What poffle,' muttered Hew.

'It is not poffle. Look at you!' Hew wore a summer suit, of dark grey satin silk, without lace or ornament. 'You look like a lawyer, or a scholar at the kirk.'

He laughed at that. 'I am a scholar, Meg, and a lawyer too.'

Meg swept this aside. 'And you have given Paul your gooseturd hat and hawking cloak. He wears them as his courting clothes.'

'Then I wish him more luck with them, than they brought to me. I am a professor, Meg. Would you have me come to college dressed in salmon slops? What would the students think of me?'

'Stuff! They think the world of you. *Clare Buchanan* telt me that her brother is devoted to you.' She stole a sideways glance at him, to see how well disposed he was to mention of the name, but Hew shrugged off the barb.

'George is a bairn, and a straw in the wind, too easily blawn. I maun dress according to my place. And I cannot imagine why you would find fault with it,' he countered, reasonably.

Still she was not convinced. 'Here dawns a cloudless play day. Giles, to mark the May, puts on a yellow coat – a sensible precaution, for judging at the butts. Yet you are dark and drab.'

'Tis prophylactic gainst the May. For fear that I should fall, and be carried off to elfin land, like the fair Tam Lin:

'When we were frae the hunting came

'That frae my horse I fell

'The quene o' faeries she caught me

'In yon green hill to dwell,' sang Hew.

Meg sighed. 'I wish you would be serious.'

'You wish I would be serious. And yet just now you railed at me, for seeming dull and sad— Hola! Whoa, there! What is that?' Hew cut their quarrel short, reining in his horse. For on the track in front of them a woman sat full squarely, skirts hoiked round her knees, peering at her toes. 'Aaeeie,' she wailed at them. She tried and failed to stand. Dun Scottis gave a snort.

'The queen of the May. Fair fou and drunken,' grinned Hew.

'Ah, do not be unkind,' his sister scolded him, 'I know her, I

28

doubt. She is Alison Peirson, a tenant of yours.' She slipped down from her horse, handing Hew the reins, and hurried on ahead. 'Mistress, are you well?'

'Quite well, I thank you, lass. What spectacle are you?'

Alison scrubbed at her eyes, pink and dim with dust. She peered at Meg distrustfully, through the clearing mist. 'Aye, I ken you noo, Matthew Cullan's lassie, wabbit wee bit blunderer, they ca'ed ye *loupy loup*. For that ye had the falland ill. They cured it wi' a spell.' Whatever harm had fallen to her did not curb her tongue.

Meg glanced back at Hew, who was out of earshot, looking for a place to tether up his horse. Dun Scottis, put to pasture, would be hard to shift. 'The falling sickness has no cure. It is controlled with physick,' she replied.

'Aye, ye would say that.' Alison lurched forward, standing up unsteadily. 'You can help me, lassie. Learn to me a charm.'

Meg could smell the liquor, curdled sour and sweaty, sickly on her breath. 'I can give you physick, if you are not well.'

'Physick will not help it, lassie. Oh, but he is ill with it! Afflicted sore and sick.' Alison began to wail with great sair rending sobbing, clinging to Meg's sleeve.

'Tell me, who is sick?' Meg fell back a step.

'Bless you, lassie, no one,' Alison corrected. 'I can gie ye money, see?' She reached into her serkinet, fishing out a purse. 'Teach to me a spell.'

'I cannot help you, then. I do not deal in charms.'

'What is the matter here?' Hew had left the horses tethered in a field. He saw a whey-faced woman in her early thirties mouthing at his sister, clutching at her sleeve. Hearing his approach, she startled and shrank back. 'What nether soul is that?'

'It is my brother Hew,' said Meg. 'We are on his land.'

'His land?' Alison looked up Hew, with dark grey doubting eyes. 'Nay, tis not his land. For it was once the bishops' land, and will be once again. There are, ye see, three kinds of laird . . .' she recollected hazily, 'and he is nought but one of them. He is not the master here, nor yet the laird of me. Inchmurdo . . . Inchmurtah.'

29

The words had a strange resonance, as though they were a prophecy. Hew urged, 'Madam, you are ill. I will take you home.'

Alison composed herself. ''Tis only a bit blister. I have lost a sock.' She lifted up her skirts, showing her bare foot. 'A braw wee sock of blue. Mind, now, if ye come across it. I would like it back.'

The wine draught had worn off; she felt the dark hurt spreading, deep inside her shirt, and knew she must be gone. She had not known what possessed her, spilling out the prattle Patrick once had telt to her, about the bishops' land. She hobbled down the path. Not far now, she saw smoke, the safety of Boarhills.

As Hew prepared to follow her, his sister called him back. 'She does not want us, Hew. You must let her go. She is not far from home.'

'I saw beneath her kirtle, Meg, her flanks flayed black and blue.'

'I know,' his sister sighed. 'But we cannot help her, if she will not make complaint. She has fallen to the May, as several others do. She is a strange soul, Hew. She came with her father, to live at Boarhills, when I was no more than a lass. The father is dead now. And Alison grows herbs to sell to the apothecaries. When their backs are turned, she makes them into remedies.'

Not so different then, from any other woman who grew flowers for simples, including Meg herself. But something in her tone provoked Hew into asking, 'Aye? What sort of remedies?'

'Mostly, harmless ones.'

'Then she is a witch?'

His sister shook her head. 'That is not a charge that you should throw out lightly. Poor Alison. She has been sorely used, and yet she does not help herself. Those words she spoke to you were almost like a curse.'

Hew reflected, 'Aye? Inchmurtah is a place. It is the ancient mansion house upon our father's land, long before he had it, fallen into ruin. It belonged to the archbishops once, and at the Reformation came into his hands. What Alison referred made a kind of sense, which leads me to suppose . . . But you are pale and cold! And you

30

are trembling, Meg.' He had forgotten, for the moment, that she was not strong, that she had been walking since the early hours. 'The sky begins to darken; I must take you home.'

They rode together on the track, where neither of them spoke. The physick wife had cast a cloud upon the first of May.

Chapter 4

Mary's Thorn

At eleven in the morning on the sixth of May, Hew Cullan crossed the South Street to the college of St Mary, to find the doors were bolted fast against the world. He rattled at the locks. 'Am I come too late?'

The porter peered doubtfully out from a grate. 'Are ye here for the speech?'

Behind him through the opening Hew could see a crowd, the flurry of black gowns, gathering like birds. Bells rang out the hour. The swallow wing took shape, and swept across the square. Since he knew better than to quarrel with the man who kept the keys, he persisted patiently, 'If it is not too late.'

The porter pulled the bolt across. His answer would have passed for logic in the schools. 'Though ye be ne'er so late, ye will not be the last. The orisons will not commence till Master Andro quits his house, and he will not do that till I have left the gate, and I will not do that until the house is filled, and a' the men and masters settled in the hall, and so you see, though you are last, ye cannot be the hindmaist yet; however late ye be, he taks the latter place. For such is his prerogative. *Primus est, et ultimus.*'

'But since the house is full ...' Hew watched the last gowns flutter, flapping up the tower.

'It is, sir, passing full,' the doorkeeper agreed. 'All our bursars here, and some of our young laureates that went into the Kirk, and all the blessed doctors save for Master James, that has privilege of absence for the month of May to get to know his wife.' He glossed this with a wink.

'And then there are they fremmit folk, fae diverse forrain parts, that come frae far and wide to hear the maister speak, that you wad not believe the babble that we hear, an' that besides the Latin a' the scholars ken; ye wadna care to wager on what tongue they may be thinking in, nor trust the words they speak. But Master Andro calls them honest, Christian men, and so we must believe it, sir. Besides that, we have students from St Leonard's, the tertians and the magistrands, and their regents too. Had we expected such a crowd, we should have kept the hall for it, and made shift for our dennar in the school of Greek.'

The common hall lay south, and at the present hour was set up for the dinner board of bread and boiled blood sausages, the earthy, iron black stench of which came creeping through the grate.

The porter counted further, flexing two fat fists, 'Of masters we have Doyle and Rollock, Rutherford and Black, Professors Groat and Bisset, Robertson and Grubb.'

'What, Bartie too?' Hew was drawn, despite himself, into the porter's list. Bartie Groat was mathematician at the college of St Salvator, and the third professor, after Giles and Hew. His post had been translated from St Mary's, after Andrew Melville was appointed there as principal. To Bartie, it was exile to the frozen North. He hankered for the sanctum of the leafy South Street colleges. The salt air and sea winds did not agree with him, provoking the rheumatics and stirring up his fleume. He felt cut off from the higher faculty of theologues, reduced to a mere pedant in the faculty of arts; his stipend was diminished, and paid to him in sufferance, his students were green striplings, nackets fresh from school. Though most of the philosophers had baulked at the reforms, Melville's warmth and vigour slowly won them round. Now Bartie had capitulated, only Giles stood fast.

'Most all of the professors here,' the porter read Hew's mind, 'apart from Doctor Locke.'

''Tis likely he was called away,' Hew excused his friend. 'Perhaps, if all are here, you might fulfil your charge?'

33

'Why, bless you, sir. Tis done.' The porter took the hint, 'Best look sharp an' run, else you may mak us late.' Hew took his chance to hurry through the gate and cross the empty courtyard to the founder's tower. The college had been built upon the site of the old pedagogy, the college of St John, the ruins of which were still apparent on its eastern flank. St Mary's, called the New College, was laid out on three sides: a high wall to the north, that looked upon the street, contained the port and lodge and Andrew Melville's house. The schools and bursars' lodging houses filled the western range, entered by a staircase in the corbelled tower. On the south side were the common hall, the kitchen and latrines, and beyond, the college gardens, extending to the burn. The land adjoined the parish of St Leonard's to the east, a boundary disregarded by the college doves, who were border reivers of a most pernicious kind. Hew knew the college well, and as he hurried to the lecture, he saw nothing out of place. He heard the fluting birdsong, and the drone of bees, saw pigeons on the bell-tower, blackbirds in a bush, smelled summer rose and cabbage kale, the soup of the latrines.

The cobbled square was empty now, the noontide sun on lattice windows casting quiet light. The lecture hall was up a flight of stairs, through the western entrance at the founder's tower. A hawthorn tree in blossom gave out gentle scent, just outside the door. A scattering of petals shivered in the breeze. Hew ran quickly up the steps, and turned into the upper school, where rows of students murmured, settled on long forms. It took a moment for his eyes to find the light in darkness, blinkered by the glare of the early summer sun. The order of the lecture room was strictly hierarchical, the front row set apart for the first ranks of the faculty. A natural gap had fallen there, dividing Bartie Groat from young Professor Robertson, who taught the New Testament in Greek. Bartie suffered from a damp, persistent phlegm, for which he tried a remedy of hardboiled egg and garlic flower, and Robertson had edged upwind. Bartie shuffled sideways, so that Hew could share his place. He acknowledged his arrival with a hoarse harrumph, filtered through the muzzle of his pocket handkerchief.

'Tis already past the hour, the lection starting late. Which means that we are likely to be late out for our dinner; the bursars will have finished all the kichin, and left us nought but bannock, soddins and cauld broth.'

Bartie took his dinner daily in the hall. On flesh days, he supped mutton soddins in a broth of kale, and on fish days, wattir-kaill, thin cabbage soup, with sops. He looked forward through the morning to his share of *kitchen* – the scraps of meat or cheese sent up to spice the dish – which halfway through the dinner hour was certain to run out.

'It is too much to be hoped for,' he continued peevishly, 'that Andrew Melville wad have thought to give a dennar for his guests.'

'Our funds are sorely stretched,' the professor of Greek testament responded to the slur, which Bartie had spat out, above and beyond the discretion of his handkerchief.

Hew said, 'Whisht, he's here.'

The master made an entrance through the nether door, and came to take his stand behind a small lettrin, raised up from the floor. His appearance brought a murmur of excitement to the crowd, for people came from far and wide to hear the great man speak. Giles Locke was dismissive: 'Half of them are spies.' Yet there could be no doubt he had a faithful following. There was scuffling at his back, where the students vied for space, and he struggled to move forward through their solid flanks. Melville was a small man, with the slight build of the scholar who was sickly as a child, and on this bright May morning he did not look not well; a pallor and a light sweat played upon his lips. Bartie saw it too, for he murmured in Hew's ear, 'There goes a man who bears upon his shoulders the sad weight of the world, or has a careful conscience, think you not?'

The mathematician's pale blue eyes were keen and penetrating through their watery film; often, there was clear sharp light implicit in the gloom. Bartie Groat was more perceptive than his snuffling countenance implied. 'Tis very like that some malignant fever wreaks its work in him. Such sickness, so beginning, is quick to spread perniciously. Observe; see how he sweats, his green and sickly air. I should make haste to leave, for fear to spread the pestilence.'

Hew answered, 'Aye, perhaps you should.' He had no time to spare for Bartie's sly malevolence, scantily dissimiled in a thin cloak of concern.

Bartie gave a snort. 'You lawyers are so keen to look for subtle evidence, you do not see the proof before your eyes. That man is sick, or something worse.'

'What worse?' challenged Hew. But Bartie had no chance to expand upon his gossiping, as Melville took his place behind the lectern at the front, as a man mounts to a scaffold, and began to speak. 'Welcome to ye, gentlemen, for it is pleasing to the heart to see so many hamely, gude and godly faces gathered in the hall. As ye are aware, I lately have returned from my duties at the General Assembly, and ye may be assured I come among ye from that same Assembly strengthened and reconforted, that ye shall find in me a firmness of resolve and steadiness of purpose in no way weakened or made faint, whosoever shall oppose me, with whatever kind of darts. And he that is against us, let him fear and quake, for God is on our side.'

This opening struck a curious note, for what purported to have been a sermon on the wedding vows. But Andrew Melville, ay contentious, could strike fire from any stone. Bartie whispered at Hew's side, 'The wedding is the hardest band that ony man may tak in hand,' and winked at him.

Melville cleared his throat. 'But of that heavy purpose, I will come to speak to you at a more fitting time. For we are come today, with gladness in our hearts. My nephew James was marrit, at that same Assembly, on the first of May. Wherefore, in his honour, I would say to you . . .'

He spoke then at some length and in the Latin tongue upon the risks and virtues of the married state, with divers illustrations, glossed in Ancient Greek. Marriage, as they knew, was not a sacrament, but a covenant, to which God was a witness, and a party, therefore sanctified. The text was plain and clear, but somehow lacked for Hew the spirit of true confidence. Andrew seemed distracted, and his tone was flat. He came to his conclusion somewhat short of the full hour.

'He has read your thoughts,' Hew winked at Bartie Groat, 'curtailing his devotions, to respect your dinner time.'

Bartie harrumphed, 'I should hope. A fine piece of stuff were that, for a man to swap his pottage for. Ye should marry, Hew,' he added unexpectedly.

'Are you so converted, then? I thought you disapproved of marriage, as a general rule.'

'As a rule, I do,' Professor Groat agreed. 'In every common sense, the married state debilitates. I have seen it happen, time and time again. First there comes the wife, and then there comes the bairn, and then you find your master is never so collegiate, nor stoops to tak his supper in the common hall. Professor Locke your brother is a case in point.' He waved off Hew's objections with a fierce flap of his arm. 'Women are the wrack, that wreaks havoc on our colleges, and we were better served in them, when no one had a wife. Yet I make ain sole exception, only in your case.'

'Indeed, and why is that?' Hew inquired, amused.

'Since you do not sup in college, more than once a week, your further dereliction might be hardly felt.'

Hew grinned. 'Ah, my thanks for that.'

'And,' Bartie went on, 'a wife might you keep you out of trouble, and from dabbling in controversies, and divers dark affairs, which if they do not see you honoured, are like to see you hanged.'

'And,' said Hew, 'for that.'

'Don't mention it. Your hanging would impart distress, and disgrace upon the college, which we could do without, and would effect in me, as I confess, a sorrow in more personal terms, for I have grown quite used to you; your wit is not unwelcome, and I am growing old, and have no use for change, though change is bound to

37

come.' Bartie blew his nose. His sudden and habitual lapsing into sentiment sometimes forged a mask for a more subtle shift. And so it happened here, as he went on, 'Moreover, it will keep you from your keeking glances at the students' sisters; *one* such, in particular.'

'I cannot imagine,' Hew protested, laughing, 'what you think you mean.'

It was more than likely Bartie had perceived the tightening of his throat, the subtle change in tone. Through a film of fleume, with piercing bird bright eyes, he picked up all that passed. What was seldom clear was how much of Bartie's gossip was benign, and how much of it was motivated by malicious spite. For the moment he did not remark upon it, but took the conversation back to the place where it began, with geometric cunning.

'And, if you were married, Giles would give a banquet with all kinds of sweets and delicats; no question of a lecture, we should have a feast.'

'If you would have a feast,' Hew recovered his composure, 'take a wife yourself.'

Bartie took this seriously. 'Alas, I am too old for that, and far too deep entrenched in single, college life. Now we must join this crowd, and try to make our way out through the thristing multitude, if we have any hope of arriving home by suppertime.' He clambered from the bench to push and grumble through the ordered lines of scholars waiting to depart. As Hew stood up to follow, Melville left the platform, coming to his side. 'I am right glad to see you, sir,' he addressed him warmly. 'Giles Locke has not come with you, I suppose?'

Professor Groat was out of earshot, which was just as well. Hew used his discretion. 'Sadly, he is not. He may have urgent business.'

'Ah, do not pretend,' Andrew Melville smiled. 'I know how he thinks.'

Hew answered this more honestly, 'I cannot think you do.' Giles' mind was supple, searching and inquisitive, its thrist for science balanced by a loving heart. He doubted whether any man was less equipped to fathom it.

'I assure you,' Melville said, 'whatever he believes in, I admire his skill. I hoped he might be here today, though I did not expect it. I require his help. But yours may do as well. I wanted some advice.'

Hew had grown accustomed, as professor in the law, to hearing colleagues' queries on the law of property, much as Giles was courted for a cure for piles. The doctor's brisk prescription, of hot coals to the fundament, made sure that the inquisitor did not inquire again. Since Hew was not so bold, his heart begin to sink. 'Do you have a question,' he suggested, 'on the law?'

'In some sense,' Andrew answered, unexpectedly, 'it is more a question that concerns the conscience. Since, in any case, it weighs upon me heavily, I should be glad to share it with you. For you are a good man, I think.'

There was an odd inflection to the words. Hew's response was awkward. 'Ah, I try to be.'

Andrew Melville frowned. 'You cannot try to be good,' he corrected tersely. 'Since we all are sinners, we are not empowered to *try* to be good. We may come to goodness, by virtue of God's grace.'

Hew saw in an instant why they were not closer friends. Still, he was intrigued. For Melville was a strong and staunch defender of the faith, and if he had uncertainties, confided in his nephew. He showed no sign of weakness, even to his friends. And though such things to Giles and Hew admitted careful argument, to Andrew they were doctrines written, read and closed.

'By God's grace,' he accepted. 'What is it you would ask?'

'Stay awhile, and dine with us,' the principal suggested. 'I will tell you then.'

They walked together to the stairwell, where Andrew was enclosed within a gulf of caps and hands, anxious to acknowledge and converse with the great man. In his absence, it appeared, he had been sorely missed. He freed himself, with kind and gracious words. 'I thank you, gentlemen, but ye maun go and eat, I will not keep you more.' The crowd dispersed at last, all but one young man, who stayed to hold the door, a thin-lipped, red-eyed youth.

Andrew Melville paused. 'This is Dod Auchinleck,' he remarked to Hew, 'a student in our college, who is training for the ministry, for whom we maun applaud. God knows, we have but few good men to follow in that cause, and a sad lack of ministers to fill our present vacancies. Our hopes are placed in Dod here, and others of his ilk.'

The young man answered wretchedly, 'I cannot apprehend it, sir, that I deserve that trust.'

'Come, Dod, there is modesty,' the principal encouraged, 'and there is lack of heart. If you do not confound the twa, you shall prove a credit to us.'

The young man shook his head. 'I dare not hope so much, for I am filled with doubts.'

Andrew Melville sighed. 'My door is always open, son.'

Though it was plain to Hew that 'always' meant 'not now', the young man seized his chance. 'There is one burning question, sir, pertaining to the lecture we have lately heard; I hoped that you might speak of it, I prayed that ye might speak of it, and put my fears to rest, and I was sair dismayed to find that ye did not; it is a matter consummate and preying on my mind,' Dod came thudding to a halt, concluding in a rush, of confusion, shame and awkwardness, staring at the floor. He seemed, in all his misery, not to notice Hew.

'Aye, son? What was that?' Andrew was a patient teacher, as devoted to his pupils as he was to his cause; and that, for all his fierceness, showed that there was good in him.

'Ye spake about the covenant that man makes with God, but not about the covenant a man makes with his wife. I mean their fleshly congress, sir,' the young man blurted out.

Andrew looked a little vexed. 'Fie, now, sir, have courage. That were understood.'

'But I dinna understand it,' Dod confided then. 'And how am I to marry folk, and gie them proper counsel, when I have had nae understanding of the carnal conversation?'

'Suppose,' suggested Hew, 'I wait for you below?'

Andrew answered grimly, 'Aye, I think that may be best.'

Smiling to himself, Hew clattered down the stair. He stepped out to the sun, into a pool of blood.

The hawthorn tree that marked the entrance cast its blossoms to the wind, each petal etched and threaded with a splattering of pink. Its heavy boughs bowed wet, its life-sap spilling red, riven at its heart. Blood had puddled, dark and sticky, in between the roots, running down the branches and the smooth bark of the trunk, to seep into the ground. Some, like Hew, had stepped in it, their frantic bloody footprints scraping on the grass.

'Praise God, it is a miracle,' a voice came from the crowd. The company stood huddled, gaping and aghast.

Chapter 5

The Seeing Stone

The hawthorn tree ran red with blood, and Hew could make no sense of it. A shadow fell across the square, a resonating stillness, though the sky was cloudless still. He put his hand, instinctively, into the cleft between the branches, where the wound was warm and wet, and felt into its heart.

'What accident has happened here?' Andrew Melville had come down the stairs, with the hapless Dod Auchinleck. It was Bartie who answered. Bartie's bright eyes were fixed like a bird's. 'All grass, it seems, is flesh. This tree has suffered some great hurt, its life force spills and spurts great gobbets of raw blood, the juglar cut full deep in its organic vein.'

Dod Auchinleck whimpered and fell to his knees, a jummil of rapture and fear. 'God save us, sir, is it a kind of miracle?'

Andrew Melville roared. His patience, when it left him, did not give out quietly. He vented his frustrations on the luckless Dod, whose want of understanding might have been excused, but not his want of faith. 'Are you such a faulter, that ye cannot call to mind the plain truth of your creed, but ye start skeich and stummering? Have I never taught to ye, that miracles have ceased?'

'The devil's ain excepted,' Bartie pointed out. 'This is his work, surely, conjured up by warlocks cunning and uncouth.' He alluded to a doctrine most of them believed, that even Andrew Melville dared not contradict, as he assured the crowd, 'Faith, if this is witchcraft, we shall sound it out and send those divils fleeing, sairly sick and sorry that they came to try us here. Yet let us be more circumspect, before we grant the devil more than is his due. It is, perhaps, some sickness of the tree, which gives a little colour to the sap.'

'It is like no sickness I have ever seen,' contended Bartie Groat, who took a layman's interest in the life of trees. 'Tis plain to any laic that the stuff is blood.'

It was plain to Hew that Bartie was enjoying this. He interrupted quietly, 'Whatever hand has left this mark I think it was a human one.'

The whole crowd turned to stare at him. A little of the tainted blossom settled on his coat.

Hew said, '*If I may . . .*' He loosened his knife from its belt, and made his way through to the heart of the tree. At his back, he heard Bartie, 'He cannot resist. He maun have an answer. None is more inquisitive. Did I ever tell you, did you never hear, about the Flemish windmill? Ask him about that!'

Though Hew did not respond, he recognised the truth in it. He felt his heartbeat quicken, knew it was not fear.

He worked on in silence, with that sharp exactness he had witnessed in Giles Locke, excising to the poison at the centre of a wound. The tree did not shrink back. It was young and slender still, and barely could support itself, its heavy blossoms drooping, dropping to the ground. Hew cut three or four of them, the crimson and the white, and wrapped them in a handkerchief, where the dark stain spread, each pink flower unfolding, colouring the cloth. He found a dark red pooling where the branches met, and here he dipped his blade, dispensing it by drops. With it came a membrane, like a piece of skin. He tied the bundle up and tucked it in a pocket hanging at his belt. 'I will take these samples to Giles Locke, who, by his analysis, will tell us what they are. It looks to me,' he concluded, 'as though some stranger came to visit while we were within. We must ask the porter what he saw and heard.'

The porter took some while to recover from his fright, after which he swore that he had had no part in this, nor had be been aware that aught had gone awry. He had let in Master Hew. He had made secure the gate. Aye, he was quite certain that the gates were made secure. They were locked the whole while, and they were locked now.

And they could gang see, if they didna trust him. (Several of them did, and were sorely stomachat to find they were locked in. Without their master's say-so, he would not give up the key.)

He had called on Andrew Melville, who was at his prayers, to tell him it was time for the lecture to begin; his house was at the north west corner, not more than a stone's throw from the founder's tower; that was but a saying, for he had not thrown a stone.

There were pebbles in the courtyard and around the tree. Were there stones there, generally?

The porter thought there were.

Hew selected one of them and dropped it in his pocket. Had the porter seen his master climbing up the steps?

He had seen him to the door, and had stayed to hold it open, standing at the tree. He had seen the hawthorn then, and not found aught amiss. There had been twa pigeons, sitting on a branch, and some others in the tower-loft, skiting fae the roof. The pigeons were a pest. Their scummering made work for him; they stoured the place with shite.

There were no pigeons now. And that was odd, thought Hew. The college dows were tame as lambkins, pecking at the feet of strangers. Rarely would they fly away. What horror then had scattered them?

Hew took a mental note, and went on with his questioning. The porter left the tower and went back to his lodging, built above the door. He had kept the watch, spied no one in the square. No one had passed through the entrance, either in or out.

The hawthorn tree had been there nigh on twenty years. The sapling had been planted by the queen of Scotland, when she still was queen; they ca'ed it Mary's thorn. It mebbe was an unco place, to plant it at a house of prayer, but had not Christ the saviour worn a crown of thorns? (At this point in the evidence, to Melville's plain disgust, the porter crossed himself.) This year was the first year it had flowered. And that was neither rare nor wondrous, as he understood it, for a proper view on it, they maun ask the gardener. The gardener was not here, for it was not his day to come. That was Thursday next and after on a Tuesday; he came by more often in the summer months. There were gardens on the south side, stretching to the burn, but you couldna cut across, all had high stane walls. Whichever way you came at it, the college was closed in.

He had heard of a disease, that the gardeners called red leaf. But he did not think the hawthorn ever suffered that disease, nor that the red leaf made a green tree bleed. The hawthorn was bewitched. He would fetch an axe, and strike the menace down.

Melville told him no. He baulked at such destruction, wanton and unwarranted, or else feared some dark magic, settled at the heart of it, that he dared not disturb. 'Are ye convicted, still,' he said aside to Hew, 'that this were not brought on by an infernal agency?'

'I am certain of it.' Though Hew was far from certain how the trick was done, he saw no sense in stirring up a fearful restless crowd, to spill their superstitions out onto the street. 'Give me leave to prove it to you, in a few days' time.' He hoped he could back up the bluff with science from Giles Locke. For now, he worked on instinct.

Andrew Melville sighed. 'As I hope you may. For it is likely this was meant by my detractors to astound my followers and undermine their faith in me. In which case, we may be advised to look to our defences, and explore the grounds. Will you walk with me, sir? The others must go too, and make a thorough search.'

The scholars were dispersed in groups of three and four. 'If you come across a stranger, bring him back to me. And, understand me, bring him back unharmed. There will be no rough justice, do you understand? The porter and Dod Auchinleck shall stay to guard the tree and so mak guid their faults.' He made it more than clear to them that they dared not refuse.

Dod Auchinleck was punished for his lapse in faith, the porter for allowing this to happen on his watch, and both of them were forced to stare the terror in the face, as penance for their sins. Melville did not think of it as cruelty, Hew supposed, but as giving them the chance to make amends to God. He felt sorrier for Dod, whose floundering for grace was scuttled by the flesh.

St Mary's was a stronghold, built to stand the storm. The townsfolk had attempted more than once to battle with it, when Andrew Melville's sermons had inflamed them at the kirk, and when a reckless student shooting at the butts had sent an awkward arrow through the baxter's hat, as he came whistling down the vennel with a tray full of fresh loaves. Melville had closed in the last remaining gap, where his own house opened on St Mary's Wynd, with a piked iron fence. Melville's house was accessed from a forestair in the courtyard, though the grandest of its windows looked out on the street at the far west corner of the northern front. All callers now must enter by discretion of the porter, through the college gate. On the east side, long abandoned, were the bare bones of the college and the chapel of St John. 'One day,' Andrew Melville said, 'we will have a kirk here, or perhaps a library.' Hew poked into the ruin, but saw no signs of life among the moss and pigeon droppings shoring up the walls. The tracery of windows shaped an arching shadow, open to the sky, and on the grassy sill which once had been God's earth he found a piece of glass, coloured like a rose. Nothing more was left.

A pigeon fluttered past. Whatever thing had startled it did not disturb it now; it settled on a parapet, flapping its white wings. 'The dows are a menace,' Andrew Melville said, 'they fly out to the fields, and beyond, to St Leonard's, ravaging the crops. The principal complains. They are a constant source of quarrel betwixt our twa colleges that we could do without. Yet they are meek as lambs.'

They walked on to the kitchens, past the college wash house, where the stench from the latrines brought water to their eyes. 'We are waiting on the draucht-raker,' Melville apologised, 'to clean out the muck. The privies can be pungent, in the summer sun.' A nether sink was clogged, and several kinds of filth had seeped up through the floor, effluvium and sediment met sour milk curds and cooking fat swilled down the kitchen drains. The sharp scent of a swooning water cut clean through it all, and made Hew catch his breath. He took a gulp of air, and satisfied himself that no one lurked inside, for no one but the raker could have lingered long.

The kitchen had its own aroma, none the less dispiriting, of college kale and sausages. A dozen blood black puddings bubbled on the hearth. Hew poked in a pot. 'Are they made up on the premises?' He was not sure what he imagined. The scudlar and the cook, with a bucketful of blood? But at this early stage, he could rule nothing out.

'The puddings are bought in, from the flesher by the cross.' The kitchen boy and cook both told the same tale: they had been together for the whole of the last hour. Where else should they have been, with the dennar to prepare?

On the south side of the college, past the common hall, were gardens filled with beanstalks, cabbage kale and leeks, which added bulk and substance to the college broths. These slender crops, though under constant siege, were nourished by the birdlime from the college doves, whose doocot lay beyond. The land to the south west, beyond the common lade, belonged to Robert Wood, the brother of the coroner, and no great friend to Hew. His wife was Clare Buchanan. Here Hew could find no access, for the garden door was locked, and no one but the pigeons saw the other side.

'This search is fruitless, Hew,' Melville said at last. 'The college is secure, and I cannot fault the servants. The bursars and economus were with us in the lecture hall. And there is no one else has access to these grounds.'

Hew paused to consider this. Of the three men in the college who had not been at the lecture, the kitchen boy and cook had shared an alibi; both had told the truth, or both of them had lied. The porter

47

had no witness but the horror on his face, and that was plain enough, as eloquent an advocate as he had ever heard. Andrew agreed with him. 'The porter is as honest as the day is long, and he has ay been loyal, though he is not wise. I cannot for a moment think that he colludes in this, nor has he the wit to think up such a draucht. As for the cook and kitchen boy, in some form of conspiracy, God knows that I see phantoms daily in my dreams, but else all reason fled, I will not think this.'

'What phantoms?' wondered Hew.

Andrew's answer was evasive. 'I have not been sleeping well. It does not matter now. But I will not accuse the porter or the cook. This search has thrown up nothing. Let us go back to the gate.'

The others had returned, with nothing to report. Whatever bird had lighted its dark feathers on the hawthorn tree had already flown. Hew looked back into the quiet sunlight, sensing there was something, somewhere, he had missed. 'Were it yet too much to hope for,' grumbled Bartie Groat, 'that we might go home? For some of us have dinner boards, waiting at our colleges.'

Melville had the porter open up the gate. 'For certain, you must go. And those of you that lodge here, to the frater hall. I am right sorry, gentlemen, that you were discomfited by this piece of mischief. Once I have the perpetrator, I will make him known to you. He shall feel our wrath. Until then, I must ask you that none of you shall speak of it, else ye may spread confusion, terror and alarm. So we rise above, and shall defeat our enemies, whatsoever men, or devils, they may be.'

There were murmurs of assent, as the crowd began to drift. Hew heard Bartie mutter, 'Aye, tis very like!' He took his friend aside. 'You never telt me, Bartie, why you came today. For certain it was not to listen to a wedding speech.'

'You are like a hunting hound,' Professor Groat complained, 'that scents game on the wind. I have not seen such vigour in you since you went to Ghent. Tis plain enough to see that you are in your element. Aye, very well, the truth. An old man's life is yet too short to waste in venting spleen. I have put by my grudge. The truth is, I had hoped that Andrew Melville might support me in the fight against the faculty. I suppose you know that they are minded to discard my post?'

'Bartie, I had no idea!' Whatever Hew expected, it had not been this.

'The fund will stretch to two professors, where it strains at three,' Professor Groat explained. 'My role is small and circumscribed, yet I maun confess to you, I know no other life. My best hope is the principals, to make a case for me. Else I maun be a pedagogue to some laird's futless lad, too feeble or to doltish to endure the grammar school. Rude bairns will hide my handkerchers, put paddocks in my bed. If I am thocht superfluous, so shall I end my days.'

'I'm quite sure,' Hew insisted, 'that it will not come to that, if there is any justice in the world.'

'If you believed in justice, you would practise law, and not profess to peddle at the university. You ken as well as I do, justice is a sham, and there is nought of consequence rewarded in this life. Rich men prosper, brave men hang.' Bartie blew his nose. 'You should be careful, Hew.'

'Should I? Of what?'

'This business of the hawthorn tree. I see it draw you in.'

'As I confess, it does,' Hew smiled, 'and I am not afraid of it.'

'You never did attend to a better man's advice. But I would urge you heartily, to seek no further answer here, but leave it well alone.' The pigeons had returned, to peck at Bartie's feet. 'So young and plump and sweet. And what would I not give, for two squabs in a pie. Yet we may be the pigeons here.' Bartie ended, briskly, 'Well now, dinner time!'

'You must hold your promise not to tell a soul.'

The mathematician groaned, 'Ah, but that is cruel! You have snuffed the heartbeat from an old man's life, stealing from his pleasure that one precious chink of light. Not speak of it! Not dine on it! You demand too much.'

'But for one day,' Hew insisted. 'I pray you will not speak of it, least of all to Giles. I would have him test the samples I have taken without prejudice, for which it is essential that he has not been forewarned. A dinner in it, Bartie, if you keep your word.'

'I shall hold you to the dinner,' Bartie snuffled off. 'But you should be aware you break an old man's heart.'

Hew found Andrew Melville standing by the hawthorn tree.

'I have sent Dod Auchinleck up to his chamber,' the principal confided. 'He was a little distressed. He is not a bad man, as I think, though at times he is a weak one. He wants a little shaping, that is all. With a little shaping, he may turn out for the good.'

Melville glanced up at the tower-loft. 'The dows have returned. I wonder if that means we are no longer under threat. You found something, I think, lying on the ground. May I ask you what it was?'

He was sharp, Hew noticed, fishing out the stone. 'This is what I found. Tell me what you see.'

The centre of the stone had been worn through to a hollow, weathered to a hole

Andrew Melville frowned, 'A seeing stone. Then this maun explain it.'

'What does it explain?'

'It confirms our fears. The stone is a charm. I have seen one before. It was tied upon a riband, round an infant's neck, to keep it from the faerie folk till it received the sacrament. The silly midwife was found out, and sorely did repent of it.'

Hew pointed out, 'There are no midwives here. Then what do you conclude?'

'That the stone is emblematic of a kind of witchcraft, and is certain proof that there is magic here,' Melville answered sadly. He did not show signs of faltering, prepared to face the devil if and when he must. His sorrow was to find that the devil came so close to him, and had taken root among people he had trusted.

Hew held up the pebble, squinting through the hole in it, to see the clear blue sky. 'It is a seeing stone.' For a moment, without thinking, he had thought of Nicholas. He swept the thought aside. 'And shall I tell you what I see? I see an endless sky, of depth and possibility; the whole world closed and captured in a winking eye. A small stone with a hole in it, sucked out by the sea, like a succar candie, on a small boy's tongue. What do I conclude from that? That this little stone did not come here by chance, but someone must have brought it here. Of faeries, witches, devils, charms, I read nothing in a hollow, worn out by the sea. This stone is out of place. And that is all I see. I will take the samples I have taken to Giles Locke. He will show us with his science what secrets are contained in it, and, if he cannot, we shall look again. For we must keep inquiring, with a searching mind. So ready we may be to keek through narrow stones, and see a world of darkness and of terrors ranged against us, when what we are looking at is mirrored from our selves. We cry censure at the midwife who pins charms upon the babby. I pray we do not fall into that same class of mistake.'

Andrew's view was clear, 'For certain, we shall not. For God is on our side. Yet I am content to leave this in your hands. Our visitors have left, and the others have retreated, to the dinner board. We should follow, I suppose. Yet I find I have no appetite for dining in the hall. May I ask instead that you come back to my house? I can offer bannocks and a decent bit of cheese.'

Hew had forgotten, for the while, that Melville had a purpose in requesting him to stay. In the safety of his house, the principal returned to it. 'First, though, we maun eat, for we are not so sparing here that we are not aware that all strong hearts need sustenance.' Andrew looked around him, somewhat at a loss. There was an air of helplessness about his hospitality. 'Somewhere, there is wine. Make yourself at home, and I will see what I can find.'

Hew was left alone, in a pleasant first floor room that overlooked the square. From the window of the chamber he could see the tower, and under it the hawthorn blossoms, darkly tinged with blood. The room inside was plain and clean, its rows of neatness overruled by straggling piles of books, which spilled out from the bookshelves onto wooden boards. There were several low-backed chairs, a lettrin and a pair of stools, in a circle round the hearth. The fireplace was unlit, swept clean of any ash, and though it looked south, the room remained cool, and harboured a faint smell of damp. On the desk were writing things, and a pile of books. As Andrew closed the door behind him a single sheet of paper blew down to the floor. Hew bent to pick it up, and saw that it was written in the Hebrew script. He took it to the light, to while away the time in waiting, trying to decipher it. It did not take him long to identify the text as one of the most difficult and troubling of the psalms. He supposed it was intended as the substance of a sermon, in which case, it was not one he would like to hear.

'How apposite that ye should light on that.'

Melville had returned, with a banquet on a tray, cobbled from the remnants he had gathered from the hall. He swept a pile of books from the board on the flour, and set out bread and collops and a lump of yellow cheese, pewter plates and cups, and white wine in a jug.

'The malmsey is quite good, though we are not one of those colleges that squanders funds on wine' – he alluded to St Leonard's – 'I had a flagon brought, to drink to James' health.' He poured a cup for Hew, and took a sip himself. 'I rarely take strong drink, but sometimes, it is called for.'

Hew took up the cup and set the paper down. In retrospect, he could not tell which proved the sourer draught.

'Forgive me, I should not have looked. The wind had blown it to the floor.'

Melville insisted, 'I have no secrets here. Yet it is of interest that you chance on that, for it has seemed to me a salutary exercise. It is not, you may see, the original, but the psalm in Greek, rendered into Hebrew. There are some small mistakes in it; that said, it

52

is a fair attempt, and one which any student might be pleased to own. You read Hebrew, do you not? You have been reading it with James.'

'A little,' Hew confessed. He had the faint sense, still, that he was found at fault, having been discovered with the paper in his hand.

'Then read it to me now. Read those parts in Hebrew that are underscored, and turn them into Scots.

'Had I expected an examination,' Hew protested mildly, 'then I should have come prepared.'

'Your patience, sir. Allow me this.'

'Ah, very well.' Hew sighed. The imposition, he supposed, he had brought upon himself.

'It is a copy of the 109th psalm of David. I have sometimes thought,' he ventured, 'that the tone of that psalm, so bitter, harsh and vengeful, does not chime so sweet with what we ken of Christ. It is a hard thing to stomach, choked with so much bile.'

'I did not ask you,' Andrew said, 'what you have *sometimes thought*, but to translate the words before you on the page.' He seemed to have forgotten that they were not in a class, but this brusqueness was unlike him, even so. Hew played the part assigned to him, and did as he was told.

'It is a prayer against the wicked, where the psalmist prays for vengeance against those who have accused him, whereupon he curses them, with many bitter words.'

Andrew urged him, 'Aye? And how do you translate them?'

Hew glanced at the verse. 'In as much as I recall . . .'

'You must not recall,' the pedagogue said sharply, as though he were the schoolmaster, and Hew the errant child. 'Translate for me, in plainer words, the places underlined.'

'Set thou the wicked over him . . . and let the . . . the opponent . . . stand at his right hand,' Hew continued carefully.

Melville nodded. 'Aye. That, now, *that* is good. You do not follow the Greek, and translate *ha-satan* as *Diabolos*, or Satan. He is the adversary; here the prosecutor, in the court of judgement. His reference is the law, as you understand. But then you are a lawyer, so tis likely you would see that. Go to, now, go on.'

'Where he shall be judged, let him be condemned, and let his prayers be turned into sin.' Here, Hew paused and frowned. Melville had no quarrel with a vengeful God, for he prompted earnestly, 'Aye, go on, go on!'

'. . . let his days be few, and another take his charge . . . let there be none to extend mercie unto him, neither let there be any to show mercie unto his fatherless children. Let his posterity be destroyed, and in the generation following let their name be put out.'

Hew set the paper down. 'I find it hard to come to terms with the singer's want of charity. And I will confess to you, tis not my favourite psalm. What purpose has it here?'

'I have no idea. Did I not explain to you? I found it on a placard, posted at my door.'

Chapter 6

A Box of Tricks

Melville read no threat in the paper at his door, and he made no connection with the bleeding tree.

'They are not the same at all. For the one may be considered an attempt to unsettle, and to undermine our faith, by the devil's magic, or some other wickedness. The other is to strengthen and make solid our resolve, through the pure voice of the liturgy, by which we all affirm the feeling of our hearts. I took it as a sign.'

He helped Hew to a collop of some cold grey meat, whose colour had leached out into the cooking pot. The flesh was limp and soft, and with a little flavour might have been digestible. It turned out to have none. Hew explored it glumly. 'As a sign of what?'

'That I should be more temperate and thoughtful in my actions, none so quick to judge. Yet where the cause is just – for you maun be aware, Hew, the psalmist's cause was just – I should not fear to act. We should strike down our enemies.'

Hew was not convinced, on either count. 'You say that this paper was pinned on your door, when you came back from the General Assembly? And that no one in the college owns to having left it there?'

'Just so. And the timing of the missive had a singular effect. Now, do not mistake me,' Andrew hurried to assure him, 'I do not suppose this comes to me straight from the hand of God; rather, I am persuaded it was written by one of my own students. Dod Auchinleck is one such comes to mind.'

Dod Auchinleck, again. And it occurred to Hew that Dod had made his presence felt both in the lecture and outside it. Perhaps he had more cunning than had first appeared. 'Have you not asked him, then?'

The principal confessed, 'I have not liked to put the question more directly, since he did not admit it when I raised it in the school. He is a modest soul. Whoever it may be, has cause to feel well pleased with it, for it was neatly done.'

Hew accepted, 'Aye, perhaps.' He felt uneasy still, for if the psalm contained a message that was backed up by the hawthorn tree, it did not augur well.

'Whoever left it,' Andrew argued, 'for whatever purpose, has strengthened my resolve in asking for your help. I would see justice done.'

'Aye? In what respect?'

'Concerning Patrick Adamson.'

'The archbishop, do you mean?' Patrick Adamson was archbishop of St Andrews and chancellor of the university. He went by several names, Constance and Constantine among them. It was said he was son to a baxter, a trade of which Hew had had more than his fill.

Melville jabbed his table knife into a piece of bread, spearing it with cheese. 'The *tulchan*,' he corrected. 'For as ye are aware, the bishops have no business in a true reformit kirk.'

Tulchan was the Gaelic word used by the reformers for the straw-calf bishops, set before the milk-kine of the starveling church. The drip drip drip of milk was creamed off by the lords, while the bishops battened on the splashings from the pail. In Andrew Melville's kirk, a bishop had no merit more than any other man. Time was when Patrick Adamson had sworn and preached the same, before the Regent Morton offered him the diocese. Then he had changed his tune.

'As you know,' Andrew went on, 'I have been at the Assembly. The rumour from the town has left me sorely vexed, for it is said the king will not submit to Gowrie's governance, nor rest content, for long.'

'I have heard that,' Hew agreed. He thought back to the last time he had seen the king, a fraught and frightened boy. *They want to take my power from me.* The boy had not been wrong. He had fallen captive to the earl of Gowrie, whose thrift and prudent government chimed well with Melville's own. His favourites were dismissed, routed from the court, Arran under house arrest and Lennox fled to France. The king had sworn he was not forced or kept against his will, a hollow proclamation no one had believed.

'His old friends are regrouped,' Melville now confirmed. 'Lennox is expected, any day, from France. This regiment will fall. Therefore the kirk is minded to act against the bishops, before they can appeal again to the king's protection. The archbishop of Glasgow has already been indicted, and called before his brethren. Now the light of scrutiny has turned to Patrick Adamson. He was called to answer to a charge of lechery, of insult to the kirk, and abandoning his flock. He wrote a letter to me, saying he was caught up in his castle, suffering from a sickness that he called a fedity, and could not compear. And so at that Assembly I stood up and spoke for him; and his inquisition was put off until another time. Yet even as I pleaded for him, I felt sair ashamed that he should so disgrace us, our kirk and university. I loved him as a brother once, and knew him as a scholar and a righteous man.'

'You took it for falset?' interpreted Hew.

'Had I taken it for falset, sir, then I should not have sworn to it,' Melville countered sharply. 'The truth is I do not know, and that were bad enough. He has kept here to his castle, and does not go abroad, but the reasons may be politick. The word is, he has sent away his surgeons and physicians, and swears he will have none of them, but seeks to cure his malady through dishonest means. Therefore, have I resolved to ask Professor Locke, to sound this sickness out.'

'That,' said Hew, 'makes perfect sense.'

'So I hope, sir,' Andrew nodded, 'Giles Locke is a fine physician. And his opinion, were it given, might be worthy of respect. But I ken full well that he is no defender of our cause. He maks his feelings felt, rather by abstention than by opposition. I do not fault him for it, for he is a civil and an honest man. But I think it likely that he will decline the charge. I hoped you might persuade him to it, and come too, as witness, to see justice done.'

Hew was roused by this. 'Giles is my friend and brother,' he defended, 'I trust him with my life. And you may be assured that he will tell you ...' *straight*, he was about to say, but Giles' diagnoses were the convoluted kind, 'he will tell the truth. His judgement as physician is not clouded by his faith, or what you think his lack of it. If you cannot trust Giles Locke, then you were ill-advised to take me as your arbiter.'

Andrew Melville sighed. 'I did not mean that, Hew. I do not doubt Giles Locke. But I would have you there to see justice done for Patrick, so that he cannot say that he has been ill used. You should know, perhaps, that in my ain poor heart I pray that he is sick, for then I had not lied for him. I pray to God for help that I may judge him fairly, to give me strength and will to seek out the truth, and that I cannot do without you at my side.'

Hew considered. 'Yet, if Giles consents to it, might Patrick not refuse?'

'It will not please him,' Andrew owned, 'but he will agree. For, if he does not, he will be excommunicat; the kirk will read refusal as his clear confession that he is a lecher, a defaulter and a fraud. It is a cold and lonely place for any man to lie in, left out from his brethren. And, as I ken Patrick, he will not want that. I bid you, put the matter plainly to your good friend Doctor Locke, persuade him he must come, nor give him cause to argue that I do not trust him.'

'Giles is a rational man,' Hew promised with a smile. 'And he will not think that, if it is not true.'

'He does not trust me,' Giles concluded. 'For that reason he sends you.'

'It is rather,' Hew assured him, 'that he does not trust himself.'

'And were it any other person,' Giles dismissed this out of hand, 'I might allow a modicum, of simple, honest doubt. But that man is a monolith. His ignorance is cast in stone.'

They were in the turret tower, Doctor Locke's consulting room at St Salvator's college, where Hew had brought the news. He had passed on Melville's message, which had not been well received.

'He asks only,' Hew persisted, 'that you make a true report of what you see and find. And he has assured me he will take your word on it. He wants justice for the kirk, without prejudice to Patrick. You cannot fault him, surely, for a careful mind?'

'Rather I should marvel at it,' Giles said with a snort. 'Aye, then, very well. I agree to make the visit, so long as you come too, to explain things to your friend – for he and I, assuredly, will find no common ground – and so long as Adamson is willing to consent to it. Which I do not think is likely; he has not consulted me. What sort of sickness is it?'

'Melville says a *fedity*. *Foeditas* is foulness, in the Latin,' Hew reflected. 'Corruption of the body, or else of his spirit. Melville knows not which.'

'The two are not so disparate, as some men would believe. 'A *fedity*,' repeated Giles, cheering up immensely. 'Then I shall look forward to it. We shall go tomorrow, first thing after breakfast.'

Giles was a practitioner of peculiar tastes. The turret tower was filled with rows of curiosities, which lined each nook and cranny of its arching shelves; unguents, oils and pickling spices, astrolabes and clocks. In the recess by the window, to make best use of the light, Giles kept his dissecting table, an old flesher's block. Hew approached it cautiously, since he was never certain quite what he would find: a poppy head or pomegranate, spilling out its seeds, or the matrix of a rabbit, with its kittens still intact. Once, Giles had a human foot, peeled back to the bone, and once the pipes and ventricles that mapped the human heart.

This time, Hew found nothing but a box of leaves, which Giles had covered over with a sheet of glass. 'What kind of plant is that?'

'Camomile,' said Giles. 'But that is not the point. The leaf is but a mask, the method of disguise. What do you see below?'

'Some sort of bulb or grub?' Coming from the box, Hew heard a rattling sound. 'A gerslouper?' he guessed.

'It is a pupa, of some sort. I wait for it to hatch.'

'What will it hatch into?'

'I have no idea. That is the experiment.' The doctor beamed at him. Hew knew no one better who could answer to his needs. He reached into his pocket for the bloody handkerchief and scraped the crusted contents out on to the slab. 'Tell me, what is that?'

It was typical of Giles that he did not reply at once, that it was plain to any onlooker it was a clot of blood. Giles was not a ly-by, and would offer no opinion without careful probing. Now he poked and prodded, sampled, stroked and sniffed, and looked closely at the specimen through a piece of glass. He dropped a part of it into a flask of water, warmed upon the fire, and stirred till it dissolved, to turn the liquid pink. With pincers he detached a small fragment of skin, washed clean of its sediment, and placed it on the block. Eventually he asked, 'Is this some sort of trick? For clearly it is blood.'

Hew acknowledged, 'I think it very likely it may be a trick. But my intent and hope was not to trick with you, but to ask you to consider, with a searching mind, whether it could be the life sap of a tree, or any substance other than it seems to be.'

'Assuredly,' said Giles, 'It is what it appears. It looks and feels and smells, congeals and dissolves, as though it were blood. And were I ever pressed, and forced to stake my life on it, then I might be prepared to swear that it was blood.'

'Aye, then, very good,' Hew grinned. 'What sort of blood?'

'The sort,' said Giles, 'that comes from cutting flesh, from fowl or fish or animal, not from any plant.'

'Not human,' Hew assumed.

'Did I say that?' Giles retorted. ''Tis like you, to go leaping at conclusions, when the proper path has not been circumscribed. When was man not animal?'

'*All flesh is not the same flesh, but there is one flesh of man, and another flesh of beasts,*' Hew pointed out.

Giles responded, 'Pah! You have spent too long in the company of kirkmen.'

'Then it *is* human blood?'

'Did I say so, Hew?' The doctor fixed his colleague with a baleful stare. There were moments, after all, when his thoroughness exasperated and Hew felt more inclined to cut through to the chase. 'Is there a way to tell?'

Giles would not be rushed. 'When we were in Paris, at the Rue des Fosses, there was a phlebotomer – a man called de la Peine – who could tell a man his nation from the colour of his blood, as our vintars can distinguish French and Rhenish wines. His patients would sit quietly till he had drawn a draucht of it, then he would sniff and say, Hispanyee, or Almanie, Flemish, Scots, or Dutch. He made a fortune from it.'

'That might be of some interest, if you kent how twas done.'

'That part I am coming to. He did it by the hats,' said Giles.

'The hats?' repeated Hew.

'He was a man of fashion; so too were his customers. The height and shape of hat differs from place to place. The differences were subtle, but his instincts were refined. They failed him only once.'

'Then all that you are saying,' Hew summed with a sigh, 'is that you cannot tell.'

'That may well depend, on what you want to ken. My father was a man with an uncommon love of sausages, and he could tell you at a glance what offal they consisted of, but I have not that faculty. From the depth of colour, I would hazard it were ox blood, though there is too little of it to confirm its source. There is no telling what or where it may come from, but for this piece of skin.' Giles had placed the membrane underneath his glass. Washed clean of its blood, it had a bluish tinge. 'From the coarseness and the strength, I should say that this was *vesica*. What plain men call a bladder.'

'*Vesica*.' Hew broke into a smile. The world made perfect sense to him. For he saw in a moment how the trick was done. 'Giles, you are ingenious!'

Giles, though slightly baffled, took this as his due. 'I think that I may have a piece with which to make compare. Which serves now to remind me, I have something new to show you.'

He lifted down a key from its wooden hook, and unlocked the door that led in to his closet. Here he kept his notebooks, papers and anatomies, and one or two rare artefacts, too strange to be exposed. And here it was that Meg had come, to nurse and care for Nicholas, through that first grave sickness that had brought him down, falling for the doctor who had saved his life. That was four years past, and Nicholas, though frail and wan, was safe and living still.

The little feather bed where Nicholas had slept was rolled up out of sight, and in its place a box stood, four foot tall by five, filled with little shotills made of polished oak, with plates of hammered brass. Giles lit the lamp, for it was dark inside the closet, peering at the letters. 'Somewhere here is *vesica*.'

Hew looked in a drawer, which sticking for a moment, shot out in his fingers, showering him with dust. 'This stuff is old and dry.'

'So I dare to hope,' Giles grumbled. 'I would thank you not to waste it. You are like a bairn, that cannot keep its fingers out.' He held up the light, so that Hew could glimpse the label.

'*Mumia*,' read Hew, and wiped his fingers hurriedly, to leave an ashen streak across the grey silk of his breeks. 'Egyptian mummy? Surely not.'

'Doubtless not,' Giles sighed. 'I bought it from a pothecar, who was had for fraud.'

'Then the *grassus hominis* . . .?'

'Is common cooking fat. The *vesica* is real enough, and must be somewhere here . . . now do not force the shotills so, or ye will spoil the box. It is a gift for Meg.'

Hew sniffed at his fingertips. 'She may not like it much.'

'Piffle, she will love it, once the rubble is cleaned out, and the simples are replaced by her own dried herbs and flowers. I will have new lattons made' – Giles gestured to the metal plates – 'but you

62

must not tell her. It is a surprise. For it is all a part of my much grander ordinance.'

'What ordinance is that?' Hew asked with a smile

The doctor said simply, 'To make your sister happy, Hew. She thinks I do not notice it. And she will not admit to it. But she has been forlorn and quiet since her bairn was born. The infant, and her falling sickness, keep her close confined. Her heart belongs out on the land, and I have closed it in, and forced it to the town; I watch her pale face drain of life, as she brings light to mine.'

'You and Matthew are her world, she would not change that,' Hew objected. But in the corner of his mind, he saw his sister standing in the physick garden, barefoot in the leaves, and wondered, for a moment, whether it was true.

'So she will contend,' Giles reflected, sadly, 'while she struggles like a reed that searches for the sunlight and is planted in the shade. When she went out on May morning I was half afraid that she would not come back. Then, when she returned, she came back with a bloom I have not seen for months, her colour and her spirit equally restored, and yet a deeper restlessness, a deeper sadness too. She misses Kenly Green. And while I cannot replicate the physick garden there, here is something lacking that I may amend. Meg shall have a still house and dispensary, built into the cellars of our home. I have hired a master of the works. The masons start next week. But not a word to Meg. She thinks I am installing conduits in the laich house.'

'Conduits?' echoed Hew.

'It was an idea I had, to carry our foul water out into the sea, which under other circumstances, I should like to implement,' his friend explained. 'Meg's happiness comes first. She has approved the project, for she counts it dear to me, and she will never guess that it is but a subterfuge. I have drawn a draft, with the approval of an architectour.' From a shelf above he took down a roll of paper, bound with leather straps, and set it on the floor. Slowly he unbuckled it, spreading out the plans.

'Here is our kitchen,' he pointed to the place, 'and this the nether hall, both on the lower floor. Between them is the trance, which is this little passage down to the front door. The trap down to the laich house is in the kitchen, *here*. The laich house runs below the kitchen underneath the trance, but stops short of the nether hall, where it meets a wall. We mean to take this out, and extend the cellar here, the full length of the house, giving twice the space. On the west side, where the wall is built upon the Fisher Gait, we will drop the floor, and build in a window, to allow the light; and here to the south, where it backs upon the rig, there will be a vent, and a lum for the distillery. Back up in the nether hall, Meg shall have her kist, and a closet for consulting, partitioned off. So that when folk come to see her, she may treat them undisturbed.'

'You seem,' reflected Hew, 'to have it well drawn out.'

'Will it please her, think you?'

Hew said, 'She will love it.' But his thoughts had strayed elsewhere. 'Do many people come to her?' he ventured.

Giles rolled up the paper and returned it to its shelf. 'More than she can help. And it vexes her when she must send them to the pothecar, for lack of some sweet herb, or pocketful of powder, they can ill afford.'

'Does Clare Buchanan come?' Hew asked out aloud, without guile or subtlety. For so he had once seen her, coming from Meg's counsel, on the brink of tears.

Giles said sympathetically, 'You know I cannot tell you that.'

'Which tells me that she does.'

The doctor sighed. 'I know you will not like what I am going to say to you . . .'

'But you will say it anyway.'

'As I feel I must. As your friend and brother, if not as your principal. I know you have feelings for Clare. And I know she comes to visit, when my back is turned.'

'She comes,' defended Hew, 'to see her brother George.'

64

No woman under fifty was permitted in the college, whether as a wife, a servant or a friend; and even Meg herself had not crossed its bounds, or been admitted further past the turret tower. For Clare Buchanan, Giles had fought for an exception, since her brother George was injured in an accident, for which, to some extent, the doctor blamed himself. George, a fledgling student there, had struggled from the start. Since Clare began to visit, once or twice a month, Hew had taken up a private room in college, the significance of which had not escaped his friend.

'Which you are aware,' said Giles, 'is quite against the rule. And though I did allow it, after George's accident, her brother is recovered now. She has no cause to come. You know that she is married, Hew.'

'We both know she is married,' Hew met his friend's gaze. 'And to what kind of a man. But you need not trouble, Giles. Since George has recovered, and he thinks her visits shameful, Clare has not called in weeks.'

'Indeed.' Giles considered. 'When did you last see her?'

'Sometime back in March. Has Meg seen her since?'

Giles did not reply to this, but changed the subject briskly. 'But we had quite forgotten what we came for. A *vesica*, or bladder, burnt into a powder, is used to treat the diabete, or water pouring out, curing like with like. Sadly ineffective. Here, as I supposed, we have one still intact. Let us take it back with us, and see it in the light.' The doctor closed the door upon his box of tricks, and, to Hew's regret, all further talk of Clare.

Close scrutiny confirmed that the membranes were alike; the substance was the same.

'Now I know what was done, or at least the part of it.' Since Bartie Groat had kept his word, and Giles was in the dark, Hew told him the whole story, ending with the samples taken from the tree.

'Ingenious,' said Giles at last. 'So that was how twas done.'

'Not how, but what,' corrected Hew. 'We now know *what* was done, but not the how, or who.'

'Nor yet the why,' said Giles.

'The why is to dismay, and make Andrew Melville doubt. To some extent, it worked. I fear it is a part with the other moves against him. Someone pinned a psalm upon his door at night that worked to prick his conscience, and to strengthen his resolve, to make an honest case in his dealings with the bishops. He took it as a sign. I read it as a threat.'

'Why should it be a threat?'

'Because it was the 109th psalm, the most vengeful and disturbing, filled with bitter curses, and the curses underlined. He thinks a student left it, and he does not take it seriously. It is a curious gift, and I can scarcely think that it was kindly meant.'

'Perhaps not,' Giles agreed. 'I suppose you have not heard him preach upon that text, since you do not pay observance at the Holy Trinity. But I remember once – it stayed long in my mind – Lermont of Balcomie left a placard at his gate, condemning his reforms. Melville cursed him from the pulpit, that he "never should enjoy the fruits of marriage, or have the joy of a succession of an honest birth". And if he were an old wife, rather than a preacher, then his kirk would have her wrung out for a witch. Perhaps it is this Lermont casts the preacher's curses back into his face.'

'Yet Lermont kens no Hebrew,' Hew objected, 'and his placards were attached to the outside of the gates. Whoever left this message, must be lodged within. Or else it were a miracle.'

'The miracle,' said Giles, 'is that whoever left it there has opened up the conscience of a man so fiercely resolute he will not give a pause to simple, honest doubt. Which gives hope to us all. Well then, we shall wait and see what the morrow brings. I will send word back to Melville, to arrange when we shall meet. As for this bleeding hawthorn, Hew, I wish you would be careful with it.'

Hew protested. 'Ha, you sound like Bartie Groat! When I have taken pains to be so analytical. I thought ye would approve of it.'

'It is not your methods that I fear. But someone took great pains to perpetrate this mischief. They have drawn you in. I have not seen you so engaged since you returned from Ghent. It almost seems as though this trick were somehow *meant* for you.'

'It was meant for Andrew Melville,' Hew assured him, cheerfully, 'and is a part of an attempt to unsettle and disgrace him. It is all to do with him, and naught to do with me.'

He could not deny that the riddle pleased him. He looked forward to discovering the author of this crime, which for its ingenuity, was worthy of applause.

Chapter 7

A Rare Roast Egg

Andrew Melville could not tell what it was had woken him, or when it was he woke. He had read until the light gave out, and then a little afterwards, though not so very long, for he was sparing with his candle, mindful of the cost. After blowing out the candle, he had knelt to speak with God. That conversation had occupied him for some while, so that when it was concluded he found the fire gone out, the room had grown quite dark, one knee bore the print of the rush mat on the floor and both knees locked and buckled, stiff and white with cold. He crept into his blankets then, where sleep came slow and fitfully, for though the conversation had been free and frank, it had not cleared his mind. God listened, but had not said much. Then Andrew knew that he must find the answer in his heart, and spent some sore hours searching for it. At last he drifted off. He woke up with a start from a slough of shifting dreams and opened up the shutters that looked out upon the square. A fine grey drizzle smudged the stars, blurring the distinction between light and dark. The rain did not fall hard enough to rattle at the windowpanes, and brought with it no wind, but a creeping, breathless hush that stilled the shrill night predators and blotted out the moon. The lantern at the gatehouse shone out to the street; there were no lamps lit in college or the porter's lodge, and at first he could see nothing but the muffled shadows of the dull night sky.

But as his eyes adjusted to the darkness, and began to fathom different shades and shapes, Andrew Melville saw, or thought he saw, a narrow strip of light that crept across the courtyard about four feet from the ground. The light was greenish grey. It did not gutter like a candle, but moved softly through the shadows like a green-eyed cat. It left behind a faintly luminescent haze. Andrew closed his eyes and opened them again. The light had come to rest, settling on the hawthorn tree. Andrew put on gown and slippers over his bare shirt, and made his way outside. He swung a yellow horn lamp clear around the square, into nooks and crevices, shining high and low, but found no trace of green. The soft rain had begun to seep into the stonework, running to the grass. From the pale face of the moon, emerging from its cloud, Andrew put the hour at close to three o'clock.

He brought the yellow lantern closer to the hawthorn tree, and placed his hand against the trunk. It came off wet, and clean.

Hew was woken by a bursar, shortly after five. He had spent the night in college, in a vaulted chamber accessed through the cloisters, next door to the chapel, on the eastern side. The room was simply furnished, with a shelf for books, a writing desk and chair, a settle made of oak that opened to a bed, a towel pin and a peg, for hanging up his clothes. A window in the corner glanced out on the North Street, with a cushion on the sill, and in front of it a sitting chair, upholstered in green silk, caught the morning light, and was kept for guests.

The bursar brought warm water and an urgent message. 'Master Andro Melville waits to see you, sir.'

'Andrew? At this hour?' Hew splashed his face with the water from the bowl, scrubbing at it blearily with the linen towel.

'He is outside in the cloisters. Shall I send him in?' The bursar was a pauper student, in his second year. His role it was to wake the college, in return for board and lodging, fetching water, fire and light. With an expert hand, he closed the settle bedstead, and stowed Hew's sheets and blankets in the locker underneath.

Hew answered with a groan. 'Tell him, I will come to him, as soon as I am dressed.'

He combed his hair quickly and put on his coat, his doctor's cap, tippet and gown.

The day had dawned cooler and fresh, the sun advancing warily through heavy flanks of cloud. Melville prowled the cloister, scowling at the wind. He greeted Hew tersely, 'Where is Giles Locke?'

'We shall meet him at his house, which is on our way. Though I cannot promise he will be awake.'

'Then he must be woken. There is no time to lose.'

St Salvator's college backed on to the Swallow Gait, which led directly to the castle on the cliff, and to Giles' house. But Andrew insisted that they go out to the North Street, turning at the Fisher Gait, avoiding Patrick's soldiers at the Swallow Port, for Patrick, he insisted, must not be forewarned. Hew judged it wise to humour him. His impatience had attracted notice in the quad, and it would not be long before Professor Groat was up, winding his old bones into his fur-lined cloak, snuffling and inquisitive. Bartie's probing questions would delay them half an hour. He hurried Andrew Melville back out to the street. 'I have something to tell you. We have solved the riddle of the hawthorn tree. Or at least, in part, worked out how it was done.'

'Aye, and how was that?' Andrew seemed distracted still, and less enthusiastic than Hew would have liked. In the waking morning light, he looked paler than before, sickly green and frail. Hew judged, accurately, that he had not slept.

'A waggish pranking trick, that a boy might boast of,' he explained. 'The scrap of skin we found turned out to be *vesica* – the bladder of a calf, or perhaps a sheep.'

Andrew prompted, 'And?'

'Did you never, as a bairn, play with bladders on a stick, or filled one at the burn, to chase and soak a friend?' From Andrew's look of bafflement, it seemed that he had not. 'Then this is how tis done; the blether of a lamb is washed out, soaked and dried, blown out full with air, and made into a ball. Someone filled a bladder up with

70

blood, and tied it to the tree. When the time was ripe, they came along and burst it – at some remove, I doubt, else they would run the risk of being drenched with blood – but to ken how it was done, we must ask Bartie Groat.'

'Then you suspect Professor Groat?' Andrew Melville frowned; his quick mind lagged a little, due to his distraction, or to lack of sleep.

'Not for one moment,' Hew assured him. 'I believe the bladder was pierced by a sharp stone, thrown at it by force, for *vesica* is tough, and would be hard to burst. Perhaps it was a sling or some other kind of weapon. Several shots were fired, and frightened off the birds. There were stones of different shapes in the courtyard by the tree, and we should not have noticed them, except that one had a hole in it, and that was out of place. It put us in a heightened state of fear. Perhaps the perpetrator tried with different sorts of stone, brought there for the purpose, not knowing which might work. Or perhaps he left the seeing stone, to trouble and perplex us, put us off our scent. We may suppose he had no time to gather in his pellets, wherefore they were chosen, cunningly and carefully; to that end, he dared not shoot an arrow, which would penetrate more cleanly, but which might be found.'

'But what,' Andrew frowned, 'can this have to do with Professor Groat?'

'Little at all, but that I hope by his geometry he may chance to tell us where the shot was fired. Whether, in particular, from up on the wall, or even from some vantage place on the other side.'

'Then you think it may be possible it came in from outside?'

'I hope it may be possible. Bartie may ken more.'

Melville said, 'I thank you, then, for that assurance.' But he looked grave and doubtful, scarcely reassured. Hew felt his grand discovery had fallen somewhat flat. The menace was at large still, he was forced to tell himself. 'What you need,' he proposed, 'is a wholesome breakfast, to fire you in your cause. Giles Locke is the man for it.'

Andrew Melville stared, as though Hew's straggling wits had finally deserted him. 'Do you not apprehend, there is no time for breakfast, Hew? To find the tulchan out, we maun surprise him suddenly. And now the sun is up, we have no time to waste.'

They had turned into the Fisher Gait, leading to the cliff, where the rigs and gardens struggled in the wind, bare blown and exposed before the cold north sea. Since it was low tide, the fisher wives were still indoors, skillets on the flame, waiting for their men folk to return home with their nets, when they would hurry to the shore with bucketfuls of salt, to ply wet writhing haddocks at the Fisher Cross. They would sit out in the sun, to gossip and tie hooks, and feed their men afresh, before the evening tides. The cottages were quiet now. A solitary child sat huddled on a step, where rarely for this quarter, the shutters were still drawn. The child hugged close her mantle, and did not look up.

They found Giles at his breakfast, in the nether hall. Matthew Locke was tethered in his father's lap, battling in the folds of an enormous napkin, which engulfed them both. Meg was baking bannocks on a girdle at the fire. On the board were butter, and a loaf of day-old bread, which Doctor Locke was crumbling in a wooden bowl. The doctor had strong views on early infant nourishment: white things as a supplement, while the teeth were cut, for milk was white and teeth were white; white meats, minced and pulped, white fish, boiled or baked; white bread, sops and soddins, soaked into a pap, almond milks and bisket, albumen of egg. Once all the teeth were cut, the infant could progress. Green foods were the devil's own; apples, salats, spinach, pears, brought on worm and colic, soured the wam for life.

Giles fed Matthew pap. Matthew opened up and closed his mouth again, like a baby bird. On the third attempt, he spat the mouthful out, and grappled for the spoon.

Andrew Melville stared, openly alarmed.

'No one bakes a bannock better than my sister.' Hew pulled up a chair.

'You are welcome, Master Andro,' Meg said with a smile. 'Canny Bett is cooking eggs. How do you take yours?'

Melville found his voice. 'Later in the day,' he replied ungraciously. 'At our college, we begin the day with prayer, and half a morning's work, before we break our fast, wherefore we come upon it with a glad and grateful appetite, not slow and soft and slovenly, fleshly plump from sleep.'

Meg's mouth opened, closed again, for the moment lost for words, like her little son.

Giles Locke said, 'Indeed?' He removed a table knife from Matthew's grasping fist and passed it back to Hew. 'The best eggs,' he remarked, 'are but lightly poached in broth, those are most digestible. Buttered, on a hot thick toast, with pepper and a dust of salt, were almost as acceptable. Or seething in a pan.'

'When we were boys at college,' collaborated Hew, 'we would roast them in their shells in the embers of the fire, where by degrees they darkened to a deep rich honeyed gold, that was creamy like a cheese. We picked the shells with pins, or else they would burst.'

Giles tutted, 'That is a method that I do not recommend. Tis almost impossible to rare roast a hen's egg. Without which you will find them hard and indigestible, binding to the stomachs of bairns and young boys. It perhaps explains a certain flaw of stubbornness, which I have sometimes marked in you.'

It was Meg who put an end to their subtle game of flyting, moved by the confusion she could see in Andrew's face. 'You must excuse them, sir, for when they are at rest, they fool and mow like bairns. Perhaps you are the same, when you share a play day with your nephew James? Hew tells me you are close.'

Melville answered stiffly, 'I assure you, not. Sir,' he turned to Giles, 'this talk is vain and frivolous, and not what I expect from you. Our business is most pressing. We must leave at once.'

'Stuff,' retorted Giles. 'There is no business can be settled before we have breakfasted, and no task that was not bettered by beginning in an egg. Sit down awhile, and eat with us. The day will still be waiting, after we are done.'

'My husband will not tell you,' mediated Meg, 'why he wants his breakfast, for he is not vain or frivolous, as you have supposed. He has been up all night at the bedside of a woman who departed from this world a little while ago. It is for that poor wife's bairns that Canny cooks the eggs.'

Hew asked, 'Was it one of the fisherwives?' He remembered the small daughter, crouching in the vennel, five or six years old.

'Nan Reekie,' Meg confirmed. 'Do you mind her, Master Melville? She came often to your kirk.'

Melville, for his sins, had the grace to blush. 'I did not ken that she was sick. Nor, indeed, that she had means to call for a physician.'

'Doubtless, she did not.' Hew felt almost sorry for him. 'Andrew,' he encouraged, 'come and sit you down, Giles has been up all night, and he must have his breakfast. Your cause will not be lost, if you have an egg. The archbishop will be abed still, after we are done.'

Melville bowed his head. 'Your pardon, mistress,' he apologised to Meg, 'for I apprehend that I have judged too hastily, and that is a fault. A little small ale, if ye have it, would be welcome, and suffice.'

He sat down on the bench, as remote as possible and furthest from the child, whose presence at the table worried and perplexed him. Canny brought the eggs, and was sent back for the ale. Meg helped Hew to cheese. 'Did Giles tell you,' she remarked, 'we are laying conduits in the laich house, to carry off our waste? It is a clever scheme of his.'

'I do believe he mentioned it,' Hew said with a smile.

'A sink is an anathema,' Andrew Melville warned. Though he had little practice in domestic small talk, it did not deter him from putting forth his views. 'At the college, we are plagued with the offence of our latrines. We are waiting for the draught-raker to come and dig them out; yet we have no idea when he will come. I would advise you strongly not to put one in your house, for it cannot be healthsome or wholesome.'

'The purpose of the conduit pipes,' Giles corrected quickly, 'is to flush the waste away, so there need not be a sink.'

'Indeed? Then I confess, I had not heard of that.'

'The conduits take the waste out to the sea, by means of a small pump. It is my own invention.'

'Did you say,' Hew interrupted, 'you were waiting for the draucht-raker?'

'We have been waiting for some while.'

''Tis likely,' muttered Giles, 'he is somewhere deep in shit. Which is what the conduits were intended to prevent.'

He was giving up his pipe dream, out of love for Meg, while Meg let him pursue it, out of love for him. But Hew's thoughts were else-where. 'The raker comes at night. How then, when he comes, is he let in to the college?'

'The door to the garden is left open. He leaves his cart outside, and takes the muck in barrows,' Andrew answered. 'Ah,' the reasoning dawned on him, 'now I understand.'

'You did not mention that, when we looked round the college.'

'For then the door was locked. But if it were then possible that someone came by night . . .'

'Then it is more than possible, the bladders filled with blood were hidden in the tree by someone from outside. Perhaps the night before,' concluded Hew. 'Or perhaps when you were absent still, at the kirk assembly, for I think your chamber overlooks the tree.'

Melville answered quietly, 'It does.'

'A *vesica* is heavy,' Giles remarked, 'when it is filled with blood. And would be hard to shift. And yet a little blood may travel a good distance, and may look like a good deal. And among the leaves and blossom, it could easily be hid.'

'If I were you,' said Hew, 'I would lock the door at night; or better, set a watch on it, and you may catch your devil, if he comes again.'

Melville struggled with his answer. 'Aye,' he spoke at last. 'I am beholden to you, both, for you begin to lift a shadow from my mind, that I confess has haunted me, in making plain to me the source of this attack. I have not been sleeping well. And I began to fear there was some evil deep within the college; last night, I saw a spirit, moving round the tree.'

'What sort of spirit?' questioned Hew.

'I almost am ashamed to say, a green and ghostly light. I went out in my nightshirt to it. It had gone, of course. I fancied it had left behind the faintest whiff of brimstane.' Andrew forced a smile. 'This wickedness has worked its magic on my fearful mind.'

'A light like that,' reflected Meg, 'may have a natural cause.'

'I assure you, madam, there was nothing natural in the light I saw.' Melville was not used to women in the house, much less those who spoke to him, to offer up opinions, which differed from his own. Giles acknowledged softly, 'You should listen to her, Andro. Meg kens more than most.'

'There is a light that comes from the bark of a tree, or from a piece of bone, beginning to decay. A lucent, ghostly lour of luminescent green that has the scent of sulphur. Could that be what you saw?' persisted Meg.

'Aye, madam,' Andrew scowled at her, 'if dead bones and trees picked up their stumps and walked. The light that I saw was moving, steadily and stealthily.'

'Then did it not occur to you, that someone might have carried it?'

'Fish heads!' broke in Hew. 'I have seen it too, at the pit at Dysart, where the earth boils black. The miners make their lamps of scales and bones of fish, to shine a ghostly light upon the darkness there, that dare not be attempted with a naked flame, and crawl up from the molten earth as it were hell itself. And had I known no better of it, so I should believe. You never saw a place on earth more dreadful nor more desolate. Those imps of hell are children, sir. And sometimes, it seems there is no clear mark to be drawn, between what we call natural, or unnatural.'

'Or,' Giles added, 'supernatural.'

Melville cleared his throat, 'My thanks to you all, for your explanations. That mark is a line that I would fain were drawn. It *must* be drawn, by faith, if not yet by your science. It is by God's will, doubtless, I am shown these things.'

All credit then to God, thought Hew, and none of it to Meg. 'If I were you,' he said again, 'I would set a watch.'

'Aye, and so I shall, when we are finished with the tulchan.'

At last, Giles took the hint. He wiped his face and Matthew's, handing Meg the child. 'Since ye are both in cap and cope, I will go and dress. It would not do to brave the bishop in our slops and slippers.' He left them with a wink.

Meg settled Matthew on her hip. 'What is a tulchan, sir?' she asked.

Though Hew sensed she was up to mischief, Melville's guard was down. 'A tulchan is a bishop in name only,' he informed her, 'as is Patrick Adamson. He is a siphon, by which the kirk's ain revenues are leached off to the lairds.'

Meg said, 'Oh. I did not know. Master Andro, I am richt glad you are come to breakfast with us. There are certain questions I have longed to ask you, since I heard your lessons sometime at the kirk.'

Now Hew knew for certain she was up to something. His sister had no love or fervour for reform, brought up in the shelter of her father's land. Matthew had remained a Papist to the last. And yet he had set Hew upon a different course, sending him to school where he was raised a Protestant, a legacy that Hew found hard to understand. For though it had ensured his safe path through the world, it had kept him distant from his father's heart. And he had felt that gulf. Raised up in a kirk which made a plain clear sense to him, he found no turning back, the gap in faith and trust was difficult to reconcile, affecting still his closeness to and sympathy with Meg. She was baiting Andrew Melville, that much he could tell.

Melville read no hint of challenge in her tone. 'By all means,' he encouraged, 'if ye are inquiring on a matter of the faith. Though if you are in doubt, you might look for guidance to your ain guid husband or – perhaps more properly – to your brother Hew, who was brought up in the faith. He likely will explain what you do not understand, and will seek to reassure you, when you cannot understand, which, as you must know, is to be expected.'

Hew could not help but smile at that. But Meg insisted, meekly, 'Yet Hew is not well studied in the doctrines of the kirk, and on its most exacting points, he may not be relied on. And I have, sir, a singular question, which requires a particular answer. Our father, you may know, was no believer in Reform. He lived and died a Catholick, stubborn to the last. He would not have his corpus buried in St Leonard's kirk, because he felt that place had lost its sacred holiness, and chose a place outside of it, resting in its shade. My question to you is, was our father damned?'

'This is monstrous,' Hew exclaimed, 'How can you think to ask it, Meg?' He could not, for the world, see why Meg should ask that, unthinkable to any man who knew their father's worth. But Melville answered quietly. 'I cannot tell you that. For we cannot know, in truth, what God's plan is for us, which of us is saved, and which of us is damned. But if you look for comfort, you may find a grain perhaps in the fact that he brought Hew up as a Protestant, which hints your father had a true reforming heart, and that somewhere deep inside, God wrought his work in him. And do not fault her, Hew,' he turned back to his friend. 'It is a proper question, that deserves an answer.'

'To tell the truth,' said Meg, as calm as Hew was furious, 'it never had occurred to me, till one of Master Melville's students telt me he was damned. I wanted to be sure, that that was his own view on it.'

Andrew answered patiently, 'And as I have said to ye, that is not my view on it. One of my students, you say?'

'I met him at our father's graveside, where I knelt with Matthew, tending to the weeds. He did not give his name. But he telt me that he hoped to take orders in the kirk, and he studied at the college, with that end in mind. He spoke to me most fervently, *ye maunna waste your prayers on him, for surely, he is damned. He lies there, steeped in sin.*

'He swore he meant no ill to me, he only meant to speak God's word, the plain and honest truth, he could not serve me better, by allowing me false hope, for to tell the truth must be the kinder thing. That he had lost a father too, and that he understood.'

'The devil he did!' Hew burst out. 'That feckless fool, Dod Auchinleck. Is this down to him?'

Andrew urged him, 'Patience, sir. Your family have been kind enough to teach me not to draw quick conclusions, you must learn the same. Some of our men show an uncommon zeal. I will look in to it; you have my word. He should not presume so much, as he could know God's will; he could not ken or see into your father's heart. For only God does that.'

'That is your sole objection to it? That he does presume too much?'

'I do not excuse it. Let me find him out, and I shall make the reprimand, I promise you, and forcefully, and I shall make him understand, where he goes wrong.'

Hew contended still, 'And is there no wrong in the hurt to Meg? Save in his frantic fervour he has overreached himself and misconstrued the logic of a zealous mind?'

'Peace, now,' Andrew sighed. 'This day looks likely to be long and trying, and I would not, for the world, begin by fighting with you. I regret the wrong that was done to your sister. Yet I cannot condemn a hurt occasioned by the truth, but only one that predicates itself upon false reason. I cannot tell her that her father is forgiven for his sins, nor give her any comfort in her hopeful prayers. Nor can I say for certain he is surely damned. For though there is little proof your father saw the light, the signs may yet be hid from us, and visible to God.'

'So you are saying,' challenged Hew, 'that though the outward signs appear that he was damned, we cannot claim to know this for a certain truth, no more can we assume a Christian man is saved? You tread a tight rope between hope and despair.'

Andrew stood up wearily. 'We take comfort in the light that God has shown to us. Tis only the blackest hearts that sink in to despair, for they will not understand, what was never meant for them. I will find out the faulter, and amend him. Meanwhile, since my purpose here is to visit Patrick, I will leave you to your breakfast now, and wait for you outside. Tell Giles Locke, when he comes.' He touched Hew on the shoulder as he passed. 'I have no wish to quarrel, Hew. But you perhaps should ask yourself, why you are so aggrieved at this. Your sister is quite calm. And, I have no doubt, she kens her ain answer. It is in her heart.'

Matthew had begun to whimper, startled by Hew's frantic mood. 'Whisht,' said Meg, 'you frighten him.'

'For pity, Meg,' Hew whispered. 'Why did you not tell me?'

'I was not offended at it. I did not for a moment think it might be true. But . . .' she hesitated, 'I did not tell Giles, because I was afeared that it would cause a storm, and I did not tell you, because I was afeared that you might think it too, since you are of that faith. And if you thought it too, I could not bear it, Hew.'

He stared at her. 'You cannot for a moment think I thought our father damned! I could not believe, not for the briefest moment, that he could be damned. For as a man cannot will to be good, so he cannot escape God's will, God willing him be good. Matthew was a good man, and he was good, despite himself, and he could not be good without it were God's will.' And that must be the truth of it, for nothing else made sense to him.

Meg's eyes were bright. She hushed and rocked her child. 'You have not lately seen his grave.'

Their father had been buried in the hard and frozen earth, in the dead of winter, shrouded from the sun. In his mind's eye Hew revisited, and he had no desire to come back to that place, bleak and cold and desolate.

'He lies there in the quiet shade, and all around are trees and flowers. It is not bare, as it once was.'

'I do not need to see,' he said, 'to know that you have done him proud. But I will come, and see your flowers.'

'I take no credit for them, Hew. They grow there naturally.'

Chapter 8

The Abbot of Unrest

The three men met like crows. They did not, like the rook, cry croaking to the wind, but settled darkly brooding at the castle gate, the lawyer and the doctor and the scholar kirkman, huddled in their gowns. Andrew was intent and thoughtful. Hew was out of sorts. Giles remained the keenest and most sanguine of the three. He brought with him a leather case in which he kept his instruments, or what he called his *equipage*, fine blades and tiny scissors, sharpened to a pin. Giles was a physician, and a pure anatomist, exquisite in his diligence, and not a barber-surgeon ready with his hands.

The castle was enclosed within an outer wall, extending to the Swallow Gait. The port upon the Kirk Heugh side, the closest to the house, stood open to the street. The three men stepped inside, where they were spied at once, and welcomed by a figure standing at the ditch.

'Good morrow to you, masters. Wait there, if ye will.'

The sentry seemed at ease, a cheerful, red-haired soldier in his early twenties, in a saffron-coloured shirt with leather jak and breeks, and a buckled broadsword swinging at his belt. He was whistling as he came, a mellow little tune. 'I will squire ye, sirs, if you would cross the bridge. A plank has rattled loose. A carter's wheel was caught in it,' he warned them, pleasantly.

He knew them, Hew supposed. All three of them had come in academic dress. Melville and Giles Locke were well known in the town, and, to Hew's surprise, the man appeared to know him too, and count him for a friend. His willingness to help was marked and unexpected. 'Is the archbishop expecting you?'

'I think it fair to say,' said Andrew, 'he is not expecting us.'

'Then he will be asleep. If ye come back in an hour, it may please him to receive you.'

'He will receive us now, if it pleases him or not. For if he does not receive us, it will please him less. Our business cannot wait.'

The soldier did not seem perturbed, nor vexed at Melville's tone. 'Then follow, an' ye will, an see what may be done for ye.'

He took them to the bridge that reached across the fosse – a steep ditch lined with earth and rubble – to the central tower. The bridge was a gangway of thick wooden planks, strong enough to bear the strain of several men on horseback, and broad enough to take the width of one or two small carts. Several of the planks were loose, so that they could be taken up, in the event of an attack, and others had dislodged, by wear or else by accident, and threatened to fall down. These the soldier pointed out. 'Steady as you go. You wouldna want to wreck your ankles, falling doun the dyke.'

As they approached the castle, Hew felt his spirits lift, curious to see what treasures lay inside. The ancient stronghold of the bishops had been rebuilt many times, its most recent incarnation now a wallowed winter ghost. It owed its courtly grandeur to the late Archbishop Hamilton, its bleakness to his fall.

The brig swept to the entrance pend, a grand triumphal central arch, with panels for a coat of arms, and five foils cut in tracery, still faintly flecked with gold. Harling and white paint had weathered to bare stone. The doors were vast and solid, fast and firmly closed.

The soldier read Hew's mind, for he said sympathetically, 'The pity is, ye canna make your entry wi' a proper pomp. But it will save ye trouble, and a deal of time, if ye come in through the wicket. And if you set your hearts on passing through the pend, the great door may be opened by the time you leave. The porter has this moment sat down to his breakfast, sirs.' He showed them through a narrow postern, opening to a vaulted tunnel on the eastern side. And here, all progress stopped. For here they met Tam Fairlie, sergeant of the guard.

'Three gentlemen are come to speak wi' the archbishop, fae the university. Masters Andrew Melville, o' the New College, and Giles Locke and Hew Cullan, o' the Auld College,' their guide imparted flawlessly. The sergeant said, '*Oh aye?*' Hew marvelled at the work to which he put the words, so small to bear the strain of it.

'I thocht to leave them here, and fetch down Master Scrymgeour.'

'Ye thocht right,' said Tam.

The soldier disappeared and left them with the guard, inhibited from moving further in or out. Melville tried to follow him, to find his way was barred. 'Patience, my masters. Ye may tak a seat.'

The guardroom was equipped with a single narrow bench, where a second man was sitting, eating bread and cheese. The porter, Hew supposed. 'We must see your master,' Andrew Melville flustered.

'When Harry comes back, sirs. A' in guid time.' The sergeant was a shank of muscle, neither broad nor tall, hardened to the temper of his battered leather black jak and as difficult to penetrate. There could be no shifting him. 'While ye are at your ease, I will have your weapons.'

'What weapons?' Andrew snapped. 'We are come as scholars, and we do not carry arms.'

The sergeant laughed at that. 'Then you will be the first, that never speared a piece of meat, nor cut hisself a pen. Your *quhingars*, if you please. Lift up your belts and coats.'

Hew laid down his dagger, and the little quill knife he kept tucked up in a pocket. Giles protested bitterly, for giving up his scissors was like giving up his thumbs, and made the soldier swear that he would guard them with his life. 'Tis likely I will want them, in my dealings with your lord.'

'Then my lord will call for them. Your weapons will be safe.'

'They are not weapons, sir.'

Andrew had no blade of any kind, and expressed his outrage at the search. 'That man is gone too long,' he hissed to Giles and Hew. 'Patrick is prepared for us.'

'What do you imagine, sir? His chambers are swept clean, of claret and of concubines?' Giles Locke was affronted still, at forfeiting his tools.

'That is what I fear.'

Melville's agitation soon became infectious. Hew began to wonder whether Harry would come back, or whether he had snared them in some subtle trap. He felt bare without his knife. But he did not have long to fret before the soldier reappeared, with a shadow at his back. 'This is Ninian Scrymgeour, the archbishop's privy secretar.'

Ninian Scrymgeour blinked at them, the startled rapid squinting of a man with failing eyes, who has come without his spectacles, and strains to see the world.

'The archbishop is not well, and he is abed. I am however author-ised to act on his behalf on any business that concerns the kirk or university, sin I am his notar, and his secret clerk.'

'And does he also trust ye,' Andrew Melville challenged, 'to safe-guard his soul?'

The clerk was faintly shocked. 'No, indeed, dear me. I do not believe so.' Ninian had the look of a relic left behind, ignored by the reformers and forgotten by the monks. He wore a brown wool kirtle, knotted with a rope, and simple leather sandals, without breeks or hose. Against Andrew's fierceness he was ill-equipped, powerless as a fluff ball in a spider's web.

'We are come to see your master, on a private matter. We maun speak with him in person, and speak with him at once. Doctor Locke is here, to tak care of his health.'

Ninian buckled. 'Yes, I see. Then I will tak ye to him.'

The humble clerk was no defence; Hew wondered, after all, whether he was meant to be, or if the castle watchmen simply played for time, and had stalled them long enough. Andrew thought so, plainly, for he muttered, 'Damn the man,' of no one in particular. The sergeant's part was done; he stood to let them pass. As they left the guardroom Hew caught Harry's eye, and for a second could have sworn he saw the soldier wink at him.

Ninian took them through the tunnel to the open air. But Hew did not have long to take in his surroundings, for the clerk turned sharply left, and through a second doorway to a turnpike stair. He stumbled as they followed up the flight of steps. Hew snatched at his arm, and felt the slight frame quiver, shrinking from his hand. 'Ye maun excuse me, masters. You caught me at my ease, and I do not have my spectacles. Wait, sirs, please to wait.'

They were left alone a moment standing in the garderobe that served the bishop's chamber on the western side. The residence was long and narrow, built into the corridor between the southern towers, and divided in compartments twenty foot in length, the central two combined, where the archbishop lived and slept. Four large windows let in light, and looked south to the town; four small ones on the north side looked down on the cobbles of the castle court. Before Hew could investigate, the little clerk returned, to show them through the door. 'He will see you now. But ye manna keep him long.'

Patrick Adamson was laid out upon a bed of state, propped up on its pillows, in a strange state of undress. He wore a ruffled nightshirt underneath a cope, a muffler at his throat, as prophylactic barrier to the morning air, and on his head a crimson flannel cap offset the mottled hollows of his fleshly cheeks, which were pinched and flushed. The bed was heaped with blankets, bolsters, cods and quilts. The chamber where it stood was airy, large and bright, lined with light oak panelling a little scuffed and worn, and hung with antique tapestries, faded in the sun. The ceilings and the window-sills were carved from darker wood, with Hamilton's device picked out in yellow paint. It might have been a pleasing, once impressive room, had it not smelt persuasively of ordure and decay. The herbs strewn round the sickbed too were withered and defunct. Though Patrick had had time enough to stage the room and bed, the odour of the charnel house could scarcely have been faked.

Giles prescribed a breath of air. Hew threw the windows open, happy to drink deep.

Patrick murmured from his pillow, 'Guid morn to you, guid sirs. I ken you will not tak it ill, that I do not get up. Your visit here is unexpected, and I am not well.' His tone was dry and languid.

Melville shot back sharply, 'Wherefore we have brocht the doctor.'

'Doctor Locke, I see. I cannot call you welcome here. For when a man awakes, to find a doctor and a lawyer and a kirkman at his bedside, then he has cause to fear that he may not have long left in the world. Good morrow to ye, Andro. What is your intent? The lawyer come to make my will, the doctor to pronounce me dead, as for your ain self, to hound me to my grave? Master Cullan, as I fear, will mak no profit from his client. This living, Andro, is not what it was.'

He smiled at Melville then, a wicked, teasing glint. Andrew kept his temper, Hew thought admirably.

'Doctor Locke has come here to examine you.'

'Then I fear that he has wasted his journey.' Patrick closed his eyes. 'For I am done with surgeons, and physicians too. I have seen enough of them to last me for a lifetime. Ask Ninian where that steward is. I have not had my breakfast yet. A few light morsels on a tray. Close the door as ye go out.'

Giles was looking through a bank of vials and bottles lined up by the bed. He opened one and sniffed. 'Who is your apothecar? This physick bears no name.'

'There have been so many that I cannot mind. I have done with them all. And now I am resolved to die, peacefully and privately. Perhaps my old friend Andrew here will kneel to say a prayer with me, to see me on my way.'

'I have come with report from the General Assembly,' Melville said, ignoring him, 'where I excused your absence, on account of sickness.'

'*Good of you.*'

Hew began to see how Patrick worked on Andrew, each small barb and insult pricking at his skin. Melville bore it patiently.

'And I felt sore ashamed.'

'Shamed were ye, Andro? Petuous as ye are? Ah, but surely not!'

'This flyting will not move me, Patrick, nor put me from my purpose here. Conscience will not cower from words and waggish wit. Are ye sick, in truth? Or are you feigning sickness, while men move against you?'

'Ye think it is a fraud? Andro, I am hurt! And yet a little touched, that ye would think to lie for me.' Patrick taunted him.

'God kens,' Andrew swore, 'that I would not have lied for you, willingly and knowingly. No more, sir, of this wantonness. I pray ye will pay heed to what I have to say. As I spoke for you last week before the hale kirk brethren, so I come to ye, and speak for all o' them. I made your plea to them, and this is their reply. Good Master Hew is here to see it is delivered to you, honestly and fairly, since he is a lawman, with no interest in the matter.'

'I never met a lawman yet,' said Patrick with a snort, 'who had no interest in a matter, where that interest was not in the lining of his purse.'

'Then clearly,' interrupted Giles, 'you have not met Hew.'

Andrew said, 'Enough. He is impartial here. And his goodwill and charity are more than ye deserve. Your present plea of sickness is suspected by the kirk, and it must be tried here by Professor Locke. If ye will not submit to trial, your guilt shall be assumed. And you will be cursed and put out from the kirk.'

'Ah, but that is cruel. Andro, that is harsh,' Patrick's wail of protest had a serious ring to it, and Andrew answered earnestly.

'The time for play has passed. Believe me when I tell you I have come in friendship, for sake of that guid man I know that you once were. But you have let greed and desire steal upon ye, to poison your spirit and blacken your heart. I pray that you are sick, as all appearance shows, and do not lie to God. I pray that Doctor Locke can somehow make you well, whatever ails your body, and that God may mend your soul.'

Patrick answered wearily. 'If I must, I must. For I would not meet my maker cast out from the kirk, when, God only knows, I suffer for my sins. Doctor, do thy worst. And if thou cannot satisfy that savage flock of crows, that style themselves my brethren, then I can have no hope of ever finding comfort in this world.' The fight and strength were sapped from him, and he looked sick indeed.

'As to the doctor's cure, I hold no hope of that. I have seen physicians, and several surgeons too. I have bled them a gallon of blood and pissed them a gallon of piss. I am too hot, or too cold, too moist, else too dry. I must be warmed or else cooled. I must be vomited, I must be purged. It is the choler, the phlegm, the black bile, the colic, the flux. I am too sanguine, or else too melancholy. Louse-leeches, potingars, joukerie-pokerie, I have consulted them all.'

Giles responded sagely, 'You have not consulted me.'

'Then make free with my closet, sir. The privy pots are filled. Sin such are meat and drink, the raw stuff of your trade, let my poor carcage be.'

The doctor shook his head. 'Ye cannot tell a sickness simply from the waters, and he that claims to do so is a liar and a fraud. No man may make a diagnosis, without a full examination. Which is to say, first, for the history, and that in the patient's own words – though *patient* in this case were not so apt perhaps – for none shall have so thorough apprehension of an ailment as he who has to suffer it. The first step to a cure is the patient's own account. Though that comes with the caveat, we speak of *kenning* sickness, rather than of curing it. The next step is the taking of the pulse, and whether it be weak or strong, quick or slow, with the perusing of the excrements, not the urine merely but all bodily discharges, as ordure, spittle, sweat, and spawn, taking note of diet, habit, air and exercise; and finally, essentially, we examine that place where the disease is keenly felt. Therefore, to begin, can you say what ails you, sir?'

'A trembling fever, and the flux, and a thristing and a thrawe in the belly, and the ripples in my back and loins, sometime hot, sometime

89

cold,' Patrick answered fretfully. 'A foulness, sir, a fedity. I ken no other word for it.'

'Excellent,' Giles beamed. 'The excremental elements we lay by for the while; I notice they are present in abundance. Perhaps you will oblige me, now, by taking off your shirt?'

Patrick stared at him. 'You wish me to divest?'

'So that I can examine you, your kernels and your wam, and also in the fundament.'

'And must I be abased, and nethered to your friends? Is this your vengeance, Andro? That I am stripped of dignity?'

Giles glanced back at his colleagues. 'It is usual,' he observed, 'to allow a little privacy. When a man is naked, he may not dissemble, yet there are some matters you should take on trust. There are some parts of his body, known to God and his physician, that a man is not expected to uncover to the world.'

Hew had no desire to see the man defrocked. He touched at Andrew's sleeve. 'Will it be prejudicial, if we wait outside?'

Melville had been slow to act, staring at the doctor with a fascinated horror. He capitulated hurriedly as Giles rolled up his sleeves. 'Aye, for sure. Indeed.'

'Tell that strutting sergeant,' Giles commanded after, 'I shall want my lance.' Patrick shrank back like a paddock, cowering in his shell.

They parted at the steps, for Melville would not stay. 'There is a foulness in this place I cannot thole nor stomach, even in the breeze. Can you not smell it, Hew? That fedity of Patrick's seeps into the stone. I will ask them at the gate to send the doctor's instruments. Here a reeking rankness vexes and corrupts.'

Hew smelt nothing but the salt in the white swell of the sea, a cool sharp cleansing wind. 'I shall wait for Giles.' He hoped that while he waited he could look around, and cross the cobbled courtyard to the northern range.

'Tell Giles Locke to send his report. Whatever he concludes, the brethren will accept. I am right sorry he has had to suffer this unwholesome stew. I have not been well-mannered to your sister or your friend. There are matters here that weigh upon my conscience; for I would do right by those who place their trust in me, and I do not always see so clearly what is right, for sometimes God is moved to hide his purpose from me. Patrick has the knack of stirring me to anger, he has always had it, and he is aware of it. I have a temper quick to arouse. That is my fault, and not his,' Andrew confessed. He looked exhausted, spent, and Hew understood how hard this task had been for him, how heavily it weighed on him. He saw him slip and stumble, passing to the gate.

For all that, once Andrew had left, a cloud seemed to lift from the day. Hew was alone to explore. A boy was drawing water from the castle well, a servant from the kitchens brought a breakfast on a tray, and Hew smelled buttered haddocks as he passed. Both were in a hurry, neither looked at Hew, but he was in no doubt that he was being watched. In the passages around him he saw signs of life, the archbishop's household at breakfast in the hall or their stations in the kitchen, or at their prayers in chapel or their ease in their chambers, coming off the night watch, falling into beds. Figures passed by windows, noting without watching, went about their work. Hew had lived in colleges almost half his life – St Leonard's and St Salvator's, the Collège des Ecossais – and he understood the workings of those worlds in miniature, where small lives were lived out, intensified and amplified, without the intervention of the worlds they replicated, narrowed and enclosed. Here Bartie Groats and Ninian Scrymgeours dreamt and spent their days. The castle, he supposed, was different in its outlook, the watchmen on its towers were trained back to the town, and outward to the sea, turning a blind eye to what went on below.

Hew walked a little on in the direction of the chapel, which was built above a colonnade, in the Italian style. The castle had been mapped out like a summer palace, pleasing in the cool haze of the early morning sun. But since the range looked north, to blistering sea winds, it could not please for long. On the second floor, above the bishop's chamber, a gallery was built to overlook the court, and to the sea beyond. Here Hew glimpsed a flash of white, flitting at the windowsill, and heard, momentarily, the careless flute of laughter, high pitched like a child's. It came like the wind, and through the clear blue sky, and was gone as quickly. He supposed that it had been the mewling of the gulls that had begun to circle, high above the cliff. The tide was coming in, and with it brought the fishing boats, and raucous fleet of sea-maws, darting in its wake, dipping with the waves.

He was not left to roam. Within minutes, he was halted by the same red-headed soldier who had met them at the gate. 'I am sorry for it, sir, but it is not permitted that ye be here on your own.'

To his credit, and to Hew's surprise, he did look sorry for it. Hew conceded reluctantly, 'I suppose not.'

'If you wanted to wait for the doctor, there is a seat in the pend. The main gate is open now, sir. Or else you can wait in the guard house. The new man on duty will give you your sword. Or, if ye prefer it, I can show you round, and tell to you the secrets shored up in the stone.'

This was unexpected, and by far preferred. 'Does the stone keep secrets?' Hew asked with a smile.

'All stones have secrets, sir, if ye ken where to look. Would ye like to see some?'

'Aye, then, very much.' Hew recalled the name: 'Harry, is it not?'

'Harry Petrie, aye. We have met before, though you will not remember it. I was with the guard that was called out to your college, when there was a fray. You may recall our captain, sir. He is no longer with us.'

'Ah, then that explains it.' The flame red hair and freckled face had struck Hew as familiar. He remembered now. The captain had discharged his pistol in the air, and brought an end to the affray between the students and the baxters, that had torn apart the college. 'I am sorry that you saw it. Though your help was welcome, it was not our finest hour.'

The soldier grinned at him. 'In truth, we were glad of it; we see no action here. But I mind that a student was hurt there. Not badly, I hope?'

'His arm was broken. Giles Locke and my sister restored it to health. He recovered completely, no thanks to the surgeon.'

'It that a fact, now?' marvelled Harry. 'Is the doctor good with arms?'

'And other things,' Hew smiled. He turned the subject deftly. 'Pray God, that he may cure your master. Has he been sick for long?'

'I cannot rightly say; we futemen dinna deal wi' him.' Harry did not seem to want to talk of that. Hew supposed he had been warned against it, by the bumptious sergeant or the feeble clerk. 'But you did know he was ill?' he pressed.

'That is my understanding. He keeps to his room. This, where we are standing, is the old fore tower.' Harry had begun his tour, with a keen abruptness that discouraged further questions. 'If you wad like tae follow, sir, I will show you where the auld stane butts upon the new, and where the wicked cardinal was wrung out like a rag.'

Chapter 9

Set in Stone

The floor above them had been lowered, Harry said. He showed Hew all the places where the building had been altered, leaving nooks and crannies in the layers of stone. 'It is not level, see? There are hollows deep enough for a man to hide in, or at least a bairn.' His interest seemed to rest in the castle's first foundations, in its bare bones and roots, sunk deep in the rock. 'There is coal, if ye go deeper. I will show ye at the pit.'

'I thought I saw a child, upstairs in the gallery. Perhaps it was a shade,' said Hew, 'a phantom of the light.'

Harry laughed at that. 'More likely what you saw was Tam Fairlie's little lass. It pleases her to play there, though it rattles the archbishop, lying in his bed. Her footsteps drum through him like thunder he says, though she is as light as the wind.'

'Tam Fairlie has a child?'

'She has lived with him in the castle since his mother died, by grace o' the archbishop, who thinks well of Tam.' What happened to the bairn's own mother Harry did not tell. 'The place where you heard her is called the lang gallery, and runs the length of the floor above the archbishop's lodging. There are fine dormer windows looking to the town, and on this side, a promontory that looks out to the sea. It is not partitioned into quarters, like the chamber underneath, but kept as one long trance, where the little lass can run about the lang o' it.'

'Can we go up?' Hew asked.

The soldier shook his head. 'It is accessed from the west, by the same route you took up to the bishop's chamber, but there is no

94

doorway on this side. You will not catch the lassie there, if that is what you hope, for she will be long gone.

'There are two things I should tell to you about Tam Fairlie's lass, the first is that you will not see her, she is quick, and wild, and fickle as the breeze. And second, if ye do see her, you maun look away, or Tam will break your nose for you,' Harry promised cheerfully. 'Now, with your forbearance, sir, I will not tak ye up here to the second floor. The chamber at the top is used mostly by the guard, for up there is a doorway leading to the parapet, where the sentry walks who keeps the south side watch. A guid view ye may have there o' the doctor's house, an' muckle mair besides. And there, sir, is the window where they say the cardinal Beaton watched George Wishart burning, while he took his supper. Which I beg leave to doubt, for the window as ye see it has been altered since, by the archbishop Hamilton.'

'It seems you make a study if it. You are well-informed.' Hew smiled.

'It is my passion, sir. My father was a mason here, and taught me all he knew. He was still a prentice when they killed the cardinal, and hung him to the wind, like washer wifies' sheets.'

The assassins, Hew had heard, had pretended to be masons, mingling with the builders who were working for the cardinal. 'Was he there, then, when it happened?'

'He was prenticed to a man who was working on the walls, and came up for his shift, to find a crowd of folk had gathered in the street. He saw a coloured cloth unfurling from the battlements; he thought it was a pennant or a flag, or mebbe else the servants beating out bright tapestries, shaking out the dust. It was the body of the cardinal, hung out in a sheet. They took him at his prayers, and slit him to his soul. Blood soaked through the stone, and stained it like a blush. *Incarnatene*, my father called that deep and fleshly red; though some have called it cardinal. You can see the trace of it, weathered to flesh pink, for forty years of wind and rain have not yet washed it clean, nor worn it into sand.

'After that cardinal was killed, then came a bloody siege, that lasted many months, and much of this front part of the castle was destroyed, together with the gun towers. My father came to work for the archbishop Hamilton, who had these parts restored. He built for himself a palace fae the ruins, and he did not suppose that he would see it fall, so little did he care for the business of reform. I have shown you where the divers curtains met, and where the new was grafted on the old, as gardeners grow new apples on established trees – he made the gardens too, that lie out to the west. My father worked for him until he was struck down, with many other masons he had brought from France and others that were Scots. Besides the castle he built bridges, as the new one at Garbrig, and much of the New College, that the cardinal began. You can see his cinquefoil up above the gate here, painted on the walls, and woven into tapestries, and carved into the panels, too, that line the bishop's hall. He did not recover, though, all the wealth and finery that perished with the cardinal, for much of that was damaged in the siege, and what was not was spoiled by the reformers, or else lost to France. Such lavishness ye will not see again, and that, we must suppose, were no bad thing.'

Hew nodded his agreement. 'Then your father helped to build St Mary's college too? I would like to talk to him.'

'He has been dead, thirteen years,' Harry said simply. 'Else I should be a mason too and not here at the garrison.'

'Ah, then I am sorry for it. May I ask what happened to him?'

'He died in an accident, at the New College. Master John Douglas was the principal there, while Hamilton was chancellor, and making his repairs. Perhaps ye might mind him?'

Hew did. John Douglas had been one of the reformers who had subscribed the Scots confession, the foundation of his faith. He had transformed St Mary's College from the Catholic seminary hoped for by John Hamilton to a college in the service of the national kirk and faith, to train men in the ministry. He had taught Andrew Melville as a fledgling student there, set him on his path and recognised his worth. He had also, when Hamilton was hanged, accepted the archbishopric from the regent Morton, and so had become the first of the *tulchans*, savaged by his church. That decision had marred the last years of his life; elderly, and frail, he was accused by his brethren of a supple kind of treachery, and a cruel indifference to his former flock. In failing health and spirits, he was called upon to preach. It was said he had died in the pulpit, during Hew's first year in France.

'The building at St Mary's never was completed, after the reforms. The cardinal intended there should be a chapel, on the site of the old chapel of the college of St John.'

'The ruins are there still.' And Hew had been among them, just the day before.

Harry's voice dropped low. 'There was more left of it then. My father was employed to take the old walls down; and sin I had expressed an interest in his work, he thocht to tak me wi' him on that day. I was, by then, eleven years of age, old enough and strong enough to be a help to him, and I can mind it well, how proud I felt that day. They do say, sir, that pride brings on a fall. I cannot rightly tell you what it was that happened, for since then, I have made a study of walls, the old and the new, and of their construction, and it never has made sense to me. For some years after, I concluded that it must have been my fault, for my father was a careful man, and skilled. I no longer think that. I was nowhere near it when the wall collapsed on him, and pressed him to the ground.'

'Sweet Jesus,' whispered Hew. 'Then you saw him killed?'

When Harry was eleven, Hew had been a student still, close by at St Leonard's, fourteen or fifteen. Had he heard about this accident? He could not remember. Would it have moved him so much at that time?

'He did not die outright.' Harry answered, bleakly. 'It took them many hours, to pull my father out, and when they brought him hame, he took many months to die.'

'Then I am very sorry. So what happened to you, then? How did you come here?'

'Master John, the principal, was unco fair and guid to me. For since I lost my father on New College land, and since I could no longer hope to come in to his craft, he sent me to the grammar school, at his ain expense. And, had I proved my worth, I should have been a bursar at the university.' Harry pulled a face. 'But it was clear to all that I had not the wit for it, and that the Latin grammar that they grafted on tae me, howsoever carefully, never really took. And, I maun confess, I was no comfort to my mother, but a sorry trial to her. I was wayward, bold and bad, and always in a fight. Then that guid John Douglas, brave man that he was, did not cast me off, as my black heart deserved, but took me to his knee and said, "Now then, Harry Petrie, what are we to dae wi' you, you silly, reckless bairn, for it is plain to see we will not mak a scholar of ye."

'And bold loun that I was, I telt him I was mindit for to be a soldier, fighting for the faith, in the foreign wars. The old man shook his head. "That will not do," says he, "Your mother's heart was broken, when your father died, and I will not be at fault, for breaking it again."

'He was the bishop by then. And so, says he, I will find for you a place at the castle garrison, where you may learn to stand and fight, and do as you are telt – which latter I confess to you, the master at the grammar school never did dint in to me, starting off too late. An' when the time comes for to fight, says he, you may do your fighting for the earl of Morton – for that was his liege – and on hamely soil. So I was taught to stand, to fight and haud my tongue, though never did take arms up for the Regent Morton, nor now ever will, sin they hanged him too. When John Douglas died before the year was up, I was kept on in the service of Archbishop Patrick Adamson.'

'And here,' concluded Hew, 'you have been ever since.'

'Just so,' Harry grinned.

Hew had warmed immensely to the red-haired soldier, and his tale had touched him. It explained his passion and his ease about the castle, which he had inhabited since he was a lad, his interest in its history, and kenning of the stone. But he was curious, too, about the father's accident, which wrought another link between St Mary's and the castle, another kind of mystery, which could not be explained. 'Can we see a little more? The chapel and the hall?'

'By all means,' accepted Harry. 'I will take you to the pit, where the cardinal was slung, pickled in a barrel, like a piece of meat.'

He showed to Hew the chapel with its high arched windows traced in coloured glass, and ornate pillared walkways, ports and colonnades; the great hall, to the east, lined in solid oak, the kitchen, vaults and oven serving from the north. A small metal postern led down to the shore, winding down a precipice of sharply turning steps.

'When the tide is out, you can pass here to the jetty on the shore. But when the tide is high, the postern is kept locked. The drop is sheer and hazardous.'

The tide was coming in, whipped up by the wind. It resounded like the pounding of a thunderous artillery, that laid siege to the castle at the northern point, more damaging and treacherous than any fleet of guns. Hew shouted to be heard. 'Who lives in the north range?'

'Servants of the bishop's household, certain soldiers of the guard.' Harry's call came faint and weak, carried on the flood and flux, '... Cardinal Beaton's ... several hundred ...'

Hew took a step back from the swell of the waves. 'And the tower on the west side?' he roared.

'The sea tower?' mouthed Harry. 'Come see!'

The parapet, he said, had been damaged by the siege, and being at the back, had never been repaired. Within it, for the most part, it remained intact, containing divers chambers for 'our special guests'. 'There is a room above as airy and as comfortable as any you may see, that has a painted ceiling and a fine fair view, while under it ... well, sir, come see ... Here is the place where the cardinal lay, his corpus stripped and drained, deep in the rock.' Harry turned the handle of a small door on the right. 'Ach, the port is locked. I do not have the key.'

Hew had wandered off, to a chamber to the left, the door of which stood open, to the morning air. The walls inside were painted white, and had a cool, reflective feel. A deep high window looked out to the sea, its roar subdued and muffled by the flank of stone. A narrow long low ledge was built into the western wall, the only piece of furniture.

'What place is this? A prison cell?' he called.

Harry answered at his back, kept a watchful eye on him, both friendly and alert. 'A place, in truth, for a gentle man to reflect upon his sins, not grand enough to lodge above nor foul enough to lie below.'

'What is this hollow here? A place where food is passed?' Hew had found the channel where the thick walls intersected, angled like a tunnel to the other side.

'It is used for that purpose,' Harry confirmed, 'since the door has no grill. But whether by design, or it came about by accident, I cannot rightly say.'

'Was someone kept here lately?' Hew felt some loose object deep inside the cavity. His fingers closed upon it. 'There is something here.'

'Not for many years. What is it ye have found?'

Hew withdrew his hand, bringing out a wreath of supple plaited hawthorn, shaped into a crown. The blossoms were decayed, and distilled a heady perfume of sweetly rotting flesh, that brought to mind the rankness of the bishop's rooms. The hawthorn, Hew supposed, produced the carrion scent that carried on the wind; the gardens to the west of them were filled with dropping trees, heavily in bloom. The sea breeze seemed to catch at and disperse the fragrance, playing with it, amplifying, as it did with sound. In this little space, it felt overpowering.

'Whatever is this?'

Harry stared at it. 'I wadna like to say. Tis likely it belongs—'

'What do you men there?'

Hew had not heard the sergeant at their back. His presence seemed to strip the room of air and light. He stood square at the door, a dark and present force.

100

Harry answered easily. 'Master Hew here has a grening to be shown in to the pit. The pity is, the doors are locked.'

'Tis well, then,' Tam countered, 'that I have the key.' He rattled at the tackle he wore hanging at his belt, a chain of heavy keys. The sound brought a pricking to the hairs upon Hew's neck.

'Though ye will want a lantern, and a piece of rope. Harry here will fetch them.'

'Indeed,' protested Hew, 'he need not take that trouble. For there is no need. I should be getting back.'

He looked to Harry for support, but Harry, for the moment, seemed to have deserted him, deaf to his appeal. 'It is no trouble, sir. And you will like to see the place, where they slung the cardinal.' This Hew began to doubt. The sergeant had a stance of rude and bluff belligerence he did not like at all. 'Ye are quite safe wi' Tam,' was Harry's parting shot. Tam Fairlie grinned at Hew. 'And what do you have there?'

Hew clenched tight his fist, closing round the crown. 'I have no idea. I found it in the channel cut into the rock.'

'Oh aye? A bird's nest.' The sergeant dismissed it.

'I doubt that any bird could weave so fine a hand,' Hew assured him, coldly; he would not be cowed.

Tam Fairlie glowered at him. 'Aye, is that a fact? Step this way, my friend, and look into the dungeon ye were keen to see.' He took a step aside, so that Hew was forced ahead of him, and harried from behind. In that small tower of corners there was no hope of escape. Hew was irritated, rather than afraid, for he recognised the sergeant as the common sort of bully, who tormented for the pleasure of it, meaning no real threat.

Tam had unlocked the door upon a vaulted hole, with no clear source of light, and little source of air, but for a channel vent that was cut into the rock. The cell was not the blackest hole that Hew had ever stumbled in, and scarcely yet a pit, but it was dank and dark, and he was glad enough when Harry reappeared, with the rope and lamp. 'Now, sir, shift yer feet. For you are on the trap.'

In the fog of yellow light, Hew became aware that he was standing on a trapdoor, several feet across. Hurriedly, he stepped aside, and pressed himself against the wall, where there was far less room.

'Good man,' Harry grinned. 'That port is heavy, see? It takes the baith of us a' our strength to shift it.'

Tam Fairlie swore at Harry. 'Ye are feeble as a lass.'

The door was lifted with the rope, and tied up on a hook, opening to a chasm cut deep in the rock. Harry tied the lantern handle to the length of rope, and lowered it to the pit, swinging in an arc. 'Come, sir, take a look.' Hew stepped a little forward from the comfort of the wall, to peer down from the edge. He felt Tam Fairlie breathing, closely at his neck, fierce and hot and sour. 'Now, sir, look at that.' Tam's hand closed on his. 'It is a long way doon.'

Into the chasm, Tam dropped the crown, sounding the depths, marking its fall. The pit widened at the bottom, in a flagon shape, eight or nine yards down. Hew saw the hawthorn splinter, brittle in the lamplight, landing at the bottom with a gentle thud, that echoed far above. 'You want to mind your step, sir. Ye wouldna like to fall.'

Hew felt his stomach lurch. 'I could do with air.' He caught the pale light glinting through the open door.

'I expect ye could,' smirked Tam. 'Harry here will see you safe. Your doctor friend awaits ye.'

'Ye did not say that he was waiting,' Hew accused him, heavily relieved to stagger back outside.

'As I came to tell ye, sir,' the sergeant said impassively, 'when ye were so incontinent to see inside the pit.'

'You maunna mind him,' Harry said, as they walked to the gate. ''Tis likely that the hawthorn crown was made by his wee lass, in one o' her strange plays. She is a tender cause to him. He does not like to speak of it.'

Giles was at the guardhouse, deep in conversation with a futeman of the guard. 'This is John Richan,' he explained to Hew. 'He has come from Orkney. He came here as a bowman, but has injured his right shoulder.'

The young sentry gaped at him. 'Wha telt you that?'

'Why, you did yourself.'

'I telt thou my name, nothing mair.'

'Richan is an Orkney name, not found about these parts. And you have the measure of it sounding in your voice. It is a pleasing sound. You hold your right arm stiff, which maks it plain to see that you are in some pain from it. You are a straight and supple lad, and I dare to hazard, not quite fully grown, though you are already taller than is common here; your growing puts a strain and a tightness in your back. In our college we are wont to hold a competition at this time of year among the students who can shoot the bow, and I have seen many a young lad, pliable and green, exert and strain himself, in lifting up a bow that is too heavy for him, or taking up the practick when his limbs were cold, or in the early morning of a winter frost, or in the summer dampness of a cooling haar. All such things are hazardous,' Giles Locke diagnosed.

Harry Petrie ventured, standing by with Hew. 'Can ye help him, sir? The surgeon could not find a cause for his affliction.'

'The surgeon, with respect,' Giles snorted, 'is a natural fool. The shoulder has been overworked. The remedy is rest.'

'Then there is no help for it. Sin ye have met our sergeant, sir,' Harry glanced at Hew, 'you will be aware we are not let to rest. John must shoot his arrows, or else be discharged.'

Giles saw the soldier's plight, and answered sympathetically. 'My wife may have a remedy.' He said aside to Hew. 'Do you recall the exercises I prescribed for Nicholas, to strengthen his weak limbs?'

'For Nicholas?' Hew frowned. 'But surely, you do not propose that Meg should place her hands on him?'

'Piffle, Hew. It is a boy. No older than the students we let through our colleges. Meg kens how to handle them. And she will be with Paul. The case will do her good, and she will do a deal of good, ye may be sure, for him.' Giles was undeterred. 'When you next have leave,' he advised the sentry, 'come down to my house.'

John Richan found his voice. 'I thank you, but I cannot, sir. It would no be right.'

'He will come, sir, on my life,' Harry Petrie swore. He clapped John on the back. 'I'll fetch him there myself.'

'This is a curious place,' Hew remarked to Giles as they quit the castle gates. 'I cannot help but think that there are secrets here.'

'Then it will amuse you.' Giles seemed thoughtful and distracted, somewhat out of sorts.

'How did you find Patrick?' wondered Hew.

'Peevish, sick and sore. There is no doubt he is ill, as I will write to Andro. But he is not inclined to consult me for the remedy, and so I am resolved I cannot help him more. The potions he is taking are the armoury of quacksalves, mostly stagnant waters, chalk and sugar pills. But he has no intention of heeding my advice.'

The doctor was offended; Hew concealed his smile. 'And what advice was that?'

'Light diet, air and exercise,' Giles reported briskly. 'Amend his way of life. His humours are as black as any I have found. Above all he should leave this place, where rankness seems to seep from every foetid pore and every foul effluvium is hardened into stone.'

Chapter 10

Men at Work

The hammering began at dawn. The builders had arrived. And so began the first of many days and weeks that drove Meg to distraction, left alone with Matthew in the din and filth of it, to battle in the stew. Giles retired each morning to his turret tower, returning once the dust had settled to inspect the works. A chasm opened up beneath the kitchen floor, where burly men were lodged, coming up at intervals to swear and whistle freely, and stamp their sweaty dirt tracks up and through the house. Giles had pinned up dustsheets to contain the stour. 'On no account go down. Canny Bett will serve the kitchen, see to all your needs.' His nights were spent in consultation, closed up with the architect, making small adjustments or additions to his ordinance, while Meg paced with Matthew, who was cutting teeth. The sheets brought no protection from the noise. And so Meg was confined to an upper chamber, with a squalling infant, feverish and cross, despairing of the laich house and her husband's plans for it, oblivious to the purpose it was meant to serve.

Halfway through the morning on the fifth day of the works, when Meg had settled Matthew to a fretful sleep, the servant Paul brought news. 'Twa soldiers fae the castle guard are asking leave to speak wi' ye. They say the doctor sent them. Will I turn them off?'

'Show them up,' Meg sighed. 'For Doctor Locke did mention it.' Giles had told her of the archer with the damaged shoulder, though he had not warned her to expect his friend. The room in which she camped was ill-equipped for guests, filled with all her own belongings and the household furniture, carried there for safety from the nether hall. It would have to serve, for there was nowhere else.

Paul brought the men upstairs. One was tall and fair, and hung back reluctantly; the patient, Meg supposed. The other had red hair, and an open, friendly face. He spoke up for his friend. 'This is John Richan, mistress. I am Harry Petrie. Your husband Doctor Locke said that we might come to you.'

'For sure.' Meg smiled at him. 'You must excuse the muddle, we have warkmen in. Which one of you is hurt?'

'John here.' Harry pushed him forward. 'Pay no heed to his manners, for he isna used to company. And he wad no have come, had I not pushed him to it, but the plain truth is that he is sair afflicted, and he cannot raise his hand.'

The young man denied this, staring at his shoes. 'There is no purpose tae wir coman but for spilling o' thy time.'

'Speak proper, man,' urged Harry. 'Else we canna comprehend ye.'

'You are not from the town here?' Meg inferred.

'Na, lady. Fae Orkney.' John spoke low and mellow, and did not look up.

'Then you are a long way from home. Will you sit down, John, and take off your shirt?'

The young man blushed bright as a rose. He was not much older than the students at St Salvator's, and nothing in his manners marked him for a soldier. 'I cannot do that, lady. It wid no be right.'

Harry laughed aloud. 'Tak courage will ye, John! He's an unco modest laddie and a stubborn limmar too. Ye must needs be quite strict with him. Shall we strip him down?'

'Perhaps,' suggested Meg, 'you would like to wait outside?' She saw she could not hope to win the soldier's trust with Paul and Harry Petrie smirking by his side. 'Paul will take you down with him, and find you some refreshment.'

'An' then come back,' conceded Paul, 'and help you with his friend.'

This was not what Meg had hoped for, but it was not unexpected. She recovered quickly. 'I shall want you to go out, for this requires a remedy we do not have at hand. Go to the apothecar, and ask for a salve of marguerites in turpentine. He will call it *bellis minor*, or *consolida*. Ask only for the leaf, we do not want the flower. And ask him to put mallow in it. When you have returned with it, you may see it work.' By which time, she would have the shirt off, and the soldier's confidence.

'Canny Bett will fetch it,' Paul proposed. Dimly, he was conscious that he should not leave the house.

'Go back down and tell her then. And bid the builders rest awhile from their incessant hammering, while I tend this man.' Meg had to raise her voice in order to be heard. She glanced across at Matthew, stirring in his crib. 'Their thundering this morning has jolted the whole house, as though they were intent on shaking it from under us. Send them out for air, with something strong to drink, and pour a draught for Harry here, and something for yourself.'

'Richt civil of ye, mistress,' Harry Petrie smiled. 'She will not bite ye, John!'

Canny Bett was peeling onions at the kitchen board. From time to time she paused to wipe away the tears on sleeves already streaked with flour and grime and soot. She was making broth according to Meg's recipe, and though she followed carefully the long list of ingredients – the foreign roots and spices, dried herbs and fresh leaves, that Canny on her own would have thrown out as weeds – her flavours never matched the height and depth of Meg's, for Canny Bett was not a natural cook. Elbow deep in onion skins, she felt no warmth for visitors, and scowled to see the soldier at the door with Paul. Never on the grand side, the kitchen now was cramped, partly by the chasm that had opened in the floor, and partly by the ale and wine butts from the cellar, which were pushed against the window, propping up the board. The larder, press and kitchen shelves were covered with thick cloth, not strong enough or fine enough to keep out the dust, which settled in the butter pail, and on the tubs of vegetables. What remained of the floorboards were scuffed and thick with dirt, the earth dredged up in clouts and trampled through the door.

'Mind where ye pit yer feet!' she snapped.

'Ye are to gang to the pottinger, for to fetch a salve of *bellis consolida*, and hae him put the cost of it onto the doctor's reckoning,' Paul informed her cautiously, conscious of the soldier standing at his back.

Canny rolled her eyes. 'Whit sort of bells is that?'

'Daisies, to you.'

The lass heaved a *humph*. She was not accustomed to answering to Paul and, true to form and habit, she answered with an argument. 'Since ye ken a' aboot it, why not go yersel?'

In a different sort of household, there would be no contest. Paul was Giles' servant, Canny Bett was Meg's, and Paul would have as clear dominion over Canny Bett as would have his master over his own wife. But, somehow, in this house, that was not how things turned out; both Meg and Canny Bett were minded to be obstinate, strong in wit and will, and both out-flummoxed Paul.

Paul would have preferred if this had been less evident. But Harry Petrie waited, civil and respectful, at the kitchen door, a decent man was that. He had taken off his hat, and held it in his hands, and he had wiped his boots, so as not to add to the dirt upon the floor.

'Wha's ta make the dennar, then?' was Canny's parting shot.

'The neeps an' that will wait. Ye will not long be gone.'

Underneath the floor, the sound of scraping stilled, and a head poked, whistling, halfway through the hatch, followed by a clod of earth.

'Ye are to stop now,' called Paul, grasping at the lull which had broken in the hammering, 'an' come up fer refection.'

'An' come up fer *what*?'

'For a brek, an' a drink.'

108

'Ach, billie,' the builder said, 'Nae need for that. The doctor left a barrel doon, maist gentle an' maist mannerly, for when we hae a thirst.'

The head ducked down again. And the hammering resumed. Paul knelt down above the hole, and bellowed like a bull calf. 'For pity, will ye stop?'

'Eh? Whit's that ye say?'

'Come up.'

The scraping shovel stopped, and there was silence for a moment, before the head appeared once more in the opening, and a pair of shoulders followed it, and heaved out to the deck. The second man came after, wiping off the sweat. 'Whit is the matter now?'

'Ye are to break off for a while, and go out on to the cliff. Take that pile of *fuillie* with you,' Paul gestured at the muck.

The workman scratched his beard. 'Wha says so, then?' He looked back at his friend, who frowned and shook his head. 'The maister says to dig until the dinner hour.' The master of the works had already quit the site, and left the heavy groundwork to his hireling labourers, the work requiring less of skill than strength.

'The mistress says,' urged Paul. 'She maun hae peace an' quiet, for to tend a soldier.'

The words did not sound right, and Paul had cause to curse as soon as they were out. The builder nudged his friend. 'Tending tae a soldier? The guid doctor's wife?'

Canny Bett intruded, in a high, indignant voice. 'Ye mauuna speak o' her in that foul filthsum voice, for wan hair on that lass's head is worth the weight of you. And *that* were lourd enough, lubbard that ye are.'

'Aye, is that right? An' ye wad tend a man, full tenderly, I doubt.' The builder leant across, and groped at Canny playfully. There was nothing in the faintest playful in her slap.

'Ye hard wee bitter bitch.' He caught her by the wrists. 'I'll mak ye tender yet.'

Canny gave a screech, less of fear then fury, swore and stamped her feet.

'Let the lassie go.'

Paul knew in his heart that he should have protected her. He knew the words, and spoke them, clearly, in his head. Yet when he heard them said, it was Harry Petrie said them. He stepped out from the doorway, to confront the builder, brave and calm and quietly. The builder turned to stare at him, dropping Canny Bett. Canny kicked him in the shin, shot Harry back a glance that bore no trace of gratitude, glared at Paul and fled, presumably to follow through the errand to the pothecar. They heard the front door slam.

'Wha the fuck are you?'

'A futeman fae the castle guard. And if ye want to tak it further, step wi' me outside.'

The two men squared up warily. The workman was the bigger of the two, broad and tall and flabby, with more brawn than wit. Harry's frame was small and balanced, muscular and lean. The outcome of a fight between them could not be assured, though the consequence of fighting would be ruinous to both. The builder's colleague plucked his sleeve. 'Leave, it, Jockie,' he suggested.

Jockie dropped his fist. 'A wee brek, ye say?' he spat back at Paul.

Paul agreed, hoarsely. 'My mistress has promised ye no loss of pay.'

'There is a barrow in the yard there filled up wi' dirt. We can tak it to the shore,' the two men agreed. But Jockie hissed, in passing, 'We are not settled yet.'

Left with Harry Petrie, Paul did not know what to say. He coloured in his shame. But Harry gave no hint that Paul had disappointed him. Rather the reverse.

'Tis a grand thing,' he admired, 'to have kenning o' the Latin, and a clear command of such a house as this. All my life, I have done what I wis telt, with a boot about my arse and a rope about my back, for want of wit and scholarcraft. Sir, I envy you.'

110

Paul found a pair of beakers in the kitchen almery and blew them free from dust. He poured them both a cup of ale. 'You do not care to be a futeman, then?'

'I am no a futeman, truth be told. I am a sentry in the castle guard. Our work is to defend the precinct o' the bishop's court, and sometimes we are called upon to keep peace in the town, but maistly we stand and watch, and watch and stand, and clean our swords and guns; and our sergeant sends us up an' doon on marching tricks and exercises, and we cannae fire the guns, for we may have no powder, save with the permission of the king, so God alone may ken what service we might do, a dozen unarmed men with one half-crippled archer,' Harry Petrie laughed. 'This ale is douce and sweet, and you, sir, are a gentle man. Your guid complice, too.'

'My complice?' echoed Paul.

'Your partner, Doctor Locke.'

Paul was warmly gratified by Harry Petrie's flattery. The soldier took him for a learned man. And why then, should he not? Paul had picked up many things from the doctor and his wife. Small knowledge was a danger, Doctor Locke believed; his wife contended, teach him, then. Paul felt for Giles and Meg a fondness mixed with pride, that verged at times on pity and exasperation, and at other times to something close to love. He doubted they could manage well without his help.

He was wearing, too, one of Hew's old coats, a doublet sewn from light blue silk, and though the tail and neck were not the latest cut, he knew that Harry Petrie would not realise this; soldiers were not noted for their fashion sense. He had taken Paul on trust, and made the same mistake as had the widow Bannerman, when Paul had turned up at her ailing husband's bedside, with a phial of physick sent by Giles. What little did it matter, if she took him for a complice of the learned doctor, for but for want of learning that was what he was. It had not been his intention to deceive her. Many servants wore their master's cast off clothes. The fact that Hew was not his master was a point of fact, that could not count against him; since Hew would keep no man by him but for the frugal Nicholas, it made perfect sense that they should come to Paul. The doctor's clothes were practical, distinctive and voluminous, ill-fitted to adapting to the role of hand-me-downs. Hew was far more slender, and had better taste.

'He is not, exactly, my partner.' Paul felt compelled to honesty as he refilled their cups.

'But you have his confidence,' Harry said, persuasively, 'and that is a thing to admire.' Paul considered. 'True enough.'

'A man might be a lord, in service to the king, or like the arch-bishop, in service to God. A servant may become a king, if only he will rise to it. The Stewarts were themselves no more than stewards to a king.'

'Even so,' protested Paul, 'I am not servant to a king.' He was encouraged all the same, and wondered whether he might reason-ably construct himself, before the widow Bannerman, as steward of his master's house.

'I have no doubt,' Harry went on, 'that ye maun be privy to all manner of rare things. And being in your master's confidence, are steward of his trust, secretar of his heart.'

'Very right an' true,' Paul nodded, full fair pleased with that.

'Then you are a lucky man, that does not hae a flock of masters baying at your back. I answer to a pack o' them – sergeant, steward, secretar – all wear boots fair thick enough to dint a beggar's arse, and all have different notions how things maun be done. The chain is long and tangled, and small comfort at its end; if a beggar does not jump when he hears it rattle he will feel it pull. Which is a lesson young John Richan has been finding hard to learn. Tis hardest for the beggar at the far end of the chain.'

Harry had veered off, to peer into the chasm that had opened in the floor. 'So what work are they doing here?' he asked.

'They are laying conduit pipes, to take foul waters out to sea. It is a scheme of the doctor's invention,' Paul told him, with a spark of pride. He answered, after all, to a fine and clever man. And that, if nothing else, reflected well on him.

'Ingenious,' said Harry. 'Shall we take a look?'

'Go down there, you mean?' Paul replied, more doubtfully. 'Why wad we dae that?'

'I dinna want to put you out, but my father was a builder too. He worked for the archbishop Hamilton. And I think it very likely that he built this house.'

'Is that a fact?' Paul marvelled. 'Ye must tell the doctor. He will want to hear that. He will show you round.'

'And that wad be a treat. But,' the soldier frowned, 'the knot is, that he is not here. And I have an apprehension, that this under-mining may be somewhat hazardous. The warkmen ye have here have neither wit nor skill. They are knocking down a wall, from what I saw and heard, and knocking down a wall requires a deal of both. My fear is, if thae clubbit blunderers dinna mind their step, the hale house will come down. That is the sum of it, plain.'

'The doctor is a clever man, and he employs an architectour, and a man of works. He would not let that happen,' Paul asserted.

'No' willingly, of course. But where are they three masters now, while these great lourdans stamp and hack? Tis plain enough to see that you are left in charge. Trust me, sir, it takes but one fool wi' a sledger an' the hale pile tumbles down. It happened to my faither, and I would not for the world see it happen to your friends. That bonny babby too.'

'What happened to your dad?'

'A wall that he was taking down fell back and down on him. It took him days to die.'

'Jesu,' gasped Paul. 'Then we maun evacuate. I will rouse the mistress.'

'Peace now,' Harry soothed, 'there is nae need for that. We need not cause alarm, until we are assured of it. The danger is not present, while they are not knocking at it. I will tak a look, and see if it is safe. It is a thing I ken about. We learn it in our training.'

For when it came to sieges, Paul supposed. He consented, nerv-ously. 'I will come with you.'

'There is no need.'

But Paul was determined that he would not be a coward, and shrink back a second time. The assurance of the household rested in his hands. When Harry climbed the ladder down into the laich house, he followed close behind.

The labourers had left a lantern hanging by the hatch. Harry took it down, and held the light aloft, to illuminate the room. There was one small window facing to the west, where the upper level rose above the ground, and a new vent for the chimney cut in the back wall. The labourers were lowering the floor, digging out a solid foot of earth. The cellar was foreshortened by a wall of stone, that heavily abridged the footprint of the house, reducing it by half, and it was this that the workmen were beginning to demolish, starting at the top. It was too dark to see into the space beyond. Harry felt his way along the stone. 'Now there's a thing,' he whistled, 'I did not expect.'

'What's that?' worried Paul. 'Is the structure hazardous?'

'Not hazardous at all. This wall serves no purpose, and is holding nothing up. Therefore its demolition can bring nothing down with it.'

'That's a good thing, is it no?'

'Good enough. But curious. Why then, build a wall?'

'I could ask the doctor,' Paul suggested.

'Well, now, and ye *could*,' Harry's tone implied that this was not a good idea. 'Does he like you to come down here?'

'Well . . .' Paul considered, 'he has not said agin it, in sa many words.' Yet he admitted to himself, his master had discouraged it.

'Ask yourself the question,' Harry went on cunningly, 'where are the pipes?'

'What pipes?' echoed Paul.

'The conduit pipes, ye said. For Doctor Locke's experiment.'

'Well, I suppose that he will fetch them once the floor is dug.' Paul hesitated, thinking. 'Well then, I suppose . . . I will not tell the doctor, then. For since there is no danger here, there is no cause to trouble him.'

114

'I think that ye do right. The main thrist an' the outcome is, our minds are set at rest. Our fear need not concern him.' Harry hung the lantern back up on its hook. 'The warkmen will be back soon. Shall we go up?'

Paul felt an alliance with his new-found friend, with whom he had defended and made safe the house. Recklessly, he ventured, 'Shall we try the wine? For I may use it freely, if an' when I like.'

This was not strictly true. Paul was a blabbermouth in drink, and whatever Giles allowed him was carefully controlled. But the new season's wine Giles had taken to the college, and what remained in the barrels was becoming sour and old, and Giles would scarcely quibble if Paul told him it was spoiled. It was never in Paul's mind to deceive his master, nor would he wish to steal from him, but he felt that he was somehow owed a drink of wine, to recompense his trouble and his fright over the wall. He poured a pint into a stoup and stirred it for good measure with a corner from the sugar loaf. 'To your guid health, sir; pass your cup.'

Harry was impressed. 'God bless ye, sir, and yours, for I will not say no.' He did not seem to mind the sharpness of the malmsey, which caught Paul's throat like vinegar. 'No sound fae the loft,' he remarked. 'I hope the laddie Richan hasna died o' shame . . . I doubt that he was strippit at a woman's beck, since he was a babby nourished by his ma.'

His tone was playful, not unkind, moving Paul to ask, 'I suppose a man like you has many a sweet lass – they seem to like a soldier.'

Harry smiled at him. 'Many o' them do.'

'Can I ask your advice?'

'Of course ye can, my son! What dae you want to ken?'

Paul drained his sour wine quickly, dregs and scum and all, and looked up from the cup. Harry was, in truth, a proper sort of friend. And that was soldiers for you. They had been together, on an operation, faced a present danger. They were friends in arms. 'There is this woman, see. The widow Bannerman.'

'Widows are brave,' Harry agreed. He reached out for the jug, and poured himself another cup of wine, without waiting to be asked.

'Ripe and rich and rare, and brimming with experience. I recommend a widow, if ye have not practised much.'

'She has her own wee house, and a bit of land. Her husband died young, and they were not long marrit. And she has nae bairns.'

'So much the better,' Harry smiled.

It was not coming out quite as Paul had meant it to. It sounded like he wanted her for her house and land, and did not want the burden of another limmar's bairns, when that wasn't it at all. He would have loved Jonet Bannerman if she bided in a cowshed wi' a pack of wailing weans, and opened up his arms to all her snot-nosed progeny if that was how it was. It would be simple then.

'I took physick to her when her man was sick,' he was trying to explain. 'And when he died, I came again, to offer my condolences. Not because the doctor sent me, but on my own account. She thinks I am his prentice, see. She thinks I will one day have a practice of my own. She does not know I cannot read. I did not set out to deceive her.'

'Aye? What is the matter then? She will not go to bed with you, unless she hears you read to her?'

'Naught like that. The matter is,' confided Paul, 'that I want to marry her. What should I do? Will she understand it, if I tell the truth?'

'How should I know?' Harry shrugged, draining his draught to the dregs. He wiped his wet lips with the back of his hand. 'A fine poison, that.'

Paul felt disappointment, cold inside his stomach, like a lump of lead. He had misjudged the soldier, laying bare his soul to him. Harry had no conscience; he was not in love, and the widow Bannerman was far beyond his ken.

'Mebbe,' Harry said, 'I will see how John is doing. Tell ye what, though – d'ye ever tak a drink in the tavern in the wynd? There is a lass there that will answer to your needs, and ye can get your practice in, and forget your troubles for a while.'

'I do not ...' Paul began. The place that Harry spoke of was forbidden him by Giles, since he had drunk there once too deep, and let loose his tongue. He had tried the tap wench too, and found himself slapped back. 'I went there once,' he mumbled. 'I did not find much luck with it.'

'Ye dinna ken the ropes. The lassie at the bar is a friend of mine. She is my cousin, Bess. When you are there next, say to her that ye are mates wi' her cousin Harry Petrie. And you shall have your drink, and what you will besides.'

'That is awfy kind of ye,' Paul acknowledged doubtfully, for he was not convinced that this would help with Jonet Bannerman.

Harry Petrie winked at him. 'Courage to ye, friend. For ye are brave and fine, and halfway to a scholar. We will mak a lover of ye yet.'

Chapter 11

Between the Tides

'No one here will force you to be stripped against your will. But it will be a help to me if you take off your shirt.'

Meg allowed her patient time to know and trust her. She felt his eyes upon her as she tidied books away and folded Matthew's clothes, to fill the gulf of awkwardness. She was conscious of his presence, watchful, at her back. He had taken off his cap and his hair shone soft as flax, silver as the hemp, as fair as any man's. His eyes were grey and careful, restless as the wind. He was sitting, straight and stiffly, on the great oak settle they had dragged up from the hall.

Matthew Locke was sleeping in the Cullans' cradle, where Meg and her brother had both slept as bairns. Meg had worked the canopy and coverlet in red, with little horses, trees and flowers, in primrose, green and gold. A fine white linen cambric kept away the dust. The infant's sleep was light and strained; his eyelids flickered warily, against a raft of dreams. His cheeks were pink and hot. His father had prescribed a pulp of hollyhock and hare brain, Meg had cooled his gums with camomile and dill, but Matthew whimpered still.

Meg searched among the few jars remaining in her almery, and found a pot of liniment. She turned back to the Richan boy. 'This salve will help your shoulder heal. But there is not much left of it. The archers at the college had a contest for the May, and took it as a prophylactic, to protect their limbs. For they are supple, young and green, and can be overstraught. The salve is kind to muscles that are raxed and sore. It must be rubbed in deep into the sinews of the shoulder and the back, and you will feel a heat, but it is a good heat, and there is no need to fear it. I can apply it for you; or, if you prefer, you can ask your friend. I do not think that you can manage it yourself.'

The liniment had come from the still at Kenly Green, where the marguerite and mallow and the tender violet buds were planted in the physick garden, and would now be flowering, spilling out their seeds. Giles supplied the turpentine shipped in bulk from France. Though Paul would bring a replica back from the apothecar, made up to Meg's recipe, it would be less effective, thinner, more expensive, and would not smell so sweet.

John Richan answered her by taking off his shirt. It took him some while, and not, Meg supposed, because of his shyness; his right arm hung futless and slack by his side. He undid the wooden buttons with his left, and eased the russet sark sleeve over his sore shoulder, letting it drop to the ground. Meg picked up the shirt, and put it with his coat of liver-coloured wool. The cloth felt coarse and thick. His back was laddered black, a mass of knots and welts.

'Canst thou no find the place?' John's speech was full and deep, as though each word was carried with a weight of meaning, ponderous and slow.' 'Where that arrow strak?'

Meg came close, and looked, but she could see no arrow wound. 'Did some hook tear the flesh? I cannot see it, John.'

'Tis trow-shot, that thou cannot see.' John said thou as *thoo*, a long soft lowing lull, like a bull-calf's bellow.

'Trow?'

'A elf. A fairie dart.'

He thought he had been struck by elfin shot. How else could he explain to her his sapping strength and powerlessness, the deep and deadening wound the surgeon could not find?

'Will you let me touch you, John?'

'And thou finds the place.'

She put her bare hands on his shoulder, felt the muscle taut and strong. John Richan did not shrink at it, but turned his cautious eyes upon her, deep and grey and serious.

'There are many natural causes will not leave a mark, and we must look for those, where with art and patience we will come to cure them. And I do not believe the cause of this is trow-shot.'

Country folk were conscious, always, of that netherland, under water, over hills, where the faeries lived. They knew that faeries crossed on winds, through copse and thicket, dyke and stream, snatching infants from their cribs, new-born mothers in their milk, gentle sleepers in the shade of hawthorn boughs and apple trees. There were witches, too, the cause of storms at sea, of cows that failed to calf and sick or stillborn children, famine, drought and flood, when nature was unnatural, uncouth and unkind. In Orkney, where the grasping kirk had not yet closed its grip, and where both land and sea were harsh and inhospitable, it was little wonder there were tales of trolls. And who was she to say the stories were not true?

Meg had learned to harness and restrain the powers of nature, and through her art and science shape them to her will. It was simpler, sometimes, to pretend to make a spell, and blow the magic off, than it was to fight it with the force of reason. But where she could, she fought, for believing in a curse would prejudice recovery. A man might die from fear.

'The hurt is inside,' she explained. 'You cannot see it like a bruise. But the shoulder has been wrenched and pulled out of its joint. What did the surgeon say?'

'He opened up the vein, and drained the arm of blood. But the infirmity persisted.'

'There are more tunes to a body than the surgeon kens to play. You will feel a heat now. Tell me if it hurts you.'

Meg warmed the ointment gently in her hand, and began to work it, deep into the shoulder, and the broad hard muscle of the soldier's back, a knot of strength and sinew taut beneath his skin. With subtle, searching fingers, she sought out the place, probing and manipulating, deep down to the bone. John let out a cry, and placed his hand on hers.

'Is that so very sair?'

'No, lady,' he moaned. 'Thou loosed the dart. The trow-shot is gone.'

His eyes were bright with gratitude, brimming with relief. Meg noticed in their grey a shard of brittle blue, subtle and reflective, changing like the sea. She lifted out her hand, feeling on its back still the gripping of his fingers, supple, fierce and strong.

'I shall quarrel with you, John, if you persist in thinking that. I have unbent your shoulder, in such a way as you might have unbent your bow, and let the muscle slacken, as you loose the strings. Now put on your things.'

The young man flexed his hands. 'Thou works magic, of a sort,' he insisted as he dressed, his shoulder slipping easily underneath the shirt.

Meg had moved away, to wash and dry her hands. The laver and a towel were set out at the fireside, close to Matthew's crib. 'The muscles were quite ravelled, and I have unlocked them. But they will go back into thrawe. You must not be disheartened then, to find them sore and stiff. It may take some while for the strain to heal.'

'I can come agin here?' The soldier asked softly.

'As often as you can, until the arm is strong.'

Matthew had begun to grizzle, fretful at her feet. He seldom slept for long. 'You must excuse me, now. My babe is waking up.'

'Aye? What is his name?' John Richan crossed the room, putting on his coat.

'He is called Matthew, after my father,' Meg smiled.

'Has thou no other bairn?'

'Matthew is our first.' It was hard to take offence at John Richan's questions, which were artless as a child's. 'He is cross and peevish,' Meg said, 'at the hammering, and his gums are hurting him, for he is cutting teeth. He wants a little cooling water, or some poppy juice.

But there is none to hand.' She rocked the cradle, hushed her child, but Matthew's grizzling threatened to break out in to a howl. 'He is not hungry yet. I should have brought the poppy water back from Kenly Green.

'It is my brother's house on the Kenly water, four miles south from here. I grew up on the land and learned of country matters, from my childhood nurse. There are woodlands there, and walkways lined with trees, orchards, flower and physick gardens, where I grew my herbs. And by the physick garden is a cool house and a stillerie, where my country foster mother taught me to make remedies, and waters of all kinds.' Talking to John Richan was like talking to a child; his gaze was deep and curious.

'Thou has na mother, then?'

'She died when I was born.'

And in those months that followed, so Meg had been told, her father could not look at her, but left her with the nurse, until that nurse had laid her, bright-eyed changeling child, dark-haired like her mother, firmly in his arms. And he had loved her then, more deeply than the life that he had given up for her. Matthew had retired to Kenly Green when his little daughter took the falling sickness, and he had kept the nurse who found the herbs to soothe her, for Annie had a way with her, that she had taught to Meg. That part of the tale she did not tell the Richan boy.

'The apple trees are full with blossom at this time of year, the broom and bay in bud.' Meg stroked the infant's cheek. 'I am sorry, John, but I will have to lift him. If your friend is here still, call him from the kitchen. Paul will show you out.'

John said, 'Bide a while.' Then, to Meg's astonishment, he knelt down by the crib, and began to rock it with his strong left hand. And as he rocked, he sang, a long, low, lilting melody that rose and fell like water flowing from the sea. The infant stilled and watched, with wide and wondering eyes. He did not want the song to end, and when it did, he mewled in protest, petulant and weak, and John Richan hushed him, stilled him with a whisht. His voice was like the

122

wind, blowing through the rafters, breathing out a lullaby to calm the fractious bairn.

'Now that is magic,' murmured Meg.

At that, for the first time, John Richan smiled. And it was like a breath of sunshine warming his pale face, that lifted up the shadows there and showed the boy within, fragile, fair and young.

'It is a song my mother sings, to soothe the weans at home. There are a lot of us.'

There was a quiet longing in his voice. Somehow it had seemed to keep the tune, the music of the song, so that though the words were Scots they sounded rare and strange, like waking from a dream to hear a foreign tongue.

'What language is it, John?'

'It is the Norish speke, the Orkney Norn. It is my mother tongue.'

'It sounds so sad.'

'It is a song about the sea, and about the wind, and of an enchantress. It is not a sad song, but the language is sad. It weeps for its own death. My father says that we must speak the language of our masters, if we do not wish forever to be slaves. So we must speak in Scots, and the Norish will die out, and only will be heard in scraps of song and stories, flying on the wind. On dark nights – and Orkney nights are very dark and long – you will hear it whispered in the crevices and cracks, whistlin' through the rafters, threaded into dreams. You will hear it in the flicker and the crackle of the fire, and in the ebb and flowing of the sea, and in the peat and stone and in the cliffs and braes, the weepin' of the sea-maws and the selkies' bark.'

Meg said, 'You are far from home. How old are you, John Richan?'

'I am nineteen.'

'Then you are very young.'

'Not where I come from. How old are you?'

'Now that is not a question you have leave to ask.'

'Then I repent the asking of it,' he accepted simply. 'But I never understand what I am not meant to ask. It is a fault in me that cannot be mended.'

'Though they try to mend it?'

John looked down at his hands. 'They have not given up. And while I live still, they will not give up. They think it is their duty to mak me like them; but I am different to them. They do not understand it. And that maks them afraid. It offends them when I speak. And when I do not speak, it offends them too. They fear what I am thinkin' and my unco foren tongue. And I have tried to mend it, but the words slip out.'

'I like the way you speak.'

'Then thou art the first. And the first to hear the Norn. I dare not sing to them.

'I think, mistress, you are no older than I am,' John returned slyly.

Meg acknowledged, with a smile. 'I am twenty-two.'

'Now that,' he teased, 'is old. My mither had five babbies when she was that age, twa were in their graves; now she is four and thirty, worn down to the bone. I do not think it suits thee to be kept here in this place. Thou's a country lass. And all this dust an' hammering will mar thy bonny looks.'

'Now I begin to see,' laughed Meg, 'why your masters venture to rein in your tongue. The hammering is temporal, I am glad to say.'

'It is na just the hammering. But this is not the place for thee. Thou're like me, as I think, thy heart is somewhere else.'

Meg had turned away. 'I thank you for the song. Matthew is quite settled now. I will walk downstairs with you, and show you out myself.'

'Art thou offended? I did not intend it. I cannot help but say such things. Thou maun take no ill by it, for thou has bonny looks, and a light in your eyes that for all the world I would not see put out. There is a loveliness in thee I have not met before.'

'You have not offended me. But if I am to help you, then you cannot ask me those kind of questions.'

'What questions am I asking thee?'

'Ones about myself. And you may not remark how I appear to you. Such comment is not proper to a married woman. You are the doctor's patient, and I am his wife.'

'Then if a woman has a husband and she is unhappy, I am not allowed to notice it?'

Meg was shocked at this, for John's reply came close to what she heard from Hew, in their quarrels over Clare. John was not like Hew, but guileless as a child. 'I am not unhappy,' she insisted.

'But thou are not yet happy,' answered John. 'I think thou are not happy. Nor where thou dost belong. For that is in the garden, with the flowers and herbs. A light came in you, when you spoke of it.'

'I am happy here. And more than this plain truth you have no right to ask. And you are not, I think, so artless and unwily that you do not know that. If you will persist with this, then we must think again about your coming back here.'

'Now thou art cross. I did not intend it,' the soldier said sadly. 'I vex folk all the time. And though I am corrected for it, still I do not learn. And if I am not well, and cannot shoot my bow, then they will send me home.'

'With a little patience, we may hope to mend you by more gentle means. I will not give up on you. But would it be a bad thing, if they sent you home?'

With the strain upon his shoulder and the welts upon his back, it was plain the archer's life was not a happy one.

'It would be the worst thing in the world. It would do dishonour to my father, for he sent me here, to learn to be a man. My father is a servant to Lord Robert, earl of Orkney, who is half an uncle to the present king, and the earl himself it was that put me to the bishop here. It would shame him too, if they sent me back. And I might die for shame.'

'What kind of man is your father?' wondered Meg. She thought about her husband, and his hopes for Matthew, and of her own father, and his hopes for Hew. Hew had gone his own way, believing to the last that his father was displeased with him. She did not doubt that Matthew Locke would go his way too. Would Giles be disappointed, then? Or would he learn to moderate his fierce pride in his son?

John Richan shrugged. 'I cannot tell you that. For the best part o' his life, he has been in thrall to that dark and errant lord, and I do not ken his mind; but that he does what Robert says. Sin he serves sic a master, no one likes him much. And here, they do not like me much, because they think I am his spy.'

'And are you?'

John was silent for a moment, toying with the buttons on his liver-coloured coat. 'Perhaps,' he said at last. 'But servants do not always tell their masters what they know. Indeed, I think they often do not do so. And if I telt him everything I saw, I do not think his lordship would believe me.'

'Can he be a master worthy of your trust?'

A smile played upon John's lips. 'He is worth no man's trust. He is a black-hearted loun. It was a dark day for Orkney, when Lord Robert came to rule. We are all of us there in his thrall. For thou maun understand, he lives between the tides.'

Meg frowned. 'What do you mean?'

'That place on the shore that lies betwixt the high and low water marks. It is the devil's land, for no living man can bide there. But Robert earl of Orkney would take it off his hands. At council, no man kens what side the earl is on, whether he is of the party of the earl of Gowrie, or of Lennox and the king. The truth is, Robert earl of Orkney is on no side but his own. Do you understand? He shifts upon the tides. He sends out spies like fishermen, to dabble in the burn; the small fry they hook up he sets by for the bait, in hopes of catching somewhat bigger fish. I cannot go back with no fish on my hook. It were better, after all, that I lay dead and withered by the fairy dart.'

Meg felt for the young archer, lost and out of place as a selkie on the land, who had come up for the sun and had been strippit of its skin, forced to live its days in a borrowed human shape. 'Then you must come again, until you are cured. I have no doubt that you will make a full recovery, with exercise, and rest.'

'I have no want of exercise, and little hope of rest. The sergeant here will work me to the bone.'

'Is there no work,' she asked, 'that does not hurt your shoulder?'

A raw smile crossed the soldier's face. 'Aye. There is keeping the watch.'

Chapter 12

The Draucht-Raker

In the beginning was the word. The New College of the assumption of the Blessed Virgin Mary was built upon the site of the ancient pedagogy, where two staunch scholars of the faith, Dod Auchinleck and Colin Snell, kept watch one moonlit night, crouching in the shadows of the chapel of St John. Their faces, pressed in hollows that had once held panes of glass, peered out pale as ghosts. The sky was overcast, the grey moon skulking shiftily, leaving Dod and Colin quaking in the gloom.

In principio erat verbum. Dod had not wanted to come. It was Hew Cullan's fault, for he had put the night watch into Melville's mind, and Andrew Melville looked for someone he could trust, and why would he look further than his own disciples, students of the college, stalwarts of the kirk? Dod had waited back, and let the others stand up first. He hoped the devil might be captured early on. But that had not worked out.

'Eh? Whit was that?'

'I said we shouldae brought a lantern wi' us.' Dod had not meant to speak his fears aloud. He placed his hand, accidently, in a patch of thistles growing in a crevice half way up the wall, and sucked at it, resentfully.

'Ach, Doad, dinnae be daft. The light would frighten aff the limmars at the gate, and put them a' tae flight,' asserted Colin Snell. Colin was bolder and braver than Dod, stauncher and more resolute in Christ. He did not suffer fools, or fear, as much as Dod did, and he had kept the watch for Melville twice before. Both times, he had

128

come back to the college empty-handed, disappointment swilling over his fair face.

'Limmars?' echoed Dod. A weakness and a trembling rippled through his knees. 'How many of them are there, d'ye think?'

'Ah dinna ken. But we will be prepared for them. We have a horn an' a stick.'

It was not what Dod had hoped for, and it was not enough. But Melville had been adamant. Scholars of the college did not carry swords.

'What will we do, an' supposing we catch them?'

'Well . . .' Colin set aside a moment to consider this, thoughtful fingers closing tightly round the stick. While Dod had hoped that he might hold the hunting horn at least, it seemed that Colin Snell had taken charge of both. 'We will tak all diligence to mak them see the light, repenting of their sins, and bowing down in Christ.'

'And what if they will not repent it? What if they are rotten, to the very core?'

'We all of us are rotten, Doad,' Colin said, complacently. 'Steeped in filth and sin. We are all contemptible, you the same as them.'

'Aye,' persisted Dod, 'but what if they are reprobate, and there is no hope for them?' He swallowed back the worry that was rising in his gorge: how could he be certain there was hope for him?

'I think it very likely, they are truly reprobate,' Colin Snell confessed. 'Yet they cannot be denied the right, the comfort and the solace of God's word. If they are reprobates, their hearts will be closed to it. Their eyes will not open, and allow the light. But if they are but belly-blind, their muffles may be lifted, and they may repent of it, and we may be the instrument that leads them to the light. Wherefore we owe it unto them, as to ourselves, and God, to bring that message home to them, and thwack them with this stick, to cow them to contrition while a higher justice comes.'

Dod was unconvinced. 'But what if they are devils, or else elfin folk?'

129

The faerie folk came at the full of the moon, to briar and hawthorn, and haunted old ruins; but faeries were shy, and would fly from the light. He had kent it all along. They should have brought the lamp.

Colin reassured him, for the umpteenth time: 'If the faerie folk come, we will blow on the horn. Scare them awa' wi' three solid blasts.'

'But suppose they creep up on us, an' tak us by stealth?'

'Pah!' Colin snorted. 'I would like to see them try.'

He would an' all, thought Dod. And if the devil were himself to come, Colin would not baulk at it, but he would stand and fight. He would grapple wi' the fiend, and grasp him by the horns, and send the devil whimpering, his boot print black emblazoned on the devil's arse. Dod wished he had the courage of his dauntless friend; a grand and fearsome preacher Colin Snell would make. Dod had not the stomach to resist the devil's charms. The devil would make mince of him. Suppose the devil came, and brought the faerie queen with him, to tempt them to their doom? For faeries were attracted to a young man on a quest. And what were they on now, in the dead of night and grey light of the moon, if it were not a quest? They were knights of Christ that ventured for their lives. He kenned the queen was after him; she came to him in dreams, insinuated, snakelike, round his helpless hips, and left her trail behind her, fouling his clean bed.

'Let me haud the horn a while.'

'Whist wi' your whining. There is someone in the garden,' Colin hissed.

Dod kept his flattened face still against the stone. He did not dare to move. His whimpering was stoppered by his beating heart, that drummed a heavy rhythm in his heaving chest, till he could barely breathe.

A small crack of light had opened in the wall, the unveiling of a door, with a lantern set behind it. Through its sly glancing, a figure appeared. Colin Snell sighed. 'Ach, tis the nightman.'

'What is the night man?' Dod felt his faint heart might burst.

'Lord, ye are green, Doad!' Colin said, scornfully. 'The gong-scourer, draucht-raker, what ye may call him. He that wis wanted to cleng out the sink.'

Dod answered, 'Oh,' filled with confusion, wonder and doubt. He watched the slight figure cross over the grass, moving towards the latrines. In the light of the pale sickle moon he could make out the shapes of a shovel and pail that swung from the gong-scourer's back. The scourer's nose and mouth were covered with a cloth. Dod considered for a moment what it what it might be like to be scouring stinking cesspits rather than men's souls. Fired by curiosity, he made bold to speak. 'He's slender for a raker, though. Perhaps it is a lass.'

Now Colin Snell would read his mind, he realised with a blush, and ken what matter lurked in it. The thought of a lass was a torment to Doad. What he might say to one, what he might do to one, what one might say or do back to him. 'A lad, I meant to say. Perhaps it is a lad,' he corrected quickly. 'The draucht-raker's boy.'

''Tis very like, his boy.'

'Then where is his cart?' Dod now dared to hope that he had got away with it. That Colin had not caught the whiff, the stench, of his sick soul.

'In the vennel, as I doubt,' Colin answered with a yawn. 'We may as well call aff the watch. For no one will come forward wi' the rakers here. We will leave it, for the night.'

Dod paid little heed, for he was watching as the figure, slender as a girl, opened up the channel under the latrines, and disappeared inside. The channel was an underbelly unexplored by Dod, deep as hell itself, belonging to a world in which he had no part. Dod held his breath until the raker's boy emerged, dragging up his bucket, and pulling loose his scarf, to take in a draught of the cool night air. How many buckets were required, for one slight lad to finish with his Herculean task? The raker's boy dragged up his load, staggered at the weight of it, and made his way cautiously across the college square.

'Wha the devil is he going wi' it?'

Colin shifted restlessly, suffering from cramp. 'Let the limmar be now, Doad. Ye are fair fu' fixed on it. Tis nothing but a laddie, wi' a bucketful of shit.'

'But where is he awa' with it?'

The draucht-raker had crossed the square, coming past the hawthorn tree, to rest by Melville's house. He set the bucket on the ground, and stepped back, looking up. The master was asleep, the doors and shutters closed.

'What is the devil up to, there?'

The answer to their question was played out before their eyes, for the raker scooped his bare hands in the bucketful of muck and began to smear it on the master's house, cawking doors and windows with a layer of filth.

Colin whistled softly. 'Wid ye look at that? Filthsum little shite.'

'Now, then,' Dod suggested, 'will I blaw the horn?' For he was eager, still, to have it in his hand.

'And scare the beggar off? Not on your life. Let you and I upend the beast, and rub his filthy nose in it.' Before Dod could respond to this, his friend had broken cover from the chapel ruin, and hurled himself, full force, in the direction of the draucht-raker. The boy dropped his bucket and turned tail in flight, but Colin was upon him like a falcon on a sparrow, and swept him from his feet. Dod, arriving breathlessly, caught sight of the raker's scared and startled face, torn out from its scarf, before that face was splattered by the force of Colin's fist. The raker had no time to howl, for Colin tipped the bucket out and over his bare head, now thick with filth and blood. Dod became enflamed with a tremulous disgust, and swelling in his veins he felt the zeal of Christ, a righteous indignation, fierce and staunch and strong. His rising spirit fed upon the stench of iron and earth, the yielding of the boy's soft flesh to Colin's boots and fist. Horror turned to rage, and terror to excitement. 'Why not swak the filthsum devil back into the sink?'

Colin dropped the raker's boy, and turned to stare at him, and for a second, Dod supposed the remedy too brutal, even for his friend, with his stout heart, to stomach, and he felt a spurt of pride. Then Colin smiled, admiringly. 'Wha would have thought it, Doad! You're not the sop I took you for. That is a fine idea.' He pulled the raker up, and grasped him at the mouth, already caked and choked. The boy let out a howl, spitting like a cat. Dod saw his white eyeballs, frantic in the moonlight, darting back and forth. One eyelid thick and bloodied had begun to close.

'What say you, sir? Since you are so fond of filth, what say you go to swim in it? Tak his legs,' said Colin Snell. Dod felt the thin limbs kicking, thrashing in his hands, the raker's boy no match for him. A dizzy rush of blood came flooding to his head. 'See how you like it, you shite!'

The two men held the raker, writhing like a fish, and Colin tied the dung clout tight around his mouth. 'Now son, haud yer whist till we are at the sink, then ye may howl yer heart out. Not a soul will hear you.'

'What in the name of Jesus Christ are you men doing there?' A voice broke through the gloom, to strike Dod still with terror, deep down to his soul. It was followed by a light, and a fearful apparition, far more dreadful than a ghost or the devil in the night, that would turn Doad's wam to water, and his blood to stone. He dropped the raker's boy, and fell down to his knees. He dared not lift his eyes to Andrew Melville's face. From the corner where he grovelled, like a serpent in the mud, he glimpsed the master standing, in his pantons and his nightshirt with a lantern in his hand. It was Colin Snell who spoke.

'We found this *trucour* smearing ordure on your house. And Doad here thocht it fitting we should dook him in the jakes.'

Dod turned his head and vomited, thick, into the earth. The raker's boy had fallen, senseless to the ground. Melville bent over him, loosening the cloth that had covered his face. 'Are you quite mad? You would murder the man, with the fumes from the jakes?'

'Not murther him, sir. But to show him the light.' Reason, sense and shame came flooding back to Dod. His cheeks ran wet with tears.

'God help us all, but this is a child.' Melville cleaned the debris from the raker's face with the hem of his own shirt. The raker moaned and stirred.

'I recognise him now,' Colin Snell declared. 'For I ken his older brother, as an honest decent man, who comes oftentimes to lectures here, to you and Master James. They are students at St Leonard's. This is Roger Cunningham. I did not see him clearly, under a' the muck.'

'Students of St Leonard's?' Melville echoed wearily. 'Can you make this worse?' He cradled the boy's face. 'Is this true, my child? No one here will hurt you, if you speak the truth.'

Roger answered weakly, dazed by Colin's blows. 'What they say is true, sir. And I am right sorry that I put muck on your house.'

Andrew Melville groaned. He wiped the boy's face tenderly. 'Then God love you, child. But why would you do that? Did someone put you up to it? Or have I done some hurt to you, that you bear such a grudge?'

The boy's eyes fluttered closed. 'I pray you will not mind it. It was a defiance, sir. It was not meant for you.'

At Kenly Green, the baxter brought a letter with the morning loaf. The servant propped it up against a jug of cream. Hew opened it and read it as he drank his morning ale. He broke the loaf, and buttered it, and read the note again; he set his empty cup on it, and scattered it with crumbs. The letter bore St Mary's seal, was written on white paper, in a crisp dark ink, and made no sense to Hew. Andrew Melville wrote, 'Your purpose is discovered, and your trap is sprung, the coney that was caught in it delivered to St Leonard's. You may have him there.'

Since Nicholas was still asleep, he tried it on the cook. 'A curt enough note for a man of the kirk. It is not like Andrew Melville to have masked himself in mysteries.'

'If there is a rabbit, I will make a pie,' the cook suggested doubtfully.

'I will let you know,' Hew promised with a smile, 'when to make
the coffin, for we may not want one yet.'

Hew saddled up Dun Scottis, fuelled by the intrigue, and set
off for the town. He stopped off at the mill, by the Kenly burn, to
allow the horse to drink. The miller's youngest son lay face down
on the bank trailing through the water with a net, for sticklebacks.

'Good morrow to you, John,' said Hew.

The small boy leapt up guiltily. 'I wasna trouting, sir, nor tickling
up the hecklebacks.'

'Are there hecklebacks?' Hew wondered, peering at the stream.

The child considered this. 'They come up fae the sea,' he allowed
at last. 'Look sharp, and you will see them. They have spinkes upon
their backs instead of scales.'

''Tis they that look sharp then,' Hew pointed out. He followed
where John gazed into the white-flecked water, and saw the dart and
flicker of a silver fish. The boy's bare legs were streaked with weed,
as though he had recently slipped from the bank, a clinging, sinewed
thread of muddy green. His face was wan and wary, and his small
fists tightly closed.

Hew assured him, 'I do not mind it if you want to fish for trout,
but you must take good care to throw the small fry back, else stocks
will be depleted for next year.' He had given up the mill as a gift
to Matthew Locke, but kept a careful interest in it, on the child's
behalf; this stretch of water too, and all the trout that lived in it, now
belonged to him.

'I mind you, and I ken that, but I wasna fishing trout,' the boy
insisted. His breeks were sopping wet, and told a different tale. His
mother, Hew supposed, would put him right on that.

'What were you doing, then?'

John Kintor opened up his palm, 'Finding stones for shot.'

'Ah, is that a fact?' Hew's interest was aroused.

'The best are in the burn; the water makes them smooth.' The boy showed up the stones. And they were not unlike the pebbles Hew had found beneath the hawthorn tree. 'What will you shoot with them?' he asked.

'Craws that peck the seed, and rooks upon the wing,' the boy admitted, warily. 'I dinna kill the dows.'

'Then you must be a clever shot, to catch a rook in flight.'

'My brother is a better one. But I am not so bad. Last night, I killed a rat that crept into the mill. My brother put its carcase out upon a stick, as warning to the other rats. Would you like to see it?'

'Another time,' said Hew. 'But may I see your sling?'

'Tis nothing but a common one. I made it for myself. But I can show you how to work it, if you will.' The boy pulled up his shirt, and unhooked a plait of hemp, which to all appearances was holding up his breeks, with a toggle knot and loop to secure it at the ends.

'Ye can mak it out o' wool, which is softer on your hands, but it will not last so long, but ye maunna use a rope, for that will stretch. In the middle is a pocket, where you put the stone. Then you fold the cord like this, an' your finger in the loop, and then you let it go.' John brought up his arm, spinning up the sling, and in one sudden rapid movement he released the stone, which followed through the air in a graceful arc, landing in a tree. 'Now you have a try.'

Hew took up the sling, and attempted several shots, but for all his play at tennis and his practice at the butts he could not get the hang of it. He succeeded, at the last, in launching up the stone, but mastered no control of where it came to ground.

John Kintor pulled a face. 'The trick is in the aim. That wis no' so bad, for a full grown man, for it is better suited as a weapon for a boy, and if ye did not learn it then, ye may never learn to have the simple knack of it. No man that was strong and powerful ever had a shepherd's sling, nor any cause to use one. Keep it, if you like. For I can mak another,' he conceded generously. 'They are not hard to craft.'

'That is very kind of you. You may have been a help to me, on business of the Crown,' Hew said with a wink.

The boy's eyes opened wide. 'Am I then your man?'

'You are indeed,' said Hew. 'And you shall have a penny, for your service to the king.'

John Kintor shook his head. 'You may have it freely, sir, for that you were kind to me, in giving me a pig. That pig has had some babbies, sir. And I have no idea how that could come about.'

'I think, before she came to you, she lay down with the boar.' Hew smiled.

'Aye, so my brother says. But I have seen the bullocks swyfing in the fields. And whitever they were doing there, it was not lying down.'

The boy ran off, bare-legged, pulling up his breeks, while Hew rolled up the sling and tucked it in a pocket. He looked forward to more practice with it at St Mary's college.

Chapter 13

Old Haunts

Andrew Melville was angry. It was not the white hot fury which was fired up quickly, and as quickly quenched, but a wrathful smouldering, deeper and more damaging, that threatened to ignite at any time. Prayer did not cool it. He was angry first with Hew, who had brought about the watch, and who, if he intended to expose the college weaknesses, had done so in the cruellest manner possible. He was angry also with his two disciples, Auchinleck and Snell, whose pell-mell ministrations on his own behalf had shaken and appalled him. Dod repented bitterly, and he had abased himself, unmanly and unmannerly, that offered little hope and provoked as little pity for him, calling for contempt. No word that Andrew spoke could lessen Dod's guilt, nor press on him more forcefully the full stent of his shame, and so he had said none, but left Dod to his torment, grovelling before God. Colin Snell, more practically, he sent off with a bristle brush, to scrub out the latrines. Still, and for the most part, Andrew Melville's anger was directed at himself. He knew, without God's hinting at it, that the fault was his.

He had carried the boy back to St Leonard's himself, hammered on the door, insisting that the principal be roused. Roger had drifted in and out of consciousness, sorely drubbed and dazed, but had recovered well enough to respond to questioning. To Andrew's great relief, he was not maimed or killed, and none of the effluvium had flowed into his mouth. Andrew had expected there would be recriminations. He knew they were deserved. For there was little friendship to be found betwixt the colleges. When St Leonard's had been mentioned, Andrew's heart had sunk. The St Leonard's principal had been steadily opposed to the reforming of his syllabus, to teaching Aristotle in the ancient Greek, and had come round only recently, reluctantly, and cautiously. If it was not the syllabus, then it was the doves. Bitter words were spoken, bitter insults thrown, over several months. Now there was a truce, of sorts, though it was not an easy one. St Mary's men had almost killed a young St Leonard's lad, and Melville had expected fully to account for that; their conduct had been shameful, he could not defend it. Since they were his disciples, their fault must be his. To his great astonishment, the St Leonard's principal had come down on his side. Roger had disgraced his college, and must be expelled. Melville had capitulated, pleading Roger's case. What was a little muck, between two fellow colleges? Roger had explained that he had done it as a challenge – a *defiance*, he had said, which was something like a dare – and Melville could discern no malice in the boy. He had played no part in the attack upon the hawthorn tree, for he had been in class, safely at St Leonard's, when the bladders burst. In which case, Andrew argued, he was undeserving of so harsh a punishment that would blight his progress through his later life. In further mitigation, the boy had lost his father. Andrew had been orphaned at an early age. And he himself had met with such a warmth and kindness he would not see a bright bairn broken in the bud.

The St Leonard's principal had Roger put to bed, and promised to look into it. But in the morning, he sent word to Andrew Melville that the boy must be expelled, without plea or remedy, that he was a menace and a viper in their midst. Andrew had returned to him, raging at him then. He had spoken bitter words that he now was sorry for, accused him of conspiracy, of covering his tracks. And the St Leonard's principal had kept his head throughout. He answered, cool and calm, that there were certain matters he would not disclose. And he would say no more, but for one scrap of information that knocked Andrew back, ending all his clamour at the college door. Melville had the message sent to Hew at Kenly Green.

He was confident that Hew would understand its meaning, and was further troubled to be called up from his prayers. He felt that he had earned a quiet hour with God.

'I wonder at you, sir, that you should show your face. Your place is at St Leonard's. There is nothing for you here.'

'I do not understand.' Hew had gleaned a little from the porter at the gate. A first year student from St Leonard's had broken in to the college, and attempted an assault on Master Andro's house. Two stalwarts of the kirk had caught him at his game, and brought him to a justice many had approved, though the guid Master Andro had not. He was fair as sour and stomachat as when he had the flux, though it was the stalwarts that were in the shit house.

'Was it vengeance for your sister? I should tell you, I have questioned Dod Auchinleck, and he has sworn it was not him she spoke with at your father's grave. You have exposed his faults, and made plain his frailty. He is brought low to his bed, and is a broken man. I knew that you had wit, sir. I did not think that you were cruel. And to use the boy! The poor fools might have killed him, Hew!'

'Honour me, and say, sir, what part I had to play in this?' Hew responded, baffled.

'That student did not work alone. Someone set him on.'

'And you think that *I* did that? Why would you think that?'

Andrew Melville sighed. 'Must I spell it out? For he is Roger Cunningham, the son of Richard Cunningham, your master at the bar. And, as I am told, he is in your charge.'

It had taken Hew some while to impress on Andrew Melville that he had no part in this. And when he had convinced him, he had not convinced himself; he was guilty of a kind of art and part, a fatal dereliction, if of nothing more. It was now two years since he had been a lodger at the house of Richard Cunningham, under his instruction at the bar. Richard had inducted Hew into the justice court, and given him what he required to practise as an advocate, a twist in fate that ultimately cost the man his life. No court in earth

140

or heaven blamed Hew for his death, but deep in his own conscience, he accused himself. He had not practised since.

Hew had taken on the care of Richard's children, James and Roger Cunningham, and their sister, Grace. But he had not seen them in a while. Roger, he remembered as a dark and subtle boy, clever and resourceful, who liked to play at chess. Grace was sweet and bairnlie; no doubt that had changed. James had been already entered at St Leonard's, and they had not met. Hew paid their board and scolage, settled their accounts, but left his interest there. He knew that he was guilty of a grave neglect.

The provost of St Leonard's plainly thought so too, for he regarded Hew with a cold and careful scrutiny, and would not hear his plea. Hew knew him as a quiet, conscientious man, who spoke thoughtful, gentle sermons at the college chapel, Hew's own parish kirk. Compared with Andrew Melville, he was mild as milk, which made his lack of mercy all the more extreme. 'That boy has no conscience. He must be removed.' What monster, wondered Hew, could he expect to find? And if there was a fault, a damage or a flaw, what part of it was his? He dredged up a memory, hollow in his mind, of a young boy brooding, darkly, on a stair.

Roger was kept under guard, in his college room. But Hew did not turn off towards the students' lodging house that looked out on the gardens on the south side of the court. The college of St Leonard's, its chapel, hall and schools, were as familiar to him as the beat of his own heart. He knew each pane of glass and stone, each broken slate and branch of tree, where Roger had climbed out, the fields and woods beyond. St Leonard's was another world and one which was a home to Hew, for he had grown up to a man behind its gentle walls. The college was set back, secluded from the street, and entered through a passageway between the building where the masters lived – known as the stone trance – and the quiet church. To the stone trance Hew turned now, returning to the rooms of the regent Robert Black, where he had spent a term, and taught in place of Nicholas. Robert Black, he knew, would tell to him the truth, and everything he kent of James and Roger Cunningham would soon be known to Hew. Old habits failed to die; Robert would hold out on him, but not for very long.

Robert Black did not seem pleased. He was sitting by the window at his writing desk, the window and the desk that overlooked the square, and though three years had passed since Hew had been there last, little there had changed. They fell back to the places they had left unfilled, as though a door had closed, and opened up again, and stripped the air of quietness, infused it with regret.

Black excused himself. 'I was going out.'

'You do not look,' objected Hew, 'to be going out.'

Robert closed his book. 'I have to read the lecture.'

'Not for half an hour.' The lecture hours, of course, were printed on Hew's mind, pressed upon his conscience, both as man and boy. The inkpot was still full, and the ink was fresh. A new pen had been sharpened to a point. Hew blew a puff of powder clean across the page. 'This looks like a beginning, rather than an end. Are you making verses?'

'It is private, Hew. Not that I expect you to respect the word.'

Hew said, 'I am hurt. Is this how you acknowledge an old friend?' Robert was a goldsmith's son, cynical and unambitious, warily resigned. He was good at heart, but liked a quiet life. A quiet life was not in prospect while Hew was around.

'I will take a drink with you, or sup with you, and argue on philosophy. I will hire a horse, and ride to Kenly Green if you will quit the college, now, and leave me here at peace.'

'You are, of course, most welcome there,' Hew smiled. 'But why are you so careful I should quit the college? Have you had fore-warning not to speak with me?'

'What warning would I need?' Robert rounded bitterly. 'Your coming is a marker of a rare kind of revenge, that will bring a trail of devils shrieking through our doors. It makes my poor heart quake, to see you at the college; you are never here, but there is trouble in your wake.'

There had been no trouble since the fall of the old principal, no sodomy or scaffery, and no suspicious deaths. The petty squalls and squabbles that took place between the colleges had melded to a commonplace, too trifling to report.

'Perhaps it is the trouble brings me. Have you thought of that?'

'*You* are the trouble, Hew.'

Hew walked back to the window, and looked down upon the square. St Leonard's was the college, still, to which he felt the most attached. And he felt no great will to feel into its pond, and prise apart the limpets clinging to its rocks. He answered with a sigh. 'Tell me what you ken of James and Roger Cunningham, and I will leave you peaceful here, and never come again.'

'That is quickly accomplished. Nothing at all. They are not in my class.'

'Then you had not heard, for instance, that they have been expelled?'

'Roger has,' corrected Robert. It did not take him long to realise his mistake. 'I will tell you what I heard, if I can have your word on it, that you will go away.' He accepted the defeat. 'And it will be quite clear to you than none of this must reach the ears of Andrew Melville, if you have any conscience, Hew, or feeling for the boy.'

Hew settled on the bed, where he once had slept.

'This is hearsay, Hew, which you will understand,' Robert Black began, 'and I cannot – dare not – answer to the truth of it. But Roger was expelled because he is involved in strange unnatural practices, and not, you may be sure, because he chose to skitter Andrew Melville's door. There are several in the college here would tip their caps to that.'

'What practices?' asked Hew.

'I will come to that. But first I will relate some facts of his history – a history with which ye might be well acquainted, had you spent more time at home among the colleges and less time in the lowlands, chasing after windmills. Roger is a quent, unkindly kind of boy. When he began last year, we lodged him with a friend, a sickly,

143

sallow lad, who fell in a decline and had to be sent home. The two lads had been close, and had had some falling out. The other students claimed that Roger put a curse on him.'

'Such slandering is vile, and a pernicious force. The master is at fault, that did not put a stop to it,' Hew said with a scowl.

'I do not dispute that,' Robert sighed. 'And, in truth, we tried. But you yourself well know how hard it is to quell a rumour that has taken root. The provost and the regents tried to help his cause, but the students in the college still refuse to sit with him. He sleeps and eats alone, and has no companion but his brother James.'

'Dear God,' muttered Hew. 'And for this the boy is blamed, when he should be pitied.'

'He does not want your pity, Hew. The pity is, he does not help himself. He might be more gentle, passive, quiet, meek. But he is not those things. It pleases him to startle and to terrorise his colleagues. He plays up to the part that they have writ for him, and seems to like the power it gives him over them. His assault on Andrew Melville was a part of that same ordinance, by which he seeks the notice and suspicion of his friends. Tis hard to understand.'

'Nothing you have said disposes me to think that he is justly used, or treated with the pity that his case deserves.'

'You do not know him, Hew.'

'But I have known him once. And nor, in truth, do you.'

Robert hesitated. 'You must be aware that he is not the child that once you thought you knew. There is an air about him, which discomfits and disquiets. His interests are significant, singular, and solitary. When they brought him here last night, he was taken to his room, where bare upon the board he had left out his materials, the substance of his craft.'

'What craft is that?' asked Hew. But in his heart, he knew; the boy that he once knew had shown an interest in anatomy.

'The matter was the body of a cat, with the eyes and entrails drawn, and the body nicely carved. From the matter, ye may seek to know his craft.'

'He has an interest,' Hew defended, 'in the natural world.'

'Is that correct?' Robert smiled. 'I do confess, I know no world where such an interest is considered *natural*. You, I am aware, are wont to move at will in darker worlds than mine. Yet I think that even you are like to understand why our provost has expelled him, and why he will not let the cause be telt to Andrew Melville; for the sake of both the college and the boy himself, he would not have him taken for a witch.'

'God help him, then,' said Hew. 'The boy is an anatomist; a cunning one at that. But he is not a witch. But tell me one thing more. You were at St Mary's at the wedding lecture, and you saw the bleeding tree. Do you think that Roger was responsible for that?'

'He may have been responsible,' Robert Black considered, 'if he is a witch.'

'Put that from your mind,' insisted Hew, 'for the bleeding hawthorn was not done by witchcraft. It was a bladder filled with blood, and just the sort of trick that might have been imagined by a boy like Roger, who likes to cut up animals and make his friends afraid of him.' He felt in his pocket for the shepherd's sling, remembering what the boy had said, *It is not a weapon for a proper man.*

'Then I do not see how. For he was kept here at the college, at the master's side.'

'And his brother James?'

'James was at the lecture, with the other tertians. He was in the hall. I cannot see a way in which he could be implicat.'

Nor, for the moment, could Hew. But he was not prepared yet to discount the possibility. 'What sort of man is he?'

'As unlike his brother as you could conceive. By all accounts, he is a model student, thoughtful, proper and devout, and well liked by his friends. I hear but small report of him, and all of that is good. He is greatly troubled by this business with his brother, and has tried to plead for him . . . He is grieving sorely at it, for his mother's sake.'

'I must thank you, Robert,' Hew acknowledged, thoughtful. 'Now I am prepared.'

'Then I will wish you luck with it. I know you will not take it very much amiss, when I say I hope you will not call again.'

Hew left Robert to his books and crossed the quiet square. He took a moment then, to look back at the stone trance and the little church, where on countless Sundays he had said his prayers, and on to the refectory, the common hall and schools. He did not for a moment think their kindness could be closed to him, that there would come a time, when he could not return.

Chapter 14

An Uncommon Kindness

The room had been stripped of its contents, apart from a low trundle bed. On the bed was a grey woollen blanket, a slim book of psalms, in the Latin, and a bare-footed boy, in breeches and shirt, who sat at the top of it, clutching his knees. A boy of fourteen, small for his age. His left cheek was swollen, blue as a plum, and his dark hair was puddled with filth. There was blood on his collar, and filth on his face, but Hew noticed no trace of tears.

'Do you know who I am?'

'*Magister.*'

As though all masters were the same. Roger did not seem to notice, or perhaps to care about, his own predicament. Perhaps he had been damaged by a blunt blow to the head. He would not be the first.

'I am Hew Cullan, lawman at St Salvator's. You may speak in Scots.'

'Do I want a lawyer, then?'

'Sincerely, I hope not. But we have met before, when you were a boy, at your father's house.'

'I do not recall.'

Was it possible, thought Hew, that those momentous weeks, that led to Richard's death, were wiped from Roger's mind? 'I stayed for several weeks.'

'I do not recall that, sir.'

'I knew your father well.'

'I do not remember him.'

147

In the court outside, a bell began to ring. They heard hurried footsteps, several doors were closed, a flurried snatch of laughter drifted from the quad. Something in its echo seemed to wake the boy. 'I must go now, sir. Or I will be late for the lecture.'

'Did they not tell you? You are expelled.'

The boy stared at his hands. 'They did. I had forgotten it.'

'Do you know why?'

'For that I put some muck on Andro Melville's door, defouling his clean house.'

'And why did you do that?'

'To make them like me here. They do not like me much.'

'There is a bangstrie in the college,' Hew reflected, 'that is no better now than when I was a student. I stayed here, in a room like this. I had forgotten how sparing, how Spartan it was.'

'There were more comforts, once. They took away my things. I do not know if they will give them back.'

'Then we will have to look into that. I shared with a friend. But you seem to lie here alone.'

'There was someone else, once,' Roger admitted. 'He fell sick of a pest, and they sent him home. I did not miss him much. I do not remember his name.'

'Why did you throw muck at Andrew Melville's house? Did someone set you on to it? Or was it your idea?'

'I thought of it myself.' Hew believed him then. For Roger's quiet answer had a note of pride in it; he was Richard's son.

'I climb out at night. There is a tree by the wall. Everyone kens.'

Hew nodded. The exit from the college was an open secret, in evidence when he was a boy. New masters came and went, and none had put a stop to it. He had climbed out there himself.

'I spend a lot of time, in the fields and by the shore. I found the garden door, at the college of St Mary's. It is left unlocked at night, for the coming of the night man, to dig out the latrines.'

'You do not shy from muck,' Hew concluded, grimly. 'That will serve you well, if you have to end your days as a gong-fermer's servant.'

Roger was unmoved by this. 'Muck is like flesh; it is what we are made of. It is a natural thing. I saw the port was open, and that gave me the idea.'

'I do not think you understand the damage you have caused.'

'To Master Melville's house?'

'Not there. If that was your intention it was sadly flawed. Do you think he cares a whistle for one spot of your manure? That you can dint a heart like his, with a stinking clod of shit? He is a braver man than you, and a better one at that.' Hew wanted to provoke the boy into a show of feeling, and he dispensed with gentleness.

'I ken that,' Roger said. 'I meant him no ill will. I am sorry that I smeared the kind face of his house, but it could not be helped.'

'What do you mean by that?'

'Master Andro's house has two sides; the proud side, that looks out onto the street, and the kind side, that looks in.

'And I am sorry that I had to put the muck upon the kind side, but there was no jeopardy in coming from the street. I did not want the collegers to see how it was done. I told them muck would come on Andro Melville's house. I wanted them to think that I could make it happen. They were all of them afeared, of the bleeding hawthorn tree.'

'Did you make that happen, too?' Hew was sure he had.

Roger stared down at his hands. 'How could I do that? I was not there.'

'Then you were not afeared, to pass the bleeding tree, alone, and in the dark?'

'I was not afeared. I do not believe their tales of magic spells. My interest is in physick and in natural philosophy.'

Hew retorted, dryly, 'So much have I heard.' He undid the pocket that was hanging from his belt, uncurled the shepherd's sling and placed it on the bed. If he had expected Roger to react to it, some flicker of alarm to show in the boy's face, then he was disappointed. The boy regarded it with little curiosity. 'What is that for?'

149

'It is a shepherd's sling. I had it from the miller's son, whose mill is on my land. I think it was used in the trick with the hawthorn,' Hew explained.

'What kind of trick was that?'

'Someone tied a bladder to the branches, filled with blood, and burst it with a stone.'

A smile crossed Roger's face. 'How did you find out?'

'With the help of Doctor Locke, it was not hard to discern.'

'That was clever, then.'

It was not clear whether Roger was admiring Hew's powers of deduction or the trick itself, but Hew felt certain he knew more than he was willing to admit. Before he could examine further, they were interrupted by a light knock on the door, and an older boy appeared, of seventeen or so, carrying a jacket and a pair of shoes. 'They said your coat was spoiled. I brought you one of mine. I beg your pardon, sir,' he said to Hew in Latin, 'but they told me you were here. You cannot know how glad I am to see you. I have pleaded for his place here, but to no avail. Is there any way that you can help him?'

Roger introduced him. 'This is my brother James. He is vexed with me for annoying Master Andro. He hoped that he might go into the kirk, and thinks that Master Andro will not take him now.'

'Hush your foolish tongue,' hissed James. 'Put on the coat and shoes.'

'I do not want your cast-offs,' Roger said.

'You should have thought of that before you dabbled in the shit – I am so sorry, sir, but he has no conception of the trouble he is in – you must put on the clothes, and go with Master Hew.'

'Why would I go with him?'

The brother shook his head, helplessly and hopelessly. 'Can you excuse him, sir? I scarcely dare to ask it, when you have done so much for us, but for our mother's sake . . .'

'What has he done for us?' interrupted Roger, who clearly knew his Latin just as well as James.

'Why, paid our fees and such.'

'But I did not know that! Why did you not tell me?'

For some reason, noted Hew, Roger seemed roused up by this, or interested, at least. He thought that *agitated* was perhaps too strong a word.

'For I supposed you knew ... Roger, what is that?' The boy had picked up the string, which Hew had left on his bed, and ran it through his hands.

'It is a shepherd's sling. Master Hew thinks it was used in the bleeding of the hawthorn tree.'

Hew thought he detected the flicker of a smile.

'Please tell me,' James begged softly, 'you have not confessed to that!'

Roger shook his head. Hew answered in his place. 'Is there any reason why he should?'

'It would be like him, after all. He thinks it is a game.'

'I understand you, perfectly,' said Roger from the bed.

His brother hesitated. 'And it please you, sir, may we talk outside?'

'This is all my fault,' James confided, once the door was closed.

'Tell me,' Hew suggested. He saw a straight young man, with an earnest, open face, worry for his brother clear etched in his frown. Where Roger was slender and small, and dark, as his father had been, James was broad-shouldered, fair like his mother, and half a head taller than Hew.

'I have not been the brother he deserves ...'

The story tumbled out as James revealed his qualms, reverting into Scots. 'In his first term he had a bedfellow who contracted a wasting sickness, and had to quit the college. He was a good friend to Roger, and Roger missed him sorely. He is not a bad boy and he badly wants a friend, whatever he will tell you; he is full of braggery. I have not been a friend to him. Some of the scholars here were cruel enough to say that Roger put a spell on him, and so had caused his sickness – as to the truth of that you may consult Professor Locke, for he looked to that boy, and he will tell you plainly that it was not so. That boy was sick and frail before he ever came here.'

'I did not for a moment,' Hew assured him, 'think it so.'

'I should have stepped in then, and put a stop to it. The truth is, I did not. I thought him weak and strange, and I felt quite ashamed, to have such a brother, that was queer and quent, and I was feared his queerness would reflect on me. And so I let him be, and woefully neglected him, ignoring those who taunted him. Do you understand me, sir?'

Hew believed he did. The brother's raft of guilt was mirrored in his own.

'So he began to play up to their taunts, and answer to their tyranny by making them afeared of him. And I have no doubt, he wanted them to think he was behind the hawthorn tree, and that was why he went to Andrew Melville's house, for he had telt the scholars here that filth came after blood, so that they would think that he had special powers. The silly, wretched bairn! He has no idea what harm he may have done.'

'He did not, I suppose, predict the bloody tree?' Hew felt certain still that Roger had a part in this.

'How could he have done? For he knew nothing of it, nothing in advance of it – I know, sir, that you wanted none of us to speak of it but rumour flew out like wildfire after we returned. Roger heard it then, along with all the rest.'

'You were at the lecture,' Hew observed.

'I was sir, and I saw the hawthorn.' James confessed. 'I did not speak to Roger of it. He needs little fuel to fire his silly games.'

'Then you acted properly. How did you imagine that the trick was done?'

'I did not imagine it. I had no idea. But I saw you take the samples, and I did believe that you would find it out. I know that you are practised, and clever, at these things. I did not for a moment think that it was magic. And as Master Andro tells us, miracles have ceased.'

'Then you are more sensible and rational than your friends.' Hew stood thoughtful for a moment. 'Is it true what Roger says, that you have a mind to go into the Kirk?'

'I have been thinking of it. But I do not suppose that it will happen now.'

'I do not see why not, if that is what you wish. Andrew will not fault you for your brother's sin. He is not the kind of man. And I could speak to him about it, if you wish. But would you not prefer to go into the law?'

'I do not think so, sir. I came, last year, to some of your lectures,' James confided, shyly. 'The *de legibus*, and the Justinian.'

'Then it is no wonder you were turned from law,' Hew smiled at this, 'in favour of the kirk.'

'By no means so. I found them interesting, and inspired with a strong, intellectual and inquiring spirit. But I am not so subtle, sir. Roger is the clever one.'

'Perhaps,' suggested Hew, 'Roger's natural instincts lie elsewhere. Did you know he kept a dead cat in his room?'

James had looked away before Hew could decipher the expression on his face. His voice was low and fearful. 'You must understand, it is not what you may think. He likes to cut things up. But I had no idea that he pursued his interest here. How can I persuade you that he means no harm by it?'

'You do not have to,' Hew assured him, 'for I understand it perfectly. Roger wants good counsel, and a guiding hand. And I can see a future for him, though it is not here.'

'You think that there is hope for him? Then I cannot tell you, sir, how grateful we must be to you.' James knelt down, to Hew's great shame, and kissed the master's hand.

'Ah, do not!' Hew cried. 'Ye maunna thank me, James. I would be a friend to you. I owed your father that. But tell me one thing more. Your brother may have hit his head. Does he always seem so strange?'

'How strange, sir?' asked James. 'He is difficult and curious, as he was before. He is a vexing boy.'

'He told me he does not recall his father. Could that be the case? Was it so before?'

A shadow passed across the scholar's face. His answer, when it came, was guarded and reserved. 'I have no idea. It is not something that we like to talk about. Here, or at home.'

Hew caught a glimpse into the loss that haunted both the boys.

Roger was still sitting, quiet on his bed. 'What did my brother say about me?'

'He said you could not possibly have been behind the hawthorn trick,' Hew reported cheerfully, 'for you are not clever enough.'

Roger said, 'Ha,' declining to rise to this. 'What happens now?'

'Shoes on, and coat on, and quick, if you please. You are my charge, and are coming with me. And I will have *that*,' Hew held out his hand for the sling.

'I think you are wrong about that,' Roger said, giving it up. 'It is the wrong kind of weapon to burst a ball of blood. You should ask your miller's son if he has a pellock bow, a bow for little stones.'

He followed at Hew's back, meek as any child, until they were about to leave the college grounds, where they met the principal coming from the kirk, who would have passed them by, with a curt nod of the head, had not Roger spoken to him, '*Vale*, professor.'

'*Vale*,' the master muttered.

'May I not have your blessing, sir, since I am to leave?'

'What? Ah yes, indeed. God go with you, child.' The provost cleared his throat.

'And may I have my cat?'

The principal forgot himself, and roared at him in Scots. 'Pernicious, monstrous boy! Your *cat*, as ye design it, is buried in the midding-sted, where sic filth belongs.'

'You did not ought to do that, sir.'

'Whist, now,' cautioned Hew. He placed a hand, restraining, onto Roger's shoulder and felt his slight frame stiffen in his brother's coat.

154

'You do well to hark to him,' the principal advised. 'Submit to his correction, with a willing heart. God go with you both. Know that I will pray for you, with little lasting hope.'

'You do not understand, sir,' Roger pleased earnestly, 'I did not kill that cat.'

'Poor benighted loun. Puir hapless, silly child. If you could only see, it would be better if you had.'

Roger grasped Hew's hand, his bluff front all but gone. 'Why does he say that?' His voice, unbroken, childlike, sounded very small.

'Because,' suggested Hew, 'it is not uncommon for a boy to kill a cat, with an arrow or a stone; it is another thing entirely for a boy to cut one up.'

Roger looked bewildered. 'I would not kill a cat. I find things that are dead, and open up the carcases, to find out how they died. I found the cat at the harbour, and it had a stone in its belly. If they had not taken it away, I could have shown it to you. I do not believe that it is possible to be a good physician, without some kenning of anatomy.'

'I know an honest man that will not disagree with you,' Hew answered with a sigh. 'But he is an exception, proof against the rule. You are disadvantaged, in the first, for the fact that you are no physician, but a first year undergraduate, who has been expelled from his studies in philosophy. And in the second, there have been physicians also tried and burned, for practising black arts.'

Roger stared at him, as understanding dawned. 'They take me for a witch!'

'I am afraid they do.'

'Then what is to become of me? Will I go to hell?'

'Not if I can help it, and you do as you are told.'

It was a mark of Giles Locke's kindness, and of his respect for Hew, that he did not dismiss the patient to the brute hands of the surgeon, but sat him straight away upon a little chamber stool, to wash with his own sponge the bruised and bloodied cheeks.

'Dear me. What stuff is this?'

'*Merda*, Professor,' Roger said, in Latin, anxious to impress, though Hew had warned him earnestly that he must hold his tongue.

'Murder?' Giles winked at him, 'Surely, I hope, not.'

'*Quod est* . . . what is . . . *done.*' Roger said, confused.

'Or else, what is dung?'

Roger flushed a little, '*Mihi ignosce, magister.*' Hew noted that the boy possessed a literal turn of mind, that clever as it was, did not respond to puns.

Giles assured him, '*libenter.*'

'A student,' he inferred, in an aside to Hew. 'I seem to know the face, though I do not think he can be one of ours.'

'He is Roger Cunningham, Richard's son,' said Hew.

'Ah.' Giles knew Richard's history, as it pertained to Hew, and let discretion veil the questions in his mind. 'Well then, Roger Cunningham, we have met before. I did not recognise you under your disguise. I came once to your house, though you may not remember it.'

To Hew's surprise, it seemed that Roger did. 'You talked about the ripples, and the bloody flux.'

'Just so,' murmured Giles. 'A pedantic schoolboy, with a whim to study physick. And now you are full grown, and a student at St Leonard's.'

'*Non, Professor, vere . . .*' Roger glanced at Hew.

Giles misunderstood the cause of his confusion. 'And you prefer it, speak Scots. We are not formal in our dealings with the sick. For sorrow is a thing that may be better expedited when expressed in the vernacular. What think you, Master Hew?'

'Beyond a doubt,' Hew smiled. 'Roger has been in the wars. He won his bloody nose from Andrew Melville's bully boys, the stalwarts of our kirk. They are a little over zealous in interpreting the text.'

Giles Locke frowned at this. 'Did Andro set them on? Then I will have a word with him.'

'In some respects,' admitted Hew, 'I set them on myself, with no thought to the consequence. And Roger here has borne the sorry brunt of it. But lest you think him shamefully and over harshly used, I ought perhaps to say he was not blameless in the matter.'

The doctor understood that caution was required, for he asked no further questions as he cleaned the patient's face, but kept the boy engaged in a cheerful line of chatter, to distract from the discomfort that he must have felt. Roger did not flinch, but let his eyes dart slyly round the doctor's room. 'What are all those things in jars?'

'Organs,' answered Giles, 'that were altered with disease, misshapen or malformed. There is a kind of beauty born of their deformity, do you not agree?'

Peculiar to Roger, it appeared he did. Hew had never taken to the pickled parts in pots, though through a close exposure he had grown more used to them. 'What happened to the pupa you were keeping in this box?'

'It hatched out to a moth. Pity was,' the doctor said, 'it flew full force into the candle flame; that brief flight was its last. Which I suppose must prove a lesson to us all.' The lesson, in some way, seemed pointed straight at Hew.

Roger overcame his shyness, and his promise to keep quiet. 'May I ask a question, sir? The word about the college is you keep a human foot here, flayed back to its layers.'

'Not that, again,' groaned Hew.

The doctor pursed his lips. 'Indeed, I kept one once, for purpose anatomical. I do not keep it now.'

'What happened to it, then?'

'It caused a deal of trouble I did not care to repeat.'

'Hear. And be forewarned,' Hew grumbled in the background.

'And it was not preserved as well as I had liked.'

'I should have liked to see it.' Roger sighed.

'You and several dozen of your snot-nosed peers. That was part of the problem,' Giles complained.

'But I am not their peer. They have no proper interest in the sphere of science, but come to gawp and snigger. I am not like them.'

The doctor paused a moment. 'Ah, is that a fact? Wait a second there.' He opened up the closet where he kept things that were precious and selected a large notebook from the row upon the shelf. 'Would you like to look, then, at the drawings I have made?'

Roger was enthralled. He opened up the notebook with a careful sort of reverence, his eyes lit up afresh at every passing page. Hew smiled to himself. The two were kindred spirits. Each had found a friend.

'Your nose and cheek are solid,' Giles concluded, kindly, 'and will heal in time. I have found no fracture, but a mass of bruising, which will soon subside. A little salve of arnica will help it to go down. You may have it, for a premium, at the Mercat Street apothecar, or from my wife for nothing, if you call at my house. No doubt Master Hew will tell to you the way.'

'I thank you for your kindness. But I have another question. Was it from a hanging that you had the foot? Was it cut down from a felon?' Roger pressed.

'*Enough*, now,' threatened Hew.

But Doctor Locke answered the boy. 'Grim, ghoulish creature! Why do you ask?'

'Because, sir, I understand how things are done. When they hanged the earl of Morton, they cut off his head, and stuck it on a spike. That was at the tolbooth, not far from my house.'

Roger's family home, on Edinburgh's Lawnmarket, looked out on the High Gate and its place of execution. God knew what sights and sounds had filtered through its gallery.

'His head was on the post for almost eighteen months. I made some pictures of it, but I do not have them still. I know that in that passing it had changed a lot. There was a time you could not have worked out what it was, before the craws had pecked it cleanly off the bone. The limbs were wrapped in candle, and were sent abroad. I wondered if a foot of his had somehow ended here.'

'We may be thankful, not,' said Giles. 'The foot was from a man who lost it in an accident, and left it with the surgeon, who sold it on to me. There is a nice exactness in enquiring of its provenance; I wonder at it, still.'

Hew broke in at last, 'Your face is clean and sound. Say thank you to the doctor now, and wait for me outside.'

Roger looked confused. 'But sir . . . I thought you said . . . did I do something wrong.'

'*Now.*'

Roger took the hint, and did as he was told. Giles Locke asked perceptively, 'What have you to tell me, Hew?'

'The boy is in some trouble.'

'So I had supposed. And he is Richard's son.'

'He tells me,' Hew went on, 'that he did not know his father, that he has no recollection of his father's death, that he does not recall my coming to his house. How could that be so? He was twelve years of age.'

'Interesting,' said Giles.

'Yet he remembered you. And he described to us the aftermath of Morton's death, that took place at that time. I wondered if perhaps he had suffered a concussion.'

Giles considered this. 'I saw no signs of one. And yet it could be true; the dreadful understanding that took Richard from him may have become detached and buried in his mind, or somehow was eclipsed by Morton's execution; which memory has served to take the other's place.'

'But to forget a father, surely, were not natural.'

'Who, in truth, can say? There is no balm or physick for the soul's disturbances, and no clear understanding of the way it works. And what is strange to us, may not be so in him. Who, indeed, can say, what is or is not natural? Nature is uncouth, and nature is unkind, and nature holds more contradictions than are sometimes shown to us. The end of our poor science is to find those secrets out. And Roger is a riddle we may yet unfold.'

'I hoped you might say that.' Hew spilled out his tale.

'Now let me set this straight,' Giles posed at the end of it. 'You want me to admit and welcome to St Salvator's a boy who is expelled, a boy who spends his leisure hours anatomising cats, and wipes the devil's arse with Andrew Melville's door?'

'That,' conceded Hew, 'is about the sum of it. So, what do you say?'

The doctor beamed at him. 'My dear friend, need you ask?'

Chapter 15

Clare

Clare Buchanan's brother George lay stretched out on his college bed, pleased with his new friend. Roger stood awkward, polite. Since the one small stool was piled with George's books, and George took up the bed, there was nowhere left to sit. He waited, with an air of deference that appealed to George, who was unaccustomed to it. 'You can move the papers, if you like.'

'Thank you.' Roger Cunningham acknowledged the concession, but did not act upon it, so that George felt obliged to rise up from the bed and move the books himself, setting down his papers in a neat pile on the floor. 'You can sit down if you like.'

'Thank you.' Before George understood he had conceded his advantage, Roger took his place on the middle of the bed, leaving him adrift, standing by the stool. George said, 'Oh, that is not what I ...' tailing off at the sight of Roger's swollen face, bloodied black and bruised.

'Were you in a fight?'

Roger shook his head. There was nothing in his manner that might clearly mark a threat, but his quiet reticence rang warning bells with George.

'Then what did you do?'

'Oh, *things.*'

'Oh.'

Doctor Locke had ruled that Roger's previous history must not be discussed, which had done little to damp down the rumour in the college. It was widely known that he was in disgrace. Some said he was a murderer, who had escaped from hanging through a narrow loophole worked by Master Hew. Some said Hew had found him living in the jakes. For now, for safety's sake, George let the matter rest.

Roger said, politely, 'This bed is quite soft.'

George resigned himself to settling on the stool. 'Aye, it is. No doubt they will send in some more furniture for you. Where are all your things?'

'They took them,' Roger said, 'but I do not know where.'

George took one last fond look over his possessions, silently accounting for the blankets, pens and books.

'You can share mine if you like,' he allowed, reluctantly.

'Thank you,' Roger said. 'But I do not like to share.' He stood up from the bed, and walked to the small window that looked back upon the cloisters. 'What is it like here?'

Roger had left a small dip in the counterpane, which George was quick to smooth, securing once again his place upon the bed. In all ways that were possible, he felt on safer ground. 'Here? It's no so bad.' And he told Roger all, of lectures in the hall and college disputations, early morning prayers and afternoons in class, of cabbage kale and sausages and of his trials with Cicero, of Doctor Locke's collections and of Bartie's phlegm, of winter days and summer evenings spent at golf and caich. Roger, all the while, stared out at the grounds. It was not clear that he heard. 'I'm sure that you will like it here,' George concluded, flatly. 'On Wednesdays, we have our sport, and practise at the butts. Did you ken, that at St Mary's they once set up butts and an arrow caught a baxter, clean richt through his hat? The loun was a' but killed.'

Roger showed no interest. 'I have not heard that.'

'It's true. But Doctor Locke says we may not set up butts here in the college, but we maun gang out to the green, for Doctor Locke says, we have had enough trouble with baxters withouten we inflame them, by shooting at their caps.

'I knocked a baxter doon once, a muckle massive man.' To George's disappointment, this had no effect. Whatever Roger's crime, it must be worse than that. That was a troubling thought. 'But since I broke my arm I cannot lift the bow, so Master Hew has learnt me to play caich. Do you play caich?'

This had struck a chord. For some reason, Roger scowled. 'No,' he said abruptly. Then, 'What like is Master Hew?'

George Buchanan shrugged. Instinct told him he should hide how much he owed to Hew, who had saved his place here, and, perhaps, his life. 'Master Hew is kind enough,' he allowed at last. 'When you go wrong, and are called to account for it, he lets you explain it in Scots.'

'That is not kindness,' Roger contradicted. 'It is a lawman's trick, to make you speak your mind. Speak Latin, and you have to take your time, to think and shape the words. You have a moment then, to plot what you will say. They cannot see you thinking out the lie, and since the tongue is not your natural one, your voice will not betray it. You have to think much quicker in the Scots.'

'Oh!' George was impressed. 'I see. That's subtle, though. I had not thought of that.'

'It does not matter much, for you,' Roger said, dismissively. 'For you are but a bairn, and he can see right through you, whatever tongue you speak. You may as well confess at once, and bear the brunt, and be done with it. There's little that will save your skin but bluther, bleat and tears.'

George said, affronted, 'I am no more a bairn than you are.'

'Is that so?' Roger turned to look at him, with shrewd dark searching eyes, deep set and unblinking in his swollen face. 'I am one hundred years old. How old are you?'

'How can that be?' George challenged him, disconcerted nonetheless.

'It cannot be. I made it up, to torment you.'

'Oh.' George did not have an answer to this strange, unblinking boy, who did not intimidate exactly, but unsettled all the same.

163

'Well, be that as it may, Master Hew is good to me. I think it is because he likes my sister, Clare.'

'Does he?' Roger came back from the window to perch on the edge of the stool, his grey eyes clear and thoughtful in his black bruised cheeks. A careful and most proper boy, thought George, uncertain why this calm reserve had ever seemed a threat.

'Then mebbe he will marry her, and he will be your brother? How would you like that?'

George giggled girlishly. 'I should not mind it much. But he never will be that. For my sister is married already, to Robert Wood, the brother of the coroner.'

His new friend smiled. 'Is that a fact?'

As May turned to June, life proceeded peacefully. Roger seemed to settle and to blossom at St Salvator's, under Giles Locke's wing. Andrew Melville's lectures finished for the term, passing without incident; his students had begun their practice in the kirk. Andrew's nephew James still had not returned, but fell into the grip of a debilitating fever, confirming what Dod Auchinleck had frequently suspected, that grave dangers were attendant on the conjugal embrace. Dod himself fulfilled his penance, under Melville's styptic eye, and preached a quaking sermon on the perils of the flesh, before a largely sceptical and unforgiving crowd. There were no further mysteries, to Hew's no great surprise, but late one balmy night the draucht-raker arrived. The sink was cleared at last, and buried in the sediment was found a little bow, which Melville packaged up, and had sent on to Hew. It was smaller than the longbows in the college armoury, but too large to be hidden underneath a coat. Primitive and light, it looked as though it might be carried by a child. Hew showed the bow to Roger, who acknowledged with a smile, 'It is a pellock bow. Country people use them to shoot rooks down from trees. They hunt for them at night, and blind the birds with lights. They shoot the bows with pellets, or else little stones. Where did you find this one?'

'In Andrew Melville's sink.'

'Then it has cleaned up well.'

'Does it belong to you?'

Roger shook his head. 'I had a little longbow, when I was a bairn. Once I shot a crow. But that was by mistake. I am no good at sports.'

His regent had confirmed that Roger's aim was poor. He made little progress shooting at the butts. Yet Hew was quite certain Roger was involved. 'I will find out the truth,' he warned. Roger simply smiled. 'I expect you will. And I would like to hear it when you do.'

Though Hew was well aware the boy was playing games with him, he let the matter rest. He wanted to discover how the trick was done, to satisfy himself, but was generous enough to accept defeat. He saw the boy was happy now, and had not been before, and that must be enough. There was a deeper magic there that coloured his wan face, transformed the lonely boy, as he showed Doctor Locke some piece of shell or bone or insect he had found.

Giles, for his part, was delighted with his pupil, and spoke warmly of his progress. He spent more time in college, and less time at home. At the little house, the building work was slow. Canny had complained about the morals of the workmen, and they had been replaced. The new ones were more civil, and more careful with their feet, but the noise and dust wore on. Hew invited Meg and Matthew back to Kenly Green, but Meg saw patients still, and would not leave the town. John Richan came to call on her, whenever he had leave. And she looked forward to the visits from the wild and lonely boy who sang to Matthew in the Norn, and told stories, far from home. In Giles' absence, Paul went out, to court the widow Bannerman, leaving them in peace. Matthew Locke cut two new teeth, and lived on, unscathed.

At Kenly Green, the physick garden blossomed and died back; broom buds clustered darkly, fruit formed on the trees. The gardeners did their best to gather in the leaves. Nicholas went on with his translation of Buchanan, filling up his hours with the tyranny of kings. The miller's son caught sticklebacks, and fed husks to the sow.

The sergeant of the castle guard kept his soldiers to the watch, and worked John Richan hard. He saw to it the bowman's hurt had little chance to heal. The brethren of the holy kirk accepted Melville's plea, and let the bishop rest awhile, acquitted of his charge. Patrick kept himself aloof, and rarely left his bed. He came out only once, on a visit to his wife, when he passed the Holy Trinity, and did not go inside. Some said that they saw his shadow running with a hare, and thought he was complicit in a dark and secret act. His sickness persevered. The physick wife came with her bottles, several times a week. Hew came across her once, selling herbs and posies at the market cross. He bought from her a bunch of rosemary and rue, yet he could find in Alison no hint that she remembered him. He hung the herbs up on a nail to brighten up his room, and they were green and fresh enough to make the room sweet still, when he received a visitor, whose coming marked a change, as though somehow the physick wife had known him after all, and cast a secret spell on him, that turned his warm heart cold as stone, and all his hopes to dust.

Hew was at the college, reading in his room, when the porter came. 'The woman is here, and is asking for you. She wants to have a word, about her brother George.'

Hew nodded. 'Show her in.'

'In here?' It was a tired formality they went through every time. The porter made a point of marking disapproval, and Hew made a point of continuing regardless. He knew that his objections would not find a voice. What happened in the college stayed within the college; and all talk of indiscretion stopped at Doctor Locke.

'As I say.'

He had time to smooth the cushions and to button up his coat before the man announced, 'Mistress Clare Buchanan.'

Clare.

She had the power to transform him to a blushing boy. It did not help that he saw her only in the college, in that bare boy's chamber he had taken for the purpose, on those rare short stolen moments when he should have been at work. He placed her in the leaf green chair, in the corner by the window where the light fell soft and searching, shadowing her face. The sunlight caught the ripples in the satin of her dress, her white hands settled quietly, gathered in her lap.

'I have come about George.'

Always she said she had come about George. The first time she had come, she had wanted Doctor Locke. She had found Hew in his place, and had thought him sharp and cruel. When she knew him better, she had found out her mistake. She had sought his help, and he had stilled her fears, and kept her brother safe. When Hew returned from Flanders, he had brought her lace. She wore it at her throat. Yet there was a reserve between them. Clare was sad and serious, and kept herself apart. There was a husband, too, between them, Hew did not forget.

'He writes to me,' she said, 'that now that he is well, my visits here are irksome to him, and I should desist, for no one else has sisters here, wailing in their wake.'

'Whatever we have taught him here, it seems it were not manners,' Hew said, with a groan. 'I will speak to him.'

'I do not wish you to. Or not, at least, on that. We both know he is right.' Clare looked at her hands, as if surprised to find them there, folded in her lap. She did not look at Hew. 'I have spoken to his regent, and he tells me George is well, and that he has a new friend. He says he lags behind a little with his Cicero, but that might be expected, following his accident, and soon to be amended with a little effort on my brother's part. He tells me you have helped him to recover his weak arm, by playing him at caich.'

'Giles Locke recommends it,' answered Hew.

'You have given up your time, for which we are most grateful. Since I think it likely I will not come again, can I dare to ask, will you do one last thing? For you have always been so very kind to us.'

167

His voice came hoarsely, then. He wondered if she saw, and if she understood, the flood and rush of feeling forced back and suppressed. 'You know I will,' he said.

'When all is said and done, will you do well by George?'

'You have not known me at all, if you have to ask me that question.'

'It is not what you think, Hew,' she sighed. 'George looks up to you, and you have his trust. I hoped you might be willing to give him some advice, since you are acquainted too with matters of the law.'

'He has that, freely, always, as and when he chooses.'

'But we both know, he will not always choose. Sometimes the right course must be chosen for him. The fact is,' Clare explained, 'our father is thought likely soon to pass away. He is of an advancing age; George was his last and late-born child and one surviving son. He stands then to inherit a considerable estate. Our fear is that the fortune will distract him from his studies, and he will squander it, long before he comes to the good sense of his majority, like our present king. For there is no clearer example of the dangers of a young man given free rein of his purse. My husband, Robert Wood, is most sensible of this, since his brother Andrew has discharged the young king's debts. I love my brother very much, but even I concede he is a foolish, bairn-like boy, and he has not the wit to manage his expenses. My husband is inclined to remind him, he has little to commend him to the scholar he was named for.'

'Aye, very like,' scowled Hew. His scorn for Robert Wood gave way to sympathy for George: the name of *George Buchanan* was a cruel trial to the boy, and one which plagued him daily in his life at college.

'He is too old now for a tutor,' Clare went on. 'Our family has concluded he must have a curator, to manage his affairs until he comes of age.'

Hew nodded. 'That is usual, in this kind of case. Your father's man of law will draw the papers up. What do you want of me?' He saw that she wanted a common man of law, perhaps a friend for George. Then had she ever wanted more?

'It is . . . it seems proper to us that the person to take charge is my husband, Robert Wood. But George will have a say in the choice of his curator. He is not a bairn, though he behaves as one. For some reason, it appears that he does not like my husband. When Robert is put forward, he is likely to refuse him.'

'What does your father think?'

'My father is not well enough to venture his opinion. But I hoped that you might explain to George that it is in his best interests to allow Robert Wood to be his curator. George will accept it, if it comes from you.'

'Did your husband tell you to ask me this?' Hew demanded. 'Did he send you, Clare?'

She did not answer straight. 'It is for the best,' she said.

'Tell him, the answer is no.'

'I thought you were my friend. I know you do not care for Robert, but I thought you cared for George. I did not think you would refuse this,' Clare accused him, 'out of spite.'

'You asked me to do well by George. And so I shall,' he said. 'I will not deliver George, and his father's fortune, into Robert's hands so that he may add them to the other things he owns – his house, his mill, his dogs and lands, his horses and his wife. Are you feared to tell him, Clare? Frightened to go back?'

'You do not understand.'

Clare was on her feet. Tears pricked in her eyes.

'If you are afeared of him, then come with me to Kenly Green, and I will see you safe.'

She was crying now. 'Please, Hew, let it be.'

'Look me in the eye, and tell me from the heart that you are not afraid of him, and I will let you be. Or, if you will, I will advise your brother to take you as his curator – no better and more proper than a loving sister to fulfil that role – if you can convince me that you are not in his thrall. I do not think you can.' He reached out for her hand.

'You do not understand,' Clare repeated softly. 'Robert is my husband, and I am his wife. He is my life. And I am with child.'

He walked her to the gate, of course. He would not for the world have let her go alone. He hid from her as best he could the turmoil in his heart.

The students saw them there, returning from the lecture to the dinner hall. Roger nudged his friend. 'Is that your sister, George?'

With mingled pride and shame, George confessed it was. 'She is not meant to come here.'

'Aye, but she is bonny though. I'm not surprised he likes her.'

Uncertain whether to be flattered or offended, George puffed out his chest. 'She's marrit to a very wealthy man. His brother is—'

'The coroner. You said. Ask what she was doing here.'

'I cannot,' bleated George.

'Of course ye can,' Roger urged. 'She is your sister, not his. Mebbe he is going out. Ask if he will play at caich.'

He pushed George in Hew's path, so that Hew stopped short, and George was forced, against his will, to raise his eyes and cap to him, '*Mihi ignosce, Magister.*'

'*Libenter*, George,' Hew responded absently. He barely saw the boys.

'*Salve, Magister*. Was that my sister?' George persisted.

Hew replied, 'It was. She will not come again – at your own request.' In Latin, he was terser than he was in Scots, and George had found his manner difficult to read. He retreated back to Roger, who whispered, sympathetically, 'They have had a falling out, and he blames it on you. No more caich for George.'

'Shut your mouth,' said George. 'It does not depend on that.'

'Oh aye? Ask him, then!'

George was in a hard place then, for he could not avoid the risk of loss of face. He knew, before he started, that the case was hopeless.

'*Salve, Magister . . .*'

'George. What is it now?'

'Are you going out? Will you take me with you, to the tennis court?'

'Not today.'

'But you will take me with you, when you do?'

Hew could not mistake the plea in George's voice, for even in the Latin, it was clearly audible. He chose his answer carefully. 'I do not think so, George. Your regent tells me you are failing in your Cicero, and laggard at your books. So no more play at tennis for a while.'

George slunk back so woebegone that Roger almost pitied him. 'Did I not tell you so?'

'You shut your mouth,' said George.

'I can help you with your Latin, if you like,' Roger offered kindly. 'For I am awfy guid at it.'

'Oh, are you, then?' George turned upon his friend in a show of such fierce spirit it took Roger by surprise. 'If you are so clever, then how come they found you out? We all ken what ye did. But folk are too decent and polite to point it out. And you were in the shit, all right. If you are as cunning as you think you are, how come that they caught you there?'

'Because he ...' Roger stopped and checked himself, for they were speaking Scots. 'Because, you silly loun, I *wanted* to be caught.'

Chapter 16

Stirring the Pot

Roger took some care with the writing of his letter. The paper he acquired from Hew, who bought the whitest quairs from Italy and France. Though it was expensive, and of the finest quality, Hew had let him help himself to several precious sheets. He gave him too a pot of alum mixed with gum and showed him how to rub the resin on the paper, so to staunch the grain before it met the ink. Roger had explained that he was writing to his mother, to inform her of the progress he had made. 'Tell her,' Hew suggested, 'that Doctor Locke, our principal, is well disposed and pleased with you, and that I am, too.'

'Thank you, sir, I will.'

'You like it here, I think?'

'Doctor Locke has shown me his anatomies and he has let me help him in some of his experiments.'

It was just as Hew had hoped. Giles had encouraged Roger to pursue his interests, and to hone his art and skills, under careful watch. The boy had thrived and blossomed underneath his hand. There were no more nighttime wanderings, no dismembered creatures kept below his bed. Even Roger's colour had improved, to a healthsome, human pink, and he had put on weight, as though he was an acolyte, a miniature of Giles.

'You have done full well, and will make your mother proud. Sign your name like this, in a fair italic script.' Hew showed to him the shape of it, and how to cut the pen. 'And she will see at once you have the makings of a scholar, and a proper man. But soon it will be summer, and the end of term. Will you not go home?'

'At Lammas, sir,' the boy agreed. 'But I want to have the letter come to her before that, so that she will look out for my coming with a glad-some heart, not troubled with the knowledge that I am a trial to her.'

Hew was touched by this. 'Then so much shall she have, and more than that besides, for I myself shall write, with none but good report of you, and so will Doctor Locke.'

'You are kind, Magister. She will be amazed. She is used to hearing ill of me, and all good things and welcome of my brother, James. They say that I am like my father, sir.'

For the first time in Hew's hearing he had mentioned Richard. Hew responded tactfully. 'You are like him in a way, a good way, as I think. There were qualities in him I recognise in you, of subtlety, and wit, of which there is no cause for you to feel ashamed, and if he saw you now, he would well approve of you.'

He could not tell the feeling woken by his words, for Roger looked away. 'May I seal my letter with the college seal?'

The master hesitated. 'Why would you want to do that?'

'Because,' the boy explained, 'when my mother sees the paper, and the college seal, she will think the worst. She will think I am dismissed, as I was from St Leonard's, and will open up the letter in a tremble and in fear, to read that I am grown into a scholar and a man, and all well and approved of, by the college stamp. When she has feared the worst, and finds the best of news, then think you how relieved and contented she will be.'

Hew had laughed aloud. 'What heartless trick is that, from a gentle mother's son! You are a wicked boy. But take it, if you will. My blessing to your mother, and to your sister, Grace.'

He gave the boy use of the seal, by which the college papers often were enclosed, the seal of his approval, sealing his own fate.

Roger wrote his letter on a quiet afternoon, when the rest of the students were about their play. George was at the butts, practising his archery. Left to his own devices, George would rather play at caich, but Giles declared it high time he resumed the bow.

'Are ye sure ye will not come?'

Roger shook his head. 'No. I have a headache.'

'You should go to Mistress Meg. She will give you something for it.'

George Buchanan was a milksop, to Roger's turn of mind, and, since his accident, was often sullen sick. He had stayed for several weeks at the house of Doctor Locke, where the doctor's wife had suffered and indulged him, with a plethora of potions, pessaries and pills. At the smallest slip or snuffle, he was grening to go back there. But he was not, considered Roger, altogether bad. With a little education, he might make a decent friend. All he wanted was direction, and a kick up the backside.

'What I need is rest.'

George left him in peace, to settle to his task. He placed Hew's paper carefully upon the writing slope, and began to write the letter he had carried in his head, embellished and elaborated, over several days.

'Sir . . .'

It was hard to work out how he should begin. Not hard to put what followed, with the bitterness of gall, that flowed from Roger's pen as easily as ink.

'Forgive me for the plainness of my words. I see no other course but to write to you direct, to tell you, you are wronged. If such hurt were done to me, then I would hope to ken of it, and see the limmar shamed and stripped, and face the justice he has courted, routed and scorned.

'I write this not from malice nor from spite, but to save you from that shame, that no man whisper cuckold when your back is turned, or call you for a coward when ye do not ken. Sir, the truth of it is that Master Hew Cullan has mellit with your wife, here at the college where he is professor, and also at the house of his brother Doctor Locke.

'This I have witnessed with my own eyes, coming from the lecture with my Euclid in my hand.'

The Euclid, Roger reasoned, was a clever touch. It hinted that the writer was Professor Bartie Groat, or someone else proficient in the mathematics.

'I saw from a window Mistress Clare Buchanan, standing in our square, supposing that she came to seek her brother George. She comes often there, on the understanding that her brother is not well, and in truth, he is a mauchtless, feeble boy, that would fare the better were he not indulged, and if ye have the governance of him, and would see him strong, ye would do well to relieve him o the care of women, and put him to strait learning how to be a man, and weather him with stripes, or ye will find the miniard weeping wi' the lassies. He wants toughening up.'

The digression on George – though satisfying in itself, and what a college master ought to wish to say – had taken Roger some way from the task in hand. He hoped that George would benefit, and suffer on the way, as he retraced his steps.

'The rule is, women may not pass into the square, and I know not how she comes there, and it were not by the express command of Master Hew, for when the principal Giles Locke is out of the college Master Hew is the first master and is left in charge. I would swear, sir, that Professor Locke kens nothing of her visits, which occur when he is with a patient, or absent from the town on business of the Crown, which since he is a great important man, is often, sir. And it is on those occasions, as though there were some secret signal made and kept betwixt them, that Mistress Clare Buchanan calls upon her brother, or, as I would have it, to engage with Master Hew, such dealings and exchanges as would make a brave man blush.

'You will ask me, I doubt, what proof do I have? The answer is the evidence of my ain ears and eyes. For to see her there – standing in our courtyard like a common whore – you maun forgive, sir, the excess and violence of the phrase, but my fears are for her brother and the students in the college, any one of whom might see and be corrupted, wherefore in my heart I felt I must speak out. I came

175

running from my staircase to cry fie upon her, when I saw Master Hew come stealing from the chapel – aye, from such a place – who caught her by the waist and lisped in her lug, *Ah, sweet luvit lass. Come in to my chamber; let us steir the pot.'*

Roger read this back, and was unconvinced. He did not think it likely Hew would have asked Clare to come and stir the pot with him. This part was the hardest part to write; unlike his scorn for George, and bitterness to Hew, which were fierce and genuine, he must make it up. Of what went on between a lad and lass, he had no experience. And as to what Hew might have said to Clare, or Clare might have replied, he had no idea, and could not ask of George. Most of what he heard from Hew, intelligent and kindly meant, was spoken in the Latin tongue. Though there were Latin epithets of a thrilling filthiness, sniggered in the cloisters and exchanged in the latrines, a woman was unlikely to respond to those. He cut out the last part, and began afresh.

'He stole upon her as she waited, watching for the prayers to end, and dropped his kisses, soft, upon her gentle neck. He took her hand and she went willing, up the turret stair. And there the two were closeted, all that afternoon.'

He hoped that was enough. It was the mirror of a moment, far off in his mind, where his father kissed his mother, coming home from work on a quiet summer evening; that was long ago, before his world had changed.

Among the letters of the college, this was duly passed, and delivered by the carrier to the hand of Robert Wood. Robert owned farmland and a country house in the valley that lay south beyond the Kinness Burn, together with the New Mill, lying to its west, which had caused him so much trouble when the miller drowned. Robert did not count the loss in simple human terms, but in cost and inconvenience, which had been considerable. The New mill had stood idle for the space of several months. Since it was not channelled to the common lade, its stopping had no impact on the other mills, but to increase their profits, while his own ran still. The

New Mill pond grew stagnant, and a red rust settled over its machinery, its locks and levers seized, and would not turn again. When Robert found a miller to take it over at last, it had to be restored. The rents were much reduced, and he had trouble in impressing on the tenants to his land, who took their corn elsewhere, that their ancient obligations still applied. His profits had run through his hands, like the finest white flour through a sieve. To make matters worse, his hopes of a windmill, coming on a ship, had been cruelly dashed. Rightly or wrongly, he blamed that on Hew.

Since Robert Wood was no man's fool, he recognised the letter for the fraud it was. The content left him irritated, rather than dismayed. It did not surprise him in the least that someone at the college shared his rage at Hew, and his contempt for George. He resented, nonetheless, the slur against his wife. He resolved to see the writer choke upon his words, which Robert would serve up to him when he was least expecting it, when he would find the cold cuts rising in his gorge. For Robert Wood was not a man who acted, fierce and hotly, in a flash of rage. He was calculating always, weighing up the cost, and how he could adapt things to his own advantage, and he was unpredictable and dangerous for that. He locked the letter in his desk, while he bided time, deciding what to do.

The letter in the desk was not disposed to cool. For each time he looked back on Clare's fair gentle face, or bent to take her kiss, he sensed it glowing hot, like a spark of kindling cool ash could not quell. He felt it like a spelk, that had worked into his thumb, until he knew there was no remedy, but to take the pincers, heat them in the fire, and tweak the malice out. He could see no option but to put Clare to the test, which, since she was innocent, she would surely pass. Then he would take a dog leash to her brother George, and find out who the liar was, hiding in his tails.

Clare was at her sewing, cutting out small clothes.

'What are you making?' he asked her.

'Some things for the babby.' She broke off, confused, at the look on his face. 'Is it too soon, d'ye think?'

Robert Wood thought it was not soon enough. It had taken her a while to fall for his child. He had sent her to consult with the professor, Doctor Locke, and also with his wife, each of whom shared remedies and views of different kinds. Doctor Locke prescribed a diet, which Robert had enforced on her, intended to provoke the getting of a boy. Meg commended patience; they had not been married long. But what remedy was that? He knew the fault could not have lain with him, for he dealt with his wife daily, if he felt like it or not, and did her through and thoroughly, both old and modern style. Robert knew he came from solid breeding stock: his brother Andrew Wood had sired a flock of weans. They never saw his wife without she had a bellyful.

He bent down over Clare, picked up a scrap of lace.

'I had it from Meg Cullan. Her brother brought it back for her, when he went out to Flanders. I thought that it might trim a sarket or a cap,' she told him, guilelessly.

'Did you go to the college, like we said?'

He sensed a shifting, then. A small prick up of fear. But there was nothing, surely, Clare should be afeared of. Had Hew Cullan harmed her?

'I did what you said.'

'And you told the lawman he must speak to George?' He could not bring himself to say the devil's name.

Clare was wary now. What cause had she had to flush? She was holding scissors, and he took them from her palm. Her felt her small hand shiver, closely clasped in his.

'I told him. But I do not think he has that influence on George that we had supposed. He may not, after all, be able to persuade him.'

That was a lie, Robert knew. He had spoken with her brother George, when he had his accident. The boy had talked of little but the man of law; his letters since to Clare had shown that nothing changed.

'Do you mean to say that the lawman has refused? Then I will ask my brother to bring force to bear on both of them. George must be instructed in the course that serves him best.'

'I wish you will not do that, Robert,' Clare replied, unhappily. 'George will come round to understanding it, in his own way, and in his own time. Please do not press him. Such a course will confuse George, and make him resentful. Do not involve Andrew in this.'

He was irked at her, then. To spite her, he said. 'I know what you did.' He did not for a moment think that she would fall for it. He saw the flush of colour fading from her face, the flutter of a heartbeat quickening in her breast. 'What do you mean?' she said.

'I took you for my wife.'

'Robert, I am your wife.' But she could not conceal, in that faux faint brightness, the quiver in her voice.

'I never thought a moment, Clare, that you would ever lie to me. Or with another man.'

He wanted her to say, of course, of course she had not. She could not frame the lie.

'Robert, on my life, I swear I never meant . . . but he did overcome me . . . I was fruel and weak.'

The blood rushed to his head. He felt a cold wind grip his belly, squeezing out the words. Clare had clasped his hands. She drowned his hopes in kisses, sweet and heavy tears.

'Forgive me, Robert. Ah, my love, do not cast me out.'

He put her from him, cold. 'You are not mine.'

'Sweet, I am yours.'

She had no wit to stray or wander free at will; whoever took advantage of her stole from Robert Wood. He came to his decision then. 'You are weak and foolish. It is not your fault.'

Her sobbing was so frantic it brought in the maid. 'Your mistress is not well. I will call the surgeon.'

The servant hesitated. 'What disorder ails her, sir, that she writhes mad with grief?'

'A disorder of the matrix, brought on by the pregnancy. Help her to her bed.'

It took four solid serving men to hold the patient down. The surgeon was concerned.

'Are ye quite sure that ye want her so profusely bled? It is not the common course for a woman in her state.'

'Look at her, man, she is out of her mind. This is not a common case.'

Clare was exhausted, worn out from weeping and her travails in the bed.

'What does her physician say? For sin she is with child—'

'He says she must be bled, for both their sakes. There is a black corruption, seething in the blood.'

'Ah, I do not ken. If I could have his name?'

'Ye shall have it in the morning, when you come again.'

At last, the man agreed, for double his account, if Robert signed a paper that he understood the treatment might prove harmful to the child.

'I will sign what e'er ye will. I do not care about the child.'

'Sir!' The man was shocked.

'I care about my wife. You can see that she is ill.'

Robert had his way, and it seemed that he was right; for once the blood was taken Clare fell in a sleep, and to a heavy quietness, all throes of passions stilled. Robert closed the drapes and lay with her all night. When morning came, he rose and dressed. Her eyelids fluttered feebly. 'Where are you going?'

'To see my brother Andrew. You must lie and sleep. The surgeon will be back soon. You will want your strength.'

'Robert, you must not . . .' She put out her hand, too weak to call to him.

'Ach, you need not fear. I will find a way to make the limmar pay, that leaves no spot nor stain, no blemish to reproach you. Since he is Andrew's man, Andrew will avenge this. He will see him hang.'

'Who will Andrew hang?' Her wits were not awake. 'But surely, you do not mean Hew?'

He stilled her with a kiss, so hard and fierce and cruel it bruised her bloodless lips.

'I will keep you by me, Clare. For you are my wife. But you will never hear, nor speak that name again.'

Robert flayed his red horse through the morning air. By the time he came to Largo it was lathered in a sweat. He left it with the groom. The family were at breakfast still, seated in the hall.

Elizabeth observed the look upon his face, and took the children out. Andrew folded up his napkin. 'Your coming is untimely. I am leaving now for Falkland. I have business with the king.'

'You have business here.'

The brothers were not friends. They had certain business interests, which it suited them to share. Andrew Wood, as coroner, was well versed in the law. But Andrew would not shed a tear to see his brother hang. 'I will hear your plea tomorrow, at the sheriff court.'

The sheriff court was held at Cupar, several miles away. It irked Robert that his brother failed to put his family first. His father's birthright and his bairns' were mortgaged to the Crown.

'It is not a public but a private matter, that must not be aired.'

'What is it?' Andrew scowled. 'For, I have telt ye before, I will not be drawn into your scheme to inveigle your wife's brother George out of his rightful inheritance.'

'Oh aye? And you had any feeling for what was rightfully inherited, you would not squander yours, and that of your poor bairns, to serve a wastrel king.'

'I will look to my ain bairns, Robert, you may look to yours.'

'So do I intend. I have come about your man, the lawman at the college.' Still Robert could not bring himself to speak of Hew by name. 'He has done me wrong, and you must put him down.'

The coroner allowed a smile, a small thin scar of pity, tempered with contempt.

'If you mean Hew Cullan, he is not my man. Though he has sometime worked with me, he is not for hire. Wherefore, I regret, I have no control of him. If he has vexed ye in some course, some sleight of dealing underhand, then it were right and just, and you have no redress. I cannot help it, Robert, if he thwarts your fleecing of the foolish George. He is an honest man.'

'Honest, is he? Aye, to couple with my wife!'

'What do you mean by that?'

In answer, Robert showed the letter, ragged and ravaged in his hands. As Andrew read, a dark confusion masked his face, and as quickly cleared.

'But you do not believe,' he scoffed, 'this bairnlie piece of spite? For it is plain as day this letter has no substance, but a coward's trick. Hew Cullan ruffles feathers further fledged than yours. He has been investigating tricks that were played on Andrew Melville. Tis likely he comes close to finding out the perpetrator, and the silly wretch has turned the trick on him. I will call him in, and find out who it is.'

'You will do nothing of the sort.' Robert snatched the letter from his brother's hand, and threw it on the fire. Andrew looked on, curious, as the flames took hold.

'But surely,' he repeated, 'you were not deceived by this?'

'You think I am too quickly taken in? So it would seem. Brother, she confessed to it.'

Andrew stared. 'She lay with him?'

'Swears it, on her life.'

'Jesus, Robert,' Andrew swore. 'Then I am right sorry for it. I had not thought that of her.'

'Do not think it of her. Think it of him. He has stolen what was mine. I want him punished for it.'

Andrew rubbed his beard. 'What does she say? That she forced him?'

'It is no matter what she says. She has no voice to speak.'

'Robert . . .' an unhappy thought had crossed Sir Andrew's mind, and he eyed his brother warily. 'Where is Clare? For you must understand, if you have overstepped the law, and put her life in jeopardy, then I maun detain you here. Brother or not, I will do my duty by the law.'

'Aye, very like you,' Robert mocked. 'You would not blink an eye to see a brother hanged. I left her with the surgeon. But you need not fear. I have not harmed a hair on her.'

'God be thanked for that. Do you want him to be charged with raping her?'

'Nothing of that sort. The world will never hear that he has made a cuckold of me. But sin you have control – ah, do not lie to me, I ken you have control of him – I want you to pursue him, and bring the devil down.'

Andrew shook his head. He was plainly thrown by this. 'I am sorry for this pass. I should perhaps have tried—'

'What should you have tried? Had you some word of this?'

'As I confess, a hint. I felt there was some feeling there. I had in mind to part them, when I sent Hew out to Ghent. I warned him off; and I had thought—'

'You warned him off! Yet gave no thought to warning *me*.'

'I took it for infatuation, schoolboy grening, nothing more. Beside which, you forget, you were suspect then of a momentous crime.'

'Aye, and thanks to him, his slanderous imputations ... I am sorely wronged.'

'As I do confess,' Andrew answered, heavily.

'I would see him gone.'

'Trust me, so you shall, without hurt to Clare. I will put this right, in my own way, and in my own time. It may take a while. But leave it in my hands.'

Robert left appeased. For Andrew made no promise that he did not keep.

Elizabeth came softly to her husband's side. She had left the children in the care of the servant. The boys, in particular, were inclined to rough play, to wrestle with their father and come pulling at his sleeves. Magdalene, the baby, had been wakeful in the night. Now she was fretful, and refused to feed. Elizabeth was worn out since she kept no nurse, had borne too many bairns in too short a time.

'Is all well with Clare?'

Andrew did not look up. He buttoned up his coat, turning back the sleeves, where a line of lace lay neatly at the cuff.

'Why should it not be?' Andrew's face was dark. Whatever thoughts had clouded it he did not share with her.

'Your brother seemed distracted.'

'He is exercised upon a legal matter. It need not concern you.'

'But if he is vexed . . . Perhaps I should go to her?'

He glanced at her then. 'You are wanted here, with the little lass.'

And that was true, of course. Elizabeth was glad, for she did not, in her heart, want to go to Clare. She would do what he willed, all that he required of her, but she was worn and tired. Andrew buckled on his sword, and turned to kiss her cheek.

'I must be gone,' he said. 'The king is at Falkland, for his recreation. He has asked me there, to join him at the hunt.'

'Why would he ask you? He has courtiers enough, and he kens you are no flatterer. Surely he knows you have work to do. What does he want?' She answered her own question. 'Money, I suppose.'

Her husband had paid the king's debts, thousands of pounds, from his own pocket and from her own dowry. She had become resigned to it, though fear of what might come to them kept her awake at night.

Andrew said, 'I do not know.' So seldom did he share with her the workings of his heart.

'He will not thank you for it. When he is king . . .'

'He is king now,' he reminded her.

'Aye, but in name. King in his own right, I mean.' The king was under governance of the earl of Gowrie. And that was a good thing, Elizabeth thought. He was kept from his old friends, his profligate

184

spending kept under check; his debts at least were reined in for the while.

Andrew was thoughtful. His words brought no comfort. 'Lennox is dead, and the king is distraught. God alone kens what he intends.'

'Lennox?'

'Esme Stuart, his cousin, that was closest to his heart. He died of a fever in France.'

It was rare that Andrew explained things. The confidence emboldened her.

'But that maun be a good thing, must it not?' Lennox was the profligate who led the king astray. 'He cannot back an army then, against the earl of Gowrie.'

'He cannot do that,' her husband agreed. 'And yet I think this news will move the king to act. He will not be content to submit to Gowrie's will. And I am convicted, there will be a change.'

'The court will be restored?'

'I have no doubt of that. The king has other friends.'

'He will not like you, then,' Elizabeth predicted. 'When he is restored. He will not like to be beholden to you, to be in our debt. And he will resent the way that you have spoken to him, openly, and plain. He will fill his court again with parasites and flatterers. He will do nothing for our boys.'

'Speak not of that!' he turned on her. 'The boys are safe. For do I not provide for you?'

'Aye, but Andrew, all our fortunes . . .' All her worries welled against her. She broke down in tears.

'Enough,' he said, 'No more. Or you will make me late.'

Chapter 17

Trials of the Heart

The king rode to the hunt without Sir Andrew Wood, driving with his hounds and falcons deep into the forest, where he walked on foot. His water spaniel, Jasper, flushed out the first bird. Jasper did not shiver at the snapping of a neck, or fear the pulse which steadied to a thudding disappointment, the heady thrill too brittle and too brief. Sure-footed and inquisitive, he brought the corpse to James. Routed, Pen rose up. She circled once and came to rest, high up on a hawthorn branch.

'Two sparrows for a farthing,' Peter Fleming said.

'Aye?' James rounded dangerously. The falconer was unconcerned. He turned his back upon the king and offered up the lure for Pen to fly back down. The bird condescended to acknowledge Peter's claim and settled on his arm, accepting a sliver of green flesh.

'Will you not take her, your Grace?'

James had removed his left glove. He picked up the sparrow in his white, naked hand, with the softness and the shyness of a woman or a child. The dead bird curled into his fingers like a leaf. 'No,' he answered shortly, 'I am weary of the sport.'

Peter Fleming sighed. He dismissed his sullen highness with a shrug, turning his attentions to the hawk. 'Pen has a broken plume.'

'Pen *is* a broken plume,' suggested James, diverted for the moment from his sulk. Peter gave no answer to this show of wit. He opened up a pouch and dipping in his fingers, stroked the bird with liniment. 'Yon spaniel came too rough to her.'

186

The king was irritated. 'It was not the dog's fault. Pen flew up into the tree. The hills are o'ergrowin here. Ye cannot see the quarry for the leaves; no more can Pen.'

'That's true enough,' the falconer admitted. He soothed and smoothed the hawk, crooning to her as he worked the wax into her wings, which Pen suffered to be oiled and stroked until they glistened like the morsels of sleek flesh with which he still appeased her, and at which she picked fastidiously. 'I doubt she is done for the day.'

'*You* may be done,' James informed him, 'while Pen may be done for. She has the heart of a pigeon. A timorous pluck of a fowl.' He looked down at the sparrow in his palm, and something in the slight corpse stirring to displease him, he tossed it back into the thicket with a gesture of disgust. He took no care to wipe the thin trail of blood from his white hand before he thrust it back into his glove. Jasper, for whom instinct overrode discretion, retrieved the bird at once and dropped it at his feet. James ignored them both.

'She is a young bird, sir, not yet come to her prime.' The falconer defended Pen.

'She is past her prime,' corrected James. 'A toothless, quailing fazart, quaking from her prey. No matter, now. This bolt is shot. So let us change our course.'

'Where would you go to, your Grace?' Peter Fleming found a plug of wool to wipe the blood and feathers from Pen's beak. Pen shook out her feet, a quivering of bells. She turned her blind eyes upwards, to the cloudless sky.

The king considered this. 'God knows, far from here. Go, bid the hunter blow his horn, and sound an end to foolish questions. Close this knotless chase!' He called out to the huntsmen returning from the hills, 'My Lords, a change of plan. We ride out to the east toward the Eden estuary, in search of water fowl.'

'That we cannot, Majestie. We maun keep at Falkland.'

The hunters closed in quietly, circling at his back. Gowrie, Angus, Mar and Glamis, those lords who had control of him, had set a careful watch, a cold and curious company to guard against his will. James looked to Peter Fleming for support, but Peter was preoccupied, attending to Pen's injury, pretending not to hear. The king could not command. His voice pitched shrill and querulous, fragile in his grief, 'Who dares say *we must*?'

They stood a moment still, embarrassed for the bairn in him, too quickly drawn to tears. Someone cleared his throat. Then a voice spoke out. A young man in a bright green coat stepped forward from the crowd. James glimpsed a piercing likeness in the ripple of a sleeve, white ruffles at a throat, a bright jewel on a cap, a delicate, cruel trickery of light. So they did taunt him, with ghosts.

The young man in the green coat bowed, and risked a smile at him. James forced a thread of coolness through his high hot voice. 'I do not know you, sir. Nor see for what good cause you move against our will.'

The green boy said simply, 'I am Rauf Stewart, your Grace.' He knelt before James, open fingered, in the damp green grass. James flexed his own fist nervously inside its leather glove. Rauf Stewart's looks were delicate and soft, his manners shaped for flattery. Jasper and Jem, the king's beloved dogs, ran fawning to his side. But James was not deceived. He whistled, and the spaniel Jem came trotting to his heels. The turncoat Jasper licked the devil's sleeve. James saw he was a devil, in his fair false looks. He set his own wits bodily against those of his king.

'Not every Stewart,' James remarked, 'may call himself our kin.' He made the words composed, aloof, despite his trembling heart.

Rauf Stewart shook his head. 'Your Majestie, I never made such claim. I am in the service of the earl of Gowrie. It pleases him to send me here to wait upon your Grace.'

'It pleases him,' translated James, 'to have you spy on us.'

Rauf coloured at the charge. 'For pity, Sire, why should you think so? I am his servant, as he is yours.'

188

'You are his spy,' declared James. He let the words hang heavy in the air, the green boy kneeling in the grass, until a second courtier came to plead the devil's case.

'This is sound counsel, for we maun keep close. There are yet too few of us to keep your Grace from harm, if ye would ride abroad. There are thieves at large, and brigands at Garbridge, for these are lawless times.'

His highness answered coldly, 'So have I observed, how lawless is the kingdom under Ruthven's rule, and all those who subscribe it, as Angus and Mar, and the *master of Glamis*.'

He knew the man, Sir Thomas Keith; the thrist would not be blunt to him. Glamis was his kinsman and laird.

The hook had found its mark. 'Those lords, who love you dearly, Sire,' Sir Thomas Keith defended. 'None that dares to speak for them would see your Highness harmed. Pray, do not let sour humours spoil a summer's play. Red trout are leaping from the lake, the deer roam through the forest, keeking through the trees, the grassy banks and meadows run alive with hares. Let us make our sport upon the Lomond hills, this fine fair day in Falkland. And it please your Highness, you shall have my lord's best hawk, to race against your Pen. Whichever bird flies faster shall be yours to keep.'

He showed up a hawk in a red velvet hood, its white and brown plumage the colour of Jem. As bairns with sticky fingers reach for shining things, the king put out his hand.

See the goshawk flutter, helpless to the lure. The whisper came so fast and faint that James could not be certain of its source. Rauf Stewart knelt before him, silent in the grass, and in the shadows falling back, the quiet hunters watched. He saw them trade glances and smiles. With a wink, they could prick him to tears. He answered them hoarsely, biting his lip. 'Let us be done here, for Pen is not fit to fly.

'Sir Thomas, we shall take your bird,' he nodded to the courtier, 'and rest her in our mews, to try another day. Since hawks are given freely, and are welcome gifts, your laird will want no recompense, save for our grace and favour, which we give to you. Sir Thomas, you may ride by us. You others, fall behind.'

The hunters blew their horns, calling in the hounds, soothing tense, taut falcons, highly strung for flight. Rauf Stewart scrambled to his feet, his green coat tipped darkly from the dampness of the grass. 'One of us should ride ahead.'

'Then let it be you.' The king swore. 'God knows, I do not want you at my back.' He watched the boy ride out, until the smooth black mare became a shadowed streak, the bright green silk a dot, beneath the Lomond hills. Then brooding, he reined in his horse, and rode back to the palace, with dark and thoughtful looks, and did not speak a word to Sir Thomas as they went.

At Falkland, he dismissed the lords, retiring to the billiard hall, in company with Jem. The hall backed onto the tennis court, and once had been a stable block; it smelled of horses still, a sweet dry pungent earthiness mellowing the gloom. High windows facing westwards seldom saw the sun, and games were played by candle-light on dreich damp afternoons, or in the glow of lantern horn, on nights too dark for caich. There were no vaults or vennels where a man might hide.

Though James was sick at heart, he did not break down in tears, but concentrated fiercely on the game in hand. He took the pieces in his hand as though he made a weight of them to anchor down his grief. He set the port and skittle out upon the cloth and leant to take his shot, to test the secret slant and bias of the board. His first strike missed its mark, rebounding sharply from the wooden rail, and rolled into a pocket on the other side. Jem, at the chap of it, shifted and stirred, let out a fart, and returned to his dreams. He did not raise a whimper at the coming of the coroner, whose left foot caught his tail. 'That is a patient wee dug.'

At his back a page boy hurried, half a step too late. 'Sir Andro Wood o' Largo, and it please your Majestie,' he amended breathlessly, 'waits upon your will.'

190

James retrieved the ball, allowing it to settle for a moment in his hand. 'Though ivory is fair and fine, it never forms a perfect sphere,' he answered to the page. Sir Andrew he ignored, for speaking out of turn.

The boy looked in a box. 'Here is *lignum sanctum* that may serve your Highness better.'

'So we dare to hope. What think ye to it, Andro?' James was flyting now, for *lignum* was the Latin word for wood.

The coroner, undaunted, answered with a smile, 'Perhaps the imperfections turn a profit in the game?'

'For one who is a player,' James agreed. He glowered at Andrew Wood, to see how this might sit with him, and took another shot. 'We missed you at the hunt.'

Wood's black coat and britches bore no speck of dust, no sign that he had hurried, riding hard or long. His bending at the knee was formal and perfunctory, for he was not a flatterer. There had been a time, and not so long ago, when James had been afraid of him. The bluntness of his manners rasped and rankled still.

'Some business kept me from ye, else ye should have found me there.' Wood made no apology, but turned to pet the spaniel, pulling off a glove for Jem to take the scent of it, stroking his soft muzzle. James was irked by this. 'Business of the Crown?' he snapped.

'Not exactly.'

'What, exactly?'

The coroner glanced sideways, where the page boy gawped, following the patter like an umpire in an argument. He was eight or nine years old, the son of some ambitious lord, and quick to spill a tale. James caught on at once.

'Go run into the caichpell, boy, and wait upon the lords. They will want new balls.'

The gawping boy said foolishly, 'There are none there, your Grace.'

'I think perhaps,' said Andrew Wood, 'you did not hear your king.' His words had depths of meaning that were difficult to plumb, for they were quiet, mild and thoughtful, and yet they brought a shiver to the child, and a moment of reflection to the king himself. The small boy blushed and fled.

'Your pardon, sir, your Grace.'

'Aye, sir,' James approved, 'you do well to warn of it. That quelp may well be Ruthven's boy. How sick am I at heart of renegades and spies.'

The coroner said simply, 'Every boy is someone's boy.'

'So I have come to fear.' James dropped his voice, to ask again, 'What business was it kept you, sir?'

Again, Sir Andrew hesitated. 'Nothing to concern your Grace. It was ... a family matter.'

He glanced up at the young king's face, quietly appraising him, sketched paler in the shadows of the darkening afternoon. The king was in his hunting clothes, and in his hand the billiard club swung like a shepherd's staff. Since turning seventeen he had tried to grow a beard, and the fluff of down and stubble left a rash upon his chin. He looked less like a monarch than a schoolboy on a stage, who comes in on his cue but cannot mind his part.

'A family matter,' James repeated, sounding out the words, as something new and strange to him. He accepted the excuse with a light flick of his hand, that left a trail of air for Andrew Wood to kiss. 'Since we are aware that you have paid our debts, your absence here this morning may be overlooked. Now that you are here, we shall play at billiarts. Look into the box there, and find yourself a ball. Ourselves, we have determined we shall keep the ivory; the *lignum* wants a lick of polish, it wants turned and buffeting, and shorn of its rough edges, else it rolls no better than a lump of wood.'

He turned back to the table, pleased with this rebuke. James found satisfaction in compelling men to play with him. Those lords who had not hesitated to lay violent hands on him, depriving him of liberty, authority and friends, were anxious to distract him now, tempting him with toys, as though he were a mewling infant, plucking at the sleeve of those who took upon themselves his rightful role of government. It pleased him to enact upon them small acts of revenge, to win from them their hawks and horses, cups and cloths of gold, though in his heart he kent it for a hollow prize. Had George Buchanan, his old tutor, caught him at his tricks, he would have served his master with a slaffert to the lug.

Did I learn ye nothing? Wad ye be a tyrant now, or would ye be a king? Ye think your duty is to them, that they maun nod and skip to thy daft bairnly tune?

The pedagogue was dead, yet James shrank from the echo ringing in his ears. He coloured at the shame of it. And he was not prepared for Andrew Wood's response.

'Your Highness maun excuse me, for I am no player. I do not think you called me here, nor take me from the service I perform on your behalf, for that you want a billie for your barnelike games. There are wasters enough here to play with your Grace.'

The blood rushed hot to James' face, as though the coroner had slapped him. For a moment, he stood wordless, helpless as to ways to answer to this insolence. Humiliation stung, and prickled in his throat. He managed to choke out, 'Take caution sir, and care, lest ye cause offence.'

'That never was my purpose,' Andrew Wood contended, 'but to prove an honest friend, and as I apprehend, it would not serve your Grace if I should pet and flatter you, and treat you as a child. But say, sweet prince, if that is what you will, then you and I shall ride our hobbies in the hall, play football, golf, and jolie at the goose, as I do with my bairns.'

James bit back his pride, though he felt stripped and shamed. He could see no option but to bare his heart. 'Do you not see?' he hissed. 'You have to see, sin ye have wit and subtlety, for all your want of grace. The good lords will suspect us if we do not play. The good lords in the rafters strain to hear our secrets. We shall drown their whispers with the thud of balls.'

The coroner looked back at him. He did not look away, as he ought to from a king, but held him in the gaze of serious grey eyes,

193

that verged upon a frown. And James was trembling now, as much from fear as rage. He felt as he had felt, though he had been a studious child, when called upon to answer at the master's chair. The question, when it came, was delicately phrased.

'What lords are those, your Grace?'

'I call them my good lords,' James had closed his eyes, to close off Andrew's face. The room bloomed with his blush, the hot rush of his heart, 'As we call *good neighbours* to the faerie folk, hoping with such flattery to fend off faerie darts. If we will not offend them, they may let us pass. Our good neighbours here are Ruthven and his spies, and all those who conspire with them. They lie behind us, in the caichpell, where you will not hear them playing, for they let their racquets fall, and press their traitorous faces close against the walls. They do not ken the stillness of the court has given them away, and I can hear through stone the beating of their hearts.'

Andrew Wood looked on. The full force of his scrutiny, sceptical and calculating, rested on the king, who dared not face its blow. But when at last he spoke, his tone was soft and mild.The mellow force of reason, tempered with his pity, brought James close to tears.

'The court next door is empty, Sire. The page boy telt the truth. Your good lords dare not play at caich without your Grace's leave. And were they at their play, we should not hear their sport, nor they the crack of ours, through solid walls of stone.'

Sir Andrew did not hear, for he was not attuned to it, he had not learned to strain and start, to prick at every sound.

James closed his white hand tightly round the billiard mace, as though prepared to strike with it. 'That is the deception, sir. And surely you were not so vain and foolish as to fall for it? To think that you might come here, without you were watched? But surely you did not suppose that I was left alone with you? That I am ever let alone? That though I sleep and pray and take my meals apart, live out my life in solitude, there are no courtly interlopers, whispering in the galleries?'

The king's cry was heartfelt. Sir Andrew was moved to take a step towards him, though whether to console or to contradict his terrors did not come to light. James thrust out with his billiard stick. 'No closer, sir, I charge you; but one word, one cry from me that aught is out of place, the guard will force the gaming house and bring you to your knees.'

'Patience, my sweet lord!' The coroner stepped back.

'Patience?' James returned. 'Aye, sir, sound advice. But patience comes not readily to kings, when they are cursed and kept, and dealt with worse than dogs. We maun fool our gaolers, and annul their fears. So, sir, shall we play?'

He stopped short of pleading, for he would not plead. But his fragile state of mind had done its work upon the coroner, who conceded gently, holding out his hands. 'Aye, then, we shall play.'

'The truth is that I cannot blame them.' James was calmer now. The billiards gave him back control, the narrow compass of the game composed and served to centre him, *this the field in which we play, this the port, and this the king . . .*

'They do well to watch, for they must know the change that is to come upon them. They lie awake at night, and hear it in the wind. Their deepest guilt will burst and bubble, their black hearts exposed.' He smiled, a little grimly. 'That you are no player, sir, we beg leave to doubt. Take care. This table has a bias, leaning to the left. However straight it seems, an honest board is rarer than an honest friend.'

'I fear your Highness gives away your own advantage.' Andrew took a shot.

'Do not count upon it. I am not a child.' James leant across the board, to nudge his own ball gently closer to the king. 'A penalty, if by your striking ye should knock him down,' he quipped. 'And *that* were bold enough.' His conquest was complete. His strokes became methodical. Between them, he paced round the stable, craning into corners, sweet with dung and hay, poking in the rubble, where the stalls had been. This was not a ploy, to put Wood off his game. The king was rarely still. He never sat where he could stand, nor stood where he could walk, nor walked where he could ride. And Andrew Wood, without distraction, knew that he could never win. He bore his losses patiently. Once, and once only, did his temper spark. The king had knocked him through the port, crowing with delight, 'Now you are a fornicator!'

The coroner set down his mace, rising to the taunt. 'I am what, your Grace?'

'A *fornicator*,' James explained, 'who kens nae more his grammar, than he does his play. *Fornix* is a vault – this little port of ivory – and you have passed it retrograde, wherefore you are *fornicate*, and so must pass it twice.'

'*Pax*, then,' Andrew scowled. 'Sir, our play is done, for we have played to five. Your good lords in their galleries have long since gone to sleep, lulled of their suspicions by my granks and granes, and by the chink of coin, that signals my defeat. Spill your secrets, speak.'

James stepped back, and listened, to the whisper of his heartbeat, to the quickening of the wind. Outside, he heard a pigeon call, a distant, mournful, fluting, faintly through the trees. He nodded, satisfied. 'They say that there are brigands at Garbridge. Tell me, is it true, or is it but a tale they tell, to stay our riding out?'

'It may be both, your Grace. I fear that there are outlaws there, though I have taken measures to contain them.'

'Then take some measures more. For I have a notion I shall want to pass that way. I feel it in my bones.' James let slip a smile. 'Lay hands on one or two, and hang them by the road.'

Sir Andrew nodded. 'And it please your Grace, I could send an escort, to convey you on your path.'

'So much had I hoped. I will send a messenger, to tell you when to come. Then, when all is done' – the king did not disclose the detail of his plan – 'I have another task for you. I wish to hire an advocate.'

'An advocate, your Grace?'

'Hew Cullan of St Andrews.'

Sir Andrew did not start at this, but answered clear and carefully. 'Your Highness is aware, I doubt, he does not practise law? And, as

I recall, you asked him once before if he would be your advocate. It pleased him to refuse.'

He did not dress the slight, but served it blunt and cold. 'You have a guid lawman, in David McGill.'

'That we do not doubt.' James took a careful moment, sizing up the ball, before he nudged it sideways with the sharp end of his stick. 'We shall want them both. McGill as the pursuer, and Hew Cullan for defence. And I am convicted he will not refuse me this, for he will understand it as a matter of the heart. I trust you to persuade him to it, since you know his mind. For I am well aware he has a will and conscience that will be not forced.'

'He has a stubborn heart, that sometime works against him,' Andrew Wood agreed. 'But Sire, the world has altered since you saw him last.'

'You think I do not ken? The light has blown out since. For Lennox, my Esme, is dead.'

James had bitten, accidently, deep down to the quick. The words acquired a hardness foreign to his tongue, a lesson he had learned, that he recited coldly, knowing it by heart.

The coroner accepted, 'I had heard that, Majestie.' He offered no condolence – he was not that kind of man – but kept a careful watch on James, alert to any change.

Gone were the floods, the raw torrent of grief, the shrill outpourings of a lost, bereft boy. James said again, 'Lennox is dead. And I mean to have justice for him.' Twin spots of livid colour darkened his pale cheeks. Yet he was quite controlled, spurred on by excitement, rather than by grief.

'Your Grace, if you intend to prosecute those lords who hastened his departure, then I do not recommend it. For by your own word, you approved their action, and were well assured of their love for you.'

James received this calmly. 'That is not what I intend. Though I am well assured, in enforcing his departure, they brought on his death.'

197

'Your Majestie, he died in France, where his wife and children were. Twere more of an unkindness to have kept him from them. What cause can you have to say he was ill-used?'

'You know how he was used, what harsh and bitter cruelties were inflicted on him, when they forced his flight. To what bitter diet he was put, and with such abruptness severed from our sight, that he withered, like a sapling starved of light and sun, forced to put its pale shoots out into the dark; he died of a disease contracted of displeasure, which is to say, his heart was broken. And it was the lords that broke him, sending him from me, with keen and poignant hardships. Yet, for all their sins, I can forgive that that. For that they knew no better of him, and believed in lies, so men are moved by envy to dispose of honest men. His death is to be pitied, not avenged.'

This answer was impassioned, but no less closely reasoned, so that Andrew Wood was baffled. 'Then what is your complaint, your Grace? What would you put to trial?'

'You might hazard,' James explained, 'that with his death, the hurt he suffered is brought to an end, and that these hooks and slanders have been put to rest. Yet still they raise their voices, when he cannot speak against them, they accuse most freely, what may not be proved. They say that he recanted all, reverting to his faith, and that he died a Catholic. That all they said and did to him was proven by this act; that he was well disposed of, having been intent to undermine our faith, and recruit our country to his hideous cause. Esme died a Protestant, honest and beloved. I know this for the truth, because I have his heart.'

'Your Grace, it is no fault in you, that you should keep a loving heart, and in your greenness seek to trust—' the coroner began.

James cut him short. '*I have his heart*, I mean to say, embalmit in a box. I do not speak in figures, like some lovesick girl. Our honest servant brought it to us, home with him from France. And since I have his heart, I mean to make a trial of it.'

That waxen sliver of the flesh, taken warm from Esme's breast, the lifeblood and the laughter sapped and withered out of it . . . It lay by James' bedside, in a lead-lined casket. He had considered wearing it, sewn into a sleeve. But in a colder light, he found it more repellent, Frankish and effeminate, insolent and fleshly, like a papish relic. It served as a reproach to him. Once Esme was exonerated he would have it buried.

There was silence in the house, so still the little dog looked up, on some account disturbed by it.

'Am I to understand,' Sir Andrew asked at last, 'you mean to put the heart of Monsieur D'Aubigny on trial, as though it were a living man, and not – forgive me, Sire – a dead thing in a box? So grief may move us to strange moods. For pity, Sire, the world will say—'

James interrupted fiercely, 'Aye, no more than that. Were that so very strange? I mean to make a test of it in court, that no man hence may question or malign his faith. Hew Cullan shall defend it; my lord advocate shall be the pursuer. I ken well what the world will say. But surely, you must *see*? That when there is a trial, the world maun haud its tongue; once Esme's faith and loyalty have been proven in the court, the rumours will be stilled. I can make a law, to stop the wagging tongues – and you may be assured that I shall make that law – but till I show them proof I cannot quell the doubts still nagging in their hearts. The trial will prove conclusive, absolute. Hew Cullan is the man that has the wit to take the case.'

'As you will, then, Majestie.' Sir Andrew bowed at last, persuaded by the force, if not the skill of argument. 'I will sound him out, and let your Highness ken whether he be fit for it.'

'Do so,' James agreed. 'For if he will not speak for us, his is not a voice we should like raised against us. Do you understand?'

'Perfectly, your Grace.' The coroner was anxious to be gone. And James, for his part, was pleased to see the back of him, a man who brought a chill wind to a summer's day. He felt his spirits lift, the weight of Esme's conscience lifting from his mind. 'Go about your business now, of keeping the king's peace. God willing, ye shall hear from us, when we are at liberty; and that will not be long.'

Sir Andrew left the gaming house, and stepped into the balm of a summer's evening light, as dusk began to close upon the sun. The coroner had not gone far before he found a courtier standing in his path, who seemed to come from nowhere, sloping through the gloom, a plump-arsed, smooth-skinned venturer.

'Hola, sir! What cheer? Not leaving us so soon?'

The coroner said, sheepishly, 'His highness has dispatched me, sir.' He cast his eyes low to the ground. 'He did not tak it kindly that I missed the hunt.'

'The king is sour and stomachat, and there is no pleasing him,' the other man agreed. 'He is out of sorts. Sometimes, he gives vent unto a passion, and a hot and trembling rage. Sometimes, he seems merry, frivolous and mirthful, snatching up at phantoms, laughing at the wind.'

'I saw none of that,' asserted Andrew Wood. 'Yet I should say, he wants diversion, exercise, and air. You should take his highness out into the field.'

'Aye, then, so we shall, when he will consent to it. He is a fickle sprite. He had you play at billiarts, I suppose?'

Sir Andrew grimaced. 'Aye, and to my cost. So many ways his highness has of cutting loose my purse, he might be a piker, were he not a king. My pockets are wrung out.'

His new friend laughed at this. 'His hand is in your pocket, or else yours is his. I feel for you; I too, have felt that sting. This afternoon, he had my hawk, a sweeter, stauncher falcon you have never seen, nor so stout a heroner, and nothing in return for her apart from his goodwill, which by this hour the morn will not be worth a pin. He has cozened us, you and me both. So, good sir crownar, where do you go now?'

Sir Andrew knew full well that he was being pumped, by the friendly courtier's smooth plump greasy hand. He could have blown him over in a puff of wind, or cut him to the quick with one shimmer of his sword. For a moment, he considered it, just to see the limmar squealing on a spit, kenning Crownar Wood was not a gentle man.

Instead, he answered honestly, for nothing put men off the scent as simply as the truth. 'Onward, to St Andrews on business of the Crown. There is a trouble brewed betwixt the bishop and the presbyters, a fierce unhaly fieriness that threatens all our peace.'

'Is that a fact? In that I do not envy you, your dealings with the kirkmen. For I would rather settle with a thousand peevish princes, than hear one canting preacher carping at my back.'

'If I had my way,' Sir Andrew winked at him, 'then I would hang the lot of them. But we maun bow to government, to kirkmen and to kings.'

'God speed you, sir! Good luck!'

'Grammercie, my lord.' The crownar took his leave, and left the courtier satisfied, to set off at a gallop on the darkening road.

Chapter 18

A Bright Bird Flown

His majeste thocht him self at liberte, with gret joy and exclamation, lyk a burd flowen out of a kaig

Sir James Melvil of Halhil

The king broke out at last, escaping to St Andrews at the end of June. He gave slip to his gaolers with a simple trick. His grand uncle, the earl of March, was grace and favour commendator of St Andrews priory and staying at his house in the old inns of the town. March invited James to come and sup with him. There were fresh wild meats, from a fair day's hunting, that would all be spoiled if they were not shared. The king was bound by kinship to honour the old man, his captors had agreed to it, and James set out at once.

Sir Andrew Wood, as asked, had made the passage safe for him, and kept at bay the brigands roaming at Garbridge, which posed less of a challenge than the king supposed, since most of them were Andrew's men, and under his control. James was in high spirits as he passed the estuary; his spaniels swam in fearless after waterfowl, ruffling up the feathers of the bright lairds on the bank. The provost of St Andrews met the company at Dairsie, to secure his highness and escort him to the town, where he would find his friends.

They entered through the west port of St Andrews, late that after-noon, on a note of triumph, for the bearers' arms were heavy with the herons they had killed, and the saddles of the mares were sleek and wet with blood. They brought with them the scent of earth and iron and victory, to startle the good people who were walking in the town, the quiet south side colleges and kirk of Holy Trinity, who had not been expecting them. James went on to supper at the old inns of the priory, where he made a merry banquet of the meats they brought with them, his great uncle, as it turned out, having nothing in. James was overjoyed, and by evening overwrought. He had written to those lords in whose support he trusted, and called them to St Andrews to convene a council, while Gowrie's privy councillors were warned to stay away. By nightfall, it was clear his plans had gone adrift.

The news had flown from Falkland, swift as James himself; his captors took no warning from it, and were on their way. Those good lords he had counted close among his friends were either late in coming or had turned up unprepared. The full force of the provost's men, together with Sir Andrew Wood, could not defend the king against the present threat, and so he was advised to withdraw into the castle, until his friends arrived, for fear he would be taken up, and kept in charge again. The priory was not fortified, and March could not ensure his nephew's safety there.

At first, the king refused. He rode out through the streets, openly and recklessly, accepting with a gracious hand the tributes of his people, who had come out from their houses with fresh lobsters, fish and fruit. The baxters brought a hundredweight of fine white wheaten flour, the vintners rolled out barrels of their sweetest wines; the king would want for nothing while he was in town. James made free with all, careless of his liberty, until his uncle March was forced to call him in.

'Would ye shut me up,' cried James, 'and keep me in that place?'

'But for the while, your Highness, till we ken your liberty and safety are assured.'

Dark forces descended, circling the town. The lords who pursued him were heavily armed, and the king was soon persuaded that he had no choice. He entered in the castle, half against his will, with a small band of men who were loyal to him, and one or two more, who were not.

At the castle, the archbishop was the last to hear the news. While James worked his charms on the startled crowds in South Street, while he was sampling wines and sweetmeats with the earl, Patrick Adamson consulted and consorted with his physick wife, experimenting with her underneath the sheets. This lewd and thorough industry was not to be disturbed for less than life and death, impending fire or flood, or, Tam Fairlie judged, the coming of the king.

Patrick took a moment to distract from his endeavours, and another half a minute to deflate. 'What, king? What, here? What, now?' he squeaked.

'At supper in the priory with the earl of March. His attendants to arrive here in under half an hour, to be followed, in due course, by a full retinue of friends.'

The physick wife was thrilled. 'I could hide in the closet there, an' keek upon his face. I never saw a king.'

'You never shall again.' Tam Fairlie stripped the bed, and tipped the woman out. 'I will scare this jack-daw back where it belongs.'

Alison clung, like a leech to a boil that sucked at the sore to the sap. 'You have no cause to call me that. I am a proper physick wife, and salve to Patrick's maladies. If I do not relieve him, he will suffer more.'

Patrick blanched and whispered, 'Do ye mak a threat to me?'

'I have not been paid.'

Tam Fairlie grasped her arm, and marched her to the door. Her belongings bundled after, tumbled from the bridge, and were buried in the fosse. 'Ye will get your due. Do not come again.'

The physick wife stood whimpering, naked in her sark. 'He will want me, you will see. He cannot keep his hands off me.'

Tam dismissed her, 'Damn you, whore!' He poured out the physick from the bishop's window, where it left a damp patch, sullen, on the stone.

It had taken Patrick all his time to dress, shaken as he was, with fear and shame and palsy; he did not think his heart could recover from the shock, or hold out at the strain. His household staff and chamberlain were frantically dispatched.

Tam Fairlie had departed to take stock of March's men, who were lolling idly in the outer court. The castle could accommodate a hundred extra guests, but Tam had no idea how many might descend. Carpets, hangings, pictures, plate, gaming tables, folding beds, all were borrowed, bought or begged, from local lairds and colleges; St Salvator's sent table napkins and a dozen cloths. The king's equipage had remained behind at Falkland; he had come with nothing but the clothes he stood up in, horse and hounds, and hawk.

Patrick was not certain what he should put on. It had been some while since he wore proper clothes. Should he be drab and dull, as fitting to a scholar of the true reformit kirk, or courtlier and gay, in honour of his king, and of the shift in fortune he had doubtless brought with him? At length he chose a satin doublet, cap and gown in black, set off with a tippet lined in silver fox. His deliberations were as nothing to the king, who turned up in a heightened state of tremor and perplexity. He did not wish to see the chapel with its fair Italian colonnade, the dormers in the gallery or fine view of the bay. He did not care to be confined.

'Do you have strong fighting men here you can trust?' he demanded.

Patrick swallowed. 'One or two.' He made a mental note to have Tam keep the bairn and perhaps the Richan boy out of sight and sound, lest their uncanny trattle fuelled the king's unquietness. His air of agitation soon translated to the bishop, who felt a little queasy and unsteady in the knees. The chamber had been swept and aired, but Patrick could not help but fear some relict of the physick wife might still be in the bed – a ribbon, lace or sock.

'Where does this door lead?' asked James.

'To the fore tower, your Grace, and onward to the chapel, where if your Highness pleases I will preach a sermon to thank God for your safe deliverance.'

'Deliverance from what? I am at no peril,' James protested.

'No, sir, ah, of course.'

'Yet,' the king conceded, 'a sermon might be apt, in the kirk of Holy Trinity. I will give you the direction for it, presently. And what is behind this curtain?'

'That is the privy closet, sir, when you may . . .' Unusually for Patrick, he was lost for words.

'Be privy?' James supplied.

'Indeed, quite so, your Grace.'

'And who was that old man we saw back on the stair? A fruel and grovelling simperer.'

'That is my privy clerk. His room is in the tower. I will, of course, vacate these chambers now, and have them swept and plenished as your Grace desires. The earl of March is kind enough to send in his own furniture, until such time as your possessions may be brought from Falkland.'

James looked vexed at this. 'I must have my bed.'

'My chamberlain tells me it has been sent for, but it will not be here before the morning, Sire.' Patrick felt a little at a loss, as to what comfort he might offer the unhappy king.

'I do not, you see, sleep in a bed like this.' The king looked help-less for a moment, frightened as a bairn. 'I have those beds, of course. But the one that I sleep in rolls up.'

'I understand, your Grace. Both the beds were sent for.'

For it was understood that the great bed of state, though it was carried through the kingdom on to every passing place, never would be slept on.

James had wandered to the windows that looked out upon the town. 'What house is that?'

'It belongs to Giles Locke, who is principal at St Salvator's College. He is an anatomist, and does work for the Crown in finding out the cause of unexpected deaths.'

'I saw him, once, in a play.' The king relaxed a little. 'In an extrav-agant hat. He is Hew Cullan's brother-in-law.'

The bishop smiled weakly. 'Indeed.'

'A man of most singular talents.'

It was not clear to Patrick which man was referred to.

'I will not want these chambers,' James made up his mind. 'There is a stench and staleness here that is far from wholesome.'

Patrick answered, blushing, 'I have not been well.'

'How, not well?' snapped James.

'It is not the sort of sickness that will spread to other men,' the bishop reassured him, 'but an internal fedity, gnawing at my wam.' He almost said, *my soul.* He felt the prick of tears, a sudden surge of confidence. His king was in his palm, and castle. James had been restored to him. He was overcome.

The king returned to his inspection. 'They are, besides,' he reasoned, looking round the rooms, 'too close to the entrance gate; the first place they will look if the castle defences are breached. Do you have guns here?'

'Aye, your Grace, guns. But no powder or shot.'

'Such things must be sent for. I saw a chamber at the head of the north west tower, that overlooks the water and is well appointed. I will quarter there. There is a gateway on the north side. Is the descent there passable?'

'When the tide is out.'

'I will, not, you understand, be kept a prisoner here. And I will die before I allow them to lay hands on me again.'

Patrick was alarmed at this. 'Majestie . . .'

'I will die first, do you hear me?'

'Nay, Sire, none of that! Know that I shall pray for you.'

'I shall want a kirkman, Patrick.' James was plaintive, childish now. 'The masters of the kirk are not always kind to me, though I am most careful and devout, and attendant to the faith, as I have ever been.'

'No one doubts that, Majestie,' the archbishop assured him. He was taken aback at the hurt in his voice.

'Since my mother is a Catholick, they suspect me of wrong.'

'That were not reasonable, Sire. All of our mothers were Catholicks, once,' Patrick murmured soothingly, though he felt ill-equipped to give spiritual advice.

'But some of them were brought since to a clearer light. The ministers of the kirk will not spare my years, but where they see small faults they put them to the light of a cold and public scrutiny, and punish my offences with the bitterest of words. They scourge my frailties openly before a mocking crowd. They show no shame or pity for the person of their king, and they are not kind. They hurt me, sir, and I am humiliated, when a word in private, or a gentle look, might better serve their purpose and achieve their end. In such a heavy climate I require a friend.' The king laid bare his heart.

'I understand, your Grace. For I too have been harried by that same monopoly. They hound a sick man cruelly, almost to his grave.

'They did beset me all around
'With words of hateful spite
'Without all cause of my desert
'Against me they did fight.'
Patrick sang out from the psalm.

James approved. 'You speak truth, sir, and wise and good words. For once I had a friend, a good sweet honest friend, who converted from a Catholick to the one true Christian faith, for love of truth and love of me, and no more loving honest friend could a man desire to see, while he was alive; and now that he is dead, they persist in telling lies, that he reverted to his faith, and put up but a paper show, to wind his pleasures close to me.'

'Does your Highness refer to Monsieur D'Aubigny?' Patrick dared to ask.

'Aye, sir, Esme Stuart, lately duke of Lennox.'

Adamson nodded. 'Aye, it is true, he has been much maligned. With a little pressure, we may yet amend that. I can make a sermon of it.'

208

'I had hoped you might.'

James looked young and vulnerable, and Patrick groping for some thread, some small scrap of grace, was astonished to discover his own cheeks were wet with tears. 'In the town, tis rumoured . . . I fear that ye may hear . . .'

'I have heard the rumours.' James was thinking still of the duke of Lennox, and did not see the bishop falling to his knees.

'Sire, I have been foolish. I have not been very well.'

The weight on Patrick's shoulders had begun to lift. He could sense, almost smell, the chance of redemption here. Without daring to believe it quite, he felt that there was hope. 'And in my sickness, have resorted to desperate remedies. I bought medicines from a woman who had a reputation for some skill in mixing herbs. I swear I had no kenning that she was a witch.'

The words were said, at last. And Patrick felt the burden lifting from his heart. Whatever happened now, he would come into his grave with a quiet conscience. He laid bare his soul before his Lord and king.

James took a step back. His voice teetered high in his nervousness. 'A witch? There is a witch, here?'

'Not near here, your Grace,' the archbishop assured him. 'My guard has disarmed her and driven her out, when we saw what a viper she was. I have severed all contact with her, and my men are under orders to arrest her on sight, if she should dare approach us. She can pose no danger to your Grace. Yet am I persuaded that she has fed me poisons that prolonged my sickness, and made me beholden to her. I have been under her spell. By God's will, and my prayers, I have repelled her. But it has sapped all of my strength.'

'Good God,' whispered James. 'What did she do to you?'

'Vile things, with such torments that I am ashamed to speak of to your Grace, that would dismay and terrify your guid sweet tender heart. God opened up my eyes to her, and strengthened me against her; I have cast her off, and prostrate myself before ye, and plead

209

your Highness mercy where I am at fault, and where my weakness has allowed this evil to take grip upon my foolish heart.'

'Let God be thanked that ye have fought her off. This is a grave fault, Patrick, and a horrible one. You know what you must do?'

'I am apprised of it, your Grace. I will denounce the witch to the kirk session, that she may be brought to trial, and dealt with in the proper manner; I will freely confess, and atone for my fault, for that I was deceived in her. I will not rest until this filth is cleansed.'

'Do that, and ye may find comfort in your brethren, since your repentance is so abject, and her guilt so great. God love you, Patrick, ye have had a close escape, so dreadful that I marvel at it. We must cut this evil out, radically and utterly.'

'I am afeared, Sire, that my enemies will seek to cast me down, and use this weakness to repel me.'

'Then we will not let them. Deliver up this witch, and no harm shall come to you, for evil doth consort to make fools of honest men. We shall find a mission for you, far off from this place.'

'Your Highness is most gracious, consummate and kind.' Patrick knelt at James' feet; and moved to kiss his hand. The king drew back, appalled. 'Foul man, do not touch me! Thou art cursed and sick. Until the witch is dead, I would not have thee near.'

Patrick gave his chambers up to house the king's front guard, and moved into the quarters of his clerk, Ninian Scrymgeour, which were small and cramped. Ninian was a comfort to him, performing countless acts of unmarked care and kindness, filling in for servants who were called up by the king. He washed the bishop's feet and emptied out his pot. The chamberlain strove hard to keep the castle fed and watered, the horses, dogs, and kitchen boys, and all the vaunting lords. Tam Fairlie found weapons and beds for the soldiers, quartered the best of them next to his own. He kept the Richan boy apart and on the watch, where he judged he did less harm. The bairn went her own way; she did not care for strange men sleeping in her gallery, and sulked for half a week; she was not impressed at the coming of a king. Once, she helped herself to a little silver ring she found lying at the bedside of a drunken lord, and Tam had to take measures, much to his regret. He took the jewel away from her, and locked his daughter in. His anger found its mark, pitiless and sure, upon the Richan boy.

John Richan kept the watch. He did not look down upon the inner court, thrang with men and horses, brewers, cooks and dogs, where several of the followers had set up makeshift camps. A constant stream of hawkers passed the entrance port, with crabs and lobsters, candied fruits, books and cards and gaming dice. Beyond them came a darker force, louring in the distance, the threat of coming storm. They sent him high aloft, to walk along the battlements, far above the town. He saw the carts come rumbling past the city walls, the steeple of St Salvator, the rows of cobbled streets and crisscross of the rigs; he heard the strike of clocks, the trundle of the hucksters' carts and peal of chapel bells. And drowning out all else, he heard the flood and flux, the pounding of the sea, that blasted at the stone, a constant, sharp artillery, echoing like drums. He saw the selkies cruising, grey heads shy and bobbing, weaving through the ships, the skidding white foam horses leaping in the waves, and heard the song of mermaids basking on the rocks. Through light and darkness, wind and storm, through endless night and cloudless day, John Richan kept the watch.

Chapter 19

Home Truths

Giles Locke was out at night, called out to a patient who was close to death, suspected of a pestilence. Giles had put the pestilence, and the man, to rest. Returning to the small house on the cliff, he felt a watchful tremor through the quiet streets. The hostelries were full, and though the inns were closed and barred against the night, the muffled sounds of drinkers drifted up from cellars, and the cracks between the shutters spilled out yellow candlelight, in thin, suspicious streaks. There were guards on every corner, and it took some time to navigate through the wynds and vennels back to his own house. Meg had left a rush light burning by the bed.

'Is all quiet, out?' Her voice came reassuring through the midnight air. He kissed her upturned face. 'I did not mean to wake you.' He brought home a coolness, dewy and damp, the scent of the night. Light drops of water had speckled his beard.

'I was not asleep. Your hair is wet,' she said.

'It has started to rain.' He took off his coat. 'And all is quiet, now. There are soldiers on the North Street, by the fisher cross. I thought they were not going to let me pass, but they knew me, I think. They were Andrew Wood's men.'

Giles had moved away to rest his gaze on Matthew, sleeping in the box crib by his mother's bed. So often he redressed the heaviness of death, coming home at night to look upon his son. He felt his heart well up, a life force pink and sweet, in the small face of his child.

'He has been good today. He is more contented now the works have stopped.'

The builders had set down their tools, in deference to the king, who would not suffer strangers at the castle gate. His frantic fits and frets had put the town on watch with him.

'The town is taut and strained, like a kind of coil, that is about to spring.' Giles yawned, taking off his shoes. He stripped down to his shirt and climbed between the sheets.

Meg asked, 'Will there be trouble, do you think?'

'I think it is averted now. The king has sent letters to the university, the provost and the kirk, in which he has affirmed his own free will and liberty. Gowrie and his enterprisers are dismissed from court. Tomorrow, as I think, James will leave for Falkland, and our little town can breathe again in peace.'

Giles blew out the lamp, and felt beneath the sheets his wife's familiar hand. 'Sir Andrew Wood was at the college today, looking for Hew. He did not tell me what the business was. Which is not such a good thing, I think.'

'Did you send him on to Kenly Green?'

'He said that he would come again; he apprehended no great haste.'

'And I suppose his brother sends no word of Clare? I have not seen her in a while,' reflected Meg.

The doctor shifted slightly, turning in the bed. 'I should, perhaps, have mentioned . . .'

'Mentioned what?'

'With the coming of the king, it had slipped my mind. I heard that Clare was at the college. I suppose she talked to Hew. He has not spoken of it, but is quiet since, and he has kept away since the king imposed the curfew. I fear that he has taken it to heart.'

'We should have told him, Giles.'

'You know that was not possible. She came to us in confidence. And you know your brother. He will not be telt.'

Meg sighed, 'Even so. You do not think that Hew could be the father of her child?'

'I have not liked to ask him,' Giles admitted. 'I would like to say that I do not believe that he could be as reckless, or as stubborn, or as wilful, or as foolish, but the truth is that I have no doubt he can be all those things, and will follow his own heart without caring for the consequence. But if it is his child, you may be certain that he will not walk away, and leave it in the care of a man like Robert Wood. Therefore we must hope that it is not, and that his brooding quietness does not foretell a storm. I meant to ask you, Meg. Do you still see the Richan boy? The bowman from the castle. How does he go on?'

He did not see her colour in the darkness of the bed.

'He comes to see me still. But he has had no leave, while the king was here. When the court has parted, he will come again.'

'Still?' The doctor frowned. 'I had not thought the course would take so long. His shoulder should be well by now. Perhaps I ought to look at it.'

'It would be well by now, if the sergeant at the castle did not make him work so hard. He has no chance to rest.'

'Then I shall have to write a letter to the bishop.'

'I think,' said Meg, 'the truth is, he is desolate, and he likes to come. He is very young, and very far from home. He comes from a wild and strange place, and life there can be perilous, but it is a natural kind of harshness, built of earth and stone and wind and sea and rain, that brings a powerful freedom with it rather than constrains.'

'You must be careful, Meg,' the doctor said. 'Else he will grow too fond of you.'

'Ah, do not be daft.'

'Or you too fond of him.'

Meg let her head rest gently on his solid chest, and listened to his heartbeat, warming in the darkness that filled the little bed. 'Must the workmen come again?'

Giles was weary now, and drifting off to sleep. 'The works have been a trial to you. But they are almost done. And it will all be worth it in the end.'

214

The king returned to Falkland then, free to come and go at will, and left the town in peace. For Meg, the blessings that this brought were tempered by the building work which started up again. No sooner had the royal court made tracks along the Swallow Gait than chaos was restored; the labourers returned and pressed on with the hammering. The noise resounded through Meg's head, and she felt faint and nauseous, symptoms of the falling sickness to which she was prone. When at last the workmen broke to wash away the morning's dust, she lay down to rest. Canny Bett took Matthew out to take the air – a bright warm summer sea breeze blown in from the east. Giles was at the college still, and Paul had disappeared in quest of Jonet Bannerman. Meg closed out the sunlight, sinking in her bed, and drifted at the edges of a fitful sleep. The echo of the hammering sounded in her dreams. She woke up with a start, to find it still reverberating outside in the street. She opened up the shutters, shrinking from the glare, to see John Richan down below, rapping at the door. His voice cut through like glass, urgent and intent. 'Mistress, let me in.'

'I am on my own . . .' She went down, nonetheless, and opened up the door to him. Her head was pounding still.

'I know that. I saw them go out.'

Had he been watching her, then?

'Aye, but not like that. I am the guard at the gate. And if Tam Fairlie sees me here, he will have my skin. Please, mistress, let me come up. There is something I must say.'

'Come up for a moment. It cannot be long.'

'Indeed,' he swore, 'it cannot. I will be missed.'

He came into the house, and followed her upstairs, where he stood by the window, looking at the street, and she saw the light glance through the half-open shutters, grazing the white crafted bone of his cheeks, the ash-coloured drift of his hair. His eyes were bright and agitated.

'A maun flee awa.' His words were a jummil of English and Norn, and Meg found it hard to make sense of the flux, of the great flood of feeling that welled up behind it, and to separate the force of that feeling from her own, perplexed at the sadness he awoke in her. She had missed his visits, more than she had known. And she had not supposed he would not come again.

He could bear it there no longer. He was going home to Orkney. It was not, she must be sure, a wanton act of cowardice. He would not for the world that she should think it that. But he did not trust himself. 'I will kill him if I stay. I will slit Tam Fairlie's throat. I will thrist into his breast, and squeeze out that black stone he keeps there for a heart. He awakes in me a kind of murderous rage, that makes me like the worst of them, and I am not their like. I will not be like them.'

He told her he had begged his passage from a fisherman from Crail. The man had brought lobsters to the castle for the king, and had promised John a boat. Harry Petrie had put up the wherewithal to pay for it.

'Why would he do that?'

'Because he is my friend.'

It seemed to Meg a hopeless scheme, childlike in ambitious scale and in the simple act of faith John Richan had invested in it. She could not see how a fishing boat could sail from Crail to Orkney, or what sum of money it would cost to requisition it.

'The earl will pay for all. He will pay the fisherman, and Harry, for the boat. For I will bring a fish, hanging on my hook. I will bring him news. What grander, better catch, than the coming of a king?'

John Richan seemed to slip into a dream, already in that boat, sailing with the selkies, bobbing in the waves. Meg felt sad and fearful for his state of mind.

His news would be long cold by the time he came to Orkney, through the barrage and the storm and the stotter of the sea, his journey would be fraught and his coming there unwelcome. She could not convince him. Finally she tried, 'I wish that you would stay a while, and think on it, consider; we will miss you John. I do not think, in truth, that we can do without you. How will Matthew sleep, without his lullabies?'

He turned from the window to face her, wild and impatient, no more than a boy. The sun lit his face and made his hair bright.

'Come with me, Meg. There is room in the boat too, for you and the bairn.'

A deep cold fear came snatching then, a sudden draught of dread. 'Now I know,' she forced a smile, 'you are not thinking straight. It is the keeping of the watch, John, the coming of the king. It has upset us all, and set us all at odds. Things will settle now the king has gone. Your arm has all but healed, and if Tam Fairlie makes life hard, I will ask my husband to speak with the archbishop.'

John shook his head. 'I know my mind. '

'This is nought but foolishness, and I will hear no more. You must leave here now. I will keep your secret, and will wish you well.'

'Ye maunna answer now,' he said.

'You have my answer, John.'

'The boat will leave at Saturday. And I will wait for you, all the night before. I will lie at the place that is closest to your heart, and will stay there until dawn.'

He said no more, but left her there, returning to the watch.

Tam Fairlie waited at the gate. He found he had no urge to raise his voice or fist; the Richan boy did not stare back at him but looked down at his shoes, blushing like a lass. He understood for once that he was in the wrong, and Tam felt almost sorry for him.

'Soldier, ye have left your place.'

'I went across the street, on an errand to the doctor's house.'

'And what errand wad that be? Was it for the bishop, son? Mebbe twas the king? I cannae hear ye, son.'

'It was none of those.'

'Mebbe, though, ye thoct, the precincts were secure enough, now that the king was gone; that there was no sic need to keep a careful watch.'

Tam offered an excuse that another man might seize, and be thankful to submit to his sergeant's friendly discipline, but not the Richan boy. The Richan boy maun stand and argue always. 'I did not desert my post,' he insisted stubbornly. 'I could see the gate still, from the doctor's house. I wad hae returned to it, if anyone had come.'

Tam Fairlie sighed at that. 'Mebbe,' he suggested, 'ye think your place is this side o' the gate, and that side of the gate, and the doctor's house, and the doctor's wife. I have to break it to ye, that it is not so.'

The Richan boy looked murder at him. Tam had not kent the laddie had the spirit in him, and he was amused by it. He did not, for a moment, care if he went lowping at the doctor's wife. In fact, he half approved of it, since it showed the laddie had the makings of a man. But he could not have him do it while he kept the watch. 'Son, ye are relieved of duty. You will follow me.'

The Richan boy was scared. Not his common wariness, but deep down in his belly, he was feart of Tam. It should have done him proud. But Tam could feel no pleasure in it.

'I can stay here if you like,' the boy was pleading now, 'an' work another shift.'

'But ye canna ye see,' Tam explained, as gentle as though Richan were his little lass, 'for ye cannot be trusted, in the first line of defence. You maun come wi' me.'

He put his arm around the soldier, kindly and protective, as a father to a son. 'How is yon sair shoulder, John?' He called him by his name.

The Richan laddie swallowed. 'Soon it will be well.'

'Aye? Tis to the good. For in the place where ye are going, ye will have to climb a rope.'

Since Meg had no hope of resting now, she retired to the kitchen and began to make broth, hoping to find calm in the dull domestic act. A fine dry-grained dust had settled over all; she had to scrub the board before she could begin. She had barely started chopping, or steadied her quick heart, when another round of knocking called her to the door. This time, it was Hew. He had walked from Kenly Green, calling in to see her on his way to college. He was surprised to see his sister open up the door herself, dabbing at her eyes with a corner of her sleeve.

'It is the onions,' she informed him. And perhaps it was. She changed the subject quickly. 'I am glad to see you here. I thought you might be vexed with us.'

'And why should you think that?'

'I thought, because of Clare.'

'I knew that she was married, Meg. Though I had not imagined she might have a child. Which may tell you how very green I was.'

There was hurt still in his eyes, and Meg was not deceived.

'I had some strange idea that I might save her from her husband. In truth, I do not know how I meant to go about it. And I took no account,' Hew admitted wryly, 'of her lack of will, or interest to be saved. And now I come to see how simple and how foolish were my feelings, I feel in part ashamed, and somewhat more relieved. I felt sorry for her, married to that man. You should have told me, Meg, that what she wanted most was to get with child. I thought that she was coming to you because she wanted an escape from her husband, not because she wanted to become more close to him.'

'We could not break her trust. And you can never tell – no one ever knows – what secrets and collusions are between a man and wife. Some are happy, that seem not; and some that seem the best of friends . . .' Here Meg faltered and broke off.

'What is the matter, Meg? For you are sad and pale.'

'I think I may have made,' she said, 'a terrible mistake.'

'What mistake is that?'

Meg composed herself, beneath his careful scrutiny. 'I think I may have put in pepper, where I wanted clove.' She peered into the broth.

'Though I do not believe that for a moment, it would scarcely matter if you had. Do you not feel well?'

'I have a little headache from the hammer. And it will not be long ere it begins again.' Meg changed the subject quickly. 'Giles telt me that Sir Andrew Wood had looked for you in college. I hope there is no matter there.'

'He wrote to me,' reported Hew. 'He said he had business that he would take up with me, but that he is now occupied, in conference with the king. And that is like the man. He likes to be mysterious. His method is to leave a man alone to find his fear, examining his conscience for some matter he has done.'

'Then there is nothing, I suppose, that you should be afeared of?' wondered Meg.

Her brother smiled at her. 'My conscience is quite clear.'

Chapter 20

The Castle on the Cliff

Tam Fairlie came to Harry to relieve him of the night watch. Harry was surprised. 'Should it no' be John?'

'He is in his pit. Mebbe ye should fetch him.'

'What, still asleep?'

The sergeant grinned at him. 'I did not say that.' He rattled at his belt, taking off a key. 'You will want a light.'

Harry said, 'Sweet Jesus, Tam!'

'Tell him to mak haste, or else he will be late. And he wouldna want to miss the early shift.'

Harry cleared the bile that was rising in his gorge and spat out in disgust. 'You are the devil, Tam. I have stood by you, but this . . . I will not keep quiet on this. I will tell the world, what primping kind of brute you are.'

'Is that a fact?' the sergeant grinned. 'Then they will laugh at ye, son. For you are as barnelike as he. I have been toughening him up. When he is a man, the lidder loun will thank me for it. I had thocht that you, at least, were made of stronger stuff. Let the laddie out, if it grieves you so much. What are you waiting for?'

'You are a consummate shit.'

Though Tam Fairlie laughed at this, his face turned dark as stone.

The Richan boy was in the pit. At first, his friend saw nothing but a pile of sacks, and dared to hope that Tam was simply making sport with him. Harry let the lantern swing from the bottom of a rope. Whatever he discovered, he would not go down, for he was

221

well aware that there was no way up, without a lot of effort on the part of a good friend. He heard a scuffle from the sacking, probably a rat. The pit was sometimes used for storing salt and grain. Though on the other hand, the rat had no way in, through flanks of solid rock.

'John Richan? Are you down there?' he called out. The hollow chamber answered, throwing back the sound. Deep down in the darkness, something stirred.

'I will throw down the rope. You maun try to catch it. Tie it round your waist.' With the help of the pulley, he could haul John Richan out, but it would take all of his strength. John Richan would be flayed from his oxsters to his wrists, and the skin would be stripped from both of Harry's hands.

The pile of sacks uncurled, and Harry saw John's face, blinking at the light. He dangled down the rope. 'Ye hae to catch it, John.'

John Richan, staring up at him, seemed not to understand. Harry thought mebbe his wits had fled.

'Haud on to the rope, John, else I will leave ye there.'

John's answer was to crouch back in the heap of sacks, and to close his eyes against the lantern's glare.

Harry Petrie swore. 'I will not ask ye again John. There can be nae helping you, if you will not help yourself.'

The rope swung and bumped, and banged against the wall. John Richan's whisper carried, faintly, to the air. 'I want to stay down here.'

'The devil you do, John. Ye will wish that you were down there when I put my hands on you.' Harry coaxed and swore at him, threatened and cajoled, until at last John caught the rope and did as he was told. It took another quarter hour before he reached the top. As Harry pulled him clear, exhaustion and relief were melded into rage. He grasped him by the throat. 'Why can you no dae it, John? Why can you not say aye and nay and be like all the rest of us? Why maun you gowk back at him, with thae great gawping eyes? Drop your gaze, and hark to him. Is it so very hard?'

John Richan stared back, blankly. Harry dropped his fist. 'I cannot always help you, John. You have to help yourself.'

He put his arm around John's neck and helped him to the door. The Richan boy woke slowly to the morning light, stepping out unsteadily. Tam Fairlie stood outside, where he had been waiting for them, watching all the while. 'There ye are, son. Did you sleep well? Ye are late for your watch. But we will excuse it, only this once.'

'For pity's sake, man,' Harry said wearily, 'let the puir bluiter go in to his bed.'

'Has he not had the hale night to sleep? And he is well now,' the sergeant objected. 'What say ye, John?'

The boy dropped his eyes. 'Ah'm well eno, aye.'

'Good lad,' approved Tam. 'Though we have not cured ye yet of your outlandish speech. The fresh air will cheer ye, up in the tower.'

Harry left them both, returning to his bunk. He would gladly tumble into it, worn out with the night shift and the dead weight of the pit, for his arms were racked and aching and his back was stiff and sore. But there was something he must do before he went to sleep, and before the day was up. The baxters in the bakehouse had already baked their bread and Harry would find breakfast there. The bishop and his household would sleep on for several hours.

Harry reached beneath his bed, and with the corner of his dagger he pulled up a hollow plank, to remove a wooden box. Inside were sheets of paper, drawing pens and ink, and a leather pocket where he kept his sketch, folded into four. He took the pocket out, and tied it to his belt. He chose a piece of charcoal, sharpened to a point, and tucked it for safekeeping in the cuff of his left boot. Then he replaced the floorboard, and went back outside.

He went first, as he always did, to the far west corner of the southern range, adding several charcoal smudges to the early draft. Later, he would rub them out, replacing them with ink. The chapel was already drawn, and coloured, on the map. He entered through the colonnade and up the chapel stair. A door led from the chapel to the central tower, and from there to the bishop's quarters on the other side, which, at this early hour, would certainly be locked. He spent a while in the chapel, simply looking out, down toward the hill and the ditch below, passing through the trance to the bishop's tower, where he heard a flutter somewhere at his back, as though a little bird had flown up through the tower. Tam Fairlie's little daughter peeped out from the stairwell.

'What are you doin'?' she asked him. 'Lookin' for jewels?'

'To be sure. Have you found some? You are like the lark, rising with the day.'

The small girl laughed at that, and ran out to the sunlight. It was for the best. Tam Fairlie did not care for soldiers talking to his child, even Harry Petrie, who had been a friend. Harry stood a moment for the lass to disappear again before he left the tower. She never lingered long, and it was rarely that they came upon her playing face to face. She flitted through the gardens, and high up on the parapets, through the vaults and cellars and up on the cliff. By God's own grace and wonder she did not fall down. She had liked to play, for a while, in the high long gallery above the bishop's hall, before Patrick put a stop to it, driven to distraction by her running feet, as he lay wan and wammilling in his bed below. While Tam was at his work, she went about at will. No matter in that, now, for Harry had no cause to climb up to the gallery. He had no interest there.

He went through the cloister to the vaulted chambers underneath the chapel, where he spent some time examining the walls. He took a measure with his thumb, and stepped out to the light with the paper in his hand, to find that someone else was walking in the morning air. He folded up the sheet again and slipped it in its pouch.

'Good morrow to you, sir,' he greeted Ninian Scrymgeour, the bishop's privy secretary. 'You are unco early up to say your prayers.'

The secretary squinted, for he had not brought his spectacles, and for a moment seemed uncertain who it was had spoken, and perhaps a little fearful that it might be Tam, though Harry was distinctive, because of his red hair. 'Good morning to you, soldier,' he agreed at last. 'I like to spend an hour or two in quiet and reflection, before the sun is up.'

'Aye, and the archbishop,' Harry sympathised.

'Ah, yes, indeed.' Ninian had embarked upon a rapid course of blinking, which signalled some embarrassment that Harry read his mind. 'It will be some time before his lordship stirs. And I do confess, I find a certain solace in this private hour.' Ninian came closer, peering up at Harry without benefit of glass. 'I think I saw you, did I not, coming from the fore tower?'

'Aye, no doubt ye did.'

'Perhaps you were on duty there?'

'I have just come off the watch,' Harry answered, truthfully.

'So I had supposed. Yet that does not explain what you were doing in the chamber underneath the chapel. Indeed, it does not explain it. I can see no reason for a soldier to be there. Indeed, he ought not be, you know. The chapel vaults are sacred.'

'Your pardon,' Harry murmured, 'if I have offended ye, for I meant no offence.' It surprised him that the timid clerk had ventured to attack, but his answer was prepared. 'I chose this hour, that I not disturb or trouble the archbishop. The truth is, I was looking for something.'

Ninian pressed him, 'Aye?'

'Do you remember that lawyer I showed round here some while back? With the doctor from the college?'

'Master Cullan? Aye, indeed.'

Well, he has lost a ring. And he is minded to believe he dropped it somewhere here.

'I will tell to you the truth. I do not think it likely. I doubt he left it at the bedside of some other fellow's wife,' Harry's wink at Ninian was rewarded with a blush. 'But that is no' the answer that he wants to hear. Well, you are my witness. I have come to look for it. And more than that, the ribald dare not ask.'

'You have not found it then?' Ninian asked, perplexed. 'Then that was not the ring I saw you tuck into your pouch?'

The little clerk was sharper than he looked. But Harry was a match for him. 'I tucked my knife into my belt. I used the blade to dig about a little in the dust. But to no avail. Then that was what you saw.'

'No doubt it was,' Ninian accepted. 'For I do not see very well. Soldier . . . sin ye are here, I wonder, could I trouble ye? There is something I would ask. The truth is, it is a matter I was meant to take up with your sergeant . . . the archbishop had mentioned it, and I had clean forgot . . . He spoke of it last night . . . By rights, you see, it ought to be the chamberlain that dealt with it, but the chamberlain will have nought to do wi' Tam Fairlie, sin the cook caught the sergeant's daughter dipping in the honey pot and he telt the little lassie he would clip her tail and Tam came to the kitchens and caught him by the throat, and telt him he wad wake one morn to find his ain tail clipped and stuffed into his mouth, and frighted him so fearfully he does not sleep at night. Wherefore it is left to me . . . and I confess that I . . .'

'Tam can be a fearsome loun to thae that do not ken him, and he is in a black mood now. What was it that you wanted from him?' This answer drove the little clerk to further frightened fumbling.

''Twas only that . . . There is a boat expected in today, to replenish the stores that were emptied by the king. And Patrick wants a soldier to open up the sea yett, afore that boat comes in.'

'Aye, then fret no more,' Harry promised, cheerfully. 'I can look to that. I will go precipitate, and see to it myself.'

'Then I am obliged to ye, for, as I will confess, I have no will to converse or dispute with that man. Good morrow to you, then.'

'Good morrow it may be,' Harry stretched and yawned. 'Sin I have done my watch, and am ready for my bed now, I will say goodnight.'

'Goodnight to you, soldier. God speed you well.'

Harry watched the little clerk climb up to the chapel, where, without his spectacles, he knelt to say his prayers, between the

226

sergeant and the bishop, wrung out like a cloth. He did not envy Ninian, put upon and weak. It was not much of a life.

It was early, still, as Harry crossed the courtyard. No one was about. He waved to John Richan, at watch on the sea tower. John did not wave back. The man on the kitchen tower was looking to the harbour, waking to the light. The sea gate was stiff, and always hard to shift. Harry had to pull at it with both of his hands. His arms were weak as water, from the effort he had wasted pulling John up from the pit.

John Richan on the sea tower saw Harry Petrie fall. He fell without a sound, and landed on the rocks. The dull thud of his landing was drowned out by the sea. For a moment, John stood still. Then he left his post, and climbed down to the shore. He pulled his friend up from the tide line, back upon the rocks, and saw that he was dead. He stood stricken for a moment, before he turned and fled, creeping like a limpet round the edges of the cliff. He had reached the harbour wall before the sentry saw him, and the sentry did not fathom what it was he saw. By the time he picked out Harry, in the grey mass of the rocks, the tide was coming in, and John far gone from sight.

The body was not brought up until early afternoon. A crowd began to gather ar the castle cliff, to witness the recovery. Harry Petrie's carcass had been taken to the haven, to the harbourmaster's house. The harbourmaster sent for Doctor Locke, whose job it was to make report on all unnatural deaths. Giles was at the college, and came down at once, with Hew. Harry's battered body was carried up Kirk Heugh and through the castle gates. It came to rest at last in the upper gallery, a cool and quiet, open-ended place, where Giles could view the corpse in privacy and dignity.

Patrick was dismayed. 'The port is open to the cliff, when this man lost his step and fell. He expected a boat,' he gesticulated, helplessly. 'Still, we expect a boat, for the court has drained us dry of all of our supplies, and all of us have worn our fingers to the bone. Ah, dear me. We all of us are tired, and all of us are exercised, and it is not remarkable that the poor man fell. Tis clear enough he slipped as he opened up the gate. He had just come off the night watch. The truth is, we have all been trauchled, with the coming of his majestie, and all the other company. The wonder is that all of us have not yet fallen to our deaths.' He gave thanks to God that Harry had the decency to wait till James had gone, before he lost his footing and went tumbling down the cliff. 'If ye could dae your work here, speedily, and quietly,' he requested Giles.

Giles sent Hew back to the gate, to see where Harry fell, while he undressed the corpse. And Hew was thankful in his heart to leave him to the task, for he could not bear to look at Harry's broken face, the bright smile cracked and blotted, scarred with soil and sand. There was, he was relieved to see, very little blood.

The place where Harry's corpse was found was some way from the steps, and it did not take long for Hew to understand that someone else had put him there, hidden from the tower, and safer from the tide. The sergeant of the guard was sent to fetch the watch, and came back with a face on him as black as any storm. The Richan boy had left his post, and could not be found.

Hew returned to Giles, who had turned Harry's corpus safely on its back, and had covered it, for decency, with a linen cloth, as though Harry was asleep, wrapped up in his sheet, with nothing sticking out but a tuft of bright red hair.

'Is it possible,' asked Hew, hoping it was not, 'that Harry could have crawled to the rock where he was found?'

'Not possible at all,' Giles said with a frown. 'For he was dead before he fell.'

He lifted up the futeman's hair, and with his pincers pulled a stone, deep embedded in his skull.

'Jesu,' whispered Hew.

'Who here is a perfect shot?'

There was no clearer answer then. It had to be the Richan boy.

Patrick was dismayed. 'This is very bad. I pray to God that news of this will not alarm the king. The young man must be quickly caught, and as quickly hanged.'

He found his privy clerk kneeling in the chapel, where he did not hesitate to interrupt his prayers.

'Here ye are. Why is it, when I want you, you are always on your knees? If ye were the archbishop, and I were Ninian Scrymgeour, you could not be more pious, nor as little use to me. Come, take down a letter.'

'Your pardon, Lord Archbishop,' the little clerk said, meekly. 'I sought the good Lord's guidance. I am sore at heart. For I cannot help but fear that I maun be in some small way accountable for that poor man's death.'

Patrick raised an eyebrow. 'Aye? And why is that?'

'It was I who telt him that a boat was expected, and that soldiers were required to open up the gate. I meant no more, of course, than that they should look out, and be ready to admit it when it comes. He misunderstood me, and opened it himself. Sin he lost his footing there, I count myself in conscience, art and part to blame.'

'That boat has not come yet, and we are out of claret, since the king has drunk us dry.' Patrick was reminded: 'Still ye need not fret, for you were not to blame for Harry Petrie's death. According to Giles Locke – and sin he is our Visitor, reporting to the Crown, on all unnatural deaths, we maun take his word for it – Harry did not lose his step, but was dead before he fell. Someone took a shot at him.'

'Dear sweet Jesu, who?'

'A proper oath and question, for a pious clerk! The suspect is yon Orkney archer. Now the loun has fled, there is a hue and cry for him. Tam Fairlie warned me that the man was feeble-mindit, no richt in the head. I should have listened to him.'

'Tam Fairlie is a brute. He plagued yon Orkney archer, all but to distraction. Harry was his friend. And if John Richan murdered him, that devil drove him to it.'

Patrick had never heard the timid clerk speak forcefully, and he received this comment with alarmed astonishment. 'You must not say that. Never shall ye say that, nor think it may be true. Tam Fairlie is a proper soldier. You are far too soft, and you can have no notion what it takes to make these puling laddies harden into men. The sergeant does his job. A fine help ye would be, if ye were ever called upon to march in our defence, quivering and scummering, and jabbing wi' your pen.'

Ninian said, stiffly, 'I should find it difficult, my lord, with one hand on my sword and the other on my spectacles.'

'Bless you, so you would,' Patrick chuckled. 'Stay with what ye ken, and ye will prosper best. I want you to write me a letter to the earl of Orkney, telling him of these events. It were bad enough that a murder should take place, so close upon the visit of the king, that it may be considered to have prejudiced his safety. John Richan must be caught, and speedily despatched. So you maun tell the earl, since Richan is his man, that if he should return to him, he maun have him brought to us in irons, or see him hanged himself. He will not take too kindly to it, and it must be feared that it is like to hinder us in our present cause, but that cannot be helped. Write thus to him, with gentleness and pleasing tricks and flattering . . . *good my sweet lord* . . . nay, *dear beloved earl . . . dear brother of my* heart . . . fah, say simply, *Sir, of your man John Richan, we were much deceived in him* . . . And we maun dare to hope it will not spoil the match between our daughter and his son. For even above that,' he concluded gloomily, 'we maun put our duty of allegiance to the king.'

The hue and cry was called, and Hew and Giles went home. Giles was unusually quiet, and since his views on death were in general philosophical, Hew began to wonder what was on his mind. At last, his old friend said, 'As a man of law, what you would advise, if I told you I intended to commit a crime?'

'I should advise you not to.' Hew saw that he was serious. 'What crime? Tell me, Giles.'

'The robbing of a corpse. Harry had a pocket, a small leather pouch. And folded in his pocket, I found this.' He showed the paper up. 'It is directed on the outside to a Master Jo. Colville, Master of Requests. *Master of Requests*. Now that is a prodigious office, and the very gateway to the Privy Council.' Giles was clearly shaken by the letter in his hand.

'I know the man,' said Hew. 'At least, his worth in court. He pitched his tent in Gowrie's camp, and now has lost his charge, and fallen out of favour with the king.'

'You are well-informed.'

'He was Andrew Melville's friend,' remembered Hew. 'And once a student here, who took orders in the Kirk. But since he sought preferment, and neglected his own flock, Andrew has not kept his faith with him. A climber after fortune. Andro does not suffer those.'

'Then Patrick's friend, perhaps?' suggested Giles.

'I should not have thought so. Colville was complicit in the raid upon the king, and put out in a paper it was wise and just. Now that the king is free, he may be short of friends. But why would Harry write to him?'

'It is not a letter,' answered Giles. 'Rather ... you must see,' he handed it to Hew, 'for I can make no sense of it.'

The paper had been marked out into squares. Those in the lower half mapped out the south face of the castle, drawn to careful scale; the fore tower and the vaults below, with several places circled, and the open fosse. On the top half was a sketch of the trance and nether hall, open to the works, in Giles' house. The places where the workmen had dug out the walls and floor were also clearly marked.

Hew exclaimed, 'This is a map of your house.'

'More precisely, the works in my house,' Giles agreed. Which, you will apprehend, demands a question. Why would Harry Petrie have it in his pocket? How can he have come by it? I have no understanding he was ever in my house, though I know John Richan was.

231

This is a skilled and detailed plat, no slight scribbler's sketch. And, I must confess, that I do not well like to come across it here. It makes me think that all our moves are closely marked and watched. What does it mean, Hew? Can it have to do with the coming of the king? What, then, should I do?'

Hew rolled the paper up and tucked it in his sleeve. 'I have no idea,' he smiled. 'My advice to you, is that to rob a corpse is a most dreadful crime, that would be the ruin of a man in your profession, and, if it came out, is like to see you damned. The saving grace for all of us is that you are quite blameless of so grave a crime, for *you* have not committed it. As to what it means, I will find that out.'

Chapter 21

The Master of Requests

Hew began with Meg, who was uncooperative. 'There is no way on God's earth that John could have killed Harry. That boy did not have a bad bone in his body. He was gentle as a selkie, and he would not hurt a soul. John has run away, and it had nought to do with Harry. He telt to me beforehand that he meant to go.'

'What did he tell you?'

'His confidence is private, Hew, and telt to me in trust. Tis no concern of yours.'

'Suppose that Harry kent of it, and had tried to stop him?' Hew suggested.

'He would not do that. Harry was his friend. He gave him . . .' *money for the boat*, she began to say, before doubt closed in dark. She turned her face away.

'Did he tell you,' Hew persisted, 'where he meant to go?'

'No. He did not say. And I am not certain what was in his mind.' Still, she did not look at him. 'He was distracted, when I saw him last.'

'Then you must allow he may have had a part in this?'

'I do not allow that he would kill his friend. And do not examine me, Hew. I am not a student in your class, nor am I a witness in your court.' Meg stood her ground.

'Aye, then, very well. But if you do know where he is, you ought to say. Twere better he were found, for no place here is safe for him. And he cannot go home, for already the archbishop has sent letters to the earl, to warn of his arrest. There is no escape for him.'

Meg made no response. Whatever the confusion milling in her heart, she would not be drawn.

Paul, by contrast, spilled out all he kent, of Harry and the builders, and the visit to the cellar, and the inn in Huckster's Wynd, where the soldier liked to drink, with a cousin he called Bess.

'He asked to see the works. He said it was his father who had built the house. I thought no scrap of harm in it, to let him look below.' Which resolved at least the first part of the mystery: where Harry Petrie found the pattern for his plan.

'You do not think it somehow caused the poor man's death?' Paul concluded anxiously.

'I'm sure that it did not.' The truth was, Hew had no idea. For want of any better lead, he went down to the inn. The streets were quiet now since all the lords had left, departing like a flock of birds that would not see another spring. They left behind a trail of dust, of empty flagons, cups and kegs, muddy floors and dirty sheets. Harry's cousin Bess was sweeping out the yard, and was visibly affected to hear of Harry's death. 'How horrible,' she said, to die in such a way. Did she ken a man called Colville, Hew inquired? The lass was too distraught, or too innocent perhaps, to hide the fact she did. 'There is a man ca'ed that . . .'

'Whit matter is there here?' An older wife appeared, who saw the lass's tears, and glared at Hew accusingly.

'I brought you some sad news.'

'Harry Petrie's deid.' The lassie blew her nose. 'And this man wants to speak wi' Master John.

The woman shot the girl a warning look. 'There is no one here that answers to that name. Go back to the bar, and tak a drop of *aquavite*. You have had a shock. How best can I help you, sir?' She turned back to Hew.

The alehouse in the vennel had no truck with passing trade; it was not a place where strangers lingered long. It was not, indeed, that they were made unwelcome; the alewife and the lasses there would serve their wants as quick enough, with just as bright a smile, yet they would sense a lull, a stillness to the place, and did not feel at ease. To those who came and stayed, from commerce, kirk or faculty, and settled in the corners, brooding with their cups, the house gave up its secrets, and became a second home. It lacked the ready roughness of the harbour inn, the raucous rant of sailors and of merchants passing through, but opened to the street, as a common drinking house, and kept its darker secrets buried underground.

The woman who had charge of it was known as Violet Rose, though the owner of the house was the vintner, Robert Zeman, famous for his imports of fine and sweet new wines, the lure that drew the masters from the colleges and kirks. Even Andrew Melville had consulted Robert Zeman, for a bottle for his nephew to prepare his wedding toasts. And Robert Zeman, true to form, had brought out just the thing, sweet and mellow, light and subtle 'like your ain sweet lass'.

Robert's link to Violet had never been quite clear; they were not man and wife; nor did they share a private life in any manner likely to cause trouble at the kirk. Robert was away a lot, and Violet was in charge. She was a handsome, well-built wife, of thirty-four or -five. And at this time of year, as every year for fifteen years, someone left sweet violets by her chamber door. These she pinned to her kirtle, or wore plaited in her hair, peeking dark and shyly from her close white cap, or planted into pots, with yellow buttercups.

'I have a letter for John Colville,' Hew explained to Violet. 'Found in Harry's things. Since there is no direction, I cannot send it on.'

'There is a man called Colville, comes from time to time,' Violet said impassively. 'And though he is not here at present, he may well be back. You can leave it, if you like.'

'I must put it in the hand of the man himself. I am,' and Hew embellished here, 'Harry's man of law, and the paper, do you see, is concerning something left.' He knew no better way to flush John Colville out.

Violet nodded. '*If* I see John Colville, I will let him ken. Whit place will he find you at?'

'Hew Cullan, at St Salvator's. I will be there tonight.'

As Hew had supposed, he was not left waiting long, for he had barely settled down to his supper in the hall, when the porter came to call for him. To Hew's irritation, Colville had not come himself.

'My master understands that you have in your possession a property of his,' the servant said. 'He has sent me to collect it.'

'Then you must tell your master he must come himself, for I will release it only to his hand.'

'My master is a busy man. He has to leave tonight, and has no time for this. If you have his property, then ye must give it up.'

'I am a lawyer, sir, and first I must establish if it is his property, in which case I will surrender it only to his hands. There are certain rules which must be observed.'

'In which case,' said the servant, 'he will see you at the inn, in a quarter of an hour.' Hew suppressed his smile. Colville had prepared, it seemed, for this contingency. Hew also was prepared, and left the folded paper locked up in his desk, having no intention of releasing it to Colville, before he understood what that might mean for Giles. He felt his spirits quicken as he set out through the gloom.

In the cavity below the common drinking house, the cellars burrowed down into a warren of small cells, where a man might brigue and deal, throw dice or tumble with a lass, or drown a sorrow in his cups, without the bray and bruiting of the fractious world. In a corner of this cavern, hidden from the glare, Hew found Master John. Colville had a cold. His eyes were dull and swollen, heavy with fatigue. Yet his response to Hew was civil.

'The lawyer, from the college? Sit ye down, my friend. Violet tells me that ye have a letter in my name. You maun excuse my manners than I did not come and fetch it. My business here is brief, and my health is poor. Do you have it here?'

'It is in my house.'

'Ach.'

Hew sensed a shadow passing over Colville's face; in the greasy lamplight, he could not be sure. The man looked frail and tired.

'Then, sir, I must ask you to direct it with a messenger; for I have nor the time nor will to follow to your house, and nor do I play games. Send it to my wife at Stirling, and I am obliged to you. I shall not be there.'

'It is not as simple as that. For it may be exhibit in an inquest of the Crown. It must be kept as proof.'

'In proof of what?' Colville asked.

'The man who left it died, and Giles Locke, who is the Visitor here, has opened an inquiry to the cause of death. The manner is suspicious. Among this man's effects were a paper with your name on it. He was a soldier at the castle, in the privy guard of the archbishop Patrick Adamson. His name was Harry Petrie.'

'Petrie?' Colville shook his head. 'The name means nothing to me. I have no dealings with the castle. What does Patrick say?'

Colville, noticed Hew, was on first names with the bishop. Given their connections, that was not so strange. They both had trained as preachers in St Mary's College. Both men were ambitious, though their paths had parted since.

'That he knew nothing of the dead man, except he was his futeman, who had been there at the castle since its last incumbent. An honest, simple soldier, born and bred. I think, perhaps, you met him, sir? I am told he drank here.'

Colville sighed. 'Do you not drink here?'

'Sometimes,' Hew admitted.

'Sometimes, so do I. The wines here, as you will acknowledge, are the best in town. Yet I am prepared to swear that you and I have never met. And shall I tell you why? For I do not consort with strangers at the bar, but take my pleasures quietly, or I am plagued by those who knew me once as *Master of Requests* to answer their petitions and advance their claims. Our masters now have stripped and broke me of that benefice,' Colville answered, wearily. 'Now I am reviled by both king and kirk, those pleas, at least, have ceased.'

That was hard indeed, thought Hew. The Kirk had well approved of Gowrie's form of government, staunchly Presbyterian, allowing them the chance to move against the bishops. Yet they castigated Colville, who had fought for Gowrie's cause, for abandoning his parish in pursuit of his ambition. Now his life and living were collapsed in ruins.

'Your dead futeman – *Petrie*, did you say? – was doubtless one of those, who looked for grace and favour. What was in his letter? For I suppose you read it?' Colville asked.

'There is nothing written on it, other than your name. The paper is a drawing of the castle and a house – a house across the way from it, belonging to my sister, and her husband, Doctor Locke.'

'You have lost me, I'm afraid. What relation was this solder to your sister's house?'

'That I do not ken. He asked to see the cellars there, where there are building works; he seemed to think his father may have built the house, and some parts of the castle, sin he was a mason. But his father is no longer still alive.'

Colville showed small sign of interest, still less of surprise. 'There, I think, you have your answer. He is making some petition that concerns your sister's house. Tis very likely that he meant to make some claim on it.'

'Could such a claim have force?' From what he kent of law – which was quite considerable – Hew could not be sure. He did not know the terms on which Giles kept his house.

Colville answered, 'I have no idea. As Master of Requests two thirds of all the pleas that I have ever heard are disputes over property, and, as I confess, I do not miss those now. The likelihood is this ... Your paper is the essence of a property dispute, the like of which I have seen many times, and shall not be sorry not to see again. I cannot help him now, since I am out of office and your friend, alas, is dead. The letter is no worth to me. Yet I advise you, keep it safe until the case is proved, for it may yet turn out to be some of – Harry, was it? – part of Harry's testament.'

238

'Shall I let you know,' asked Hew, 'the outcome to the inquest?'

'Assuming it can find me, I'll be glad to have the news. I know you, sir; your fame has gone before you. I saw you at the court house once, with Master Richard Cunningham. Ah, what year was that! The year they struck poor Morton down and our king was sore misled, by unhappy influence. And now sic fortune comes again; now those of us who spoke for Gowrie's cause must joggle for our lives. I go presently to Edinburgh, to answer to what charge the king may set against me, and to plead my case, that is a good and honest one. I am sick, in soul and body, as ye see afore you, and harbour no great hope of it.'

So fate twined and turned, and taunted with her tricks. The thought of Richard Cunningham was sobering to Hew. For Colville, he felt sympathy. There were worse things, to his mind, than to have nailed one's colours to the earl of Gowrie's mast.

'Then I am sorry for it, and I wish you well.'

'I thank you well for that. I pray that you may prosper. Believe me sir, I do. I cannot tell you, sir, how glad I am we met.'

There was an odd note to his voice, which Hew could barely catch, and could not well interpret, perhaps it was the ague, closing in his throat.

'And that you solve the riddle of your fallen friend. Tell Andrew Melville, he will have his wish, for I shall surely lose my living at Kilbride; such pittance as it is. And tell him, he and I were ever more alike than he has had the courage to suppose.'

'God save you, sir.'

'Adieu.'

Hew's thoughts turned to Harry as he climbed the stair. His interest in the castle stone was heightened and unusual, the story of his father's death sufficient to account for it. Had he harboured some false hope of claim to Giles' house? Surely, if he had, he could not have died for it. Colville, Hew remarked, had shown no interest in the letter once he had established what the contents were. And it was plain to see that he had troubles of his own; the death of Patrick's futeman did not ripple in his mind. Then what were Harry's dreams, and Harry's fears and hopes?

Hew sought out Petrie's cousin Bess, but did not find her at the bar. A helpful lass explained, 'Violet sent her home. Her red-rimmed eyes and dripping nose were puttin' aff the customers.' Her father was a fisherman, living by the fisher cross. Hew would find her there. Since Bess was out of sorts, and not up to her best, the lass would take her turn, if he preferred to stay. Hew thanked her, and declined. 'She no doubt is dismayed at her cousin's death.'

The serving lass sniggered. 'Is that what she called him?'

On his way back to the college, Hew passed by the fisher cross and called in at the house. The fisherman was in his bed, and none too pleased to answer to his knock.

'I am right sorry,' Hew consoled him, 'to have heard about your loss.'

'What loss was that, then, son?'

'Your cousin that was killed.'

The father said '*Piss off*,' and slammed the door on him. But Hew had not retreated far when the lass herself appeared, shuffling across the cobbles in her stocking feet. 'You should not have come,' she sniffed. 'He was not a cousin, in the proper sense.'

'I am sorry, Bess. Harry was a good man. You must miss him sorely.'

'He was not, you understand, like all the rest. I do not say that we were like to have been married, it was not like that, but Harry was a friend.'

'I liked him, too. He showed me round the castle once.' Hew understood her will to talk, and drew her out with gentleness. 'He told to me the history and secrets of the stone, and showed such deep felt fondness for the place, I felt it meant the world to him.'

'Aye, that is true. He loved that place. His father was a builder, sir and Harry had a passion for all kinds of works. He telt many tales.'

'Did he ever mention he had claims upon a house?'

240

The lassie wiped her nose upon a grubby sleeve. 'I do not think, so, sir. He said that he had *expectations*, but I paid no heed to it. Harry had elusions, he was always talking grand.'

'What elusions did he have?'

'That he would come to money, sir, had grand important friends.'

'Like Master John Colville, perhaps?'

'That I do not ken.' Bess was guarded now, warned off by the name. Hew tried another tack. 'A gentle man was that, and vexed at Harry's death. A brave man, so he said.'

'Did he say that, sir?' The simple lass brightened. 'Then that was civil of him. I mind he asked me once if Harry had been in that day, but I no idea that they were friends. I must go in now, sir.' Bess recognised, perhaps, that she had said too much. 'My daddie will not like it that I traffick in the street.' She shrank back to the shadow of her father's house.

Colville, then, had lied, for Harry Petrie's name had not been strange to him. On his return to the college, Hew took out the paper from his desk, but looking at the map, could find no further clue from it. He slipped it for safekeeping in a book of Latin verse, and returned it to the desk, where it lay forgotten in the coming days, its presence there eclipsed by far more close concerns.

John Colville sat in darkness in the stillness of the vault. He did not turn his head, nor raised the wine cup to his lips, but sat in sombre thoughtfulness, till Violet brought the light.

'Look at you there, in the dark. Ye have let the lamp blow out.' She lit it from the flame, and looked into his face. 'Ye havena touched your wine. *Aquavite*, a posset, that is what ye want. I will make a bed for ye.'

'No.' He lifted his right arm, and took her hand in his, sheltered her small hand, withered as a leaf, dry and coarse and red. 'I cannot stay tonight.'

'Tsk.' She pulled back her hand, and set straight the stool, put her cup on a tray, wiped down the board, tidying briskly. 'What, will ye gang now, catching your death?'

'Aye, mistress, probably.' He smiled at her. 'Here.'

He took off the fur tippet he was wearing round his neck and placed it round her shoulders. Violet let her cheek rest briefly on its pelt. 'I cannot wear that.'

'No. But ye can keep it.'

'Your wife will wonder what has become of it.'

'She may wonder, Violet. But she will not ask.'

She kept it for a moment there, before she took it off, and lifted up her skirts, her bare legs in plain sight. John Colville smiled. 'Wicked, wicked woman. Have ye no small shred of shame?'

Violet tied the tippet close around her waist, smoothing out the kirtle she pulled down to cover it. 'I will keep it warm for you, biding your return.'

'Aye, then, lass. Dae that.'

'I suppose,' she understood, 'we will not see you for a while?'

'Not for a while.'

'What was in the letter, then? Was it that important?'

'What?'

Colville seemed already far away, intent upon his journey, wherever he would go. She wondered if he would be cold, without his little scrap of fur.

'No, it was not important. But ye did well not to tell the man that I had met with Harry, and you have my thanks for that.'

'I wad not tell your business,' Violet promised, 'not if they put me to the jayne, and broke my banes wi' torments. I wad save ye, see?'

Colville smiled at her, sadly and tenderly. 'You would spill my secrets at the first turn of the screw, and I ask no more. I would not hae your sweet blood shed, your white bones snapped for me. But ye have naught to fear, for ye have naught to tell, and will not be asked. I drank here; Harry drank here; that is all ye know, and all that ye should ken.'

Violet nodded. 'How did Harry die?'

'That I do not know. But a man like that, that lets his fingers dip into so many men's pies, he shouldnae be surprised when someone nips them off.'

242

Violet shivered. 'Ah, I liked him, though. Ye maun be careful, Johnny.'

'When am I aught else?'

He kissed her lightly on the cheek, and Violet felt the scent of him, the tickle of his beard, long after he had gone.

The servant brought the horses, wordlessly. It was cold on the highway, as the night began to fall; his master had no tippet, but the fever burned his cheeks. The country road tailed off. Colville smelled the air, the hot curling of the smoke stacks, drawn from sleepy chimneys, farmhouse suppers on the wind, heard the seabirds calling, scattering at dusk. They were some way on the road before the servant asked, 'Will I come wi' you, sir?'

Colville shook his head. 'Bless you, Thomas, no.'

'I do not mind it, sir. You will want a man, to bring you drink and such. And they will surely notice that are not well.'

'Ye are a guid man, Thomas. Go, tell my wife.'

'I will dae that, sir. That matter at the college wreaks no ill, I hope? Only Violet telt me, Harry Petrie's dead.'

'What? Ah, no harm to it. In truth, no harm at all. I think, in truth, the contrary.'

'Then I am glad to hear it, sir. They say that Master Cullan has a sharp and ready wit.'

'That I do believe. Yet he will serve us well,' Colville answered, sadly. For he had liked the man. He felt sorry, in his heart, for what he had to do.

Chapter 22

The Still House

Hew slept the night in college, to be woken up at dawn, by the frantic knocking of his closest friend.

'What is the matter, Giles?' Hew was dredged up from sleep by the force of his passion; he had never seen his friend so exercised before.

'She has left me! Gone! Run off, with a murderer! And in my heart, I knew that I did not deserve her. I should never have subjected her to that relentless hammering.'

'Begin at the beginning,' Hew suggested, kindly. 'Where is Meg?'

'If I knew that,' Giles retorted, 'I would not be here.' He was clutching at a letter in his quaking hands, and in his agitation working it to shreds.

'A letter, Hew! She wrote it in a letter. Am I such a tyranniser, that she could not tell me to my face?'

Giles could speak no more, but sank down, hard and heavy, on the folding bedstead, which creaked a little, straining at the sudden weight. Hew rescued the letter and began to read. He recognised the writing as his sister's careful script. She had written letters to him while he was in France, under their father's kind instruction, practising her French. To Hew's shame, he did not remember ever writing back.

The letters were well-formed, with no blots in the ink. His sister wrote a firm and unexceptional hand.

'Dearest Giles

'It grieves me to have had to leave you in this way, at such a time and place; I hope you understand that I could not have done so, without a greater heartbreak was at stake.

'John Richan is a lost and frightened boy. He has been maligned, and misused by his tormenters, and I cannot allow him to face this test alone. I think you will not believe me – as Hew will not believe me – when I tell you John is blameless of this crime. That fortune somehow has aligned against him, and he is bereft, and left without a friend. Yet even Hew will recognise that sometimes tis the case, a man may be maligned, when he is not at fault, when all inquiries are misled, and all hopes misinform. John Richan is a good and honest man; there is a strangeness in him, that I will confess, but since I know you recognised a strangeness once in me, I know that you will not condemn on that account alone, but understand that a strangeness can hold in its heart a peculiar sweetness, that cries out for our charity, deserving of our love.

'John made a declaration to me, not long before he left. He wanted me to sail with him, to his Orkney home. Now he is suspected, he must find some other path. And I do not believe that he can do so on his own. He is frightened, lost. Therefore, I must go to him.

'If you love me, as I know you do, then you will not attempt to follow, for you will know that to do so will put all our lives in jeopardy. Take heart, and trust me, Giles.

'I am sorry, too, that I could not take Matthew, and he will not have his Minnie when he wakes. But I know he will be well enough the while with Canny Bett, and, of course, with you. He likes to hear you read to him, and he cares not one scrap for Hebrew, Greek, or French, so long as they are spoken to him in your ain dear voice. Then am I well content, to leave him in your hands. He will not miss his Minnie when you are close by. You are half the world to him, as he is all of yours.

'Dearest, as you love me, do not take your troubles out on Paul. He knows not where I am, and he cannot help you. He is not to blame in

245

this, as you, and he, may think. He is a good friend to us both, but none the less deserves a life of his own.'

'What does she mean?' Hew broke off, 'about Paul?'

Giles shook his head hopelessly, 'As it turns out, Paul was not there. He has never been there. He has been disporting with some Jonet Bannerman, while all the while this lovelorn boy was coming to my house. I have dismissed him, of course.'

'You cannot for a moment think that Meg intends to stay with him?' Hew's eyes, though he protested it, were baffled, grey with doubt. 'She would not leave her child!'

'Do you not understand? She could not take him from me, Hew. She left him here for me, a final act of love.'

Hew was quiet then, for he recalled the sadness in his sister's face, her grening for the life that she had left behind. What was it she had said, of Clare and Robert Wood, 'No one ever knows what secrets and collusions are between a man and wife. Some are happy, that seem not; and some that seem the best of friends . . .' Are not happy, she had meant. Surely, she had not referred to her own life with Giles?

'Well then, we shall look for them. We shall call a search.'

The doctor shook his head. 'John Richan is a fugitive. And, if she is found with him, then she will be accused of art and part, complicit in his crime. Besides, she does not want it, Hew. I would not have her back against her will.'

'Then we will wait a while, and trust in her return,' Hew consoled his friend. But as the day wore on, he became less sure.

John Richan had pulled Harry's body clear of the high water. He did not want to leave it in that place, where the devil might have claimed it. Though Harry's heart was warm still, John knew he was dead. The corpse was hard and dense, a solid flank of flesh that took John all his strength to drag clear of the tides. He owed him that, at least, for Harry had that morning dragged him from the pit. John found a

246

quiet resting place close against the cliff. He wiped the weed and silt from Harry Petrie's face. Harry's cheek had cracked and splintered in the fall, and his mouth had slackened, showing broken teeth, but there was not much blood. John had done his best to make the corpse more comfortable.

John Richan understood the tides. He worked his way round to the harbour, clambering over rocks, between the water marks. Most of the boats had gone out with the flood, and would not return for several hours. The haven was still as he passed, slipping unseen by the white-footed cat and inquisitive black-headed gulls. He was at the shoreline before the town above was properly awake. He made his path along those parts the devil called his own. And when the waters turned, he retreated to the cliffs, clambered over rocks, sheltered from the flow in crevices and caves. He understood the sea, and he was not afraid of it, though he could see the sea-trows, dancing in its foam, and heard the mermaids singing, sitting on the rocks. He had heard them in the cavern at the bottom of the pit where their lonely lullabies had come to comfort him. He scented in the early morning salt the sleek skins of the selkies, who came out to sun themselves, glistening through the haar.

He followed closely to the cliff, until he saw the tower and smoke, the woodlands that marked Kenly Green, and then he found a place to climb up from the shore. He crept into the wood, and found a place to shelter, deep among the trees, and crouched as darkness rose, a blank and still new moon across the summer sky. When the last of the pale light was failing, he fled, through the gloom that ushered in the night, through the fading shadows of an avenue of trees, and found his way by stealth to that enchanted place where Meg had kept her physick garden, where the buds were nipped, and heavy still with dew. At the bottom of this garden, he found the cool house and distillerie, quietly detached. The cool house shelves held bottles still, of pickled broom buds, pears and plums. He had not eaten since the night he had spent lying in the pit.

The still house had a furnace, and the means to light its fire, but John feared that the smoke might be noticed from the house. He lit a tallow candle with a piece of flint, and kept his night light low, level with the ground, while he looked around the room for the safest place to sleep. A dark and dragging weariness worked upon his bones, a heavy, cold exhaustion sudden and compelling as a witch's curse. The still house had a cleanness and a coolness that were foreign to him, containing an equipment of uncanny, unknown things; long, lipped phials of coloured glass, flasks and pottles, copper cones. John crept behind the shadow of a kettle cauldron and curled up in a corner, where he fell asleep.

It was chance, after all, that Giles had been called out. Had he not gone out that night, then Meg perhaps would not have left the house. As it was she could not sleep but took the stub of candle up to write her letter in the darkness, several hours before the dawn. She left the letter in the crib; she knew that Giles would see it there, coming from the deathbed that had kept him up, to find a strength and comfort in his little son. She did not like to think of him, returning tired and cold, to find his warm bed empty, his beloved gone.

Though the night was dark, she dared not take the lamp, for fear of waking Canny Bett, sleeping by the fire. She waited till the night was on the brink of dawn before she ventured landward, out into the fields.

And Meg had known, of course, where she would find the boy. She knew, without words, the place that he would wait for her, that place that he had known was closest to her heart. She walked through woods and fields, the well-loved, well-worn path, that she had known and followed since she was a child. But Meg was weary now. The trouble in the town had begun to tell on her, her limbs moved slow and heavily, her head began to ache. She was thankful in the end when she came to Kenly Green, and opened up the door to the distillerie, to sink down to the floor. She saw a white light flicker in the morning wind, the colours of the sun upon the pewter pots. Meg fell to the ground, where the sunlight danced with her, picking out the rhythm of her jangling limbs.

The sunlight woke John Richan from a slough of dreams. For the first hour, he had fallen to a deep and dreamless sleep; then the dreams began. He was buried in the pit, where the heavy earth had squeezed and crushed each breath, each faint fall and flutter in his frantic breast, and where the rush of water filled his heart with thunder and his heart with blood, until the darkness had itself become a sound. He was standing on the sea tower, high and light as air, where the winds came whipping and the sea birds wept. He was fighting with the devil, over Harry's corpse. He woke up on the floor of a magician's workshop, where evil was distilled in glass and pewter pots. Between him and the light he saw her witch herself. The devil had possessed her, and thrawn her like a fish, a limber fair-skinned herring, writhing on the ground. John Richan drew the knife that was hanging at his belt, and crept up to her thrashing throat to cut the devil out.

Nicholas awoke to a cloudless summer day. For the first time in months, he discovered he had slept, restfully and dreamlessly, and woken up refreshed. His thoughts were light and clear. He put the final touches to his George Buchanan, translating the last epigram, of Seneca, on kings. It came in to his mind that he might like to write a prefatory verse, but he dismissed the thought as vaunting, vain and proud. Instead he wrote a line, with plain and simple modesty, inscribing it to Hew, 'first, and dearest, friend', content to quote as epigraph Buchanan's closing words, which he translated into Scots: 'This ilk I tuke in task for thee alane. Gif thou hast lyking of it, I halde me weill content.' I undertook this task for you alone. If it meets with your approval I am satisfied.

When this was done, he went downstairs, and found he had surprised the servants and himself, by feeling well enough to take the air outside. He walked into the gardens, through the gentle breeze, and came to the distillerie, where his presence put to flight the startled Richan boy, who passed him like the wind. Nicholas found Meg, in the throes of the falling sickness, pale lips flecked with blood. He picked her up and carried her, through leaves and flowers and herbs, and brought her to the house, where his good heart gave out.

Meg woke up at last to find both Giles and Hew were sitting by her bed.

'Nicholas was here.'

Giles took her hand in his, but found, for the first time, for all his long acquaintance with and competence in death, that he was overcome, and could not find the words. It was left to Hew to tell his sister then, how Nicholas had given back the life that he had borrowed from her, when she nursed him from the brink in Giles Locke's turret tower. The servants said that Nicholas had brought her to the threshold, writhing like a fish, had carried her as lithe and limber as a child, no shiver of the effort of it showing in his face. A light shone in his eyes, and he stood proud and tall, before he set her down. According to the kitchen lass, who was prone to fantasy, a flight of angels came and swept him from his feet, a delusion that the kirkmen were soon to hammer out. Meg remembered nothing but the smile upon his face, which gentle light had stayed with her until she went to sleep, and softened the convulsions that ravaged through her dreams.

'I came to find the Richan boy,' she recalled at last. 'To warn him, that it was not safe for him to go to Orkney. The falling ill came on, when I was at the still house.' Through all her raft of dreams, dredged up in to memory, she found no trace of John.

'I thought I had lost you, Meg. I thought that you were gone.' Giles took her in her arms.

She looked at him, bewildered. 'Why would you think that?'

Hew left them to their tears, and went down to the laich house, where the servants had laid out the body of his friend. And there he

250

found no part of him, no fragment that was Nicholas, in that worn out place, shabby and discarded, like a suit of clothes, its owner having grown and gone, to finer, better things. He knelt down in the quiet dust and spilled his heart for Nicholas, the childhood friends that they once were, and what they had become. His heart was quiet then. He went into the garden, to the cool house and distillerie, finding life and solace in the plants and trees. In the corner of the still house, hidden in a cloth, he came upon a jar of plums, the relict of the Richan boy, the only trace and shadow he had left behind.

Nicholas, like Hew, was a true child of reform, and entitled to a resting place beneath St Leonard's kirk, in the college chapel where they met as boys. Meg had questioned how a body could find rest, in earshot of a ranting clerk, a loud and heavy thunderer. Hew had smiled at that. 'He cannot hear it, Meg. And the text is milder here than in the Holy Trinity.' It did not matter now. The fragile ghost of Nicholas long since had departed him, what remained was rag and bone, and soon would fall to dust. At Meg's request, he was buried at the far end of the kirkyard, next to Matthew Cullan, underneath the trees. Hew did not object. He understood at last what Meg had always known, that no God in his heaven could have closed his doors against those two good gentle souls, whatever were their differences; that Andrew Melville and his Kirk must bare and bow their heads. In accordance to that Kirk, to which Nicholas subscribed, no prayers or psalms were said, no choir of earthly voices sang them to their rest, but there were sparrows in the rowan, fluting high above, and far across the fields, the mellow calling of the doves, riffling through the yellow corn, came faintly on the breeze.

'We never found the man,' said Hew, 'who disturbed the quiet here. We must make a search for him.'

'We must not,' asserted Meg. 'For he is of no consequence. And there is nothing he could say, to hurt my heart, or harm this place.'

He looked into her face, and saw that it was true.

Chapter 23

A Wicked and a Guileful Mouth

The term drew to a close, and in the last week of July the students of St Salvator's had gathered at the gate, preparing to depart. Meg brought flasks of ale, and fresh baked bannocks tied in cloths, for those who had no horses and were forced to go on foot. The richest brought their grooms and bearers for their bags, and set off at the gallop for their manors, halls or towers. At the new foundation, the reformers had proposed that the vacation be curtailed, to keep the sons of gentle folk from sluggardry and sloth, but, mindful of the cost, the colleges resisted this. Their livings did not stretch to further bed and board. For the poorest college bursars the vacations were a trial, though Giles helped where he could.

Hew had hired two milk-white mares for James and Roger Cunningham, who would break their journey over several evenings, and at several inns. James had joined his brother at the chapel door, where Hew dispensed instruction, letters and advice. Once the students had departed, Meg came to his side. 'Who was that with Roger Cunningham?'

'His brother James,' said Hew. 'Why do you ask?'

'No reason,' Meg said, absently. 'They do not look alike.' She took her brother's arm. 'While we have a moment on our own' – Giles had taken Matthew down to see the horses – 'I would like to speak to you.'

'Not more secrets, Meg,' he teased, but realised in a heartbeat she had something on her mind.

'It is a matter, rather, of discretion. I do not like to mention it to Giles, after all that happened. For I would not hurt his feelings for the world. But I cannot help but wonder what became of John. You have not heard, as I suppose, if he has been found?'

'As I understand it, he has not been found.'

Her friend had disappeared, and left no trail behind. The fisherman at Crail was traced, and had confirmed the Richan boy had sought to buy a boat from him. But he would not confirm that they had struck the deal, or that any bond had been advanced to pay for it. In all events, the case was immaterial, for John had not turned up to lay claim to the boat, the boatman had it still.

'The common thinking,' Hew reported, 'is that he has drowned, his body deep entangled at the bottom of the sea, or he is spirited away, with neither hair not sound of him. And I am sorry for it, Meg.'

'I am sorry for it too,' his sister sighed. 'For then he is condemned, without a trial. I know you will not hear it, Hew, but I do not believe that John killed Harry Petrie.'

'And why do you suppose I will not hear that?' questioned Hew.

'Because I had supposed you thought like all the rest.'

'And when,' he risked a smile at her, 'have you known me do that? The truth is,' he was serious now, 'that I am not convicted of it. If John was in the tower when Harry Petrie fell, then he could not have fired the shot that struck him down. It does not want Bartie Groat's degree of skill in geometrics to work out that the pellock did not come from up above him, but from somewhere on the ground. The sergeant of the guard was doubtless well aware of that, and yet he spoke no word of it, which must throw suspicion on his whole account. Which is not to say, of course, that John is not a suspect, but that we must find proof of where the bow was shot – I would hazard, on the south side of the place where Harry fell. No one saw John there. And since the southern aspect is in clear view of the guardhouse, that gives pause for doubt.

'And there are other questions. How could John afford to buy himself a boat? You telt me Harry Petrie had put up the money for it. Why would he do that?'

'From kindness, Hew,' contended Meg. 'The simplest and most natural reason in the world. Because he was his friend. It is no more nor less than you would do for Giles.'

So much might be true, thought Hew. For Meg, with her kind heart had known John Richan best. And Hew would buy the boat for Giles, without a second thought. But he could well afford to; Harry was a futeman in the castle guard, and could scarcely have afforded, on a futeman's pay, to advance a loan that John could not pay back. What were Harry's *expectations*, telt to Hew by Bess? Was it for the money that he had been killed? And what had it to do with the paper in his pocket, and his dealings with John Colville, the Master of Requests? These questions he kept close, and secretly from Meg, for fear that he would frighten her by mention of the map, which showed the building works in the cellar of her house.

'Is there not a way,' Meg pleaded, 'you can find the truth? For rumour and report are sure to travel after him. The news of the disgrace will follow to his family, far away in Orkney, who will suffer at the shame of it.'

Hew accepted, 'I can try. But ye maun be aware, the truth is not always what we would hope, and is sometimes not what we expect.'

'That danger I can face,' insisted Meg.

'In that case,' promised Hew, 'I will ask the crownar, Andrew Wood, to give me leave to go into the castle, and put further questions, for I cannot think that the archbishop will be willing to agree to it unless it has the sanction of the Crown. The time is ripe, for Andrew Wood is coming here to speak with me today.'

'Then I am content.' Meg hesitated. 'I did not want to say . . . but there is something more.'

'Hm? What more is that?' Hew already was distracted, planning the first steps of his investigation, working out the plat that he would put to Andrew Wood.

'If I tell you something, something else apart, will you give your word, you will not act upon it?'

'I cannot promise that, without knowing what the matter is.'

'Then promise you will think on it, and will do nothing rash.'

'I promise I will think on it,' he smiled.

'The matter then is this. It is Roger's brother James. We have met before.'

'Aye? And where was that?'

'At our father's grave.'

She had his full attention now. His sharp wits working quickly understood the truth of it, but did not want to hear. 'He was at the interment, perhaps. For his father was one of the bearers.'

Meg shook her head. 'It was not at the burial. James was the young man I spoke of, who telt me our father was damned. I wondered how he knew that I was mourning for my father, when he telt me he was sorry, he had lost a father too. Now I understand, and there can be no doubt of it. I recognised his face. But do not blame him, Hew. That poor, unhappy boy!'

Back in his own chamber, Hew packed up his things. His papers, clothes and books were wrapped up in a box, sent ahead by carrier, home to Kenly Green. The light green cushioned sitting chair he gave to Bartie Groat, who received it in a spirit of amazement and affray, to find himself possessed of so delicate a thing. Bartie stayed in college through the summer months, and took solitary suppers in the empty hall, from the last dregs of the barrels and the scrap bags of the grain. Once, Hew had invited him to stay at Kenly Green. Bartie had refused. He was working on a thesis on the mathematick arts, no word of which had ever made it to the page.

Ordering his room brought order to Hew's mind, where Meg's revelation had begun to make some sense. Though he suspected Roger, he had not suspected James; together, it became apparent how their trick had worked. James had been a presence all the while: he had been at Matthew's grave, and in St Leonard's kirk, and to several of Hew's lectures, watching unobserved. He had taken classes also over at St Mary's, had studied ancient texts, and, it now seemed clear, had penned the Hebrew verses pinned to Melville's door, though Hew suspected it was Roger who had put them there. He had no doubt the curses had been meant for him. The boys had set a challenge – a *defiance*, Roger said – designed to drawn him in. They knew that he was vain enough that he could not resist. And James was at St Mary's when the hawthorn bladders burst. At first, Hew had discounted all those at the lecture, lacking both a method and an opportunity. Now he understood that this was a mistake. Suppose that James had slipped away, to visit the latrines? In the crowded stairway, would he have been missed? Suppose he had remained there while the talk took place, and crept out to the quietness, to fire his brother's bow, returning just as easily to drop it in the sink. Roger, Hew supposed, had left the bow before for him, when he brought the bladder in and tied it to the tree, and pinned the Hebrew psalm at Andrew Melville's door. The green lights Andrew Melville saw perhaps were Roger too. Had James sent him back, to find the hidden bow, or had he been disturbed, in some other piece of mischief? On that occasion, it appeared, he had not wanted to be caught.

The younger brother, noticed Hew, had taken all the risks. The lecture hall was full, and it would not be hard for James to stand up on the stair and slip among the crowd as they were coming out. Who could say, for certain, whether he was there? And who could fault a man, if he had been missed, for having the misfortune to be called to the latrines? The bladder filled with blood was plainly Roger's plat, and he had been full proud of it. His brother was the bowman, and the better shot. No wonder James was wary: *please do not tell me he confessed to that.*

The brothers bore a grudge for their father's death, so much was apparent in what James had told to Meg. And what had Roger said to Andrew Melville's face? 'Ye maunna mind it, sir. It was not meant for you.' Then Bartie had been right, the hawthorn was a snare, and all of it was done, on purpose, to catch Hew.

He wondered, to what end? For if it was to remedy, and counter his neglect of them, then they had achieved it, and all to the good, for Roger was much happier than he had been before. But that did not account for the translation of the psalm, which Hew had little doubt was intended as a threat. Was Hew the dark opponent, who had stood at Richard's side condemning him to death? Or was it Hew himself the boys had brought to judge?

His reflections were cut short by the coming of the coroner, who walked in without knocking.

'Are we undisturbed?' Andrew Wood was not a man who wasted time on niceties.

'*I* was,' answered Hew.

'What I have to say to you must not be overheard.'

'There is no one near.'

Sir Andrew Wood did not sit down. This seemed to Hew a natural part of his intent to daze and daunt, and he would not be cowed by it. 'What can I do for you, sir?'

'There are two pressing matters that I must discuss with you,' Andrew Wood replied. 'The first concerns the death of the duke of Lennox. The king is careful to impress upon the common multitude that Lennox died a Protestant, true to his ain faith.'

Hew nodded. 'So much I have heard, in his proclamation.'

'The king does not believe that it will be enough to quell the people's doubts, though it must still their tongues. He wants to put it to the test, in a court of law.'

'That is very interesting,' said Hew, who began to have a sense of what matter was to come. 'But I cannot see how it refers to me, since, as you are aware, I do not practise law.'

'The king is of a mind that you are fit to practise it, if you will or no. I have made it plain enough that I do not agree with him.'

Hew grinned. 'Thanks for that.'

'The king has in his possession Esme Stuart's heart, which it is his pleasure that ye should defend.'

'Has the king gone mad?'

Sir Andrew did not smile. 'I did not choose to ask him that. But his state of mind is somewhat frayed and fraught. I had half a hope that the concerns of his new council might distract him from his cause; unhappily, that has not proved the case. I can tell him, if you will, that I have not found you fit, or that you have refused, but it is as strongly in your interests to accept the case as I doubt it may be to refuse.'

The choice, as Hew could see, was not a happy one. In truth, he had no will to defend the duke of Lennox, whose conversion from the Catholic faith he took to be a fraud, designed to win the confidence and favour of the king. He pondered on a way to stall the king's intention, till such time as James should mellow to a calmer frame of mind.

'Pray tell his highness, though I am not prepared for it, I will give it thought. The duke of Lennox's heart will want a strong defence, and, as I suppose, a sharper wit than mine, and one more fully versed and practised in the law. It will want, besides, a man to go to France, to find the matter out.'

'I am not persuaded,' the coroner said, drily, 'that his Highness is concerned with finding out the truth of it.'

'But he must concede, a kenning of the truth, whatever that may be, is an essential part of the defence. Send him my good will . . . and tell him I will look into the law, and see what can be done.'

'That defence will hold him for a while. Very well,' the coroner agreed. 'I will put it to him it will take you time to forge a proper case, and in that while we may hope that his Grace will think better of this course and come to his right senses.'

'Thank you, sir.' Hew bowed. 'There is a matter, though, that I would like to raise with you, since I have a sense that it concerns the king's security.'

'Aye? And what is that?'

'It concerns the death of a man called Harry Petrie, at the castle here.'

Andrew Wood was silent for a moment. And Hew, who was not afraid to look into his face, was conscious that the words had

258

somehow a struck a chord. He sensed a tightening there, though the expression did not change, that indicated to him that the coroner was listening with a sharp alertness he had not betrayed before. But when at last he spoke, his voice was neutral, flat. 'That death is in the archbishop's jurisdiction. And, I am told, was caused by a young Orkney archer, who has since fled. Why do you infer a danger to the Crown?'

'For I am not convicted that the Orkney archer killed him. I think that Harry's killer may be in the castle still, and may present a threat. Harry was in contact with a man called Colville, that was Master of Requests.' Hew proceeded carefully. Again, he noticed Wood take note, an almost imperceptible reaction to the name.

'What kind of contact?' Andrew frowned.

'That I cannot tell you, sir.' Hew was not prepared to speak about the map until he had established what it meant for Giles. 'But give me leave and licence, and I will find out.'

The coroner said then, 'The man you speak of, Master John, is presently in ward. He has given himself up in answer to the charge that he has dealt with Gowrie, and against the king, and that he did not represent the interests of his Grace, and of the duke of Lennox, honestly and fairly in his embassy to England, which was undertaken during Gowrie's rule.'

'As I understand,' said Hew, 'the king is ill-disposed to him.'

'The more so, because he has maligned the duke of Lennox. Colville's is the voice,' Andrew marked the irony, 'against whose accusations you must make defence, when you put on trial the dead duke's heart. Wherefore, I will give you leave and obtain for you the commission you require to search the castle, on the sole condition that you will report to me, and to no one else. Speak Colville's name to no one, including the archbishop. Do you understand? The king's defence is paramount.'

'I understand you, sir.' Hew could not help but feel a shiver of excitement.

'Then papers will be drawn, and sent to you at once. I leave you to your packing,' Andrew Wood replied. He seemed, of a sudden, anxious to be gone.

'There were two things, as you said,' Hew reminded him. 'What, then, was the second one?'

The coroner let slip a smile, the slightest flicker of his lips. 'I almost had forgotten that. You ought perhaps to know, that someone in the college here has formed a grudge against you. A letter has been sent to my brother Robert.'

'What kind of letter?' questioned Hew, a darker mood descending at the thought of Clare.

'A letter which asserted you had congress with his wife. Can you tell me now there is no truth to it?'

'I swear upon my life,' he answered quietly, 'there is no thread of truth to it. When was this letter sent?'

'It was sent some weeks ago. But I have had, you will observe, more close and pressing matters on my mind. It was, in truth, of small account. The ranting of a jealous child. But there can be no doubt it came from St Salvator's. It bore the college stamp.'

Hew felt sick at heart. He saw Roger's dark head huddled at his desk, and understood the lengths the boys had gone to trap him, plotting from the start to catch him in their snare. The full force of their feud against him now was made quite clear to him, and for a second he forgot the fears he had for Clare. He struggled to compose himself. 'I believe I know what person sent the letter. It is a student here, who feels I owe a debt to him. Forgive me, sir, I cannot say his name.'

'Then I must take your word on it, and leave it to your conscience to avenge.' Andrew watched him narrowly. 'The pity is, that Robert had dismissed it as a fraud, until his wife confessed to it.'

'I do not believe you, sir.' Hew curled tight his fists. He saw that Andrew Wood intended to provoke, and swallowed back his rage. He did not, for a second, think the worst of Clare.

'What devil has he done to her? If he has done her hurt . . .'

260

'Clare is safe and well.' Sir Andrew Wood appeared to smile, and Hew conceived a hatred then that he had rarely felt.

'This passion, sir, will do you no good grace, sin it reveals the workings of your heart,' the coroner advised him. 'I did warn you once, that you were too attached to her. But have no fears for Clare. For sin she is a woman, and she is his wife, Robert has concluded she is not to blame in this.'

'For certain, she is not to blame. You must inform your brother that the letter is a lie.'

'So I should have done, sir, had she not confessed to it.'

'She did not confess to it!'

The coroner regarded him, with shrewd and careful scrutiny. After a moment, he nodded. 'It is possible, I doubt, that Robert has invented that, to press the charge against you, and enlist me to his cause. Leave it in my hands, and I will speak to Clare, and if there is no truth to it, will plead your case to Robert. What action would you bring against the letter writer?'

'And it please you, give me leave to deal with that myself.' Hew scowled.

Sir Andrew shook his head. 'You are a stubborn tyke. Aye, then, as you will. I will leave you to make peace of the muddle in your mind, for, as I perceive, there is confusion there.'

Hew's mind, it was true, was thick with clouded thoughts, but though his mind was dark, he saw through clear enough. His thoughts had turned from Clare to James and Roger Cunningham. At the start of the next term, he would call them to account. Most likely, when it came to light, they would be expelled. Both boys were distracted by their father's death, but Hew was shaken to discover just how deep that went. This was more than a call for his attention, but a calculated plot, that had worked for his destruction, and he could not let it pass. The boys must have a hearing that was full and fair, whatever was the consequence for Hew. And if they were combined, a fierce destructive force, by setting them apart, could there be a chance for either boy? Giles might speak for Roger, since he saw the good in him. Andrew Melville too, perhaps, might agree to counsel James. Hew dared to hope the boys would see the wrong they did. For, if they could not, then they were living testament to Andrew Melville's tenet that a man's end was decided in the moment he was born, and Hew, for all his faith, could not believe in that. Or else they were the instruments of that unruly Fate, that lifts a man up high, to spin him to his ruin.

Sir Andrew spent the night in town, at his brother's house. For though they were not close, there was a pact between them, certain business interests that they kept and shared. Robert had the wealth and Andrew had the influence to press those interests home. Andrew had brought wine from the inn in Huckster's Wynd. He poured a draught for Robert, but declined to drink himself. The servant brought in supper, and the two men dined alone, on salmon in a green herb sauce, for Clare was lying down. They spoke of business at the mill, and politics at court.

'How does the king now?' Robert asked.

'He is fretful still. He has reconvened his council, and dismissed those lords, that he perceives did move and act against him.' Andrew's tone was flat. He never had disclosed the side that he was on, nor whether he approved of Gowrie's prudent government, which left his brother Robert both intrigued and irked. No right thinking man could fail to see that Gowrie had done service to the king, however harsh the means by which he had effected it. Now James was free to deal again with parasites and flatterers.

'And the earl of Gowrie?'

'Gowrie he has pardoned, for the while. But since his Grace has taken up again with some of his old friends – Arran in particular – he may change his mind,' Andrew answered, neutral still. He reached across the board, to fill his brother's glass. 'I heard tell that the English queen is sending an ambassador to remonstrate with James, displeased with these events. She takes it ill that he has chopped and changed his Privy Council, without consulting her.

And while she will not say that he should have been held against his will, yet she is convicted that they had his good at heart. She warns him too against the earl of Arran. Her man will speak her mind. And you may be assured, the king will not like that.'

Robert took a sip. 'Aye? What man is that?'

'She sends, as I have heard, a man called Francis Walsingham, that is her privy secretar. An old man in his dotage, and of no account. The matter is, his coming will not please the king. We may see trouble yet.'

'Ye are well informed,' Robert answered sourly, jealous of his brother's closeness to the court. I do not dare to ask the source of your intelligence. I doubt you are too occupied with wiping James' arse to trouble much with matters closer to your home.'

Andrew shook his head. 'I have not forgotten it.'

Clare joined them after supper, sitting close to Robert, quiet by the fire. The colour, life and energy had wilted from her cheeks. Andrew Wood had seen the bloom of pregnancy transform his wife Elizabeth into a dew-eyed blossom, blowsy and full blown. It was not a transformation that he cared for much, but he knew it boded well for the prospects of the child. He saw no such bloom in Clare.

'I was sorry,' he remarked, 'not to see you here at supper. I hope that you are well.'

She did not raise her eyes. 'I thank you, sir. I was not well. But I am quite well now.'

He dared to ask her, 'And the child?'

Clare stole a glance at Robert. 'As I think, the child is well. I have felt it quicken.'

'Robert tells me,' Andrew said, 'it will want a foster mother.'

Clare did not look up. 'So I understand.'

'It is quite common,' Robert said, 'to put a bairn to foster, when it has a mother neither well nor fit for it, as has proved the case.'

'Indeed, it is quite common,' Andrew Wood agreed. 'I have spoken with Elizabeth, and she will take the bairn, to bring up with her own, if ye should so please. Our youngest child is not yet weaned, and she has plenty milk.'

Clare looked up at that, but it was difficult to read the expression on her face. 'To bring up in your house?'

Robert was drunk, and increasingly belligerent. 'I have no doubt Elizabeth will thank us for the money, now that the king will be racking up new debts.'

Andrew did not rise to this. 'It was kindly meant.'

'Your kindness, sir, were better spent in seeing to your charge. It is harder for a woman to recover fit and well, when the cause of her disgrace remains at large and liberty, and vaunts about the town. You do not keep your promise, sir. If you will not contain him, then I must myself.'

'Patience,' Andrew smiled. 'Learn to play the long game, Robert. For that young man has slipped his head into the hangman's noose; a little patience now, will make secure the knot.'

Clare turned white at this, and presently excused herself.

When Andrew too retired to rest, he found her waiting by his bed. 'You should not be here,' he said.

'Robert will not ken, sin he is dead drunk. I would that he were dead.'

'You do not mean that, Clare.' He touched her on the cheek, and she shrank back a little.

'He will take the child.'

'But it will not be lost. I will take it to Elizabeth.' His voice was cool and practical.

Clare nodded. 'Then I must thank you for that. It was none of it, you see, what I had intended. I wanted Robert's child. I came to ask you what you meant about the hangman's knot?'

'Words. To keep your husband quiet,' he assured her.

'I do not believe you. For you do not say things that you do not mean. I want to have your promise that no harm will come to Hew.'

Andrew shook his head. 'I cannot promise that.'

264

'I have no will to hurt him, Andrew,' Clare pleaded. 'He is quite blameless in this.'

'Aye? But you confessed.'

He was quite detached, like a man of law, setting out a case. Perhaps it was a test, or he believed it too. He very seldom showed to her the workings of his heart. Clare would not be beaten by him. 'That was a mistake. Robert tricked me to it. For I did not fully understand the question that he put to me. I do not dissemble well. I am not like you. But you should be aware, if you will not help Hew, then I will tell the truth.'

Roger lay down with his brother in the Dysart inn. He was stiff and weary from the hours spent on the road. He was not used to riding; nor was he as athletic as his brother. The bed was rough and thin, and he suspected, far from clean. Below they heard their fellow travellers, drinking after hours. Roger crept in closer next to James.

'Wid ye stop wrabiling?' his brother complained. 'Keep your vermin to yourself.'

Roger closed his eyes, and thought about the teeming life that squirmed among the sheets. 'There are fleas in the bed here.' Maybe, he could catch one, and keep it in a jar. He could fill it up with blood, and feed it till it burst.

'Nae more of your filth.' His brother pinched him sharply, promising a bruise. There was comfort, still, in lying next to James. The older boy had taken time to notice him. But when he did, he had admired his brother's subtle skill, his cunning and his craftiness, his deftness with a knife. He and James were partners, and a perfect team.

While other students slumped in taverns, chased in caichpells, played at golf, Roger's play days were spent working at the flesher's block; on carcases and specimens dissected in his room, slitting through the lamplight in the midnight hours. The bladder had been delicate, and difficult to fill, but Roger had perfected it, through a little spout. Though he had taken care to map the path of flight, he could not be certain that the ball would burst. His brother had achieved it, with a perfect shot.

The hardest part, for Roger, was to keep his counsel close, and not to take the credit for the cunning of his trick. Though it pleased his pride to have defeated Hew, it vexed him to the core that he dared not point this out.

James said, 'I did not see your friend, when we were setting off.'

'He went home early, to Dunkeld. His father is not well.'

'Your little friend is fortunate, in that he has a father still.'

James could be overweening, sometimes, with an elder brother's insolence. But he was bigger than Roger, and more ready with his fists, though he was not as clever. James could not have thought up the bladder on the hawthorn tree, and, if he had thought of it, could not have made it burst without Roger's help.

'He will not have one long.' Roger felt a sudden pang, and fondness for poor George, who had left the college looking quite forlorn. He was thankful Robert Wood had not taken his advice, and weathered him with stripes, since George's future prospects now seemed bleak enough.

'Doctor Locke has said,' Roger changed the subject, 'that if I work hard and acquit myself well, he will recommend me for the course in medicine at the Collegium Scoticum, in Paris. He lived there, at the Rue des Fosses, and shared a room with Master Hew.'

'You silly little bairn,' James snorted, 'you will never be a doctor.'

'That is all you ken. I do not see why not. Professor Locke has promised he will ask our mother. And also, he has said—'

'All that will count for nought, when he kens what you have done. Do ye think that he will keep you, when he knows you wrote that letter that was meant to hurt his friend? The same friend that he lodged with in the Rue des Fosses, and that is his own wife's brother? He will not want to ken you, when he knows what ye have done.'

Roger felt a cold fear gripping in his bowels. 'He will not ken I wrote that letter.'

'Puir sad fool. Of course he will.'

'I thought ye would approve of it.'

James allowed, 'I might've done, if ye had used more subtlety. You should have asked me first.'

'I do not think the letter ever got there,' Roger said. 'For naught has happened since. And Master Hew is free, an' gangs about, an' that.' He said a silent prayer, sorry in his soul for the letter he had sent, and not just for himself; for deep inside his heart, he knew that he liked Hew.

'We will hope so, then,' his brother answered generously, 'and give some closer thought to what we ought to do to him, when we next return. Ye must proceed with subtlety.'

'Must we do more?' Roger asked.

'We have just begun.'

Roger lay still for a while. He felt his brother's breath, gentle, at his side.

'Will I go to hell for the things that I have done?'

'I have telt you before,' grumbled James. 'You do not go to hell for the things that you have done, but because God has forsaken you. And if he has forsaken you, he did it long ago, the moment you were born. And if he has not chosen you to be in the elect, ye cannot go to heaven yet, however hard you try, and whatever good you do.'

'Suppose, though,' Roger said, 'that he wants me to repent?'

'It is too late for that. And, do not forget,' his brother warned him, crossly, 'this was your idea.'

'Was it? I do not recall.'

'Of course it was. For you were ay the clever one. Father thought so too. You were left at home, when our father died. You saw what hurt was done to him. You telt it all to me.'

'I do not remember.' Roger felt confused. The horror of that moment he had blotted from his mind. 'I thought he had laid charges, foul and falsely, at our father's door. But mebbe I was wrong. I did not understand it. I was just a bairn.'

'You did not have it wrong.'

'You did not tell me, then, that he had paid our fees.'

'Aye, and out of guilt. Your fee will not be paid, when we have destroyed him. You must make that sacrifice, for our family's sake.'

Roger was alarmed at the venom in his voice. 'But by paying for us now, he may make amends. He may be a friend. Suppose we let him, James? He could find you out a living, when you go into the Kirk, he could pay my fees in France. I could be a doctor. Is that not enough?'

His brother answered fiercely, 'It will never be enough.'

James had been in St Andrews when his father died. The St Leonard's principal had told him what had happened, hurriedly and clumsily. James had felt at fault. He had made the journey home to find his mother desolate, and his brother and his sister in a parlous state. He had gone for comfort to the high kirk of St Giles, and kneeling down to prayer, had found his cheeks were wetted with a flood of heavy tears. The kirk at that time was split in several parts, one of which had served the prisoners in the tolbooth, and the vicar of that quarter caught him at his prayers.

The minister had said, 'Courage now, my laddie, wherefore dae ye greet?' A kindly sort of man, he had clapped him at the neck, in something in between an embracement and a slap.

'I am sending up a prayer, for my father, who has died.'

'What faith were ye brought up in, lad?'

James had opened up, confiding in him then, 'The true reformit kirk. I am a student at St Andrews, at the college of St Leonard.'

'Then ye should be ashamed. For you ken well eno' ye cannot save his soul,' the man had railed at him. 'What was your father's name?'

James had mumbled something, sorely sick and shamed.

'Ah did not catch ye, laddie. Was he from round here?'

Their house was just a stone throw from the high kirk and the tolbooth, from the place of execution and the earl of Morton's head. Roger had spent hours there, sitting in the gallery, drawing with a pen. Their mother burned the sketches, and he made them all again.

James had faced him, then. 'His name was Richard Cunningham.'

'*That* man.' The minister had spat, on the floor of his own kirk. 'Then ye maun pray to God, that ye be not accursed, and your seed as well. For I can tell you plainly, *that* man is in hell.'

'You cannot ken that,' James had insisted. 'You cannot claim to know the Lord's will. A man may do wrang, and be saved at the last. He works in mysterious ways.'

'Oh aye? Do not presume to preach God to the Kirk. For I have seen enough men die, to ken when one is lost to God, fated fae the first. Better that the sinner never had drawn breath, than that he should have lived to sow his foulsum seed. Now, son, wipe your tears, for there is no amending it.'

This kindly man had given James a little book of psalms, which he had taken home, and taken to his heart.

Chapter 24

High Water

Andrew Wood left Hew with little time to brood, for the next day he sent letters authorising him to act on his behalf in all inquiries pertinent to Harry Petrie's death. Hew came in to the castle on the first of August, which was Lammas tide. His overtures were civilly if warily received. 'Go where'er you will,' the archbishop allowed. 'My people and my palace are at your disposal.' The coroner's commission had already done its work, and Adamson was eager to appease the king. Hew was left to wander through the castle grounds. He remembered with a strack of sorrow Harry Petrie's tour, his keenness for the stories and the secrets of the stone. Harry's map had centred on the south east front, which seemed as good a place as any to begin. The wind was warm and light, and gentle through the colonnades, the pale sun glancing softly from the painted glass, the stench of Patrick's fedity all but washed away.

Hew had no real sense what he was looking for. He recalled that Harry's tour had kept him on the ground, and resolved to go upstairs, and look up in the gallery. But he began with the old fore tower on the eastern flank, which Harry had informed him was the first part to be built, and which had been prominent in Harry Petrie's map. He climbed up to the upper floor that linked the bishop's quarter to the first floor chapel, through a series of small doors, with one or two dead ends. The floors were built at several different levels, joined by wooden ramps or by low stone steps, to form a thoroughfare. The inner space was furnished, with a small lettrin, camp bed and chair, and in a recess on the left, which Hew supposed was once a door, a narrow shelf of pens and books, above a wooden box. Hew pulled out this kist, but found it bare inside. It covered up another gap, reaching back beneath the floor, where his fingers closed upon a piece of cloth, which opened to reveal a pile of little stones.

Hearing footsteps on the stairs, Hew wrapped up the stones and put the parcel back. As he pushed back the kist, the bishop's clerk appeared, wrinkling up his nose to hold on to his spectacles, flaffing with his hands. 'I beg your pardon, sir, but his lordship sent me to inquire if I might be of help to you,' the clerk said, blinking rapidly, 'now that I have done with taking down his letters. Is there anything that you would like to know?'

'Can you tell me who this room belongs to, sir?'

'Well, sir, to his lordship.' Ninian looked perplexed.

Hew rephrased the question. 'Who stayed in it last?'

'Well, that is hard to say. For with the coming of the king, all is disarranged. But in general, it is used by the sergeant of the guard, for he likes to keep a close watch on the bishop.'

'Yet as I suppose,' guessed Hew, 'these books will not be Tam's?'

'The books? Ah, no, indeed. Those are some books that belong to the archbishop, that he likes to keep to hand. Psalters and such, for when he is not well enough to climb up to the library.'

Patrick had his study in the small retiring chamber on the western side, which he could access easily, without recourse to stairs. His prayer books, Hew had noticed, he kept by his bed. Why would he leave others, in the keeping of his charge? Hew took one down and opened it. A narrow strip of ribbon floated to the floor. Ninian snatched it up.

'Sir, may I speak plain?' He made low his voice. 'These walls have eyes and ears, and there are guards above. There is a present danger here that I dare not disclose. For there are goings on no Christian man can bear, and I am much embittered at it, fearful for my life. As I am part to blame for Harry Petrie's death, and sent that puir man out, my heart is full with it, and I will take that burden to the grave.' His clouded eyes grew damp at this affecting speech. 'But it will ease my conscience to explain it to you now. Ah, that puir soldier, sir! The most civil man among them, in a pack of fiends! Tam Fairlie is a devil, sir.'

'Now why do you say that?' Hew noticed that the clerk had snaffled back the book, and slipped it on the shelf. The ribbon strip had disappeared, through some sleight of hand.

'For if John Richan were at fault, then twas Tam that drove him to it. Turned the laddie's mind. You did not ken, I suppose, that he put John down in the pit, the night before he fled. The same day that he died, Harry pulled him out. His puir wits must have left him, when he fired that shot.'

'If he fired it,' murmured Hew. 'The shot came from the ground, and somewhere close to here.' His thoughts had turned to Tam. If Tam had put John Richan in the pit, then it was no wonder Ninian was afeared of him. And, if that were so . . .

'But if it was not John, then none of us is safe.' Ninian flapped and twittered, like a frightened bird.

'Is there something that you fear, that you do not like to tell me?' Hew pursued him gently.

'On my life, not here. For there are echoes carry in these hollow chambers. You would be astonished sir, the crevices and channels that deceive the unsuspecting. For one such as myself, who cannot see full well, these hollows all are filled with high attendant dangers; thankfully, I hear, and am alerted to their sounds. No Christian soul may prosper here; for all it is the bishop's house, it is the devil's too. May I crave your pardon, sir, and ask you one small question, praying for your patience, if you find it strange? Was there any object found on Harry's body, that was out of place?'

At this, Hew's ears were pricked. 'What sort of object, sir?' He examined Ninian closely, scrunched behind his spectacles, squeezed on like a vice.

'A piece of clothing,' Ninian said, which answer Hew had not expected. 'That some soul may have kept, as a kind of charm. In short,' for Hew was baffled now, 'I mean to say a sock.'

272

'A sock?' repeated Hew.

'Aye. Just so. So short, so silk, so blue.'

'I believe not,' Hew admitted, for his mind was on the map that they had found in Harry's pocket. He knew nothing of a sock.

'And such was not found on the shore, or down among the rocks.'

'Not to my knowledge.'

'Then perhaps it washed away. Listen!' Ninian froze, and Hew heard a small sound, that might have been a mouse, or the flutter of a bird, somewhere high above.

The little clerk knelt down. 'It is not safe, for there is evil here, a dark kind of magic. They will harm me, sir, and I should not have spoken of it. There are witches here.' Ninian's voice was fraught with terror, shrill and highly charged.

'Is there somewhere we can talk, where you can feel safe? My sister's house, perhaps?' suggested Hew.

'I cannot let them ken that I have come to you,' Ninian fumbled helplessly, 'and there is no place near . . . but there may be one place, where the fearsome covenant will not dare to follow, if on hallowed ground.'

'Then I will meet you,' Hew suggested, 'at the Holy Trinity.'

'I do not dare consort with you, in a public place. Rather,' Ninian pleaded, 'let us meet tonight, in the grounds of the cathedral. The archbishop is invited out to supper at the priory, to discuss the king's expenses with the earl of March. I shall slip out after dark, with a ticket of account I shall say he has forgotten, and will meet you by the gate. If Tam Fairlie is on watch, it may be after ten, for I would not have him find us for the world.'

'Aye, if it will please you,' Hew accorded, kindly. He had come to the conclusion that the little clerk was mad.

Hew retreated from the castle to the house of Meg and Giles, with whom he shared a quiet supper in the nether hall. The building work was finally complete, and the nether hall returned to its former light and glory, with the apothecary's cabinet given pride of place.

273

Hew was taken down to see the new distillerie. The entrance had been moved from the kitchen to the trance, and a wooden stair installed. In the cellar down below there were windows to the Fisher Gait, level with the street, and a furnace at the back, vented to the yard, where Giles had made a cool house from a little shed. In a corner of the room was a wooden compost bed, for heating up the simples to the first degree, that gave the place a mellow, earthy smell. There were several pottles, vessels and alembics, wrought in varied shades of pewter, clay and glass, and a shiny cone of copper, pointed at the top. The walls and wooden floorboards had been painted white, and the walls were lined with shelves, with bottles of stilled waters, unguents and oils. The old walls and partitions had been taken out, opening up the whole of the footprint of the house.

'The space is more than twice the size it was. Here we are, you see, below the front part of the nether hall, which was quite closed off before,' Giles explained to Hew. 'The floorboards are uneven here, which is a little vexing.' He gestured to a gentle dip, where the boards appeared to sag. 'The workmen found it hollow, when they laid the floor; we thought it very likely the first lot of builders caused it, digging out the earth, and filled it up with powder, rubble and sic stuff, and all the muck and debris that they did not care to shift. I fain would call them back, and have it levelled properly, for though it is quite safe the boards begin to give a little, which has spoiled the look. But Meg,' he spared a fond glance to his wife, 'was not all that keen they should begin again.'

Meg came to his side, and slipped her hand in his. 'The works are perfect, Giles, and perfectly complete. And where there is the hollow is just right for the great pottle, which sits nicely in the bowl. Now come you both upstairs, for it is time to eat.'

They settled in the nether hall, where Canny Bett had set the table with a bright green cloth, and Meg served buttered haddocks in a mussel broth. The fish was fresh and succulent, the mussels sweet and pink. Matthew Locke was wakeful still, and settled in his father's arms as Meg fetched bread and cheese.

'Did I tell you,' Giles asked, proudly, 'he has spoken his first word?'

Hew swallowed down his scepticism, with a fine white wine.

'That is quite remarkable. What word did he say?'

He looked upon the prodigy, who met his frank gaze stolidly, with wide, mistrusting eyes. Whatever word it was, he would not say it now.

'Ba,' Giles said triumphantly.

' "Ba"?' repeated Hew. He wondered, for a moment, if he had misheard, but a glance at infant Matthew's fair impassive face suggested he had not. 'And "ba" is a word in what language, precisely?'

Giles admitted, 'That, now, is the question that has troubled me all day. I have come to the conclusion that it must be Hebrew. I tried him with a grammar of that ancient tongue, since his mother has complained when I read to him in Greek. Now the danger is that he becomes a Melvillite,' he concluded, gloomily, 'and I must put him straightaway to a course of Cicero, before it is too late.'

'You cannot really think he spoke to you in Hebrew,' Hew objected, pouring out another cup of wine.

'On balance,' Giles said seriously, 'I believe he did. I have, however, one small nagging doubt. For it is faintly possible the word I heard was *bab*, in which case it was Scots, and he was speaking of himself. That is some concern; I hope he will not grow up to think himself the centre of the world.'

'Matthew is assuredly the centre of his world, and certainly of yours.' Meg brought in a tart of cherries on a tray, with oatcakes, cheese and bannocks and a pot of cream. 'I have telt him,' she confided, 'that all babies babble, but he will not heed,' and she helped her husband fondly to a piece of pie.

'He is not all babbies,' Giles said, slightly huffed. 'He is Matthew Locke.' He brightened at the cherries spilling on his plate, sticky, sweet and plump. 'If and when ye must eat fruit – for Meg believes we must eat fruit, it is a country quirk of hers – then eat them red

275

and cooked. Matthew is the subject of a proper fit experiment. Did ye ken that James the Fourth was a linguist of some aptitude, a man of many skills? He put two infants on an island with a nurse who could not speak, to see what language they would end with as their natural tongue. And some say they spake Hebrew, though that could not have been possible. An interesting experiment, albeit deeply flawed.'

'For certain, it was flawed,' laughed Meg. 'They had no mother with them.'

The hour struck ten o'clock, and Hew prepared to leave. 'I have some pressing business that I must attend to. Though I may be out late, I am not going far.'

'By all means,' promised Giles. 'But what is your business, Hew? Might it not be dangerous? Shall I come with you, or will you take Paul?'

'There is a set of non-sequiturs,' smiled Hew. 'For if there was a danger in it, I would not expose you to it, and Paul would be a hindrance, rather than a help.' Giles had pardoned Paul for his neglect of Meg, and he was once again made welcome in the house, though he would not stay long, for he had pledged his troth to the widow Bannerman, and Jonet had accepted him.

'No, and no, and no. I am well convicted that there is no danger. Hang out a lamp at the door, for the night is a dark one.' Hew left them to their loving quarrels and the comfort of their board, content that all was well with them, and the little house.

It was a dark night indeed, for the new moon gave no light, and the lamplight in the streets was pale and intermittent, pooling on the cobbles in a wash of grey. There were lanterns at the castle, at the taverns and the cookshops, and over doors and windowsills the smoke of yellow candles smudged into the gloom, a weak and watered light. Hew walked up by the North Street, where the lights were stronger, and away from the impenetrable darkness of the cliffs. At the old inns of the priory, where the archbishop went to supper with the earl of

March, the cloisters were well lit, for the earl had marked the passage with a row of brazen lanterns, lined against the wind with little panes of glass. The lanterns tapered out on the north side of the church. Hew entered at the furthest wall, where the walls were breached, in the shadow of the great cathedral, stripped bare of its grandeur, and its roof. He found an upturned stone, and settled down to wait.

At the castle, Ninian Scrymgeour felt in great fear for his life. He had used the bishop's closet for the third time that evening, knotting and untangling the thin string of his belt. He found it oddly comforting to hold it in his hands. The closet felt to him the safest place, though of course the bishop had no kenning that he used it. When Tam had found him there, he had been so afeared that he had shat himself. He had not thought that Tam would foul that private place. But Tam had no respect for either man or Kirk.

He spent so long at his stool that he was almost late, and he did not see Tam Fairlie coming from the hall, with butter saps and honey for his little lass. Tam glimpsed Ninian's shadow as he scurried past, and set down his plate. 'All quiet, here?' he asked the guard. The soldiers in the guardhouse packed away their cards, and tried to sit up straight. 'A' quiet, aye. His lordship isna back.'

'Did I not see, this moment, someone pass the gate?'

'Maister Ninian Scrymgeour ganging to the priory, for ter bring a ticket that the bishop had forgot.'

'Ah, is that is a fact? A muckle fearsome venture for a timid clerk.' Tam Fairlie rubbed his beard, and buckled on his belt. 'I doubt I will go after him, and see the fazart safe.'

The half hour had already struck before the clerk appeared. He was carrying a staff, and a little lamp of horn that cast a sallow shadow on his frightened face. He put his fingers to his lips. 'I fear that I am followed. Do not make a sound.' Hew could hear the wind, and the slow swell of the sea, as it grumbled at the cliff, clamorous, insistent, for the tide was coming in. The water filled the darkness, drowned out other sound. Ninian Scrymgeour fled, his horn light darting faintly, from the precinct walls. Hew cried, 'Ninian, wait!' and followed the shy light out to the Kirk Heugh, towards the ruined chapel of St Mary's on the rock. There were lights far below at the harbour, where beacons burned brightly to guide in the boats that came in by night on the incoming tide. And at the castle, too, a pinpoint prick of lamplight, steady as a heartbeat, flickered from the parapet, moving round the tower. Between them was a blackness, deep distilled and dense, and deep within this darkness Ninian's horn lamp danced. Hew cried out again. He kept close to the track, and one hand on the wall. He saw the faint light stop, and picked out in the gloom the old kirk on the rock, to which he felt his way, carefully and stealthily. He stepped into the shadow of the old kirk's weathered footprint, reaching out to Ninian. There the light went out.

Ninian's cries were dulled by the clamour of the sea, and Hew could not identify the place from where they came. They were perilously close to the sharp edge of the cliff, and in the muffled darkness, Hew could sense the drop, the transitory falling in the flood of sound. 'Where are you, Ninian?' he called. His own voice resounded, hollow and strange.

'Help me! Murther! On my life!' Ninian's words came far and faint but Hew heard footsteps somewhere running.

'I will go for help.'

In answer came a scream that splintered the night air. Hew dropped to his knees, and feeling through the darkness, found the blown out horn lamp, next to Ninian's stick. 'Call to me,' he cried. 'Cry out; I will find you.' Ninian gave a moan, tremulous and pitiful. Hew used the stick to probe, feeling for the ground. He could see a little light that was mirrored in the sea from the beacons at the harbour, and he attempted to look out among the shadows of the cliff, looking for the place where the little clerk had slipped, as he saw shapes and movement in the heavy darkness, and began to find his bearings in the thunder of the waves. He heard a whistling at his back, like the drawing of a breath, and something struck him hard in the middle of his neck. It struck him to the ground, or where the ground had been.

The rushing of the sea, or the rushing of his blood; he could not tell at first which it was he heard. The chapping of the sea sent a light spray at his back, lapping at his heels. His left foot came to rest, on a shelf of rock, his right foot dangled loose, and could find no place. Both hands wrenched and gripped, in grass and leaf and mud, and clung and burrowed hard into a clod of earth. He felt against his skin the sharp face of the cliff and clung to what was hard, fearing what was not. He dared not turn his head, and knew he could not move. 'Help me,' he cried out.

And, to his relief, the little clerk appeared, and he had lit the lamp again, and held it in his hand.

'Dear me.' The clerk set down the lamp, and knelt upon the ground, to reflect on Hew's predicament. 'I cannot rightly think what I ought to do. You see, I left my spectacles, and that was why I fell. I do not see too well.'

'If you give me your hand, I can pull myself up. But I cannot hold on here for long.' Hew heard the water, close at his back, the swell of the sea, as it broke on the rock.

'That will not do. For I am, you see, such a very small man, and I have not the strength of a young man like you. But I have a better idea.'

Hew did not see, from the slope of the cliff, as the little clerk pulled out his knife, but he felt the blade prick, and the warmth of his blood, as Ninian stabbed blindly at both of his hands. He reacted from instinct, as well as from pain. His left hand gripped hard at the red clod of earth, while he straightened and lunged with his right, and grasped at the little clerk's belt. As he clung to it hard, it came loose in his hand, and the little clerk fell, soundless and down, a heavy cross wind that blew at Hew's back. Hew closed his eyes as he felt his life slip, and his foot and his hands and his heart working loose, as strong fingers grasped and gripped at his wrists, and lifted him up, like a child. He found himself thrown on a soft patch of ground where he clung for his life to a pair of thick boots.

'Sweet Jesus Christ,' Tam Fairlie said. 'Wad ye have me over too?'

He pulled Hew to his feet, where his legs gave way, and held him at the cliff edge by the collar of his coat. 'Not the devil's chance.'

In the sullen lamplight they saw Ninian's broken body dragged out by the ocean and returned upon the rocks, tossed upon the shadows of the restless sea. Tam picked up the hemp that had fallen through Hew's hands. 'This is Ninian's belt.'

But it was not a belt. It was a shepherd's sling.

Chapter 25

Private Lives

'Do you mean to say that you have killed my clerk?'

'I did not kill him. He tried to kill me.' Hew was shaken still. His legs had given way on the way back to the castle, and the sergeant of the guard had all but had to carry him. Tam had marched him straight to the bishop's chamber, where the bishop in his nightcap scrutinised him now. Patrick was not pleased. His household was in jeopardy; the king would not look favourably upon a second death, and it was more than likely that the castle would be forfeit, if he could not keep it safely for the Crown. He had lost two futemen, and a privy clerk, and given up his physick wife, a source of some regret. The physick wife must die a grim and futless death, and he must look elsewhere to satisfy his needs. He was working on a sermon to extol the duke of Lennox. He doubted whether James would think it warm enough. How could a man be glowing, when a cold hand gripped him, grappled in his bowels?

'Ninian, a murtherer? That timid, mild, sweet man?'

Hew showed up the sling. 'This was Ninian's belt. It is the meek man's instrument. Like David and Goliath.'

Patrick answered irritably, 'I have heard that story, sir. My clerk, ye may recall, could not see past his nose. Then how do you suppose he found the target for his stone?'

'In truth, I do not know.' Hew glanced back at Tam, who had saved his life, and left his help at that. It was hard to fathom what the sergeant thought, what he had observed, or was prepared to tell. He had heard Ninian's cries, of *help me!* and *murder!*, and he had seen

281

Ninian go over the cliff, like a stack of onions rolled up in a sack. The stab wounds on Hew's hands were evidence of sorts; but the clerk might have inflicted them in simple self-defence. Hew could not predict which way Tam's mind would turn.

The bishop had come home from an unrewarding supper, to be woken by his sergeant as he settled down in bed. The rummle of the fish plat rippled through his bowel, and resurfaced, salmon-like. Adamson excused himself, retiring to his closet. Within a moment, he emerged. 'It seems my privy secretar has made free with my closet, discharging there a privilege that I did not bestow. He has left his spectacles.' He held up Ninian's glasses in their leather pouch. 'I daresay in the darkness he had little use for them, for there the blind man is advantaged and surpasses other men.'

'Not so little use,' said Tam, 'as he has for them now.'

'May I see those?' Hew took up the spectacles and pinched them to his nose, squinting through the candlelight, to see the world as Ninian had, thickly through a slab of glass, hoping to cast clearer light upon the clerk's distorted mind. For what must it be like, to see the world so darkly? What he saw astonished him. 'Were these his only pair?'

The bishop confirmed it. 'He was, you understand, a man of simple means. His eyes had grown quite weak. A villainous affliction, in a privy secretar, for it was a trial to him, to read and write a letter. I kept him out of charity.'

Hew returned the spectacles. 'Then look, sirs, if you will.'

It was Tam who saw, and put the facts succinctly. 'This is plain clear glass.'

Patrick said, bewildered, 'Why would a privy clerk put out he could not see?'

'That, sir, is a question.' Hew moved back a step, and began to look around.

The chamber was divided by a light partition, lined with panelled oak, that sectioned off the closet in the corner to the east. Access to the privy was provided through the corridor, which linked it to the fore tower on its southern side, and to the little room where he had found the books. The partition-wall of oak was in line with Patrick's bed, but Hew did not remember seeing it before.

'Is that panel new? I do not think I saw it, when we came with Andrew Melville.'

The chamber had been stripped since then. The walls and floor were bare, and the scent of rotting sweetness – of the hawthorn bough, thought Hew – had finally dispersed. He remembered, too, the crown of hawthorn blossom hidden in the rock, that Tam had taken from him, dropped into the pit. The castle stone gave up its secrets, randomly and one by one, like the coloured shards of glass that were thrown up on the beach. Ninian had killed Harry, with his shepherd's sling. And why had he done that?

Patrick answered, 'Aye, there was a cover on it then. A tapestry of silk. It was sent out for repair. The castle was refurbished for the coming of the king.' He surveyed his lodging gloomily, counting up the cost. 'The lords that slept here said the hangings harboured dust. There was, ye may recall,' he gave a little cough, 'a staleness to the room, that wanted airing out. The servants took the arras out, to shake it at the parapet, and there it was discovered there were muckle holes it in.'

'What made the holes?' asked Hew.

'Wha devil should I ken?' the archbishop countered testily. 'Some monster of a moth. The tapestries are old, no more than scraps of threads; the holes were at the top, and in the darkest parts, and over the dark panel never would be seen, though they were fat and muckle ones.'

'Big enough,' Hew pressed, 'for a man to peep through?'

Patrick stared at him. 'What kind of a man would be peeping through a tapestry?'

'A filthy one,' smirked Tam.

'And it please you,' Hew suggested, 'Let us look into your closet. We may find the answer there.'

283

It grieved the bishop's heart to take a prying company in to that secret place, which no man ought to share. 'Ye maun take a candle there,' he agreed, reluctantly. 'It is dark inside.'

The entrance to the closet was a heavy woven curtain, opposite a window looking out towards the town. The window could be opened, and the curtain flattened back, to allow the wind to draft in extra air. Tam Fairlie did so now, letting in the blackness of the summer night. He brought in a lamp to supplement the candle sconces on the far stone wall, and set it on the ground. Inside were Patrick's privy stool – his dry stool covered with a cloth – his laver and his water pots, and two or three more resting places, where a man might sit and think, at peace and at his ease. A corner held a hassock, where he bared his soul, and the back wall marked the place, underneath a canopy, where he bared his body, in the wooden bathtub kept beneath the stairs.

Hew took up a stool, of the ordinary sort, and explored the wood partition that faced back to the room, feeling at the top of it. It did not take him long to discover and dislodge the panel that was loose. From his vantage on the stool, he could see quite clearly to the bishop's bed. 'I think you had a keeker, hiding in your closet. A most perverse and inward sort of spy.'

Patrick's face turned several shades, from puce to grey to bilious green, before he squeaked indignantly, 'Whit kind o' man wad spy upon a malade in his bed? A sair and sickly languisher?'

Tam Fairlie answered with a snort, 'Whit kind o' man, indeed? And you think that this keeker murdered Harry Petrie?' he inquired of Hew. 'Why wad he dae that?'

'I think,' reflected Hew, 'that mebbe Harry caught him in the act, of something that he was not supposed to see. He appeared to think that Harry had something of his; he mentioned a blue sock.'

'I ken naught of that,' the archbishop answered quickly, 'and I'll warrant, nor does Tam.' The two men swapped a glance, and the sergeant shook his head.

'Then it remains a mystery. For no such sock was found. I think he had a secret cache, in the chamber next to this.' Hew led them back in to the tower, and opened up the cubby hole. The piles of stones had gone. 'Well, we have his sling, and that must be enough. This was his room, I suppose?' He looked back at Tam. 'He telt me it was yours.'

'The lily-livered shite. This was Ninian's place. It gave him ready ingress to the bishop,' Tam retorted. 'And a pleasant view. I caught him in the closet when the physick wife was here, but thought that he had come to have a shit.'

Patrick cleared his throat. 'Indeed, I see it all. And what kind of a man,' he squawked, 'would take his pleasures so, to watch a sick man in the throes of strained and desperate remedies? I am sore aggrieved, that we have been deceived in him. Speak nothing of this, sir,' he beseeched of Hew, 'for it is an old man's shame, to be spied on in his bed. I will send a letter to the earl of Orkney, to warn him that the Richan boy may not have been the villain that we had supposed, and you may tell the crownar that the case is closed. Now, sir, it is late, and you have had a close escape. God speed you to your rest. Tam will take you down. But pull the curtain, pray!' He sank down to the horror of it, in his feather bed, leaving Tam to close the drapes, and blow the candle out.

It was several days before Hew fully understood what Ninian had been spying on, and why the bishop had insisted that the case was closed. Justice took its course. The physick wife was taken up and accused of witchcraft, brought back to the castle to await her trial. Her name was read in kirk. And he remembered then the cloudless summer's day when he and Meg had met with her, coming home-ward with the May, dizzied, drunken, black and bruised, and she had lifted up her skirts, and mourned her blue silk sock.

Alison was not afraid at first. At first, she had supposed that it was one of Patrick's games. And why would it not be, when they put her in that place, the hollow quiet cell, with the window to the sea, and the narrow bed of stone? She expected, fully, Patrick to appear to her, dressed as Little John, or a mummer from a masque, or in his bishop's gown. He had not been at the kirk, and Alison was sad at that, and had to face alone those dour and dreadful men. There are three types of kirkmen, Patrick might have said, and of all those types, those elders at the session were among the worst. She wished that he had been there, to explain it all to them. But, for several days, she kept faith he would come. Patrick was like William, who came back still, in the night, and for many years, after he was dead.

After several days, she began to fear that she would not be fresh for him. She wondered, after several more, whether he lay sick, or otherwise distracted, that he did not come to her. In between her wondering, she sang, or wept, or prayed, depending on her mood. She lay down on the bed of stone, and when she fell asleep, dreamt strange and fitful dreams, befuddled and bewitched by lack of warmth and food. In the morning, when she woke, she found that he had left her things to eat and drink, in the angled cubby hole where she had put the hawthorn crown. The hawthorn crown had gone; she worried he was vexed at her, for throwing it away. But surely, all the world must ken, that no one but a libber brought the hawthorn in a house. Sometimes, there were other things, a flower, or stone, or shell. And once a piece of coloured glass, from the chapel window washed up on the beach, worn smooth by the sea. Alison held up the glass, and let the sunlight fall upon it, painted blue and green. It might have been the cassock of a long dead saint, or a piece of water, thrown up on the storm. It was not the emeralds and sapphires he had promised her. But she took it for a token she should not lose hope. Fine things would be hers, if she could be patient now. She put the stones and the shell and the piece of coloured glass into a little pile, and when a seagull feather floated to her windowsill, she put that in as well. She looked forward to the gifts another day might bring.

Patrick, in the meantime, was otherwise engaged. It was a source of some regret to him that there must be a trial, for he could not be certain what the witch would say. Tam had scoured the castle, looked in every crevice and in every crack; he had not found the sock. He wondered if the Richan boy had squirreled it away. Patrick preached a sermon to appease the king, on a crowded Sunday at the Holy Trinity. It was not a great success. He telt them that the duke of Lennox had kept to his faith, and had died a Protestant. To illustrate his point, and give it further force, he brandished the duke's testament, a rolled-up piece of parchment borrowed from his desk. A woman in the front row saw it and called out, 'I have seen that paper, sir. I sent it ye myself.' The wife was Tibbie Strachan, married to the dyer, and the paper was the bill for his May Day coat; he would never dare again to dress as Robin Hood. He had too much on his mind to spare a thought for Alison, or to stop to wonder how she spent her days.

Help came, at last, by night, and from a longed-for source that Alison had not expected, had hardly dared to hope for, in the long dark days. Tam, who first had brought her here, whose sweet face smelt of wood and smoke, came to let her out. The sentry on the tower was lying sound asleep, for Tam had slipped a potion in his evening drink. He would find a rough awakening at the changing of the guard. The loss of Harry Petrie and the Richan boy had left the section short, and Patrick filled the gaps with lubbers from the street, hiring by the hour, to help keep the watch. The man on guard tonight had not been hard to dupe, already in his cups when he took up his post.

Tam had helped her out, shivering and blinking, to the moonlit square. He locked the door behind her. 'Dinna mak a sound.'

He stilled her cries with looks, and with his own thick hand, clamped across her mouth. 'Still, ye silly wench, and ye would be free.'

She wriggled in his grasp, like a captured bird, beating her shrill wings against his soldier's back. At the ladder to the sea he unclasped her mouth a moment, to unlock the gate, and her shrieking had aroused the bishop in his bed, had it not been for the wind, and the black thrust of his fist, to shut her up again, that left her on her knees, weeping as she clung to him.

'For God's ain pity, Tam, do not cast me down there.'

'Listen,' he closed his hard fingers tight round her mouth, and turned her face to his.

'You have two hours, till the tide comes in; by then you must have found your way around the cliff, and tak your carcase clear, and where ye gang from there then God alone may ken, but make it far from here.'

Her eyes were wide and wild. 'Ye want me to climb down there?'

'If you will save your life.'

But I cannot, Tam, ah, do not make me. It is the place where that soldier laddie fell, that sweet bonny red-haired soldier. Tis cauld, Tam, and dark, an' I cannot climb.' Alison clung to him.

Tam shook her off. 'I can put you back right where I found ye, or I can leave ye here, to fend fer yerself, an' ye can find your ain way out, then God speed and good luck to you.'

'Where is Patrick, Tam? Why does he not come?' The physick wifie wept.

'Ye dae not get it, do you? Twas Patrick did accuse ye, and cried ye for a witch. Cauld are ye, now? Then bide where ye are, and let the fire tak ye, and ye may be warm enough then.'

She understood at last, and climbed onto the first rung of the ladder, cowering close into the jagged stone. Her face was wet with tears. 'I cannot dae it, Tam. Ye maun help me back.'

But Tam had locked the gate, and gone into the night.

The rough tongue of the wind lapped and leapt at Alison, lifting up her skirts. She clung to the hard iron of the ladder, unable to climb further either up or down, until her fingers stiffened, bone white in the darkness. Inch by inch she shifted, edging her way down, pressed into the shadow of the jagged cliffs. At her back she heard the water, flowing still and smooth. Her sobs were carried seaward, borne on taunting winds, like wicked boys that nipped her, snatching at her clothes.

The witch was noticed at the harbour, clinging to the rocks, ship-wrecked and sea-green, rising from the waves. She was witnessed, briefly, passing through Boarhills. From there, she disappeared.

Patrick was called out at dawn, to an unpleasant scene. The sentinel was doubled up, spewing in the courtyard, opening up his belly to the scornful wind. 'Something that I ate.'

'He was drunken fu,' Tam Fairlie grumbled. 'I doubt the lusty beggar took his flagon tae the watch. He will be sorry o' it now, an' the deal the sorrier if I had the charge of him. For even the Richan boy wis better than this trash.' He felt, in truth, an absent fondness for the hapless John.

Patrick stepped a little sideways, upstream of the spray. 'He is a hireling?'

'Aye, sir, an' God kens, no man of mine. This is the trouble when ye put your trust to outlanders. Have I not always said it?'

'Ceaselessly, Tam,' Patrick groaned. 'When he has done with vomiting, send the beggar home. Dismiss him, without pay. But all is well, I hope? That is, with the witch?'

'She is quiet,' Tam admitted, 'that is no like her. I think it were well that we did look in to her.'

'*You* will look in to her,' Patrick corrected, loath still to come up too close.

'She is confined now, and no cause to fear her,' Tam assured him.

'Wha spake about fearing her? Naught is to fear but the sight and the stench of her. Damn it, man, open the door!'

But when Patrick saw inside, he felt sore afraid, and sickened in his heart. There was nothing in the room but the little ring of objects – stones and flowers and shells – that the physick wife had used to make her magic spell, and a feather from the bird, on which she must have flown.

When Tam Fairlie came at last to lie down in his bunk, he found his little daughter curled up fast asleep, and wrapped in her fist he saw something blue. He shook the bairn awake. 'Up, now, slugabed.'

'Daddie.' She clasped her thin arms tight round his neck but still did not open her palm. He lifted her up, and into his lap, and opened her fingers out, counting each one. 'What have you there?'

She poked out her tongue at him. '*Mine.*'

'It is not yours. Where did ye find it?'

She giggled at him then. 'It was in a hole, where the wee man kept his things, the wee man with the spectacles, that wis the bishop's clerk. He thocht it was a soldier took it, an' he threw a stane at him.'

'And how wad ye ken that?'

'I saw him,' she said simply. 'I wis in the gallery.' She snatched out at his fingers. 'Daddie! Gie it back!'

He held it out of reach. 'And you have kept it, all that time?'

'I thought that I might give it to the lady in the sea-tower,' she admitted, candidly, 'but it is awfy bonny though. I thought that she would like it, though, for she is awfy sad.'

'You saw that lady too?'

'I heared her greitin through the wall. I gave her things, for she was sad.'

He smiled at her. 'She liked the things.'

'And is she not sad, now?'

'She is not there now. And that is a good thing. For here is no place for her.' Tam felt the child's breath, hot on his neck, the warm, sticky grasp of her hands. 'Do you mind I telt ye once, that your mother has a sister, that lives far away? Tomorrow, I will take you there. She will have you stay with her.'

The little girl said fiercely, 'I will *never* stay with her. I will stay with you.'

'You will stay,' said Tam, 'wherever you are put. I cannot keep you here with me. Tis no place for a lass.'

Chapter 26

Friend and Foe

September came, and Paul and Jonet Bannerman were married at the kirk of Holy Trinity. Hew gave Paul a brand new coat of sea-grey coloured silk, and lent his home at Kenly Green to hold the wedding feast, out of sight and censure of the spiteful kirk. Meg came early in the day to dress the house with coloured ribbons, sweetmeats, fruits and flowers. The miller's son had sent a piglet, and the smoke of roasting pig flesh, on a bed of early pippins, spiralled through the tower.

When all the wine was drunk and all the songs were sung, when Paul and Jonet Bannerman departed for the little house where they would spend their married life, and Meg lay down with Matthew, falling into sleep, Giles discovered Hew, sitting by the embers of an early autumn fire.

'You are quiet there.'

'I was thinking,' answered Hew, 'what kind of horrors work their wrack upon a poor man's mind, that he should turn the world askew, distorting what is true and kind, as though he saw life thrawn and twisted, through the devil's optic glass.'

'You mean Ninian, I suppose?'

'Aye, Ninian,' Hew agreed, though it was James and Roger Cunningham he had had in mind.

Giles settled down beside him in a high backed chair. 'I have given it some thought. Ninian was suffering a foul sort of affliction. He took his pleasures inwardly, spying on the bishop and the physick wife, which, as I suppose, excited and revolted him. He was both stirred up and repulsed by the feelings it provoked. It was almost as if that fedity of Patrick's seeped into the stone, corrupting all it touched. Ninian's own weak will could prove no match for it. It fanned and fuelled his lust.'

'Andrew Melville is enraged,' reported Hew, 'that Patrick has escaped the sanctions of the Kirk, though it is common kenning he is an adulterer, who consorted with a witch, and allowed her to escape. He is out of reach, under the king's protection, and survives unscathed.'

'Not quite unscathed,' said Giles, 'since Alison escaped. The king has put the castle back into the keeping of the provost, to secure it for the town, and Patrick and his crew are out upon the street.'

Hew raised a smile at that. 'Tam Fairlie too, I hope?'

'Tam Fairlie too,' Giles assured him. 'He was Patrick's man.' He had watched the little party trundling from the gate, from the window of his house, with a certain satisfaction.

'Then my heart is glad at it,' said Hew. 'Although he saved my life. Ninian telt me Tam put John Richan in the pit, and that Harry pulled him out, on the morning that he died. And though that may have been another lie and subterfuge, put out by the clerk, it has the ring of truth to it, and is the kind of cruelty I can well believe of Tam. And, if that were true, what terrors then were wrought in that poor boy's mind, when he made his escape?'

Giles tutted. 'Keep that close from Meg. I believe it too. For it explains a fact that I had not accounted for. The skin was stripped back raw from Harry Petrie's hands, as though he had been grappling hard to grasp the rock, though he was dead already when he fell.'

Hew was silent then, to think of Harry Petrie falling from the cliff, and the frightened Richan boy, who had dragged the body safely from the sea, in service to his friend.

'Ninian,' Giles observed, 'was well placed to look in upon an unsuspecting world, pretending all the while that he could not see. His case is interesting. I read a story once, in the *Flowers of English*

History, about a young queen of the May who rode naked through a town. A man peeping out at her, with low and lewd intent, was blinded at the sight. A cautionary tale and a curious parallel, to Ninian's own delinquishment, patterned in reverse. Perhaps, when I have time, I will write a pamphlet on it. Ninian hid his secret even from himself, and was prepared to kill, to spare it coming out.

'His pleasures were embodied in the charms he kept – the ribbon that you found, and the witch's sock – which were emblematic too, of his sense of guilt. If Harry took the sock, then he would have to kill him, according to the reasoning of that sad disordered mind. Harry found him out, and blackmailed him, perhaps, accounting for the money he had promised for the boat.'

Hew was not so sure. 'Ninian was a poor clerk, and had none to give. And I do not believe that Harry blackmailed him. Though Ninian seemed to think that Harry had the sock, it was never found. I think that Ninian saw him searching in the tower, where Harry made his map, and mistook his purpose there. Which begs the question, what *was* he looking for?'

Giles admitted, 'Ah, I had forgotten that,' and his face fell a little.

'Put it from your mind,' encouraged Hew. 'You never saw the map, nor ken of its existence.'

'I am touched at your concern for me, Hew. But it is hard to put it from my mind, when it shows the workings in my house. Have you no further light on what it means?'

'Harry had a passion for the stories of the stone, and must have known of secrets there, that went back many years. Then you do not suppose . . .' Hew saw the lines of worry etched in Giles' face and broke off with a sigh. 'It does not matter now. For Harry took his secret with him to the grave. Whatever was his purpose, only Master Colville knows, and since Colville is imprisoned, and in peril of his life, I do not think it likely he will choose to tell us.'

When all the guests had gone, Hew found himself bereft. He mourned the loss of Nicholas, whose life and breath were patiently distilled within each quiet measure of the stone, consoling in his father's death, and wondered how so light a trace could leave behind so sound a gulf of absence in the house, so deep a draught of emptiness. He mourned the loss of Clare. And there was nothing here that could quicken his sad heart, or move his restless spirit to a new excitement, the adventure that it craved, or hold it fast with love. Meg and Giles and Matthew Locke had forged a solid band that would not, at his parting, threaten to unlock, and would still be as strong for him, whenever he returned. Hew resolved to go abroad; to Flanders or to France, to travel through the world, as a free adventurer. His spirit stirred and lifted at the thought. He would stay in town until the start of term, to see what he could do for James and Roger Cunningham. And though he faced that prospect with a heavy heart, he would not shrink from it. Then he would resign, and give his place in college up to Bartie Groat, so that Bartie's future would be safe assured, when the reformation made its cruellest cuts.

The serving lass supplied the last part to his plan, coming from the garden with a basket full of plums. 'There is sic an abundance of fruit, I cannot start to think what we will do with it. The kitchen wants direction, from the hand of Mistress Meg. Do you not think, sir, that her coming here breathes life into the house? Her little babby, too. Without her, it will wallow to a bitter wind. Or the fruits will all be wasted, gross and overblown.'

Hew agreed with her. He spent a solemn afternoon with his man of law, his steward and his factor, who looked after the estate. And, when they were done, the whole estate at Kenly Green, the house and all its lands, belonged to Meg.

'We will not tell her right away, but will stay upon a time, when she cannot well refuse,' decided Hew. He slept that night content, and quiet in his mind.

The next morning, Hew was woken by a loud and frantic hammering. The house was full of men, and the coroner among them. He knew, before they asked, what it was they looked for, and he offered up the book with Harry Petrie's map. 'This is what you want. Now please go away, and do not alarm my servants.'

Sir Andrew took his time. He opened up the little book, Buchanan's Latin verses.

'You are fond of George Buchanan,' he remarked.

'I admire his Latin. He was master here, when I first came to St Leonard's. He left in my first year, to be tutor to the king.'

'The king himself does not recall those years with fondness.'

'Yet,' suggested Hew, 'he has the learning now to appreciate the verse. Buchanan was a forbidding scholar to a first-year student; to a little boy of four, he was doubtless a ferocious one. When the king is older, he will look on him more kindly.'

'Perhaps.' It might have been a careless conversation, with an acquaintance passing on the corner of a street, were it not for Andrew's men, who were tearing down his books, and the weeping of Hew's servants, herded in the hall. The coroner retrieved the map, and nodded, satisfied.

'There is no call,' he called in his men, 'for this destruction, none at all, and if one of you will break a glass or cause affray to ony servant as he gangs downstairs, then he will make amends for it. One of you maun bid the groom to saddle up a horse, for Master Hew will ride with us, when he and I are done here. Something more dependable, than that stubborn dun horse he has chosen to affect. It is time that hobbie is put out to grass.'

'They will not harm Dun Scottis?' Hew was moved to ask.

Sir Andrew smiled at him. 'Why would they do that?'

On the way to town, the charge was put to Hew. Master John Colville, entered into ward, had for the last few weeks been caught up in a fever, and too ill to speak. Now he had recovered, he had made his plea. He had sworn to the justice clerk that Hew Cullan of St Andrews, had brought to him a map, and had tried to sell it to him. The map marked the entrance to an ancient shaft that ran below the castle from the doctor's house. Hew Cullan meant to use this trance to undermine the king, and restore him to the captors he had lately fled. Colville, so he said, repenting of his fault, had refused to take a part in it. Had he not been unwell, he would have spoken up at once. He was speaking of it now, as proof of his devotion and loyalty to the Crown.

'It was Colville's map, and Colville's plat and crime,' protested Hew.

'So much you might say. And so I might believe, if the map had been with Colville, and was not with you.'

Then Hew understood. When Colville found he could not have the map, he had made sure that it stayed safe with Hew, and made Hew his security.

'His name is on the paper.'

'Where he will say you wrote it.'

'I found the map,' protested Hew, 'on Harry Petrie's body.'

Andrew stopped his horse, and turned to stare at him. 'Did you? Did you, Hew? Then I am surprised that you did not mention that. For did I not ask you, expressly, to come to me with aught ye heard of Colville? Anything at all.'

Then Hew was lost for words. For he could not reply without exposing Giles, and he began to see that things did not look well for him. They came to Giles' house, where more of Andrew's men already had begun to open up the floors. If they found no shaft, then the whole account would be called back into question. If they found a shaft, then Hew would straightaway be taken into ward. The charge would be of treason; so much was assured.

At the small house on the cliff, the men had lifted up the slabs, and were sifting through the earth of the floor to Meg's distillerie. Giles and Meg stood watching them, white-faced. Hew spoke up at once, before Giles had time to think. 'I found a map of this place on the corpus of the soldier, Harry Petrie. And I have sworn, of course, that you were not aware of its existence.'

Meg looked at her husband. 'Giles . . .'

But Hew had made it certain Giles could not protest, in drowning out the truth of the defence his friend could make for him; nothing he said now was like to be believed. And Hew had little hope the shaft would not be there. There had been a tunnel; Harry was aware of it. It was the secret in the stone. He had been being looking for the entrance on the castle side. It was somewhere by the fore tower, somewhere by the fosse. He was looking still to find it on the day he died.

Andrew murmured, 'Close, I think.' A surveyor was brought in, to make the house secure. He lay down on the floor, which had opened up a crack. 'Go softly now, and bring the light.' He squinted through the gap. 'Aye, there is a shaft. I cannot say how deep, nor how far it goes. There is rubble in the hole, and a mass of heavy rock. The tunnel has been filled. It looks like ancient works. I heard a story once, that a mine was built to undermine the castle, following the siege when Cardinal Beaton died. But that was long ago, and I did not believe it.'

Hew remembered Harry's tale of the killing of the cardinal, the hanging of his carcase like a pennant from the tower. The siege and mine that followed he had crucially left out. He looked into the hole, and felt Sir Andrew's hand as it closed upon his shoulder. 'We will dig down deep. But you, my friend, will not be here to see.'

Once Hew was placed in ward, Sir Andrew rode to Perth, where he met the king. James was fretful still, and moved around his court, fearful to be captured if he stayed still for long, subjecting all around to his habitual restlessness, no sooner off the boat than packing up again. He brought with him a long and weary trail of dogs and cooks and furniture that followed him uphill. He had, Andrew saw, a high colour to his face, marking a mood of precarious excitement. He was laughing, as Wood entered, with the earl of Arran, but did not seem to take much pleasure at the jest.

As the coroner approached him, James dismissed the earl. 'Later.'

For a moment, Arran looked as though he would object, before he took his leave, with a light kiss to the air, and a slight bend of the knee. He caught Sir Andrew's eye, with a slanting insolence, that clearly spoke, 'No secrets, sir. For all that you reveal to him, he will tell to me.'

James was shrewd enough to wait until the door was closed. 'Well?'

'There is a mine shaft, Sire. It is not new, but part of an old plat to break in to the castle.'

James shuddered. Since he had report of Colville's confession, he was thrown once again in a perpetual fear, that he was undermined. 'Then we were deceived, most hideously and treacherously, in the man Hew Cullan.'

'So it would appear. He had asked to speak with you, Sire.'

'Speak with me?' The king's voice rose shrill, 'I will not hear him Andrew, do you hear? I will not listen to his smooth persuasive words, allow him to deceive me with his serpent tongue. Let him go to his trial. He is a traitor, a defender of traitors, never to be trusted, never to be heard. To think I had entrusted him with Esme's heart! No matter,' he retracted, 'for I am persuaded that was not a good idea. Arran thinks the people would be like to laugh at it.'

The coroner smiled grimly. 'On this occasion, Highness, Arran may be right.'

'The archbishop made a sermon on it, and the people laughed at him. In truth, I do not think that Patrick Adamson is a good vicar in Christ. I have sent him away, for a cure. Yet,' reflected James, 'he telt one idea of his, that we may commend. Hew Cullan has a good plot of land, that belonged to the archbishopric. When he has been broken, Adamson shall have it back, and offer up its profits to the Crown.'

The king was playing, all the while, with a bauble in his hand, a marble or a stone, for he was ay a fidgeter. He loosed his hand, and let it slip. It fell on to the ground, and Andrew picked it up.

'Keep it,' the king said. 'It is irksome to me.'

The stone in Andrew's hand turned out to be a ruby. 'It is a pretty thing.' Andrew had the measure of the king. He knew when to ask, and when to hold his peace. He stood and waited now, and in a moment James' passion broke out.

'It is a reproach to me. I will not be reproached.'

Sir Andrew waited still.

'There was lately here an Englishman called Walsingham, that is the queen's own secretary. A whining, carping man, that sought to tell me how I ought to keep my court, and how to wear my crown, and I telt him – you may be sure, sir, that I telt him, that I am the king, and that it is my crown, and I will not be spoken to by blustering old men.' The king became less certain now. 'And I will not be spoken to by queens.'

Sir Andrew said no word to this. And in the silence that ensued, the king's colour darkened, and he bit his lip.

'I had put by for him, respecting his commission, a ruby in a ring. Now the earl of Arran has telt me, that seeing my displeasure at the talks with Walsingham, he took it for a jest to seize upon the ring, taking out the ruby, and replacing it with glass. Which is a fine jest, but in my heart, I own, I cannot think it politick.'

'Suppose,' suggested Wood, 'I took this stone to Walsingham, and put the matter right again?'

'Aye? Would you do that?' The king accepted eagerly. 'I think that would be best. You are a good friend, Andrew, and have ever been, for you are quick to see and understand our mind. You will find that man staying at an inn, somewhere in the town. You cannot miss the inn,' a brief smile crossed his face, mocking and incredulous. 'His car will be outside; he came here in a coach.'

The inn, as James predicted, was not hard to find. In the yard outside, where most men kept their horses, Andrew found a coach that had caused a blockage filling the whole street. It was not the coach itself, nor the English footmen who were left to guard it, that had blocked the road, but the massing crowds who had come to marvel at it, the little boys who leapt at it, and plagued the guards with stones. It took the coroner some long while to work his passage past. For all that, as he passed, he paused to steal a look at it, its wrought-iron wheels and shaft, and polished shanks and roof. The windows were obscured, with heavy velvet cloths.

Sir Andrew Wood gave his name and found himself admitted to a private chamber, where he came at last to see Sir Francis Walsingham, a man with whom he had had detailed correspondence, going back some while, yet whom, until this moment, he had never met. He saw a sallow, sunken face, a frail man in his early 50s, sick, beyond a doubt, but by no means in his dotage, of a keen intelligence, shrewd and sharp in mind.

Walsingham said, 'What do you want? You have courage, coming here.'

Andrew placed the ruby on the board in front of him.

'And what is this? A change of heart?' the Englishman inquired.

'I think, rather, it is a mark of the king's trust in me.'

Walsingham nodded. 'Keep it that way. Was there aught else?'

'A favour I would ask. For the man Hew Cullan.'

'Ah, now that's a pity,' Walsingham replied, 'for the qualities which have led that young man into this parlous position, are precisely those qualities which did recommend him to us. We should well have liked to bring him to our cause, since we have lost Colville, and most likely Fowler.'

'Hew is the perfect replacement for Fowler,' Andrew argued. 'Since his father was a Catholick he can move among them and he will not be suspected. He has lived in France. And since his faith is strong, there will no danger he will be corrupted.'

'Aye, his faith is strong. But he is stubborn, as I think, and as you say, he will not be corrupted, so I think he will not turn for me. Besides, it is no matter now, for he cannot be freed from his predicament without hurt to Colville. For the service he has done I must attend to that. We will support Colville's account, and entreat with the king to secure his release. And, if we do that, we cannot sue for Cullan.'

'As I understand,' Sir Andrew nodded, at the answer he expected. 'Yet suppose that it were possible to secure them both?'

He explained his plan. The secretary's eyes narrowed as he heard, and then grew wide with disbelief. 'A frantic plan is that. It is preposterous. And it will not work. Tell me, what worth is this young man to you, that you should take such trouble with him?'

'It is a complex family matter,' Andrew said.

Walsingham accepted, 'That I understand. We are all of us bound in such ties. My daughter Frances lately has been married. It is, I am aware, an advantageous match, and yet I have my doubts on it. We all of us are bound up in our children's fortunes, and must help them where we can. They are our weakness, and also our strength. Very well, sir, let me think on it. I will send word. I will leave on the 15th, and will not stay that day, for any living man. Here, take this stone, for I have no use for it. I will, of course, commend your kindness to the king.'

Sir Andrew took up the ruby up and slipped it in his pocket. He would give it to Elizabeth. Or, perhaps, to Clare.

In Andrew Melville's house at St Mary's college, a council of war was in progress. Melville had unlocked the door securing his apartments from St Mary's wynd, on the western side, and the small band of conspirators had entered, one by one, secret from the porter at the gate. The conspirators made up an unexpected company: the phlegmatic Bartie Groat, the cowardly Robert Black, Melville and Giles Locke, who no one had supposed would set aside their differences to share a common ground. The common cause was Hew.

Melville, true to form, had drawn the line at Meg. His principles would not admit a woman in the house, whatever was at stake. But he had intimated kindly and civilly to Giles that he was willing to console Meg on the prospects for Hew's soul, if the outcome of the trial was not as they would like, and Giles was civil in his answer: he did not think that would help. They could not meet, of course, in the small house in the cliff, which was in the process of a thorough excavation, and it was too far to walk to Kenly Green.

The four men were resolved to march upon the justice court, demand to see the king. For all their wit and courage, and their faith and hope, their four sharp minds combined, most poignant and most searching in the Christian world, could think of no defence they could apply to Hew.

Hew would have been amused, and touched, to see his friends unite for him. But at the present moment, he was not dismayed. He was kept in the whitewashed cell, where Alison had slept, and provided with lights, writing things and books, a pillow and a blanket for his bed. These courtesies, he knew, were thanks to Andrew Wood; his gratitude to Wood did not extend to trust, but he was thankful, nonetheless, for he would not have liked to have languished in the pit. The solitude and quietness allowed him to reflect. When Andrew Wood returned, he was prepared for him.

The coroner brought papers with him in a leather case. He came straight to the point. 'I have made inquiries. Your story of John Colville is borne out. He dealt with Harry Petrie, and the map was made for him.'

'Then Colville has confessed to this?' asked Hew.

'He has not confessed, and I think he is not likely to. The map is his insurance,' Wood explained.

So much Hew had understood, and worked out for himself. 'But since he has confirmed this, you can inform the king.'

'It is not as simple as that.'

Hew answered Andrew quietly. 'I thought that might be so.' In the hours that he had spent waiting in the cell, he had realised that the map had never been intended as a threat against the king, for Harry Petrie had begun it many weeks before the king had thought of coming there, when first he saw the works in Giles' house.

'Who was Colville working for?'

Against the western tower the sea began to swell. Hew had grown accustomed to the rush of tides, that battled and withdrew. Sometimes, in the night, he was woken by a force that drowned and muffled thought, and sometimes by the lull of a still and deathly quietness. Now, he felt the thunder quicken in his heart.

'He was working,' Andrew said, 'for a man called Francis Walsingham,' a candour in his voice he had seldom shown before. 'An Englishman. Colville sent reports, on divers different things. Harry spied for Colville in the castle, reporting on the bishop, Patrick Adamson, and some dealings that he had with the earl of Orkney.'

Hew shook his head. 'John Richan thought that Harry was his friend,' he concluded sadly.

'Aye? Perhaps he was. Do not suppose, Hew, that these matters are not clouded by affairs of friendship, love. By matters of the heart. For often those things are the very things behind them, are the moving force. Until ye know the cause, ye shall not judge. For whatever reason, Harry made the map to send to Walsingham. Harry was himself, I think, the force behind it, and the English had no cause, particular, for wanting it, but Harry had a passion for the secret of the stone, and Colville saw no harm in letting him pursue it. In truth, the harm was caused by the bishop's clerk; the map came to light at a delicate time, and Colville had no choice but to protect himself.'

'And all this, you will tell the king?' Hew suggested, drily.

'You know that I will not.'

'I asked you once,' said Hew, 'whose man you were. You would not tell me then. Will you not tell me now?'

The coroner replied, 'You may recall I told you then, that you were being watched. It was Walsingham that watched you. He followed your adventures when you were in Ghent and he is well disposed to bring you to his cause. He can save you, Hew.'

'And what would make you think,' Hew responded coldly, 'I would choose to deal with him? I never was, nor chose to be your man, and I will not become an English spy. I will take my chance, and tell the king the truth.'

Andrew Wood said quietly, 'I do not think you will, for two reasons. For the first, I am all you have here to protect your family. I have telt the king that they have had no part in this. But it will not be hard to sow that seed of doubt. Indeed, I am persuaded that it has been sown. And for the second,' he reached in the case he carried at his side, 'you are Colville's insurance. This, sir, is mine. It was taken from your house at the time of your arrest. There were witnesses enough that you may not deny it. Perhaps you will remember it?'

Hew recognised at once the paper in his hand. It was Nicholas' translation of the George Buchanan, his diatribe against the tyranny of kings.

'This is a work that the king detests. He is very tenderly at present, when it comes to works that claim that a king should be constrained; he has had it banned. You, sir, have had it translated from a language that contained it to the provenance of scholars to one that will disseminate it to the common multitude. That, beyond a doubt, is an act of treason.'

'It was nothing meant . . . a task for a sick friend.'

Sir Andrew read aloud, ' "This I have done, for thee alone." Those words are enough to see you safely hanged. And so you see, my friend, you have little choice.'

Hew insisted hoarsely, 'I will take my chance, and see you at my trial.'

'Then you are a fool, and I leave you to your prayers. Perhaps, you ought to ken,' was Andrew's parting shot, 'that the wily Patrick Adamson has laid claim to your house, and after you are dead, he will have his hands on it. What sir? Smile at that?'

'It is the witch's curse. But Patrick will have none of it. I have no house or land. I gave it all to Meg.'

'Ah, you have been clever then. Though you must be aware,' the crownar pointed out, 'your foresight will be taken as a mark of guilt.'

He closed the door on Hew, and left him to the trouble of a restless sleep, where presently he woke, and found his darkest fears, that were not for his life, but for Giles and Meg.

At night, Hew was taken from the castle on the cliff by a band of the king's men. He was strapped to a horse and his hands were tied behind, and carried in a convoy on his way to trial. The roads were quiet then, the skies were dull and dark, and the horses walked on for three or four hours until Hew's arms and legs were numbed, and he had lost all sense of how far they had come. The devil struck at Dysart Moor. Hew recognised that place, bleak enough in daylight, where the moor hung close its heavy pall of smoke. The horses knew it too, pricking with their hooves at the hot wallowed ground where the coal pits smouldered, spilling out their dust. A little in the distance Hew saw pale green shadows, moving in the trees, the children of the coal pits working through the night. What difference to their world was this outer shroud of darkness, but a cooler earth beneath their blistered feet? The lights came closer then, like little candle moths, and then they were unleashed, not children of the pit, but devils that from hell ascended, hot and fierce and furious, and Hew smelt blood and heat and heard the clash of steel, a horse that reared and screamed, and tasted earth and blood. Hands were laid upon him, and his carcase lifted, dragged through gorse and shrub, until the hot earth split and something warm and sticky poured into his throat, the belly fire and fleume that came from hell itself.

He was in a sack. The sack was full of stones, and was bowling down a hill. The stones would break his bones. He wanted it to stop. He did not want it to stop. At the bottom of the hill was something worse.

He was on a hurdle, on his way to execution. Each trundle of the hurdle rattled at his teeth. Soon, it would stop.

It would never stop.

He was in Hell.

Dimly, through the blanket, he heard someone speak. A whining English voice, that came out with a long list of complaints, that rattled with the motion of the cart. The complaints were loud and querulous.

No kind of roads, and no kind of manners.

What we. Had. Expected. From. The Scots.

You will like England. For. Things are civil there.

Civil.

We burn witches there, and do not suffer them to traffic in the streets.

Did hell, for the Scotsman, have its own attendant Englishman, petulant and querulous, pricking with complaint?

'I hope you are not sick. The discomforts of this mission have been difficult enough, but your sickness in the carriage would make the thing intolerable.'

Hew opened his eyes.

He was in a cart, and the cart had a high ceiling to it, domed and lined with cloth. There were curtains at the side, and a little light came through. Too little light. Enough. Above him sat the Englishman, on a bank of furs. He had furs wrapped around him, from which he looked out, sallow, sour and pinched.

Hew's wits were blurred and shaken from the draught that he had drunk. Dizzily, he hazarded, 'Is this how you supply your fill of foreign spies?'

'Preferably, not. I am glad that you are with us. You are free to leave at any time. I should tell you though, that you are fugitive and will be killed on sight. Two of the king's men died in the skirmish.'

Why?

'Andrew Wood has some command of the renegades in Fife, but he has no control of them. Some are enterprising, more than we would like. In truth, the king's men did not put up a fight. Most of them believed that they had been bewitched.'

Why?

'It was all Andrew's doing. He dared not take the chance of allowing you to testify. Nor, in truth, did I.'

Understanding cleared the muddle in Hew's mind. 'He could have had me killed.'

'He could have done,' Walsingham agreed. 'For him, that would have been by far the simplest solution. I understand that he felt under some kind of obligation to a woman he calls Clare. I do not inquire into his domestic affairs.'

Meg. . . .

'Your family are quite safe. They will, I regret, be troubled for a while, about your disappearance, but when some time has passed, you will be able to write to them. Once Colville is released, we will work towards a way to restore you both, to secure for you a pardon. Such things are sometimes possible. Until that time had come, you will work for us.'

'I will *never*,' Hew insisted, 'work for you.'

'As to that, we shall see. But I will point out that working for me need not, in any sense, conflict you in your principles. You need not betray your king. Indeed, you are not in a position to do so. You have never been at court, and at the present time may not return to Scotland.'

'Aye?' Hew questioned warily, conscious of the sense in that.

'You might, perhaps, be sent into the Low Countries. You did good work there, with our friend Robert Lachlan.'

'With your friend? Robert is not your friend,' Hew protested. Lachlan was a man for hire who had gone with him to Ghent. Though Hew had first suspected him, the two men had grown close.

'He is a man who sometimes has provided us with intelligence. I understand from Robert that he saved your life.'

'Aye, from Spanish rebels.'

'He has saved it once again. For if I had not had his report, you would not be of interest to us. You have met the prince of Orange, and impressed him. You have solved a riddle of a Flemish windmill, and shown yourself adept at working out such schemes. You keep your counsel close. And you have lately had instruction in the

307

ancient languages, which shows you are adept in learning writing schemes. These things make you suitable for what we have in mind. We want a man that has a wit for ciphers.'

'Ciphers?' echoed Hew.

'We will teach you how to write, and how to understand them. You, no doubt, will come up with some others of your own. Would that be so bad?'

And Hew, struggling up to sit up upon the bench, wondered if it would. Could it be so bad to be in England for a while, knowing in his heart that his friends were safe? He felt the stirring heartbeat of a rare excitement. 'Have we far to go?' he asked.

'We have just begun.'

Historical Note

The Ruthven Raid

The 'Ruthven raid' took place in August 1582, when a group of Scottish noblemen, the 'Lords Enterprisers', led by William Ruthven, earl of Gowrie, detained the young King James VI against his will at Ruthven castle, and forced a change of government, removing Catholic influence at court. The king's beloved favourite Esme Stuart, sixth sieur of Aubigny, earl and duke of Lennox, fled to France, where he died in May 1583 'of a disease contracted of displeasure'. His ally, James Stewart, earl of Arran, who had overthrown the king's last Regent, Morton, was placed under house arrest. Gowrie's interim regime, austere and ultra-Protestant, was approved by Andrew Melville and the Scottish Kirk, and by Queen Elizabeth of England, who supported it financially. Gowrie, as Lord High Treasurer of Scotland, was motivated partly by the profligate extravagance of James' friends at court.

In June 1583, the 17-year-old King James broke free from his captors and escaped from Falkland Palace to St Andrews castle. He appointed a new Privy Council, with the earl of Arran once again its spokesman. Queen Elizabeth sent her first secretary, Sir Francis Walsingham as ambassador to James, 'willing him to stay from any strict proceeding against the lords who were pricked at for the raid of Ruthven' . . . 'but he was of a sickly complexion, and was not able to endure riding post, therefore he was long by the way, being carried in a chariot'. Walsingham, his influence and power, were greatly underestimated by the Scots.

Characters

The following characters are based on real people:

James VI of Scotland b.1566
King of Scotland 1567–1625. King of England (as James I) 1603–25. Son of Henry Stewart, Lord Darnley, and Mary, Queen of Scots

Esme Stuart, sieur of Aubigny, earl and duke of Lennox
Court favourite of the young King James, and cousin to his father Darnley. French convert from Catholicism mistrusted by the Protestants

James Stewart, earl of Arran
Follower of Esme Stuart. Accused the Regent Morton of art and part slaughter of the king's father Darnley. Captain of the royal guard

Robert Stewart, earl of March
Great uncle of James VI. Commendator of St Andrews cathedral priory; assisted James in his escape from Falkland

Robert Stewart, earl of Orkney
Illegitimate son of James V. Unpopular ruler of Orkney; political allegiances unclear

William Ruthven, earl of Gowrie
Lord High Treasurer of Scotland, leading instigator of the Ruthven raid

John Colville
Presbyterian minister who rose to power in the Scottish court and passed on secret information to the English. Supporter of the Ruthven raid; Master of Requests to the Privy Council

Francis Walsingham
Principal Secretary and spymaster to Queen Elizabeth l

Patrick Adamson
Archbishop of St Andrews; chancellor of the university of St Andrews

George Buchanan
Historian and humanist scholar. Tutor to King James Vl. Author of *De Jure Regni apud Scotos* – on the law of kingship among the Scots

Andrew Melville
Presbyterian scholar and reformer instrumental in the new foundation of the University of St Andrews and in the General Assembly. Principal of St Mary's College. Uncle of James Melville, whose diaries inspired the Hew Cullan stories

Alison Peirson
Accused by Patrick Adamson of curing him of sickness by the use of witchcraft. Escaped from St Andrews castle in 1583. Recaptured and convicted in 1588. Alison's 'confession' gives a detailed account of her trips to fairyland

Sir Andrew Wood of Largo
Sheriff and Coroner of Fife. Also, Comptroller of Scotland, in which capacity he settled the king's personal debts, bringing his own family to the brink of ruin. Great grandson of the admiral, the first Sir Andrew Wood, from whom he inherited his property and title.

The Woods were staunch supporters of the Stewart kings, and their dealings in this story are not based in fact.

Elizabeth
his wife

Robert Wood
his brother, owner of the New Mill at St Andrews

With thanks to Dr Ian Drever of Dalkeith, for introducing me to his family name of Richan, which as a surname has apparently died out. According to George Black, *The Surnames of Scotland*, in early 20th century Kirkwall, Richan was 'a very puzzling name . . . never found out of Orkney . . . yet the *ch* is not Norse when pronounced as in *loch* – as it is in this name' which gives us a clue as to how the name should sound. The earl of Orkney, in 1574, had a William Richane on his staff.

Glossary of Old Scots words

Ain	(one's) own
Almery	a cupboard
Aquavite	whisky
Art and Part	participation in (a crime)
Bairnlie	childlike
Bangstrie	bullying behaviour
Bannock	a round, flat cake of oat or barley
Barnelike	childish
Baxter	a baker
Belly-blind	blindfolded
Billie	a close friend, comrade
Bisket	hard biscuit or rusk
Blawn	blown
Blether	a bladder
Blockhouse	a small fort or defensive building; one of two circular gun towers built on the south face of St Andrews castle, largely destroyed in 1547
Bluiter	a beggar
Bluther	to weep, blubber
Brave	fine or elegant
Braw	variant of *brave*, fine or elegant
Brigue	to intrigue
Bruck	rubbish, trash. An Orkney word
Bruit	clamour, noise or rumour; to spread rumour
Bursar	student who receives a 'burse' or bursary
Burse	a purse; an endowment for support of a student or scholar
Butter saps	bread fried in butter and dipped in sugar

Caich	tennis
Caichpell	a tennis court
Carcage	a dead body
Cawk	to smear with excrement
Chap	to rap or knock
Cleng	to clean out
Close	an enclosure, court or courtyard next to a house
Clout	(1) a cloth
	(2) a small patch of land
Clubbit	clumsy
Collop	a slice of meat
Compear	to appear before a court
Complice	a partner, accomplice
Convicted	convinced
Craw	a crow
Crownar	a coroner, district officer charged with maintaining certain rights of the Crown, such as keeping the king's peace, serving writs on malefactors. Usually combined with the office of sheriff
Curator	the legal guardian of a minor between the age of 14 and 21
Defiance	a challenge or dare
Delicat	a delicacy
Ding	to strike or beat violently
Dissimil	to cover up by pretence
Distracted	deranged, disturbed in mind
Doubt	to think
Douce	sweet
Dow	a dove
Draucht	draught and draft, in all senses related to *draw*. Here:
	(1) a plan or design

(2) an architectural plan

(3) a receptacle for excrement, channel for drawing off filth

Draucht-raker	a cleaner of privies; nightsoilman
Dry stool	a chamber pot set in a stool, a commode
Economus	a college steward or bursar (in the modern sense); housekeeper
Elusion	a delusion
Falland ill	epilepsy
Falset	falsehood
Fazart	a coward
Fedity	foulness, corruption, both physical and moral
Filthsum	filthy
Fleume	phlegm
Flux	excessive discharge from the bowels
Flyting	railing or scolding; a battle in words
Fosse	a ditch built for defence
Fou	full [of drink] = drunk, intoxicated
Foulsum	loathsome
Fra/frae/fae	from
Fremmit	foreign, strange
Fruel	weak, feeble
Fu	full
Fuillie	excrement, manure
Fummill	to fumble
Futeman	a footman as attendant, or as an infantry soldier
Futless	useless, footless
Gang	to go
General Assembly	Supreme Court of the Church of Scotland following the Reformation of the kirk in 1560, marking the beginning of the Presbyterian Church in Scotland; in 1583 meeting twice a year in Edinburgh

315

Gerslouper	a grasshopper
Gingiber	ginger
Girdle	a griddle; a circular round plate for baking cakes or bannocks
Gong	a latrine
Gong-fermer/ gong-scourer	a cleaner of latrines
Gooseturd	a shade of yellowish green
Gowk	to stare
Granks and granes	moans and groans
Greit	to shed tears
Grening	yearning or longing
Guid neighbours	good neighbours: name given to the fairy folk, intended through flattery to guard against malevolence
Haar	sea mist common on the east coast of Scotland
Hale	whole; sound in body, healthy
Haly	holy
Hammermen	members of the metal workers' craft
Haud	to hold
Haven	a harbour
Heckleback	a stickleback
Heugh	a hill
Incarnatene	flesh- or crimson-coloured
Jak	a soldier's sleeveless jerkin, padded or plated
Jakes	a latrine
Jayne	an instrument of torture
Jolie at the goose	an early version of the board game, Goose
Joukerie	trickery; underhand dealing
Juglar	a magician or sorcerer who works by sleight of hand (here, punning on jugular)
Jummil	a muddle or confusion
Keek	to peek, glance

Keeker	a peeping Tom
Kendal	green wool cloth from the town of Kendal; a particular shade of green
Kenning	knowing; knowledge
Kernels	'kirnels of the thie': the groin
Kichin	a kitchen; an allowance of cooked food, such as meat or fish, that supplements a staple such as bread
Kirk	a church; here, especially, the Reformed Church of Scotland
Kirtle	a simple woman's dress of skirt and bodice, worn on its own or underneath a gown
Kist	a large chest or box
Kittill	fickle, sensitive or difficult to handle
Knotless	futile, pointless, groundless
Laic	a layman
Laich house	'low house': a cellar
Laird	a lord; the Lord
Latton	a kind of yellow brass hammered into plate; a thin sheet made of this
Laureate	a graduate
Laver	a basin for washing
Lettrin	(1) a lectern or book rest (2) a small, lockable writing desk
Libber	a sorcerer
Lidder	cowardly
Limmar	a villain or rogue
Loun	a lout or rogue
Loup/lowp	to leap, jump, spring at
Lour	to lie low, lurk
Lourd	heavy
Louse-leech	a doctor, physician [from Gaelic *lus*, 'herb']
Lubbard	a lout
Lug	an ear

Lum	a chimney
Ly-by	an onlooker, bystander
Magistrands	students in their fourth and final year of study for the degree of MA
Man/maun	must
Manchet	the finest wheat bread
Manna/maunna	must not
Master of Requests	Scottish officer of state whose role includes receiving petitions from subjects of the Crown and presenting them for consideration by the Privy Council
Matrix	a womb
Mauchtless	feeble, weak
Mellit	dealt, had intercourse with
Midding-sted	a midden
Mindit	disposed, inclined
Miniard	effeminate
Minnie	child's name for mother
Mow	to joke, engage in banter
Muckle	great big
Muckle mair	much more
Muff	a covering of fur; pubic hair; vagina
Murther	murder
Nacket	a stripling, youngster
Nether	lower
Nether (vb)	to abase, humiliate
Nether hose	stockings
New foundation	reform of the universities following the Reformation of the kirk
Norish	Norse, of the Norn language
Norn	variety of Norse language native to Orkney, now extinct
Notar	a notary; here, more generally, a scribe or clerk

O'ergrowin	overgrown
Overstraught	overstretched
Paddock	a frog or toad (a shell paddock is a tortoise)
Pantons	velvet slippers
Pedagogy	place of instruction; name given to the teaching body of St Andrews University, at its earliest date; name given to the College of St John
Pellock	a pellet
Pend	an arched roof or vault
Petuous	compassionate
Physick	medicine
Piked	spiked or pointed
Piker	a petty thief
Pistolett	a small firearm; former name for pistol
Placard	a sheet of paper printed or written on one side, for public display; a poster or handbill
Placket	an apron or an underskirt; a slit or an opening in a woman's dress to give access to a pocket or for sexual intercourse; by extension, the vagina
Plaister	a medicinal plaster; ointment spread on muslin and tied to the body
Plat	(1) a plan (2) a dish or plate
Pluck	a mouthful
Port	a gateway or entrance, especially to a town
Posset	a drink of hot milk curdled with wine
Pothecar	an apothecary
Potingar	an apothecary
Pottle	a pot or vessel, and its contents
Privily	secretly, privately
Privy	(adj) intimate; private; secret (noun) a latrine

Privy Council	the board of advisors to the king, with economic, administrative and judicial powers
Quail	to grow weak
Quair	a quire; a measure of paper
Quelp	a whelp
Quent	crafty, cunning; queer
Quhimper	to whimper
Quhingar	a dagger or short sword
Raker	a cleaner or scavenger; a clearer of cesspools
Raxed	strained, stretched
Reconfort	to strengthen or inspire with new courage or confidence
Regent	(1) in the ancient Scottish universities, a master who took a class of students through the full four-year course of instruction leading to the degree of Master of Arts (2) Someone appointed to rule during the minority of a monarch: the regent Morton
Ribald	a waster; a fornicator
Ripples	a disease of the back and loins, believed to result from sexual excess
Rummle	to rumble
Sair	injured [of body part]; severe, harsh, extreme(ly) or excessive(ly)
Salat	a salad vegetable
Sark	an undershirt or shift
Scabbart	scabbard or sheath; vagina
Scaffery	the act of obtaining benefit by fraud
Scathless	unharmed
Scolage	school or college fees
Scudlar	lowest rank of servant; drudge
Scummer	to defecate; hence 'scummer pan': a chamber pot

Sea-maw	the common gull
Secretar	a trusted scribe or servant; a confidential clerk
Selkie	a seal
Serkinet	a small jerkin or bodice
Shairds	small pieces or fragments
Shakebuckler	a nickname for a serving man who is easily antagonised
Shotill	a drawer or compartment
Sic	such
Sin	since, considering that
Sink	a sewer, cesspit or drain
Skeich	timid, shy
Skift	a small light boat
Skite /skitter	to defile with excrement
Slaffert	a slap, box on the ear
Sledger	a sledgehammer
Slops	wide, baggy breeches fashionable in the late 16th century
Soddins	scraps of boiled meat; food that has been boiled
Sops	bread soaked in milk or wine
Speir	to make inquiries
Speke	speech, way of expression
Spinkes	prickles, spines
Squire	to escort
Steir the pot	stir the pot; stir up; copulate
Stew	a stench, a blast of stinking air; a cloud of filth or dust
Stomachat	offended, resentful, put out
Stoup	a flagon or pitcher
Stour (rb)	to spray
Stour	a cloud of dust
Strack	struck
Stummar	to stumble or stammer

Subtle	ingenious or clever
Succar candies	sweets made from clarified sugar
Succats	candied fruits
Swak	to dash, hurl violently
Swyfing	copulating
Tam Lin	protagonist of the ballad by Thomas the Rhymer, who rescued his true love from the fairy queen
Tertians	students in their third year
Thole	suffer, bear patiently
Thrang	crowded
Thrawe	a throe or spasm
Thrist	(1) a pang or throe, a stabbing sensation, thrust (2) thirst
Thristing	jostling, pushing
Ticket of account	a bill of expenses
Tippet	a narrow strip of cloth worn across the shoulders; the pennant of an academic hood
Traffick	to do business with, negotiate
Trance	a passageway; the stone trance: the entrance to St Leonard's College
Trattle	to prattle
Trauchled	exhausted
Trow-shot	struck by a fairy dart [Trow = troll]
Trucour	a traitour
Tulchan	Gaelic word for a straw calf, used to coax a cow into giving up its milk. Disparaging name for titular bishops after the Reformation
Unco	uncouth; strange, unfamiliar, unknown; extraordinary
Vennel	a narrow lane or thoroughfare
Visitor	an inspector or examiner; a physician appointed to establish the cause of suspicious

or unnatural deaths. Giles Locke was
appointed Visitor of St Andrews at the end of
Fate & Fortune

Wabbit	feeble, weak
Wallowed	withered
Wam	the stomach
Wammil	to feel sick
Ward	custody, imprisonment
Warkmen	workmen
Wattir-kaill	cabbage soup made without meat
Wha devil	what devil! What the devil!
Wrabil	to wriggle
Wrackful	vindictive, harsh or cruel, vengeful, destructive
Wynd	a narrow street or alley
Yett	a gate